GW 10/14/06

W9-BGA-018

The
HIGHLAND ROGUES
WARRIOR
BRIDE

LOIS GREIMAN

HIGHLAND ROGUES

THE WARRIOR BRIDE

AVON BOOKS

An Imprint of HarperCollinsPublishers

This is a work of fiction. Names, characters, places, and incidents are products of the author's imagination or are used fictitiously and are not to be construed as real. Any resemblance to actual events, locales, organizations, or persons, living or dead, is entirely coincidental.

AVON BOOKS
An Imprint of HarperCollins*Publishers*
10 East 53rd Street
New York, New York 10022-5299

Copyright © 2002 by Lois Greiman
ISBN: 0-7394-3023-8

All rights reserved. No part of this book may be used or reproduced in any manner whatsoever without written permission, except in the case of brief quotations embodied in critical articles and reviews. For information address Avon Books, an Imprint of HarperCollins Publishers.

Avon Trademark Reg. U.S. Pat. Off. and in Other Countries, Marca Registrada, Hecho en U.S.A.
HarperCollins® is a registered trademark of HarperCollins Publishers Inc.

Printed in the U.S.A.

To Leandra Logan,
whose talent is only exceeded
by her unequaled capacity
for listening to me whine.
Grab onto a star, Mary,
but make sure I have a firm grasp
on your coattails first.

Lachlan MacGowan's

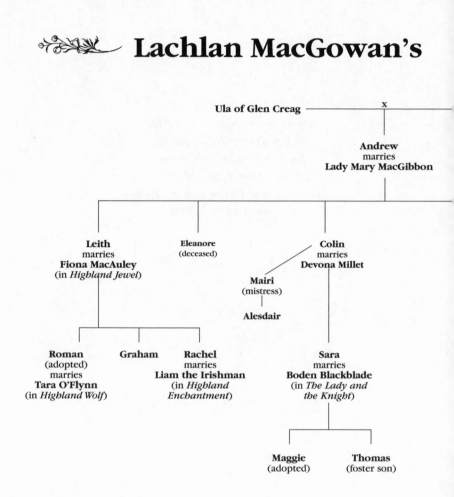

Ula of Glen Creag ——————— x

Andrew
marries
Lady Mary MacGibbon

Leith
marries
Fiona MacAuley
(in *Highland Jewel*)

Eleanore
(deceased)

Mairi
(mistress)

Alesdair

Colin
marries
Devona Millet

Roman
(adopted)
marries
Tara O'Flynn
(in *Highland Wolf*)

Graham

Rachel
marries
Liam the Irishman
(in *Highland Enchantment*)

Sara
marries
Boden Blackblade
(in *The Lady and the Knight*)

Maggie
(adopted)

Thomas
(foster son)

Family Tree

Malcolm of Irondell

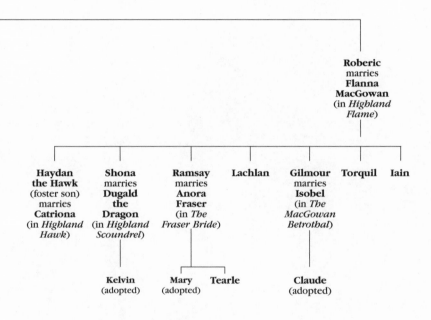

Roberic
marries
**Flanna
MacGowan**
(in *Highland
Flame*)

**Haydan
the Hawk**
(foster son)
marries
Catriona
(in *Highland
Hawk*)

Shona
marries
**Dugald
the
Dragon**
(in *Highland
Scoundrel*)

Ramsay
marries
**Anora
Fraser**
(in *The
Fraser Bride*)

Lachlan

Gilmour
marries
Isobel
(in *The
MacGowan
Betrothal*)

Torquil

Iain

Kelvin
(adopted)

Mary
(adopted)

Tearle

Claude
(adopted)

The Prophecy

He who would take a Fraser bride,
these few rules he must abide.

Peaceable yet powerful he must be,
cunning but kind to me and thee.

The last rule, but not of less import,
he'll be the loving and beloved sort.

If a Fraser bride he longs to take,
he'll remember these rules for his life's sake.

For the swain who forgets the things I've said,
will find himself amongst the dead.

Meara of the Fold

Prologue

In the year of our Lord 1535

Though the great hall of Evermyst rang with laughter, Lachlan MacGowan stood in silence amidst the merriment. Aye, friends and kinsmen had journeyed long and far to view the wedding of his brother Gilmour to Isobel of the Frasers. Forbes and MacKinnons and Setons were there. The chief of the fierce Munros, Laird Innes himself, had arrived with his own handsome bride, and stood head and shoulders above the crowd. Even his sisters had joined the throng. Quite bonny they were, at least by the neighboring Munros' standards. The warlike clan was not known for its fair looks, after all, but for its prowess in battle. Still, a truce of sorts had been crafted between the Frasers and the Munros. And now all were eager to catch a glimpse of the maid who had captured the heart of the rogue of the rogues, but Lachlan was far more interested in another.

From a distant corner of the high-beamed hall, a woman's laughter could be heard above the melee. Ale flowed in abundance. Upon the high table, grape-stuffed partridges jostled pureed quince and pies of Paris. Guests talked and teased and riddled, but Lachlan remained apart as he searched for the one called the warrior. The one to whom he owed his life.

But try as he might, he saw no trace of the other; thus his gaze drifted to the two young women who stood upon the dais not far away. Isobel and Anora, the Fraser sisters. His brothers' brides. Twins. They stood together, fair and bonny and bright as a promise. Almost identical, they were, fairylike in their beauty, delicate of face and form. As he watched, they leaned close together, speaking softly. Anora stroked Isobel's hair, and they shared a smile. It was a simple gesture, and yet it stirred something deep inside him, for it spoke of tenderness and femininity, and a dozen other traits far beyond his grasp. But he knew the truth; they were not gentle maids.

Nay, he did not envy either Gilmour or Ramsay. Hardly that, for these maids would not make their lives the simpler. His brothers had battled for the right to these women. Indeed, Lachlan himself had joined in the fray. Mayhap he would have lost his very life if it had not been for the intervention of the warrior called Hunter.

For a moment he scanned the hall again, but the warrior was nowhere to be seen. An enigma he was, wont to appear during times of battle, and with his brothers' wives about, there would be many confrontations, for despite their bonny features and willowy forms, they were not the kind to bend easily. They were made of stuff stern enough to wither the stoutest knight. Both brothers bore scars from their delicate hands. Nay, he did not envy his brothers' fate, for he was Lachlan Mac-Gowan, the rogue fox, and far above battling with a *woman*. When he wed, it would be to a lass whose hands were as gentle as her countenance.

But then he heard again the sisters' laughter. His gaze was drawn to them, pulled inexorably across the hall. Each bride wore a delicate chain of silver about her neck, but upon their hips, they wore small daggers and in their eyes was the gleam of trouble. Aye, they were not what he sought in a wife, but God's mercy, they were beautiful beyond—

"Mooning, Lachlan?"

He refused to jump when startled from his reverie, but turned slowly to find two of his brothers beside him.

"If I did not know better, Quil," said Ramsay, not glancing at their younger brother, "I would think we had caught the fox daydreaming."

"Aye," Torquil agreed, and grinned. The expression was almost as irritating as Gilmour's. Their mother should have known far better than to birth such a riotous passel of sons. Five of them there were, and each more troublesome than the last. "And daydreaming whilst he stares at your lady, Ram."

Lachlan kept his own expression carefully stoic. 'Twas never wise to encourage his brothers when they were in "playful" spirits. "I was not daydreaming," he corrected, "merely contemplating."

"Then perhaps you should wipe away your spittle and turn your attention elsewhere," suggested Torquil. Although he would never achieve Lachlan's musculature, he rarely felt the need to keep his tiresome wit to himself.

Ramsay chuckled. Jealousy, it seemed, was not his weakness. Though Lachlan wondered if he would say the same if he *himself* had found a Fraser bride, he kept his notorious temper in careful check. Their mother would be unhappy indeed if he initiated a brawl at his brother's wedding. Past experience assured him of that, so he nodded sagely and relaxed the muscles that bunched like sailors' knots in his tightening shoulders. "At least I have no scars to show for the attention I've showered on her," Lachlan said.

Ramsay smiled. The expression was serene, natural, ultimately content, and it made Lachlan's stomach churn, for he himself was less than composed. Indeed, ever since talking to Gilmour some moments before, he felt as fidgety as a baited cat. He turned his attention aside again, searching the crowd. Where was that damned warrior?

"'Tis a small price to pay," said Ramsay, and glanced once toward his wife. She yet stood with her sister, but Gilmour had joined them on the dais.

"What's that?" asked Lachlan, turning back.

"The scars," Ramsay said, and drew his gaze from Anora with an obvious effort. "'Tis a small price to pay to have her by me side."

"Indeed. She could stab *me* in the eye with a quarryman's wedge," sighed Torquil. "So long as she shared me bed, I'd have no complaints."

The elder brothers turned in tandem toward Quil. Ramsay's face, Lachlan noted, was emphatically expressionless. Emphatic expressionlessness was never a good sign in a MacGowan.

Quil tripped his gaze to his eldest brother, cleared his throat, and tried a lopsided grin. "Did I say that aloud?" he asked.

"Aye, wee brother," said Ramsay quietly. "It seems your mouth outpaces your good sense yet again."

Quil's smile widened. "I only meant to say . . . you are a lucky man, Ram."

"Aye," Ramsay agreed dryly, "and you will be lucky to remain unscathed if you do not keep a rein on your tongue, lad."

"'Tis true," agreed Lachlan. Good sense had rarely stopped the brother rogues from throwing themselves into a fray when the opportunity presented itself, and Lachlan was hardly the exception. "You'd best be careful what you say, Quil, or Anora may yet become vexed and challenge you to a duel."

Torquil chuckled happily. "Surely you are not saying that Ramsay here allows his wee bonny bride to fight his battles for him."

Lachlan grunted as he skimmed the crowds again. "Ask him about the scar on his scalp sometime."

Ramsay said naught, so Lachlan continued. Despite his vow to keep out of trouble's ubiquitous path, there was a demon gnawing at his guts. "The scar she gave him when she struck him with a bedpost in an attempt to keep him from battle."

"A bedpost?"

"Aye," agreed Ram amicably. "It seems me wife was concerned for me welfare even then, but fear not, Lachlan, there is someone just as worried about you—the warrior." He cast his gaze sideways. "I believe he calls himself Hunter."

"Ho!" crowed Torquil in a burst of unleashed delight. "A warrior! Interested in the rogue fox?"

" 'Tis true," said Gilmour. Lachlan turned to watch his third brother enter the fracas. God have mercy, Mour sounded just as ecstatic as Quil. "During the battle of Evermyst, Lachlan was rendered unconscious. But the warrior appeared in the darkness." Mour had been "gifted" with a flair for drama and put his hand to his hip as if grasping an unseen sword. "Like an angel of mercy he appeared and fought off all comers, then, lifting our brother lovingly in his arms, he cradled him against his bosom all the long way to Evermyst."

Torquil couldn't have looked happier if he'd been declared the king of bean. "Truly?"

"Aye," said Gilmour. "Every word. I believe this brawny Hunter fellow has deep feelings for our brother. Indeed, I think he is not—"

"Mour," Lachlan interrupted quietly. "I've no wish to wound you during these festivities."

Gilmour laughed, looking not the least bit concerned. It was, perhaps, the quality Lachlan hated most about his brothers; they consistently failed to realize their physical inferiority. "Ah, but if you wound me on me own wedding night, me bride will be much displeased, and you'll be left to explain the reasons."

"What reasons?" Quil asked, all but breathless with anticipation.

Gilmour motioned for his younger brother to lean close.

Lachlan tensed, but just then he caught a glimpse of the warrior through the crowd and rushed into the mob, leaving his brothers to their gossip. Devil take it! He'd stop these damned rumors here and now!

Concealed in the shadows near Evermyst's great, arched door, Hunter watched the revelers in silence. He was dressed in dark leather, his face shadowed by a broad-brimmed hat, his hands gloved, his feet shod in black boots that reached just above his knees. He was a warrior, dour and watchful, with few acquaintances and fewer friends.

The Munro was here. Hunter heard his voice boom in the noisy hall, but did not turn. Innis Munro no longer threatened Evermyst. Nay, since he'd lost the battle for Lady Anora's hand, there had been a truce of sorts between Evermyst and Windemoore, and though that truce did not, in any way include Hunter, he ignored the giant chieftain for a moment.

Laughter echoed to the high beams of the festive hall and Hunter shifted his gaze to find the source. 'Twas Gilmour who laughed. Gilmour of the MacGowans, the bridegroom, the rogue of the rogues. But why would he not be merry? The earth's treasures were his. Wealth, power, and now this maiden bride at his side. Hunter didn't glance at her, for he knew exactly how she would appear—just like her sister—fair-haired and bonny and far beyond the likes of him. He tightened one fist and turned to watch Ramsay make his way through the crowd toward Lachlan. Aye, he knew the brother rogues, if not by acquaintance, at least by reputation. Ramsay was the intellect, Gilmour was the charmer, and Lachlan . . . Hunter narrowed his eyes. Lachlan was not a pretty lad. Indeed, by the look of him, his nose had been broken on more than one occasion. He was shaped like a wedge, his shoulders broadly muscled, his hips lean and sculpted. Although all those about him had donned bright ceremonial garb, he wore naught but a free-fitting tunic, open at the neck and tucked into the MacGowans' traditional tartan. Deep greens and blues, to blend like magic into heather and heath. His plaid was belted by a broad band of leather and held in place by a silver buckle fashioned in the shape of a wild cat's snarling face.

Lachlan was the fighter.

And yet Hunter had saved him—had arrived just in time to ward off Lachlan's enemies and carry him to Evermyst. What did the fighter think of that? Would there be trouble? Oh aye. Lachlan had voiced his thanks. But behind the gratitude there had been something more. Curiosity certainly, but also resentment. The rogue fox did not like to be beholden. Perhaps he should have left him to fight his own battles, but—

"So you are the warrior."

Hunter turned abruptly at the female voice, then shifted his gaze downward, for the speaker barely reached his chest. Indeed, she was as wizened and gnarled as a windblown tamarisk.

"Speak up, lad," she ordered.

"Aye." He glanced up once, making certain all was well. He must be cautious, for he was a fool to chance being here at all. "Some call me the warrior."

"And I am Meara of the Fold."

"I know who you are." The words came unbidden and were colored with a shadow of emotion. Hunter held his tongue and said no more.

"Do you now?" she asked, and narrowed her ancient eyes until they were but slits in her furrowed face.

"Aye." He made certain his tone was casual now,

though a thousand unwanted emotions steamed through him. "You are the one who nurtured the ladies of Evermyst."

"Nay!" Her expression changed. Perhaps there was pain there. Perhaps there was sadness and regret, but perhaps he was seeing naught but what he wanted to see. "Nay. I did not nurture *them*, but only Anora." She lifted her much-folded chin and looked him in the eye. "Isobel I sent away at birth, but perhaps you know that too."

Hunter tightened a fist, then loosened it with a careful effort and focused all his attention on this one adversary, for perhaps, if the truth be told, she was more dangerous than all the other combined. "I have heard the tale."

"Aye." She nodded slowly. "Aye, and so you have."

Hunter drew himself to his full height, looming over the wizened form. "Did you have something to say, old gammer?"

She pursed her parched lips and nodded. Something shone in her eyes, some emotion too deep to guess. "Spirit you have," she murmured. "Spirit and pride."

Her eyes were eerie and far seeing, and he dare not let her look too deep. Thus he turned to leave, but she snagged his sleeve in gnarled fingers.

" 'Tis said you saved our Lachlan."

He twisted toward her. "Some say that I did, but if left to his own defenses he would have rallied on his own, most like."

"Modesty." Her ancient voice dropped to little more than a whisper. "Aye—"

Hunter yanked from her grasp and turned to leave, but she snatched at his sleeve again. "I've a mind to hire you."

He glanced back at her. "What?"

"You heard me, lad."

"Hire me? Why?"

" 'Tis said you are not afraid to battle. Indeed, 'tis said you are hired to kill in the name of king and country."

"I have killed," he confirmed.

She nodded solemnly. " 'Tis said you are a great warrior."

"And why, pray, would you need a great warrior when you are surrounded by the brother rogues?"

"Perhaps 'tis they what need the protecting."

"What?"

"Trouble comes," she murmured. "I feel it in me soul."

"Your soul," he scoffed, but suddenly he felt an unnatural draft of air. It drifted across the back of his neck, setting his hair on end.

The old woman glanced up as if worried.

"What manner of trouble?" he asked.

She shifted her gaze toward the twins where they stood on the dais. "I know not."

"Are the maids in danger?"

"Tell me, warrior." She pinned her uncanny gaze on him, and it was all he could do to keep from shifting his away. "Would you care?"

"Nay," he said. "I do not even know them."

"And what of Lachlan? Do you care for him?"

"If you've something to say, old woman, do so and have done with."

"Evil comes to Evermyst."

"Nay," he murmured. "Evermyst is all but invincible."

"Invincible." 'Twas her turn to scoff. "Naught is invincible, warrior. Surely you know that."

"What evil?" he asked.

"I know not. 'Tis why I would hire you to abide here with us."

"Here?" His stomach lurched, his muscles cramped. If there was one place in the world that he did not belong it was here. "At Evermyst?"

"I will make it well worth your efforts, lad."

Unnamed emotions burned like spirits through him, but in that instant he heard the brothers laugh. He shifted his attention. From across the room, the MacGowans watched him, and then, as if from a nightmare, Lachlan stepped toward him.

"Nay! There is naught I can do for you," Hunter rasped and, turning, disappeared like a wraith into the crowd.

Chapter 1

In the year of our Lord 1536

Maybe humility wasn't Lachlan's best attribute. True, he was as strong as a bull, as crafty as a fox, and as silent as a serpent, but perhaps he was not quite as humble as he might be. Then again, what did he have to be humble about? He grinned as he pressed aside an elder branch.

Somewhere up ahead was his quarry. Lachlan had been following him for many hours now, and though he had inquired long and searched diligently, he'd learned little. The man traveled alone, he was reputedly a great fighter, and most called him naught but "the warrior." Lachlan snorted silently.

The warrior, indeed! If memory served, he was not tremendously impressive to look upon, being neither tall nor particularly brawny—although the other had never stood near Lachlan for more than a pair of moments. Indeed, the warrior avoided him, had fled from Evermyst's great hall, if not from Scotland entirely. Why? If the man had been willing to save him in battle those long months ago, why did he refuse to converse with him?

Lachlan scowled into the deepening darkness. From somewhere up ahead he caught the faintest whiff of smoke on the cool autumn air. He turned his head ever so slightly, concentrating, for he'd finally found the warrior and was not about to lose him now.

The man had started a fire of . . . elm wood, if Lachlan wasn't mistaken. So Hunter, as Gilmour had once called him, was preparing to dine, and had no idea that he was now the hunted. The great warrior's instincts were less than impressive, for despite the darkness that had settled in around him, Lachlan knew just where his quarry was. He knew just where he had left his steed, still saddled in the wee dell not far away, and he knew . . . Lachlan canted his head ever so slightly and closed his eyes.

Aye, he knew what the other would eat—mutton and cheese—crowdie, perhaps. He opened his eyes and smiled into the darkness. There was a reason Lachlan was called the fox and it certainly was not for his lithe form. Nay, he'd been blessed with the build of a bullock, but that did not mean he was unable to slip like a shadow through the heather.

Straightening silently, he did so, taking a pair of steps before stopping to listen again. No sound issued from the warrior's camp, but Lachlan knew just where his prey was.

'Twas lucky for this Hunter fellow that Lachlan meant him no harm. Indeed, he planned the very oppo-

site, for even though his brothers had taunted him relentlessly about the battle of Evermyst, he hoped to finally
repay the warrior, to even the score, so to speak.

True, the warrior had been less than appreciative of
Lachlan's thanks, but that didn't lessen the debt. Hunter
had attempted to help Lachlan; Lachlan would help
Hunter. It was as simple as that. And perhaps in the
meantime the other could learn a skill or two. After all,
there was none in the Highlands who could match Lachlan's ability as a tracker. Barely a sound whispered up
from beneath his feet as he stepped forward, and he
smiled at the absence of noise. Aye, perhaps he would
teach the warrior how to walk so silently. Perhaps he
would teach him how to track. And perhaps, if he were
an apt student—

Lachlan wasn't certain whether he felt the point of the
blade at his neck, or the fingers in his hair first. But two
facts were indisputable, there *was* a blade and there *were*
fingers.

"Who are you?" The voice was unknown, deep and
low and deadly. The knife was sharp enough to draw
forth a droplet of blood with the slightest nudge.

Lachlan dare not swallow lest another drop follow the
first. He raised his hands and swore in silence. "Put away
the blade and I'll not harm you, friend. I've no quarrel
with you." He had tried to learn diplomacy from
Gilmour, but perhaps he'd not been the most gifted student, for the other seemed undeterred.

"Then why do you sneak into me camp like a flea-
bitten cur?"

Silence stole into the woods. "*Your* camp?" Lachlan
asked.

No answer was forthcoming.

"You are the warrior called Hunter?"

"Aye."

Damnation! "Then you've naught to fear from me," Lachlan said.

There was a moment of quiet, then the other laughed and slipped his knife harmlessly away. "That much is pitiably apparent," he said, and turned back to his fire.

Lachlan watched him go. 'Twas said the man had carried him to Evermyst. 'Twas said the man had saved his life, but perhaps gratitude was not Lachlan's primary virtue for even now he could feel his temper rising.

"What say you?" Lachlan asked, and followed the other through the darkness.

Not a word was spoken for some time, but finally the warrior glanced up from his place on a log. From beneath the curved visor of his dark metal helm, his eyes were naught but a glimmer of light tossed up from the fire now and again. His nose guard shadowed his face, and the fine metal mesh attached to the bottom of his helmet did naught but continue the mystery.

"Why have you come, MacGowan?"

Lachlan scowled. So Hunter *had* recognized him. Perhaps this warrior was not so poorly trained as he had assumed. Indeed, perhaps he was somewhat adept. "In truth," Lachlan said, remembering his mission with some difficulty, "I have come to return your favor."

"Ahh."

The fire crackled, and although it was difficult to see past the fine chain metal that hid the warrior's cheeks and neck, Lachlan thought he caught a hint of a smile. "Something amuses you?"

"Rarely," said Hunter, and carved a slice of mutton from a bone.

"Then why do you smile?"

Silence again. Lachlan tightened his fist. Indeed, if he hadn't come to save this fellow, he would be well tempted to give him a much-deserved pop in the face.

"Leave me," said the warrior and stood.

"Perhaps you did not understand me," Lachlan said, his tone stilted even as he did his best to smile. "I wish to repay your favor."

"Are you so bored, MacGowan?" Hunter's voice was little more than a murmur in the darkness.

"What's that?"

"Why else would you come but for boredom's sake?"

Lachlan straightened his back, but he was quite certain his smile had slipped a notch. "I have come for chivalry's sake," he said. "To repay you for—"

But his words were interrupted by laughter.

"For a man who is rarely amused . . ." Lachlan began, then shrugged, as much to relieve his tension as to finish his thought.

"You have come for vanity's sake," said Hunter.

"Vanity?"

"To prove yourself me equal."

Perhaps Lachlan was more vain than he knew, for he had never considered a need to prove his *equality*. He smiled. "I assure you, you are wrong."

Hunter watched him for a moment. The fire flickered between them. "I have made me a rule, MacGowan."

Lachlan waited, but if the other planned to continue, it was a hard thing to prove. And perhaps patience was not MacGowan's stellar characteristic. "What is that rule?"

"I do not kill a man whose life I once saved."

The sliver of anger that had wedged into Lachlan's system expanded a bit. "You think you could best me?"

There was not the least bit of mirth in the man's smile—only arrogance mixed with a bit of blood-boiling disdain. "Run home to your father's castle, lad. I have no time to teach lessons that should have been learned long ago."

Lachlan flexed his hands. "It has been some years since I have been called a lad."

"Has it?"

"Aye."

Hunter laughed quietly, as if he shared some private jest with himself. "And therefore you assume you are a man?"

"Would you like to test the theory in battle, mayhap?"

"And here I thought you came to save me."

"Aye, well," said Lachlan and tilted his head at the strange twist of fate. "That was before you spoke."

The warrior grinned, as if savoring his amusement. "I will allow you the choice of weapons."

Firelight danced across Hunter's teeth. They looked tremendously white in the darkness. "Will you now?"

"Aye. What will it be? Claymores? Broadswords? Fists?"

"Did you not hear me rule, MacGowan?"

"Aye. I did. You vowed not to kill any man you once saved. But I assure you . . . You need not worry on me own account."

"Such an impressive combatant, are you?"

"My opponents have said as much."

"Any that were not your maidservants?"

"It surprises me that someone has not taught you better manners long ago."

"Aye. At times it surprises me as well."

Lachlan nodded. "What do you choose then?"

"Choose?" he asked, and poked leisurely at a burning faggot. "I choose for you to leave off and find another to amuse you."

"The *warrior*," Lachlan said, as if musing to himself. "I have heard a good many rumors about you. Me brother Gilmour has a host of interesting theories, but none mentioned your cowardice."

"Go away, lad, before I lose me good humor."

" 'Twould not be a fight to the death," Lachlan assured him. "I would not wound you unduly."

"Truly? How noble of you."

"But if you will not choose a weapon I fear I shall have to do so for you."

Hunter turned toward him, his face barely illuminated by the crackling fire. "And if I choose a weapon as you wish, will you vow to leave me be?"

"Aye. If you do me the favor of a battle it will be me own pleasure to refrain from speaking with you ever again."

"Very well then." Hunter rose languidly to his feet. Lachlan tensed and placed one hand on the hilt of his sword. "I choose wits."

"What's that?"

"Me weapon," said Hunter, "is wits."

Perhaps it wasn't too late to strangle him and be done with. "Wits," Lachlan said, "is not a weapon."

Hunter shrugged. "Maybe not for a MacGowan."

Anger cranked up a notch in Lachlan's gut. "Wits it is, then."

"And you vow to leave at the contest's end."

"Happily."

"Very well then, MacGowan, if you answer this riddle correctly, you may tell all your wee friends that you have bested the great warrior called Hunter." He said the words strangely, almost as if he were mocking himself. "But if you answer wrongly, you shall act as if you were not bested upon the battlefield. You were not at death's very door, and I did not save your life."

Lachlan gritted his teeth, but he managed to nod. After all, if the truth be told, he had already tried to do just that. But the memory kept eating him like a canker, though he was not sure why.

"Then here is your riddle," said Hunter. "What has neither tooth nor horn nor weapon of any sort and yet has caused more deaths than the most fearsome of brigands?"

Lachlan scowled at him as he ran the riddle around in his mind. What creature was he referring to? The Lord God had given them all defenses of some sort, so perhaps he was referring to a person. Was this some manner of religious debate? Perhaps he had best look deeper. Aye, that was it. The answer was something that could not be seen even with the keenest eye.

Something like . . . the wind or the cold of winter. Cruelty, perhaps.

But nay, they were not quite right. Lachlan glanced at Hunter, but the other was prodding a log into the fire with distant unconcern, as if he had entirely forgotten the contest, as if time held no—

That was it then. Time. It destroyed all things and yet it did not bite nor tear nor pierce.

"The answer is time," he said. "It causes more death than any other."

Hunter glanced up from his idle task. "Time," he

mused. "'Tis a fine answer and better than I hoped to hear from you, MacGowan."

Lachlan's nerves cranked up. "It has no weapon."

"You are wrong," Hunter said. "Time's weapon is a man's own age. The answer is vanity."

"Vanity." Lachlan repeated the word, his voice a rumble in the darkness.

"Aye," said Hunter. "Surely you have heard of it."

"Are you suggesting that I am vainglorious?"

"Nay, I am not suggesting, I am stating it outright. You are vain and you are foolish."

Lachlan took a step toward him, but the other did not back away. Nor did he reach for a weapon. Instead he raised his chin slightly. "What now, MacGowan? Do you hope to kill me for stating the truth?"

He stopped in his tracks. "I am not foolish."

"But you admit to the vanity."

"Because a man knows his value does not mean he is vain."

"And you know your value?"

"Aye, that I do."

"'Tis good," Hunter said. "Then let that be of solace to you on your way to your father's castle."

Lachlan drew a cleansing breath. "Mayhap we should begin anew," he suggested. "I assure you, I did not come to harm you."

The warrior shrugged. "To harm or help—it matters naught, for you are capable of neither. Now, if you possess the slimmest scrap of integrity, you will honor your vow and leave me in peace."

Lachlan remained where he was.

Hunter stared at him. "It is not that you are afeared of

the dark, is it? Do you need a guide to find your way from me camp?"

"I admit," Lachlan mused, "that keeping you safe may well be a near impossible task."

"'Tis good to hear you finally admit your shortcomings."

"Not at all," argued Lachlan. "I could keep you safe if I but set me mind to it, but surely there is not a person with whom you have conversed that does not wish to see you dead."

"Luckily for you, it is not your concern."

"Nay. It is not," agreed Lachlan, and, turning into the darkness, vowed never to do another good deed.

Chapter 2

Vainglorious! Him. Lachlan of the MacGowans. Hardly that. 'Twas that Hunter fellow who was vain. And why? If the truth be told he was probably afeared of fighting. That is why he had refused a battle.

Of course, Lachlan could not blame the warrior. After all, Lachlan thought grimly, watching the sun break over the eastern horizon, Lachlan's reputation as a warrior had surely preceded him. 'Twas really quite clever of the wee fellow to suggest a riddle instead of a test of arms. One couldn't blame him for being cautious, but it certainly would have been satisfying to hear the little weasel admit his fear.

Vain! Him! Well, perhaps he was, but at least he had a reason for his vanity, while Hunter . . .

Lachlan snorted. He could best that warrior fellow with one arm disabled, but perhaps beating him into mash

would not be considered Christian. Thus he would refrain
from that particular pleasure. Still, it would soothe him
considerably if he could scare the other a bit. But there
again, that too might be considered less than kindly.

On the other hand, thought Lachlan, rising restlessly
to gaze back in the direction from which he had just come
the night before, humility was surely a godly attribute, so
if one looked at the situation in a certain light, perhaps it
was his Christian duty to show the warrior the way to humility. Aye, he decided, and smiled into the dawn. Humility may not be his most notable quality, but he was not
opposed to helping others find that same saintly attribute.

It was a simple task for Lachlan to find the warrior's
campsite from the previous night, of course. Following
him thereafter, however, was not as easy as he might
have expected. But then, Lachlan had never liked an
easy course. It was the challenge that made a victory re-
warding. And too, it was good to know the man had felt
it necessary to be somewhat cautious after their meeting.

Lachlan smiled into the darkness. Aye, the warrior
was doing his best to cover his tracks now. Indeed, he
had ridden his mount down a narrow, swift-flowing burn
for some ways, but Lachlan had still managed to find the
spot where he'd turned his steed out of the water. Aye, he
had found it and he had followed the tracks, and soon
he would see his quarry again. Not to exact revenge for
the other's sharp tongue. Nay, that would be churlish,
and though he may not be as charming as some, Lachlan
liked to believe he was a thoughtful sort.

Content with his thoughts, Lachlan tied his stallion to
a rowan that grew beside the burn and glanced upstream.

Aye, the irritating warrior had returned to the rivulet's

edge, but not to ride through it again. Nay, this time he had stopped to water his mount, but he had also made a terrible mistake. He had stopped for the night—beside the burn. It was foolish, for though Hunter had anticipated Lachlan's approach once, it would not happen again. This time Lachlan would be prepared. He would use all his considerable skills, and he would prove himself the better man.

Unfortunately, it would almost be too easy this time. After all, the campsite was quite near the stream and the sound of the water flowing would cover any slight noise Lachlan's footfalls might make. But that was Hunter's mistake.

Easing through the woods, Lachlan held his breath. He was close now, within a furlong for sure, an eighth of a mile, and not too far to use the utmost caution. Thus, he tested the direction of the scant wind and circled noiselessly about so that the breeze trickled into his face instead of onto his back. Not a frond whispered as he passed through the bracken, not a stone was misplaced. Aye, he had been cautious before, but now he was beyond silent as he slipped through the night.

And then, not thirty rods in front of him, Lachlan spotted his prey.

Hunter. He was there, and the situation was even better than hoped for. The warrior was bending over the rushing burn. By the fickle glow of the moonlight, Lachlan could see the man reach into the water. Aye, even though the other was turned away, Lachlan could tell he was washing up. Indeed, his back was bare as he scrubbed at his torso, and what a scrawny back it was!

Lachlan stared in disbelief. Without the padded leather jerkin, the man was as narrow as a sapling. His skin was pale in the deepening darkness and even now, with the moon well hidden again, it was clear that his arms were no brawnier than a strapping lad's.

Sweet mother Mary, he was pitifully lanky. It was almost a shame to frighten the poor waif, and yet . . . the fellow was disturbingly conceited and Lachlan had made a vow to do his Christian deed and teach him humility.

Thus, quiet as a shadow, Lachlan stepped from the woods. The night was silent but for the rush of the burn. Not a sound issued from his footfalls, and he smiled as he stepped up within inches of his quarry. Ahh, how sweet reven—*Christian duty* felt, he amended.

"So here—" Lachlan began.

In that instant the warrior spun about. His sword flashed in the moonlight.

Lachlan leapt back. Snatching his own blade from its scabbard, he parried desperately. Their weapons clashed and clashed again. Sparks flew like shooting stars. Lachlan's sleeve was torn asunder. Pain streaked up his arm, but he hesitated not a moment. Heaving upward, he twisted sharply to the right. Catching the other's sword near the hilt, he dipped and dragged, and suddenly the warrior's weapon was spinning into the darkness and Lachlan's was poised at the other's throat.

Lachlan paused, breathing hard. "Perhaps a game of draughts would have better suited—" he began, but at that moment the moon broke free of the bedeviling clouds and shone with ethereal light on his opponent's— breasts!

Lachlan stumbled backward, reeling as if he'd been struck.

"Holy mother!" he rasped and let his weapon drop

from bloodless fingers. "Gilmour was right! I was saved by a woman!"

Hunter swept up her sword and with a movement as swift as a serpent's strike, she tipped her blade under his and tossed it at him. It sang into the air only to pierce the ground not three inches from his feet.

"Take up your weapon," she ordered, but Lachlan only shook his head.

"You're . . . a woman."

"Aye," she growled and advanced, sword at the ready, "I am the woman who is about to best the great rogue fox."

If her words were meant as a slur, he failed to realize it, for his head was still spinning.

"But you have . . . breasts," he said.

"Pick up your sword!" she demanded and stepping forward, fitted her blade below his jaw, just as he had seconds before. "Or shall I kill you here and now?"

Lachlan tilted his head back slightly, but even so he could see her breasts. And they were beautiful, full and fair and moon-kissed in dusky hues. "Kill me then," he said softly. "And have done with, for I'll not fight a maid."

"Damn you!" she swore, pressing forward. "Defend yourself."

"Nay."

"Retrieve your sword!"

"I will not."

For a moment her blade trembled against his throat, but finally she yanked it away with a curse and pivoted about. Lachlan watched her go, watched her bend and lift and pull her tunic over her head and past her waist.

He closed his eyes and remembered to breathe, but his mind was reeling.

"Why—" he began.

"Don't speak!" she snarled and, retrieving her weapon, stalked back to him. "Or I swear by all that is holy I shall carve your tongue from your head."

He nodded once. Aye, maybe ten minutes ago he would have gladly welcomed such a challenge, but ten minutes ago she had been a man. Life was indeed full of surprises.

"You'll tell no one." Her voice was as deep as the night again, gritted and quiet, but it seemed different now, imbued with a earthy sensuality that he had somehow failed to recognize. Breasts! Sweet Mother. Who'd have guessed—besides Gilmour, of course. Mour had said that Lachlan's brawny savior had been a woman, had all but driven him mad with the taunting, but—breasts!

"Do you hear me?" she snarled, lifting her sword.

"What's that?" he asked, and she took a threatening step forward.

"I said, you'll tell no one."

Her beauty was hidden from him now, and yet it seemed as if he could see them still, moon-drenched and perfect. "About what?" he asked and tried a smile, but he would never be a success on the stage.

"Damn you!" she swore. "Make your vow or die now."

He was silent a moment. He could feel his heart beating in his chest, could hear his breath and hers.

"Tell me this first," he said finally. "Why would you hide such beaut—" He paused, searching for words. "Why would you hide your true sex?"

"It matters not," she said. "Only that I do and that you shall keep it so."

How could he not have known? "But I owe you me life." Perhaps he should have been mortified to have been saved by a maid. In fact, when Mour had taunted him with his theory, he had been, but now, for reasons he could neither explain nor condone, he felt some pride for it. After all, she had saved *him*. Not Gilmour, the rogue of the rogues, nor Ramsay, with the "soulful" eyes. But him. Why? "I owe you," he repeated, setting aside his thoughts for later dissection. "And I shall repay you."

"Nay!" Her tone was sharp. "You failed to answer the riddle correctly, thus you agreed to go."

"Aye," he said, "but I won the battle of swords and now you shall agree to allow me to repay the favor."

"Never." There was passion in her tone. Passion that had been entirely lacking on the previous day, passion that Lachlan would have thought was impossible to awaken from such impenetrable stoicism. "You shall return to Isobel's castle."

"Nay, I—" He paused. "*Isobel's* castle?"

There was a momentary silence. "To Evermyst, or wherever you choose to go," she said.

"Why do you refer to it as Isobel's?"

"You will leave!" she ordered, but Lachlan barely heard her.

"Anora was lady of the keep long before Bel came along. She was raised there as the only child of the old laird and lady. None knew she had a twin until a few months hence."

She said nothing. He took a step toward her, though she raised her sword in defiance.

"Did you know her? Had you met maid Isobel before she found her way to Evermyst?"

"Mayhap you do not realize this," she said, her words measured, "but I do not wish to discuss this subject or any other with the likes of you. Nor do I—"

"Who are you?" he asked.

She said nothing.

"How do you know me sisters by law? I'd not seen you at Evermyst but at Gilmour's marriage to Bel."

"I am called the warrior," she said. "Hunter if you must, and no one to be trifled with."

Trifled with. The phrase brought to mind an entirely different meaning than it would have if she'd said the same thing yesterday. Breasts! Glory be!

"So you came to Evermyst during the battle. But how did you know we were in need, and why did you save me? And—" A thought came to him suddenly. "The warrior . . ." His voice was little more than a whisper. "The warrior at Dun Ard long months ago. When we first found Lady Anora. That was you."

She neither denied nor confirmed.

" 'Twas you who was following the lass. 'Twas you on MacGowan land. You who caused her fall from her palfrey."

For a moment the world went silent, then, "I will have your vow, MacGowan, or I will have your life."

"But what of your rule not to wound the very man you saved?"

It seemed a logical point to him and not one to justify the growl that issued from the maid.

"Quiet!"

"You would break your own rule?" he asked. It didn't seem strange to him that his tone was naught but conversational. He and his brothers had engaged in many such debates while they caught their breath before battling again. "You would break your own rule just to keep your secret safe? Not to mention the fact that I would be dead and—"

"I would slay you just because you irritate me!" she snarled.

"Why—"

"So you should not irritate me!" she said, her voice rising.

He didn't mean to grin. "In truth, me lady," he said. "I irritate—"

"Do you always prattle so? Give me your vow and be gone."

"I cannot," he said.

Sweeping back her sword, Hunter lunged toward him, and in the same moment Lachlan titled his head back. Her blade swept past him, missing his throat by a breath.

Silence fell over them and then she turned with a snarl and strode into the darkness.

As for Lachlan, he remained as he was. True, he had not believed she would kill him, but when a sword sweeps past one's throat, one has time to reconsider his judgment. In fact, in that flashing second, one has time to consider many things.

Who was she? Why was she dressed as a man? Why had she followed Anora? Why had she come to Evermyst? And . . . He glanced rapidly about. Where the devil had she gone? Listen as he might, he could hear nothing, and suddenly the idea of losing her caused panic to stir in his gut.

He employed no stealth as he rushed back to his steed, and though it took him some time to find her, he did so finally. She didn't turn at his approach. Neither did she acknowledge his presence. Instead, she traveled through the darkness as if he were of no more significance than a bothersome midge.

They rode for hours until a glimmer of dawn finally lit

the eastern sky. Something rustled in the undergrowth. An arrow hissed into the air, and in an instant a hare lay skewered to the earth.

Lachlan glanced toward Hunter, but she was already unstringing her bow and setting it back in place behind her leather-clad thigh. Throwing a leg over her pommel, she jumped to the ground and pulled a dagger from the top of her tall boot.

He dismounted as well, drawn to the hare. And as he approached it, one singular fact made itself clear. It had been pierced directly through the heart.

"A fine shot," he said, and she turned abruptly toward him.

"Why do you follow me?"

Her fist, he noticed, was wrapped tight and hard about the hilt of her knife, and the blade was surprisingly close to his chest. He glanced at it, cleared his throat and found her eyes. "Because I owe you?" He had meant to growl back, but the image of her breasts gleaming in the moonlight had somehow unmanned him. Although he was gifted at many things, he had never been particularly adept where women were concerned.

"You do not owe me," she hissed.

"Aye. I—"

"I absolve you of the debt."

He remained silent for a moment. "Where are you bound, me l—"

"And I am *not* your lady!"

"Then what shall I call you?"

"Do not call me. Leave me be."

"I cannot," he said simply.

"You cannot." Her voice was low and quiet. "And why is that?"

"Because you saved me life."

"Aye," she agreed, "but just yesterday you were willing to forget the debt."

"All was different then."

"Naught was different—"

"You were a man."

"Me sex makes no difference," she said, and turned abruptly away. "Indeed," she added, "if you are wise you will forget what you saw at the water's edge."

He didn't mean to do it, but somehow he snorted, and in an instant she had pivoted back around. Her knife was up again, and her teeth were gritted.

"You have something to say, MacGowan?"

Perhaps he should not, but in fact, he did. "Aye," he said, and glanced down at her. She was not a small lass, but neither was she huge, standing several inches beneath his own height.

"And what, pray tell, is it?" She gritted the question between her teeth. Nice teeth, he thought. Straight and white.

He shrugged slightly. "The truth is this, lass—wise or foolish, I shall *never* forget the sight of you."

She was utterly silent as she stared at him. Beneath the shadow of her dark helmet, he could not quite decipher her expression, but finally she spoke, her voice soft with just a hint of the femininity he had inadvertently discovered. "Why?"

Because she was beautiful. The realization surprised even him, for he had never gotten a good look at her face. In fact, until last night, he had never cared to.

"It is something that a man remembers," he said simply.

Silence again, then, "Why?"

"Because you . . ." He motioned stiffly toward his own chest. "You were unclothed."

"I do not see why that should be so amazing. I assume even the notorious MacGowan rogues are unclothed from time to time."

"Aye," he agreed. "But that is entirely different."

"We are not so different," she said, and turned abruptly away.

"Oh yes," he argued and followed her through the underbrush as she retrieved the hare by her red-feathered arrow and strode off to her steed again. It felt quite strange discussing such a topic, but then, she was obviously a strange maid. "You can take me word on this, lass, we are completely different."

She stopped her mount in a small clearing and removed the bridle before facing Lachlan. The dark stallion ambled off, his saddle still in place. "Nay. Structurally, there is little difference between us."

"You jest." He let his gaze dip to her chest, but it did him no good, for they were hidden well out of sight. It saddened him to think about it.

"Aye," she said, her stance stiff. "Little difference atall except for . . . a few small details."

"Small!" he snorted, then cleared his throat at her sharp expression. "Your pardon," he said. "But if memory serves . . . and it most certainly does . . . the details were very . . . well proportioned."

She watched him for several long seconds, then turned away again, leaving him to stare at naught but the quiver of arrows that was strapped across her back. It was crafted of fine leather and stamped with knot work designs that somehow reminded him of deep water conchs all laid in a row. The quiver ended at her lower back, and though her long, bullhide jerkin revealed little, it seemed now that he could discern a thousand idiosyncrasies that belied her guise—the grace of her stride, the sway of her hips, the—

"So you are like the others."

"Others?" he asked and, lifting his gaze from her backside, suddenly felt the sear of some bitter emotion he could not quite name. "What others?"

"Other men. You are obsessed with a woman's form."

"Hardly—"

"You've but to be in the vicinity of them and your mind turns to miller's bran."

" 'Tis not—"

"You are a man trained to battle," she said and nodded up from her task of collecting firewood. "Aye, you have had some tutelage. And despite my initial suspicion you are not completely inept. But one sight of me chest and . . ." She scowled as if baffled, as if talking to herself. "I could have killed you with ease."

"Not . . ." He grimaced, remembering. "Not with ease."

She laughed. "Are you daft? You practically begged me to slit your throat. And why? Because me chest is conformed a bit differently than yours?"

"Nay, 'twas not the reason. 'Tis simply because . . ." Very well, perhaps he *had* been a bit discombobulated. "You are the fairer sex."

"Fairer!" Anger punctuated the word. Her teeth were gritted and her hands formed to fists. "Fairer than what?"

"I meant no insult, me l—"

"I am not your lady!" she growled.

He almost stepped back a pace at the force of her emotion. What had he said to make her so irate? " 'Tis simply that me mother taught me to revere the fairer . . . the female gender."

"Well your mother was a fool!"

If a man said the same he might well be compelled to teach him better manners at the end of his sword, but now he merely scowled. "Me mother is many things," he said. "But a fool, she is not."

Silence fell between them.

She tilted her head. "You cherish her?" she asked. Her voice was strangely soft and he nodded in some confusion.

"Aye. Certainly. And you?" he asked, but she had turned away already.

"You change the subject," she said. "Because you know I am right. Men make fools of themselves for no reason more substantial than the sight of a woman's body."

" 'Tis not true."

She laughed. "Oh, aye, it is and you well know it. One glance of a woman's bosom and all thought flies from your head."

"I was merely surprised," he countered.

"Surprised! You looked as though you'd swallowed your heart. Had I not wished to kill you I would have laughed at the sight of your face. Tell me, MacGowan, have you not seen a woman's breasts before?"

He mouthed something, but no words came for a moment.

"Well?"

"Of course," he said. "I've seen . . . scores—"

"Then why did you all but swoon at the sight of mine?"

" 'Tis a far cry from the truth. In fact, I barely . . ." He wasn't sure, but he may have winced at this point. ". . . noticed."

"Truly," she said, and scoffed. "So I could disrobe this very instant and you'd not be the least distracted."

"Nay I—" he began, but the possibilities suddenly

penetrated his brain. Beneath his plaid, his interest raised its horny head. "Are you considering it?"

Hunter's gaze held his and then, slowly, irrevocably, she lowered her hands to the buckle on her scabbard. It came away in her fingers and fell to the ground.

Lachlan stared like one in a trance, and then, like a butterfly, her fingers moved the slightest degree. For a moment, he was almost aware of danger, but already the narrow blade had been slipped from the hidden sheath and was flying through the air. He heard the hiss of its passage as it skimmed past his ear and sped with vicious intent into the tree behind him.

He turned to glance at the reverberating hilt, then back at her.

"Go back to your mother, MacGowan," she growled, and turned scornfully away. "There are dangers afoot and I have no time to keep you safe."

"If you would cease trying to kill me there would be no need to worry for me safety."

"Trying to kill you!" she scoffed, and laughed. "If that were the case, laddie, you would already be dead."

He smiled. "I think not . . . lassie."

"I am not—"

"Not a lassie, not a lady. What are you then?" he asked, and stepped up to look down at her from a closer angle. "For you surely are not a man."

"Nay, I am not," she hissed. "For I have more important things to do than preen my fragile ego."

"And what things might those be?"

" 'Tis none of your concern, MacGowan, but I'll not have your death on me hands. Go home to your clansmen. Tell them you bested Hunter the great warrior if you like."

"Why would me life be endangered if I remained with you?"

She watched him for a moment, but finally she turned away with a shrug. "I travel south, down to the borderlands. They have no love for bonny Highlanders who wear their plaids like a badge of honor."

"Why?"

"Are you so coddled as to have no knowledge whatsoever of the world? There is no love lost between England and Scotland. Surely you know—"

"Why do you travel south?" he corrected.

" 'Tis none of your concern."

"Perhaps 'tis true," he agreed. "Nevertheless, I shall remain with you until me debt is paid."

"So you insist on continuing this foolishness until you have saved me life?"

"Aye."

"Then I shall threaten me own life and you . . . in your manly way, can convince me to go on living." She glared up at him. "Then we can have done with it here and now."

"I think not," he said and turning, pulled her knife from the tree behind him. Holding her gaze, he sent it shivering past her toe and through her boot's exposed sole.

She didn't flinch. Indeed, her gaze never left his. Even when she bent to pull the blade free, she continued to watch him.

"Aye," she said, and straightened slowly, "you've had some tutelage, MacGowan. Mayhap the border reivers will not find you such easy fodder after all. It seems I shall find out, whether I want to or not.

"You skin the hare. I'll kindle a fire. We can bed down here until nightfall."

They made a meal of rabbit and dark rye bread. Their mounts grazed where they would. Both steeds had seen enough of life to avoid the toxic bracken that flourished there, and although Hunter's dark stallion fed contentedly on the tough grasses that grew sporadically amidst the ferns and mosses, Lachlan noticed that he did not venture far from the maid's side. Instead, he lifted his head often to make certain she was still in sight. He was a fine animal, long of limb, but not as broad as his own Mathan. Three white socks marked his legs, and knotted into his long forelock was a pierced agate. 'Twas strange, he thought, and glanced at Hunter where she rested some rods away. She herself wore no ornament, and yet her mount was adorned. But something flashed into his mind then—the image of her bare bosom. He was wrong, he realized suddenly, for between her bonny breasts there had been a pendant of some sort. Lucky pendant, he thought, and with that image firmly in mind, he rolled himself in his plaid and went to sleep.

Lachlan was never sure what awakened him, but when he became fully alert and glanced at the spot where Hunter had bedded down, he knew the truth immediately; she was gone. He cursed in silence as he straightened his aching back, then turned to find his steed and . . .

He swore aloud this time, for the grove of rowan trees was empty.

Aye, she'd taken both horses and left him afoot.

Chapter 3

Knight Star arched his great, high-crested neck and
snorted.

Evil comes to Evermyst.

Aye, Hunter remembered the old woman's words, and
though she'd tried to ignore them, she had failed. Thus,
her mission, and her journey south, against all her better
judgment.

Knight snorted again.

She spoke softly and urged him on. Dark as a winter
night, he was a large steed, over seventeen hands at the
withers. The Munros had bred him for battle, and in a
state of pique or boredom or both, she had stolen him
from them. Aye, through the years there had been times
she'd been thought of as a hero, but history demanded
that there be just as many times she acted the villain, just
as many times she sought revenge. And though she bore

the scars for her misdeameanors, the acquisition of Knight had been worth the injury. He was strong and bold and loyal, and he was not tired, for she'd not pressed him. MacGowan was afoot; there was no need to hurry.

Knight didn't drop his head or glance at the stallion beside him. Nay, he remained absolutely alert, his ears pitched forward, his eyes bright, watching for trouble, as any true hero would.

Hunter stroked him again, then glanced at Lachlan's steed. He was blood bay in color and built like a bear— not unlike his master, she thought and let her mind wander momentarily.

Aye, she'd taken MacGowan's steed. Maybe she'd done so to keep him safe. Or maybe it was to prevent him from interfering with her plans, or maybe, if she were to be completely honest, it was for no reason other than spite.

Oh aye, Hunter could be spiteful. As could the warrior, as could Maid Rhona, as could Master Giles. Yes, she was all of those, all of those and more. And she would be home soon at Nettlepath, where she'd spent most of her youthful years, where she'd learned many things, not least of all how to survive. But before then there would be trouble.

She could smell it, or perhaps it was another sense that allowed her to feel the nearness of her enemy, something more bestial. But whatever the case, she knew someone was watching her, would have known even without Knight's warning. She stroked him absently. Who it was that awaited her arrival, she wasn't certain, thus she rode on, looking neither right nor left, but drawing in perceptions with barely conscious ease.

He was in front of her, but not on the path, and . . .

It was at that very instant that MacGowan's horse nickered a welcome, and it was at that instant that she realized her mistake. Lachlan had found her. She almost smiled at the realization. So there was some truth to the rumors about him. Not that she too couldn't have run down a pair of horses herself. After all, 'twas easier for a man to navigate the underbrush than it was for a charger, and maybe, just maybe, she had intentionally slowed her pace.

Both horses' ears were pricked forward now, watching the woods ahead and to the left. Aye, MacGowan would exit the trees just about there and . . .

But in that instant something rustled behind her. Without turning, she realized the truth. She'd let her mind wander, and she was surrounded.

"Ho there." The man who appeared on the trail before her was mounted bareback. His steed was spavined, his hose dark, and his quilted jak of plaite well worn. These reivers could not afford full armor, but the metal links sewn into his jerkin would make him hard to kill. "Yer travelin' late, me lord."

She straightened slightly. She could sense them all around her now. There were five . . . nay, six of them. At least two more were mounted. That much she knew, for Knight's ears flickered side to side. But what of the others? If they were afoot her chances were better.

"Aye," she agreed, and tightening her legs against her mount's stout barrel, kept him walking toward the speaker. There was no point in letting them get settled in. "I was hoping to reach the village of Jedburgh yet this night."

"Jedburgh? 'Tis a good five leagues yet. Too much for a man alone, especially should he be afoot."

The threat was implicit, but Hunter ignored it, pretending ignorance. So he was after the horses, and probably more.

"Five leagues," she repeated. Her every muscle was tense. Aye, she was ready for battle. Mayhap she would even welcome it, but she would not give up Knight. Nay, she would keep him, but not for something so foolish as loyalty. Nay, loyalty was for saps and coddled noblemen. She would keep him because without him she was dead. For she knew something about this sort of brigand. Aye, they were tough and they were adroit, but with the boundaries ever shifting between Scotland and England, the border reivers had long ago learned to be ruthless. They would not leave her alive, and only a few meager yards separated her from the nearest one.

"Well," she said, and shrugged, loosening her muscles with an effort. "I suspect there's naught I can do but press—" she began, and dropping the bay's lead, spurred Knight into action as she whipped her sword from its scabbard.

The man shrieked and drew his weapon, but Hunter was already upon him. Knight crashed into his mount, knocking him off balance, then leapt forward, toward safety, but suddenly another horse appeared to their right.

Hunter kneed her steed toward this new challenge and swung her sword in a hissing arc. The man screamed and tottered sideways, but she didn't leap in for the kill. She did not crave revenge, but only survival. One quick cue and Knight pivoted left, swinging his huge forefeet high and leaping forward, but in that second she felt a weight on her leg.

A brigand, afoot! He had grabbed her knee. Too close for a sword. She clubbed him with the hilt of her blade. He faltered, but suddenly the first horseman was there. He yanked the reins from Hunter's hands. She spurred Knight forward. He reared and bolted, wrenching his reins away. She was almost free, but in that moment, a footman appeared in their path. Knight pivoted sideways, trying to avoid him, but his great hooves became tangled in the undergrowth, and he stumbled. Hunter grappled for control, but hands were already reaching for her, pulling her from the saddle, dragging her toward the earth. She hit the ground hard. Her sword spun from her hand. She rolled and leapt to her feet. One glance told her Knight was well out of harm's way.

"As I said . . ." The mounted man was afoot now and grimaced as he drew the back of his wrist across his lips. Blood smeared along his arm, and when he lowered it, she saw he was missing a tooth. "It'd tek a good deal of time to reach the village without a mount, but I'll tell ye what . . ." He stepped forward. "It'll tek a sight longer when ye're dead."

"Dead!" She made her voice warble a bit.

Toothless grinned, and the truth was abundantly clear. These were not just brigands, come to steal from her and better their lives. Nay, they were here to enjoy her pain, and fear would only improve the sport.

"I wish you no harm," she said, and backed up a scant step as she glanced to the side as if weighing her odds. But she already knew her odds, and they were not good. Four men formed a semicircle around her. Toothless was in front. Another sat his steed some rods to the right.

"He wishes us no 'arm," repeated the first fellow and

chuckled. There was no humor in the sound. " 'Tis good to know, ain't it, lads?"

"Please!" Her voice trembled. "Let me be and I'll give you me steeds."

"Or we could kill ye and take the steeds and whatever else ye 'ave on yer person," said Toothless and took a step toward her.

"Nay!" she pleaded, and held out an unsteady hand. "You'll not catch Knight without me."

Toothless stopped for an instant, then he snorted and stepped closer.

"God's truth!" she rambled. "He was bred and trained by the Munros."

"The Munros?"

There was silence for a moment, so she rambled on, and perhaps the panic in her tone wasn't altogether fictionalized. "So you've heard of them! They are my kindred and they'll not take it kindly if I do not return."

"You're a Munro."

"Aye. I—"

" 'Tis me lucky day then, for I've not yet killed one of the warrior clan."

"Is that what you want?" she asked, and turned desperately to scan the faces that surrounded her. "What will do you more good, me own death or a fine mount to ride or barter?"

"Methinks we can 'ave both," said one dark fellow. He was unshaven and squat and limped as he stepped nearer.

"Not true," she said, and turned jerkily back toward toothless. "Here. See this. Come," she called, raising her voice. It trembled again. "Knight Star, come hither."

Nothing happened, but then there came a rustle in the

woods. The black stepped into view. His reins were dragging, and for a moment he paused as he stepped on one, but then he bobbed his head and came forward like a well-trained hound.

"Halt," she said, and her voice sounded stronger as Knight stopped and she turned her attention back to Toothless. "Let me go and he is yours."

The brigand grinned. It was not a pretty sight. "Call him over," he ordered.

"Nay," she said, and Toothless lifted his dirk.

"Call him or—"

"Not until you vow to set me free."

"Vow?" Someone chuckled behind her. The sound shivered up her spine. "Aye, give the fancy lord your vow, Kirk."

Toothless grinned as he tightened his grip on his knife and stepped forward. "Aye, that's what I'll do lads, I'll—"

But in that moment Hunter shrieked. The sound echoed like a falcon's cry in the woods. Knight lunged forward. Toothless spun toward the beast, but too late. The stallion struck him with one pistoning hoof. The brigand went down screaming. Men scattered as the stallion slid to a halt before her. She made a dive for the saddle, but in that instant an arm encircled her throat, dragging her backward. She felt a blade against her neck and heard a whispered threat, but she wasted not a moment. Instead, she swung her feet up against Knight's ribs and shoved with all her might.

Her captor stumbled backward, then tripped and went down. For a moment his grip loosened on her windpipe. Snatching her dirk from the scabbard at her waist, she twisted wildly about. He died in an instant.

She scrambled to her feet, searching desperately for

Knight, but he'd already been mounted by another. She shifted her gaze to the others who stood before her. There was death in their eyes.

She lifted her bloody blade. "Come on then!" she hissed.

There was a moment of quiet, then screams burst from them and they came, swords drawn.

She kicked the first one aside and ducked the second, but the third was there immediately. She parried and twisted away. Pain sliced across her back, knocking her to her knees.

Death thundered up. She heard the boom of its hooves and raised her face to snarl at it. The rider bent toward her. His sword hissed through the air and then . . . like a fallen leaf, it dropped to the ground in front of her.

She tried to reach for it but her arm would not react. Someone shrieked. She twisted about, ready to fight as best she could, but chaos had erupted about her, and as sudden as death, the men lay sprawled on the trampled bracken.

"Hunter."

Someone spoke. She turned in bewilderment, and there, not an arm's length from her, was Lachlan Mac-Gowan.

"You are injured."

She struggled to rise. "Where is he?"

He pressed her back down. "Stay put until I see to your wound."

"Where is he?"

"Calm yourself. He is dead."

"Nay," she muttered, and found her feet despite his efforts to keep her down.

"Steady, lass. They are all dead."

" 'Tis not true. Knight would not—"

"Night?" he said, but in that moment she felt a warm draft on her neck.

Hunter turned and he was there, larger than life, his dark eyes gleaming. She raised a hand to straighten his forelock, and Knight pushed his head forward. Resting his jaw on her shoulder he breathed, loud as a bellows into her ear. She stroked his wide brow and felt her knees begin to buckle.

"Damn!" MacGowan swore and, reaching up, dragged the horse's head from her shoulder. "Mount up."

"What—"

"Get up there," he said and pushing her toward the saddle, tugged Knight's head forward. "Unless you're planning to carry him."

The ride to Jedburgh was not as far as the brigand had suggested. Neither was it a comfortable one. Nevertheless, Hunter survived the journey and managed to dismount in the gathering darkness without assistance.

"We are in need of lodging." MacGowan's voice was clear enough as he spoke to the innkeeper, so apparently she was still lucid. "For me companion and meself."

The proprietor had seen ninety years if he'd seen a day, and each one seemed to weigh as heavily as sand upon his stooped shoulders. "What is it that troubles you?" he asked, and glared askance into Hunter's face.

"There is naught amiss," she said, and straightened with an effort.

"You're as pale as oyster broth. Are you ill?"

"Nay. Merely weary," Hunter said and, moving carefully, pulled her cape more firmly over her shoulder.

"We want no trouble here," warned the innkeeper.

"I've enough problems what with naught but a simpleton and a doxy to lighten me load."

"I am well, old gaffer," she said, employing her gruffest tone. "Will you house us or nay?"

He squinted at her for a moment, then nodded stiffly. "Aye. Don't get your comb up, young cock, I've a room for you."

"We'll need two," she said, but he glared up at her with new ferocity. "What's that?"

"We'll need two rooms," she said, her voice hard.

"Well, I've got but one to spare. You'll take it or you'll not. Which will it be?"

"I—" she began, but Lachlan interrupted her.

"We'll take it," he said and reaching out, tugged Knight's reins from her hand. "I'll see to the steeds."

"Nay," she argued, and yanked the reins back. "I'll care for me own mount."

"You need rest," Lachlan gritted.

"You rest, MacGowan, I've no need for your—" she began, but he nudged her slightly. She glared down at his elbow, then looked in the direction he was staring.

The old man stared back. "What's wrong with the two of ye?" he asked.

"Nothing," Hunter said, drawing herself up again.

The ancient innkeeper snorted. "You act like a pair of dolts."

"Listen, old man—"

"Me apologies," Lachlan interrupted again, and taking Hunter's arm, steered her toward the stables. "We are but weary. We'll see to our steeds and find our rooms short—"

"*Room!*" the old man corrected, then turned to shuffle toward the wattle and daub inn that listed wearily over the partially cobbled street. "And I'll have me monies in advance or you'll be sleeping with the beasties."

"What the devil is wrong with you?" hissed Mac-Gowan.

"Me?" She yanked her elbow from his grasp and though she regretted the movement, she kept her pain to herself. "There is naught amiss with the likes of me."

"You've been wounded, if you disremember."

"I am well."

"You've been wounded," he repeated, "and you need a leech to see to your troubles."

"Nay, I do not," she said and leading Knight into a wide, loose stall, she turned him about and loosened his girth. Removing his saddle was trickier. She grimaced and Lachlan was beside her in an instant, pushing her away as he lifted the gear from her stallion's back.

"The old man is right," he said and tossed the bridle atop her saddle blanket. It was scarlet in color and made of fine wool. Long ago she'd abandoned the blankets woven of straw, for they chaffed Knight's stout back, and an injured horse was a weakened horse. "You are a dolt."

Bending painfully, she lifted a handful of bedding from the floor. Twisting it into a knot, she rubbed circles into the stallion's neck. Knight sighed and cocked a hip, but MacGowan was less content.

"Sweet mother," he said, and yanked her cape aside.

"Leave off," she growled and jerked away, but pain skittered across her shoulder and she stopped to hug her arm against her side.

He stared at her. "Get to the inn."

"Mayhap you've forgotten your place, MacGowan. You are naught to me. Certainly no one to order me about."

"If you do not care for it it will fester."

"That is me own choice, then."

He shrugged. "I have a rule." His voice was low so that none else could hear. "Not to allow any maid to die if I've recently saved her."

They were her own words twisted about and come back to haunt her. "I care not for your rules."

"I have another rule. To make certain that the maid tends to her wounds else I'll expose her as the fraud she is."

"Do you threaten me, MacGowan?"

"Go in," he ordered. "Your mount will be fine without you."

She shifted her gaze to the stallion. "Ill care makes him naught but less valuable."

"So 'tis simply his value you are considering," he said.

"Of course."

He snorted.

"You think I lie?"

"I think you would have carried the animal on your shoulders had he been over tired."

"Coddling is for fools and Highlanders."

He cocked his head at her. "And which of those might you be?"

She considered arguing, but there was that in his eyes that spoke of lies exposed, so she lifted her chin and left the stable while she still could.

Even though there were lads in the livery, Lachlan saw to the steeds himself, for unless he missed his guess,

Hunter would blame him if aught was amiss with the dark stallion when she returned. Strange, he had not thought her to be the sentimental type, but she seemed firmly attached to the steed called Knight.

With the horses fed and groomed, he made his way to the inn. Fatigue wore at him as he reached his rented room, but he did not enter immediately, for she would be there, and even in his weakened state, he was entirely unsure he could share a chamber and not be moved. Standing beside the arched door, Lachlan lifted his hand to knock at the portal, but a shuffling noise distracted him, and soon the ancient innkeeper appeared from around a corner.

"I'll have me monies first," he rasped, his hoary fingers outstretched.

"Of course," Lachlan agreed, and opening his sporran, brought forth a coin.

The ancient proprietor took it without a word, but remained where he was. "Well? What be ye waitin' for?"

Lachlan glanced toward the door and back. "What's that?"

"Go in, ye daft bugger," he said, and shuffled away.

"Oh. Aye," Lachlan agreed and clearing his throat loudly, pulled up the latch and stepped inside.

Hunter sat upright in bed, her eyes narrowed and her dirk already in hand. Judging by first impressions, she'd removed nothing but her helmet and sword—maybe her spurs, if he was lucky.

He eyed her as he crossed the room.

"Hear this," she said. "If you so much as touch me hand I will skewer you to the wall."

He snorted. "I saw you try to lift your saddle, laddie. You'd be fortunate to skewer a fat onion to a trencher."

"I am not so wounded that I cannot best the likes of you, MacGowan."

" 'Tis good to hear. Take off your cape."

She rose slowly to her feet, and damn the luck—she still wore her spurs. "As I said, you'll not be touching me."

They stood nearly nose to nose.

"And why is that?"

"Because I know how men are." She smiled grimly. "In fact, I am one meself most days."

"And pray tell, how are men?"

"Not to be trusted where women are concerned."

"Ahh, that again," he said and reached for the silver clasp that held her cape in place.

She raised her knife and her brows in slow tandem and he crossed his arms against his chest and stared.

"You are the most difficult . . ." He searched momentarily for the proper word. ". . . *warrior* I have ever met," he said.

"It is you who are difficult."

He made a sound like a winded horse, but she ignored him.

" 'Twas not I who asked you to interfere in me mission."

"Nay, but 'twas—What mission is that?" he asked.

She scowled. His shoulders and chest were near as broad as a stable door and yet she doubted if he packed a thimble's worth of fat. Nay, it was muscle that rippled beneath his tunic and she would be lucky to hold him off for so much as an instant, with a blade or without, if he decided to force his hand. She'd been raised as a lass for the first several years of her life, and as a lass she'd learned her weaknesses. 'Twas as a boy she'd found her strength, and 'twas as a boy she'd survived.

Oh aye, things could have been worse. She could have been abandoned to die in infancy. But she had not. Nay, her blood kin had seen fit to give her to another. To an old man called Barnett. An old man who did not want a girl child, an old man whose wits were addled by loss and hopelessness. An old man who longed for the return of his son. But the son was dead, and she could not replace him, no matter how hard she tried, no matter what skills she acquired or what battle she fought. And in the end she'd been abandoned both by Barnett and by herself, until only the warrior Hunter was left. With no room for softness or giving. No room for a maid or the wee lass she had once been. But Hunter did not miss her and she would not turn back.

"I did not ask you to interfere with me life," she said, and kept her voice low and steady. Nay, she could not hold him off by force, for her own strength lay in wit and dexterity, but if he wanted a battle, he would have one. "In truth, I begged you to leave."

"Begged," he scoffed. "You wouldn't know how to beg if Saint Peter himself were your tutor. What the devil were you thinking standing those brigands alone?"

She stared at him, awestruck and silent, then, "Might you believe I invited the bastards to accost me? Do you think I asked them for trouble?"

"Aye! That is exactly what I think, for if you wanted no trouble you would have kept me at your side."

Perhaps her surprise showed on her face. "To protect me?" she asked scornfully. "To be me champion?"

"Aye," he growled. "Mayhap I could do a better job than your knight in yonder stable."

"He has been more loyal than most."

He watched her carefully, as though her words told him a thousand secrets she did not want spilled. She tensed.

"So he is a Munro steed," he mused.

She considered denying it, but he had heard the truth spoken to the brigands, and lies were naught but more difficulties. "Aye," she said. "The Munros bred him."

"Their mounts are usually white."

"So I am told."

"And well treasured." He paused. "Why did they give him to you?"

She said nothing as she seated herself on the edge of the bed.

"So you are a Munro," he said.

"Of course," she agreed, and laughed. "After his mother's death, and before his father attacked Evermyst's folk, the fierce Innes Munro, the barbarian bastard of old, nurtured a wee girl child, then raised her to battle like a man. Perhaps they trained me to combat their Fraser foes."

"Evermyst and Windemoore are foes no longer," he said. "Not since Anora's marriage to Ramsay. Not since he gave up trying to win a Fraser bride and became the peaceful bridegroom of Lady Madelaine."

"Perhaps," she said.

"What do you mean, perhaps?"

"Not all Munros are thrilled with their laird's new and gentler ways."

"How do you know this?"

She shrugged. "Did you not say I was one of them?"

"If you are not a Munro, then who are you?"

"I am a warrior, and not to be underestimated."

"Aye," he growled. "And nearly a dead warrior for your foolishness."

"So 'tis true," she scoffed. "You would be me champion?"

His scowl deepened. "Mayhap."

Tension sparked between them. "Have you any idea how long I have been protecting meself, *champion*?"

For a long moment he said nothing at all. Instead, he remained perfectly motionless as he watched her, as if any movement might distract him from his thoughts. "Nay." His voice had dropped and his eyes were narrowed. They were solemn and dark, nearly the same hue as his sable hair, held back from his face with a single strip of untanned hide. "Tell me how long you have been on your own, lass."

For a moment there seemed to be no air in the room and for that same length of time she almost longed to tell him of her life, of being left with an old man who did not want a lass, of her futile struggle to become what he wanted her to be. But she knew better than to air the truth. She forced a laugh. "'Tis none of your concern. Indeed—"

"But I am curious," he said. "How long has it been?"

"Long enough so that I do not need your assistance, of that you can be certain."

"That did not seem to be the case a few short hours ago."

She was silent for a moment, remembering. Aye, it had been a tight spot, but she had been in tight spots before and lived to tell of it. She needed no one. Not the family that had forsaken her, not the baron who had betrayed her, and certainly not this man. She had proved as much before and she would do so again. "Leave me be,

MacGowan," she said. "If you wish it I will agree that you saved me life. You can return to sipping ale before the fire in lofty Evermyst and tell the lads how you saved the warrior from sure death. Perhaps if you tell it well the maids will sigh and swoon at your bravery. I'll not call you a liar."

"Aye," he said, "and do not forget that you stole me steed."

She *had* almost forgotten. Indeed, he had run a goodly way to catch her. What the devil was he made of?

"Next time I will ride faster," she vowed.

He raised a brow at her. "So you delayed, did you? Were you waiting for me, lass?"

She laughed, and he canted his head at her.

"What are you so afeared of that you would endanger your life to avoid me?"

"Afeared? Me?"

"Aye. You. Who are you really?"

"I am Hunter, the warrior."

For a moment neither spoke. His gaze was as sharp as shattered glass.

"Aye," he said and nodded slowly. "The warrior. And so you must disrobe so I may see to your wound, for 'tis obvious, there is no difference between us."

Chapter 4

Lachlan watched her as he waited for her reaction. She wore no hat this night. Neither did her chain ventrail hide her face, though her cheeks were smudged with dried blood and dirt. Her hair was but a little longer than his, reaching a hand's length or so past her shoulders, but where his was dark and bedeviled with waves, hers was smooth and straight and as bright as barleycorn just brought into the barn. Her cheekbones were high, her jaw strong, and her mouth full, but it was her eyes that fascinated him, for they reminded him of something, though he couldn't say exactly what. Silver blue, they were, and as bright as the even stars.

"Why do you stare?" Her voice was low.

He shrugged, trying to look casual. "No reason. Take off your cloak. I'll see to your wound."

"As I have already told you—"

"Aye. Skewering and all that," he said, and set his fingers to the clasp at her throat. She knocked his hand away with her arm, and though her knife never touched him, he scowled at her.

"Tell me, then, do you call yourself a liar?"

"What's that?"

" 'Twas you who said there was little difference between us. If such is true you have me most solemn vow that I will have no interest in you."

Silence.

"In truth," he added, "You could dance naked about the room and I would be naught but bored."

She still said nothing. Her face was as somber as a stone.

"Well, perhaps I would be a mite . . . surprised," he said, and in that instant he thought he saw the slightest hint of a smile and the dimmest shadow of a crescent dimple. "Maybe . . ." He shrugged, feeling breathless as he watched that foreign expression ebb and wan. "Maybe I would be a bit . . . repulsed."

The corner of her mouth lifted a quarter of an inch and then she dropped her head, as if she could not trust him to see such a dastardly weakness as humor.

"So I am to believe you have no interest in other men, MacGowan?"

"Interest?"

She shrugged. "There are those who favor their own sex. Men dallying with their servants. Knights . . . enjoying their squires."

He stared at her.

"Surely you've heard such tales."

He could not help but grimace, and perhaps she could not help but laugh, for she did so and the sound tantalized him; it was hardly the deep chuckle of a warrior, but the silvery laughter of an untried maid. 'Twas little wonder she hid behind those dour expressions and low mutterings if she wished to feign masculinity, for it was an utterly feminine sound, light and joyous and filled with iridescent beauty.

Lachlan stared transfixed.

She cleared her throat, dropped her gaze, and lowered her brows. "What are you looking at, champion?" Her voice was low again. He yanked himself from his trance with an effort.

"Think of this. If your wound festers you will need to have it seen by a healer of some sort. Surely then another will learn your secret. But if you let me help you . . ." He shrugged. It was becoming a familiar gesture, disarming, he hoped. But then, the word *disarming* was a bit disconcerting now that he thought about it, for she still held the knife, and though her laughter may be utterly feminine, her fighting skills were not.

"Why?"

"What?"

"Why do you wish to see me wound?"

He scowled. "What are the possibilities here?"

"There is no reason you should help me."

The statement made him pause. "I suspect you are right, laddie, except for the fact that you are another human being and it be me Christian duty to do so . . . and that you were unjustly attacked and did your part to rid Scotland of rabble that may have harmed others in the future . . . and that you once saved me from—"

"Very well."

He stopped abruptly and turned his ear toward her for he was certain he had not heard correctly. "Your pardon?"

"You can see to me wound," she said. Drawing a deep breath, she sheathed her knife and set her fingers to the clasp at her throat. Knot work was etched into the fine silver.

Lachlan nodded once. " 'Tis good," he said, but though his tone was casual, he felt an odd tightening in his chest. "Sensible. Wise."

She stared at him strangely. He cleared his throat, and in a moment her cape was laid aside. Setting her fists to her hips, she turned away.

"Well?" she said.

"Well?"

"See to it."

"Oh! Aye," he said, and stepped quickly forward. Padded and protruding well past her shoulders, her sleeveless jerkin was made of thick, rough bullhide, but the brigand's blade had sliced easily through it. That much Lachlan could see, though he could discern little else. "You must remove your garments."

She said nothing, but merely glanced over her shoulder at him. No emotion showed on her face.

"I can see nothing like this," he explained.

"Tell me, champion . . ." Her voice was low and quiet. "Do you think me a fool?"

Her expression was absolutely sober, as if her question were one he was to answer, and for some foolish, inexplicable reason it almost made him smile. Almost. But she still had her dirk close to hand and he liked to think he wasn't an absolute lackwit.

"Nay," he said.

"Then mayhap you think I find you irresistible."

Lachlan gently tugged at the sliced edge of the dark

jerkin. Beneath the heavy leather, she wore a simple, bone-colored tunic, and beneath that there seemed to be another layer of cloth. Did she already wear a bandage?

"Is that it then?" she asked.

Her tunic was bloodied and tattered. He scowled. "MacGowan?"

"What's that?" he asked, distracted.

She pulled away to turn toward him. "Do not think I am like the others. For I do not find you irresistible."

"I did not . . ." he began, then, "Others?"

They watched each other cautiously for several silent moments.

"What others?" he asked.

"Your past conquests."

"Ahh," he said, and nodded once. "Those."

"Aye. Those. It does not matter if there were dozens or scores. In truth, champion, I find maids to be a silly lot, and the things that excite them, sillier still."

"Excite them?"

She drew herself up slightly. Nay, she was not a small woman, but without the cape she had lost some breadth. Her jaw was square and firm, her cheeks slightly hollowed, but her neck . . . He stared at it. Without the metal ventrail, it looked as delicate and smooth as a royal swan's.

"Aye, I admit that you have some power in your arm, and your face . . ." She stared at him a moment, then shrugged. "It is not hideous to look upon, but that does not mean that I will beg for your touch like the maids of your past."

He stared blankly.

"Do not underestimate me, MacGowan. I am a warrior and not easily charmed," she said and, setting her hand to her dirk, pulled it forth again. "Do you understand me?"

Was she suggesting he was charming? Him? Oh, aye, he was strong and he was stealthy, but truth to tell, women did not always appreciate the fact that he could best them in arm wrestling or startle them at will.

"Do you understand?" she asked again, and pressed the point of the blade to his chest.

He paused a moment, still thinking. She pressed harder. He dropped his gaze to the dirk, then lifted it slowly back to hers. "Aye," he said finally, and nodded. "I think I do."

They stared at each other for one endless moment, then she drew a deep breath and replaced her dirk.

"Very well then," she said and removed her jerkin. A moment later, she grasped the bottom of her tunic and pulled it upward.

Lachlan didn't realize he was holding his breath until he heard her soft gasp of pain.

"Here then," he said. Brushing her hands aside, he gently tugged the tunic over her head and tossed it aside.

When next he saw her face it was ultimately pale, and her eyes, silver blue in the dim light, were unbelievably large.

"Are you well?" he asked.

It took her a moment to speak, but when she did her voice was brusque. "Aye, of course," she said and turned away.

Lachlan lowered his gaze to her back, but despite the removal of her shirt, he could see little of her injury. A long strip of white fabric encircled her chest. It was wrapped over her shoulders and criss-crossed against her torso again. She was trussed up like a Yuletide goose, and from the top of the bindings a narrow leather sheath protruded. So that was where she kept her wee sgian dubh—her black knife. She hid a dirk in her boot, her short sword lay on the floor, and housed with her beloved Knight in the stable was her longbow. The woman was armed like a battalion of foot soldiers, but it was her back that held his attention, for the lower portion of her bindings was rent and bloodied. The cloth frayed apart for several inches and along the edges of the cut there was a smear of dried blood. He spread the tear apart carefully, but he had seen enough injuries to know this one was far from life threatening. His gaze skimmed down from the cloth, smoothing past her waist and over her buttocks.

"Well?" she asked, but her tone was softer now.

He drew himself back to her wound, but it was difficult to see, so he brushed his hand down her hair and gently skimmed it past her shoulder and out of the way. A silver chain lay against the velvety skin of her neck, and he was stunned, and yes a bit mortified, to find that it was just there, beneath the spun gold of her hair, that he longed to kiss her.

"Must it be stitched?"

So deeply absorbed was he that he nearly jumped at the sound of her voice. "Truth to tell . . . Hunter . . ." It was difficult remembering to refer to her as a man, for though her torso was mostly hidden, he could catch glimpses of her flesh, and where it showed it looked as smooth and soft as a kitten's coat. "'Tis impossible to tell with the . . . ahh . . . bandages in place."

Silence entered the room. 'Twas a good sign. At least she hadn't yet skewered him to the wall as earlier suggested. But if he gave in to his yearnings, she might do so yet. Thus, he cleared his throat and stepped back a pace, lest he fall victim to his nether parts' foolish urgings.

"We have little choice here," he said. "The wound must be cleaned and tended."

She didn't speak, but turned to glance over her shoulder at him. Thick, deep gold lashes fringed her quicksilver eyes, and her hair, long as his forearm, fell over her shoulder in a cascade of sunlight. Her shoulders were as smooth and pale as winter's first snow, and below the bandages, her waist was as small and curved as the bend of an hourglass. But it was not just those stunning elements of femininity that made the breath squeeze shut in his chest. It was the striking contrast of the warrior and the maiden, for though her skin looked as creamy as a babe's, below she was encased in scarred leather.

Her bottom was round and firm. Her legs were as long as a blooded mare's, starting at the provocative *V* and sloping down to where her battered boots rose above her knees.

Beneath his plaid, his desire stirred restlessly. He cleared his throat, and then they spoke at once.

"Listen—"

"Do—"

"What?" they said in unison.

He took a deep breath and carefully held her gaze. Aye, one would think it would be safe to stare at her back, but one would be entirely wrong, for even now his desire was whispering foolhardy things to his foolhardy brain.

"Mayhap you should employ the aid of another," he suggested.

"What's that?" she asked, and scowled. The curve of her cheek was hidden by a wave of flaxen hair, and somehow the sight of that alone was nearly his undoing.

He swallowed hard. "I am not greatly gifted as a healer. Perhaps I should send someone else to examine you."

"And have another man discover me true—"

"Man!" The word escaped him without warning. Her brows rose abruptly. He scowled and began anew. "Nay. The bindings will have to be removed, therefore I assumed you would want . . ." He paused, rephrasing wildly in his mind. "That is to say, I thought a woman would be more . . . knowledgeable in the ways of herbs and the like."

"A woman?"

"Aye, you could . . . remove the rest of your clothing." He truly hoped his voice didn't squeak when he spoke, but he felt like an untried boy, hard and needy and aching with hopeless desire. "You could tell her you fell. There would be no reason for her to know you were aught but a misfortunate maid who had—"

"But I came here in the guise of a man."

A man! With an arse like that? No one in his right mind would believe such foolishness. The fact that he *had* made it no more believable. The thought almost made him laugh, but he was finding it difficult to breathe, so laughing was out of the question, and it was a good thing too, because regardless of the delicious curve of her buttocks, she did not seem to possess a woman's renowned ability to forgive.

"Aye," he agreed, and took a cautious step backward,

putting a bit of judicious distance between himself and the temptation that was her. "Aye, you did that, but no maid saw you enter. I could tell them that the man I came here with was . . . in the stable and that I had a . . . companion who needed—"

"A companion? From where?" she asked. "Everyone in Jedburgh will know their own citizens. Nay." She shook her head. " 'Twill never work."

"But . . ." He was starting to sweat. Holy Mother! He'd followed her afoot for many a league and had not felt this winded. But her buttocks were as curved and sweet as a ripe apple and her waist all but begged for his touch.

"Is it so hideous then?"

"What's that?" he asked, and snapped his gaze to her eyes.

There was worry there and the first glimmer he'd seen of true fear. "The wound," she said. " 'Tis bad, that is why you've no wish to tend it."

"Nay," he said and shook his head. " 'Tis not that, lass, *lad*. Indeed, I can barely see it, bound as it is. 'Tis simply that . . ." He ran out of words.

"What?"

"I'll fetch help," he said, and turned with rapid relief toward the door.

"Nay."

He stopped abruptly, bumping into his erection.

"You are a man of arms. Certainly you've see the like of this before."

Turning, he let his gaze fall to the breathtaking curve of her buttocks. No, actually he hadn't, he thought, and tried not to wince.

"You're not squeamish about blood, are you?" she asked, and turned slowly toward him.

"Nay," he said, but his tone may have been less than convincing.

She stared at him for a moment. "Good then. You can see to it."

He still delayed.

"Or I will care for it meself."

He drew a deep breath through his nostrils and chastised himself. What the devil was wrong with him? Aye, restraint might not be his finest quality, but surely he could resist her. After all, she was practically a man, he remembered, and made himself look directly at her. It was a bad idea, for she looked no more masculine from the front than from the rear. Indeed, standing there with her arms crossed against her bound chest, she looked as vulnerable as a child and as provocative as a siren. How could he have known that a woman trained to battle would only increase his yearning?

"MacGowan?" she said, her tone suggesting that he had been lost somewhere.

He spurred his gaze to hers.

"Nay. Nay," he said. "I . . . I will see to it." He nodded, but somehow he couldn't quite make himself cross the floor back to her, for if he did he couldn't be certain of his actions.

"Very well then," she said and uncrossing her arms, pulled her sgian dubh, sheath and all, from its hiding place. Dropping it to the floor, she found the place where the end of the cloth was tucked beneath the tightly wrapped bands. She tugged it free, then began to unwrap the bindings.

Lachlan held his breath as her fair skin was uncovered, and then she winced.

He spurred his gaze to her face and saw the pain etched there.

Sweet mother, he was a dolt.

"Me apologies," he said, but his tone was strained. "You need help."

"Nay." Her voice was firm as she continued the process, but then she winced again and paused in her task to exhale softly. "Aye," she said, her tone softened. With her eyes downcast, she turned her back toward him. "Help would be appreciated."

Chapter 5

Lachlan drew a steadying breath as he stepped forward. "Very well then," he said and slipped one hand beneath her arm to retrieve the end of the cloth. Their fingers brushed. A shiver of excitement shimmered up his arm, but he ignored it. If he couldn't withstand the touch of her hand, he was going to have a devil of a time with the rest of this process.

Balling the cloth in his fist, he pulled it behind her back, passed it to his other hand and slipped it beneath her opposite arm. Another half inch strip of skin was revealed. He closed his eyes for a moment and wound the bandage about her again. It went over her shoulder this time, and as the fabric was pulled away, more fine curves were revealed. Her arms were strong and firm, her shoulders smooth and lovely, but he didn't touch her. Instead, he eased the cloth around her body once again. His arm brushed beneath hers and his breath came harder. Again he unwrapped, bending slightly closer, and this time his crotch touched her bottom. His erection jerked on contact. He ground his teeth, closed his eyes, and continued, but finally he felt the bandage resist. He glanced down and saw that the cloth was adhered to her wound. Tugging gently, he pulled the linen from her flesh. The cut was several inches long, but no great amount of blood had been lost and the pain didn't seem excruciating as he eased the cloth back around.

One more circuit and suddenly her shoulders were bare. They were not delicate shoulders, not weak shoulders. The bone was substantial. There was little slope to them, and the muscle that curved down to her arms was as firm and graceful as a doe's.

He swallowed hard and reached about her again. Through the fabric, his wrist brushed her nipple. He jerked at the impact. She stiffened, but despite his expectations, she made no attempt to decapitate him. In fact, she didn't pull away, but remained like a life-sized doll in the circle of his arms.

Lachlan licked his lips, said a silent prayer to a surely mischievous God, and eased the cloth around her one last time. 'Twas not such a difficult task, he told himself as he gazed into the distance. No troublesome ordeal. It was like peeling a quince or unwrapping a . . .

But in that instant, the tail of the binding fell away, and her torso was bare. His biceps inadvertently brushed the swell of her breast and his cock kicked like a mule against his plaid.

He froze. Aye, he knew he should pull away, but, strangely enough, he found such self-preservation impossible. He was paralyzed, with his arms about her, breathing in her essence, feeling the softness of her hair against his throat.

Reaching out, she found her tunic with her fingertips and pulled it to her chest. The last of the cloth unwound from her waist and he stood like one in a trance, staring at her back.

It, like the rest of her, was beautiful. Sleek and smooth, it sloped down to the sharp curve of her waist like an ivory spoon.

"Tell me," she said.

"What?" he asked, and fretfully caught her gaze as it slanted up from beneath the heavy fringe of her lashes.

"Surely you can see it now."

"Oh, aye," he said, and glanced down at the wound. "And?"

Her heavy tunic and her bindings had saved her much pain. Indeed, the wound was barely a scratch and would surely heal well with no help from him. It almost seemed a shame.

"Will it need tending?"

"Ahh . . . Yes it will."

She glanced over her ivory shoulder at him, and there again he saw the worry.

"But you needn't fret," he added at guilt's nudge.

Her brow puckered slightly. "Do not coddle me, Mac-Gowan," she said. "You can tell me true. Is it a grievous wound?"

"Not . . . grievous," he said, and let his gaze slide over her buttocks again. "Still, I think—"

"Does it fester?"

He pulled his attention upward, only pausing momentarily on the dramatic dip of her waist.

"MacGowan?"

"Nay," he said. "It looks fresh. If we clean it thoroughly it will mend well."

"You are certain?"

"Aye, you needn't worry."

She nodded once. "Then I shall douse it with spirits and bind it anew."

"Alone?"

"Of course," she said, and glanced at him again. "If 'tis small and not festering—"

"Well there might be a bit of . . . festering." Oh aye, he knew he was pathetic.

She stared at him.

"And you cannot reach behind," he continued. "Nay, I'll not have it."

"You'll not have—"

" 'Tis your rule we live by now."

She raised her brows slightly in curiosity.

"If one saves another it is his right and duty to make certain no harm befalls him, at least for a spell."

"That is not my rule," she said, but he failed to hear her, for his entire attention was bent on the beauty of her skin, the firm stretch of her muscles.

"I'll fetch what is needed," he said, and yanking himself away, turned abruptly toward the door.

On the far side of the portal, Lachlan slowed his pace and gave his head a mental thump. Sweet mother! What was wrong with him? She was wounded. She was uninterested. She thought herself a man!

Still, the sight of her bare skin . . . His erection ached again and he shook his head at his own foolishness. Nay, she was not for him. But hardly could he leave her. After all, she was a maid, and a wounded one at that. 'Twas his duty to see to her, and if that duty involved bathing her and . . .

Nay, not bathing her! It only involved tending her wound, and that much he would do. After that his duty would be complete and he could return home with a clear conscience.

Aye, that was all he wanted, he vowed, and strode determinedly off to find the necessities that would heal her and hurry him on his way.

Alone in the bedchamber, Hunter exhaled heavily. She was tired, exhausted really. But her wounds were not serious and her mission would not be delayed.

Evil comes to Evermyst.

Was the old woman right? She didn't know. Wasn't sure, though she'd spent a year trying to find out. For a long while, she'd thought it all foolishness. Now she wasn't certain, but she would learn the truth soon enough.

She would allow MacGowan to tend her and then she would be rid of him, for he would only make her task more difficult. Aye, she determined, and nodded to herself as she pressed her tunic more firmly to her breasts. They felt strangely full and unusually heavy, like a foreign weight against the bare skin of her arms. But then she'd never found much use for them, she thought, and almost laughed as she sat down on the bed.

Steadying a flagon of spirits, an unwieldy bucket of warmed water, and a half dozen other items, Lachlan fumbled with the door latch. The bucket tipped slightly, loosing a few drops of water onto his wrist and spilling forth the medicinal scent of camphor.

He remedied the situation, managed the door latch, and stepped inside. From the corner of his eye, he saw that Hunter sat upright in bed. He was just about to speak when he realized she was asleep.

Nay, she had not lain down, but neither was she awake. Her cheek rested against the head of the bed. Her shoulders were bare, and though her right arm was holding her tunic against her bosom, some kindly miracle had caused the garment to slip slightly toward the mattress, revealing the soft upper curves of her breasts.

It was then that he stopped breathing. It was then that his desire roared back to life. Not coincidentally, it was also then that his plans began to crumble like a house of sand, for lying there silent and defenseless, she looked like a fairy child who had found her father's clothing. A fairy child dressed in leather. And aye, the fairy child was soiled and she was the very devil with a dirk but . . .

She awoke without warning. Her eyes snapped open and her gaze flew to her blade where it lay on the floor. He tensed, but she did not leap to her feet and demand a duel to the death as he had suspected she might. Instead, she relaxed visibly. Her eyes, still heavy with sleep, lowered, and seeing the wanton ways of her tunic, she pressed it slowly upward again.

"You've returned." Her voice was low, her heavy lashes dipped slightly over her sleep softened eyes.

"Aye." No threats? No curses? "Are you feeling well?"

"Very well," she said and sat up slowly. "I dreamt."

She said no more, but somehow those simple words intrigued him. The thought of her asleep captivated his imagination, while the thought of her playing in dreamland stole his breath.

"What did you dream?" he asked.

The suggestion of a crescent smile curved her lips. The expression did strange and unwanted things to his innards, and his nethers. "I dreamt of a castle," she said.

"Oh, and what castle was that?"

For one fleeting moment the smile remained, but in a short while she sobered. "It matters not," she said, and straightened from the headboard. "The sooner we see this done the sooner you can find your way home."

He yanked himself from his fantasies. "Aye," he agreed, and nodded. "Here then." He set the wooden bucket aside and lifted an earthenware flagon in one hand. "I brought something to cleanse the wound, and 'twould do no harm to the palate either. 'Twill ease some of the pain."

She nodded once. He sloshed a draught into a drinking horn and handed it to her.

"You had no trouble securing the spirits?" she asked and, releasing her tunic with one hand, took the offering. The shirt slipped a fraction of an inch. Lachlan's erection grew in direct proportions. Interesting.

"Nay," he said.

"And what of a meal? Can we yet sup?"

"I convinced them to bring us a trencher."

"Kind of them."

"Oh aye," he said, and after filling a basin with water from the bucket, dipped a rag into it. "The old man's all but a saint."

She almost smiled before trying a sip of the wine. "Truly."

"Turn a bit," he said, and she did so, twisting slightly on the mattress so that she presented her back. Smooth and fair, it scooped dramatically down toward hidden treasures. His heart rate bumped up a beat, but he scoffed at himself. This was no great ordeal. It was just a back, after all. Just a back. The water felt warm as he wrung out the cloth and touched it to her flesh. She flinched slightly. He grimaced and drew away.

"Me apologies."

"Nay." She was sitting very straight now. "I was only startled."

But he knew he had hurt her and when he touched the cloth to her back again he did so with cautious gentleness. "They had no chamomile for the water. Lady Fiona would box their ears if she knew of their negligence. Still, I was fortunate they had camphor. 'Twill keep the swelling at bay."

She remained very still as he washed the edges of the wound. There was some inflammation, but only a bit and soon the area was clean.

"Lady Fiona," she said. "Your uncle's wife."

"You know of her?" He could not help but be surprised.

"Only a bit. She is a healer, I believe."

"Aye," he said, and leaned away, feeling somewhat breathless.

"You are finished?"

If he was, did that mean she would don her tunic? "Nay," he said, and finding a fresh cloth, dipped it into the bucket. "There is a bit of blood . . ." He drew a breath and touched the rag to her neck. "There." He washed it gently. She turned her head to watch him. Her eyes were huge, her lips slightly parted, her tongue a coral shell all but hidden behind pearlescent teeth.

Sweet mother of God.

"And . . ." He steadied his hand as he leaned forward

again. "There," he said and smoothed the cloth across her cheek.

She said nothing.

"And there." Lachlan eased the warm rag across her brow. It was high and regal. He placed a hand to her jaw and she shifted slightly, turning sideways on the bed. That alone was nearly his undoing, for while the sight her back was alluring as hell, the thought of her breasts all but stole his breath away.

Oh aye, she still held her tunic to her chest, but she seemed to have forgotten its purpose, for the fabric was pressed up against her bosom, and somehow that only managed to push it well into view. Above the linen garment, the uppermost portions of her breasts looked as soft as a dream. Between them, a silver chain formed a fortunate V and disappeared mysteriously into the folds of heaven.

Breathe. Breathe, he told himself and pulled his gaze from the tantalizing chain.

"There," he said and, remembering his mission, dabbed gently at her nose. It was, he thought, a perfect nose, straight and small, but not weak or silly. Just below it, in the delicate teardrop dell above her lips, he washed away a smear of blood, and then it seemed wrong to ignore her chin. He bathed it gently, drawing the cloth along the sharp edge of her jaw and then down the endless length of her throat. Slowly, ever so slowly. Her head was tilted back slightly, her breasts were pressed high, and in between there was an endless tract of ivory flesh, as soft and perfect as a fresh bank of snow. He trailed the rag down the length of it, removing a trace of dirt. His knuckles brushed her flesh. It was the simplest contact, and yet he felt the impact like a fire in his gut.

They were close, so very close.

"MacGowan."

He snapped back to reality. Had he been leaning in?

"Aye?"

"Perhaps I should finish washing . . . Oh, me hands . . ." she murmured and gazed at her fingers where they curled about the drinking horn. "They are soiled."

Lachlan took the horn from her like one in a daze. Setting it aside, he slipped his hand around hers. Without the leather gauntlets, it did not seem quite so daunting, but neither was it a delicate hand. Taking up the cloth again, he washed it down her wrist and across her knuckles. Her fingers curled slightly against his palm. There was a scratch on her thumb. He slipped the rag over it, washing it gently, and then it simply seemed like favoritism to ignore the other digits. Wrapping her index finger in the warm cloth, he dragged it over her knuckle and onward, across the smooth bed of her nail.

"Dirty." He could think of nothing else to say. In fact, it was difficult enough forcing out that simple word.

She nodded once, then licked her lips. He watched breathlessly as her tongue swept against the edge of her teeth and over the sunrise brightness of her lips.

Strange. There seemed to be an odd lack of air in the room.

"Perhaps—" she began, and tugged at her hand, but he interrupted and tightened his grip ever so slightly on her wrist.

"Still dirty," he said and moved on to her middle finger. "Can't allow that." Her hand lay soft and limp against his palm. His own looked large and square beneath her wrist. A row of calluses graced the ridge of her palm, but the omnipresent gauntlets had kept her hands supple and fair. The pads of her fingers pressed upon his wrist and he tightened against the pressure on that sensitive area. "Mother always insisted that we wash thoroughly."

"What?" She glanced up, and in her eyes was a rapt uncertainty that made his heart pound against the containment of his ribs.

"Mother . . ." he said and, finding the hard bar of lye soap, slipped his hand over it before lathering her ring finger. "She taught us to wash well." He massaged the delicate digit. Her lids dipped momentarily and for the same small span of time she drew a breath between her lips. As he watched, his mouth went dry, but in a second, she recovered and tugged at her hand.

Once again he tightened his grip. "Surely yours did the same," he said and, turning her hand over, rubbed a slow circle into her palm.

She watched the movement, watched the suds appear in a cyclonic score and seemed to sigh under his ministrations, but perhaps it was his own sigh that escaped.

"Did she not?"

"What?" she repeated, as if from a daze.

"Did she not insist that you wash?"

She blinked at him and stiffened slightly. Even in the center of her palm, he felt her muscles tighten. Fascinated, he enlarged his circle, encompassing her callused pads. Then he eased down her fingers again, pressing away the tension. She seemed to relax against her will.

"Nay," she said, her voice low. "She did not."

"Ahh, well." He shrugged and moved back to her middle finger. "Mothers be strange. Me own did not mind if we brothers beat each other as senseless as plow shears, but she liked to see us clean. What of yours? She must have allowed you your battles also, else—"

"That's enough," she said, and pulled her hand from his grip. In her hurry, her tunic slipped a bit, but she pulled it back to her chest, pressing her bosom higher still.

"Me apologies," he said.

Perhaps she had meant to rise, to draw away, but she froze now, staring at him with mercurial eyes. "Why do you apologize?"

Near the delicate swirl of her ear, her hair was slightly damp from his cloth. One gossamer wave curled beside her cheek. He raised his gaze from it to her eyes.

"You've no wish to speak of your mother," he said.

Her expression showed her tension.

"Thus we shall not."

The shadow of a frown formed between her brows and suddenly he had a burning urge to kiss it away.

"Still," he said, resisting the temptation. "You owe me."

"I?" There was a glimpse of the warrior in her face again, a trace of the brooding gladiator she was thought to be. "Owe you?"

"Aye," he said, but he kept his voice soft as he reached for her hand again. Surprisingly, she did not pull away.

"You owe me the opportunity to keep you alive for a wee bit longer."

She canted her head at him. "Is me wound so grievous then?"

"Nay," he said. "But you need rest if you are to mend."

She still watched him, and he searched somewhat desperately for an explanation.

"You must not overtax yourself," he said. "And you need to wash."

"Bathing is not usually horrendously tiring."

"Bathing!" The thought burned through his mind like a scorched elm. "Did you wish for a full bath?"

"Nay. I but meant . . ." It was her turn to be at a loss for words. "Nay. Of course not."

Was that a blush on her cheeks? The idea intrigued him and he stared.

"Nay," she repeated, and tugged at her hand.

He tugged back, but he could not completely resist the temptation to smile. "Very well then," he said. "We shall have to make do with what water we have here."

"I do not think—" she began, but he had already begun to lather her palm.

Her lips parted as if to go on, but nothing issued forth except for the tiniest sigh.

"Relax," he said, and cupping her hand in both of his, smoothed his thumbs outward. "I'll not harm you."

She straightened slightly. "Not even if you try."

"You should not be so certain, lass. After all, your trusty dirk is not close to hand." He caressed again, smoothing outward before finally changing to her left hand. "Then again, neither do you wear your tunic."

Their gazes met and locked.

"And if memory serves I seem to have a bit of trouble battling a half-clothed maid."

For a moment she simply breathed, then, "I am not a maid."

"Me apologies," he said and let his gaze skim her breasts for the briefest of moments, before shifting his attention to her hand again. "Forgive me forgetfulness."

"Do you—" she began, but at that moment he massaged the knotted muscle beneath her thumb and somehow that simple movement seemed to leave her breathless. Still, she found her voice in a second. "Do you mock me?"

"You?" He shook his head in utter earnestness. "Nay. I but wonder why you have chosen the path of a warrior."

"Mayhap it was chosen for me." She shrugged. It was naught more than a simple lift of her shoulders and yet it seemed to change everything, including the rhythm of his heart.

He continued to breathe and congratulated himself on his efforts. 'Twas not as if he was unaccustomed to the company of women, but . . . Well, perhaps he'd somewhat neglected the art of seduction.

"Chosen for you?" He lathered her wrist. A needle-thin scratch marred the satiny flesh, and he washed it carefully. "How so? Did your father wish for a son?"

She too seemed to be concentrating on the bathing process. Her expression was solemn. "'Tis difficult to say what me father wished for."

Lachlan scowled, trying to read her meaning in her face, but he could not guess. "He was dead before your birth?"

"Nay." She shook her head. "I believe he was alive at the time."

The scratch on her wrist bothered him, for it lay between the delicate blue veins and seemed to threaten her very life's blood. Of course it did not. But how many other times had her life been threatened? How many other times had she fought alone and unaided? Washing away the soap with the cloth, he ran a fingertip along the reddened course.

"You *believe*?" he said.

"In truth, I have never met him."

"Not met him, and yet he lives?"

"Not any longer."

He glanced up.

"I did not kill him."

Lachlan raised his brows. "I did not think you did, lass."

"Oh." She cleared her throat and dropped her gaze.

"I am but surprised that you chose not to introduce yourself while he yet lived."

She shrugged as if it were of no great interest.

"Your sire . . ." Lachlan said, smoothing the cloth gently up her arm. "Who was he?"

"It matters not."

The skin at the bend in her wrist was as soft as a cygnet's down, and he found that, against all good sense, he longed to kiss it. "Why do you not wish to tell me?"

"Because it does not matter."

He eased his thumb along the crease of her joint, and for an instant he thought he felt her shiver. The idea sent a tremble of excitement through him, galvanizing his desire, quickening his heart.

"But what if you meet a man you wish to marry and—"

"Marry!" she said the word like the knell of death.

He raised his eyes to hers, surprised by her tone.

"Aye."

"I will never marry, MacGowan." Her entire body had stiffened. Her mouth was pursed and her nostrils flared.

"Whyever—"

"Because I am a warrior!"

He shrugged. "Warrior or not, you are still a—"

"Nay!" she said and yanked her arm from his grasp. "Do not say I am a maid. I am a warrior," she repeated, but her arm remained across her chest, pinning her tunic to her bosom, which was rising and falling with the drama of her feelings. "Just as you are."

"I do not mean to—"

"I am like you," she insisted.

He could not help but shake his head.

"Aye, just like you," she insisted and leaned toward him. But if she meant to emphasize her point with that movement she would be sadly disappointed, for now he could see her breasts from above, hugged together like pearly lambkins with the silver chain trapped between.

"Lass—"

"Warrior!" she corrected, "with the same training and skills. Nay, better skills than you."

"I do not doubt your—"

"The same strengths, and aye, the same weaknesses."

His gaze fell to her breasts again. Even mostly hidden, they were truly beautiful, full and fair and tempting beyond belief. "I doubt you have the same—"

"The *same* needs!" she hissed and, slipping her feet to the floor, snatched up her dirk. Her breasts dipped nearly into full view. Lachlan held his breath, then remembered to inhale when she straightened.

She stood now with her dirk in one capable hand, but still it was hard to concentrate on the threat, for she looked all the more glorious with her eyes ablaze and her hair strewn about her pearlescent shoulders. Indeed, he ached with the intensity of his need. If she would give

him but the slimmest indication that she felt the same
heated desire, he would not delay a moment. In fact, if
she would simply put aside the knife, he would be encouraged. But she held it just below her chest. Conve-
nient really, for this way he could watch the dirk and her
breasts at the same time.

"Lass—" he began, but she interrupted.

"You think we are different." Her tone was very low,
her eyes utterly steady. "You think me form sets me apart
from you, but this I swear . . ." She paused, her eyes narrowed. "We are the same, you and I."

"I . . ." he began, then paused as her meaning came
home to him, like an arrow to the heart. "The *same*
needs?"

"Aye," she said. "Regardless of the shape of me body,
I am no less. We are no different."

Holy mother!

He rose slowly to his feet. All this time he thought
he'd been seducing her, when in truth, he'd only been
making her angry. She had no interest whatsoever in
him. No interest in any man.

Nay, she was attracted to women!

Chapter 6

H unter watched him back away.

"Me apologies." His voice was low and a muscle jumped once in his lean jaw.

She scowled. Although she had belittled his abilities at first, she had since learned he was not the kind to retreat. Indeed, in the past he had all but begged for battle. Why not now? He outweighed her by a good four stone. True, many men did and found their size gave them little advantage, but with MacGowan it would be different. His additional weight was not wasted on fat. Instead, it was formed of naught but muscle, and much of that was packed into his chest and arms. Aye, he had the grip of a bear, and yet he was as silent as a cat when he wished to be. It was a strange meld of capabilities, and she could not deny that it intrigued her somewhat. Had she time for a man in her life, she would not be adverse to making *him* that man.

"I did not mean to . . . That is . . ." He motioned toward the bed where they had been seated. "Me apologies," he said again and nodded brusquely as he backed away. "I will go inquire about the—"

But at that moment a knock sounded at the door. Hunter tightened her grip on her dirk and shifted her gaze to the portal. Lachlan did not so much as turn. Instead, he set his hand to his own knife, as if welcoming a challenge, so long as it did not come from her.

"Who comes?" he asked. His voice was as deep as the night outside their lead-paned window.

" 'Tis your dinner, me lord." A young woman answered. She was probably not the type he'd care to challenge either, Hunter mused, but his tone was no lighter when he spoke again.

"A moment," he said and, keeping his gaze pinned to Hunter's, motioned for her to get into bed.

She raised her chin and her dirk at his imperious manner, but he only lowered his brows as if mildly irritated.

"They might not be as enlightened as you," he murmured. "Indeed, if they see you thus, they might mistake you for a woman."

She considered a half dozen appropriate rejoinders, but the maid spoke again, and Hunter finally stepped toward the bed. Lachlan swept the blankets aside, allowing her to slip beneath the woolens. In an instant he had covered her nearly to the top of her head.

"Enter," he called.

The door creaked open.

"Good eventide, me lord. I was told to bring this meal to you and your . . ." She paused for a moment. Hunter could imagine her skimming the room, seeing the helmet, the jerkin, the gauntlets—spread upon the chamber floor. "Companion."

"Me thanks," said MacGowan, but his voice was little more than a feral growl.

Being bested by a woman surely made him contentious. But in truth, she had hardly bested him, though if she tried it would be a battle to remember, for she was not some frivolous wench ready to simper at his merest scowl, and the sooner he realized that the better.

On the other hand, she had not meant to scare him off. Indeed, perhaps she would have almost welcomed a bit of a tussle. Perhaps it would not be so hideous to feel his hard body against . . .

But nay. She was being foolish and there was no place for foolishness in the life she had made for herself.

"I hope the meal be to your liking." The maid's voice was dulcet and ultimately feminine.

"'Twill be acceptable I am sure." His response was little more than a grunt.

"'Tis a fine bit of mutton stew and barley bread I've brought. It seemed like a good bit of food, until now when I lay eyes on ye. Master Crighton did not say you were such a braw one."

Beneath the blankets, Hunter stiffened, then, tugging the woolens a half inch lower, she gazed through the tangle of sheets toward the speaker. She was small and soft and buxom with a pink bow of a mouth and fluttery, lily-white hands.

"Me name is Grace," she said and paused. No response came. "And what might I call you, me lord?"

He delayed a moment as if distracted, then, "I am Lachlan, of the MacGowans."

"And your . . . companion?"

"Your pardon," he said gruffly, "but me friend is in need of me attention."

"He is wounded?" Her mouth made a sympathetic circle as if she could not bear the thought.

"Only slightly."

"Then I must assist you."

Beneath the stifling blankets, Hunter tightened her grip on her dirk.

"Nay." MacGowan's voice was firm and a far cry from flirtatious.

"Then there is naught you want from me?" Grace drew out the word *naught* slightly as if he might be too daft to realize what she offered. Not that the flirtations bothered Hunter. Nay, 'twould not matter to her in the least if the little tart ripped off her clothes and began humping his leg, but 'twas a sorry way for a woman to act.

"Nay," said MacGowan. "This will do nicely. Me thanks."

Hunter scowled. 'Twas not often that men turned down such obvious invitations. Why would he?

The maid paused for a moment, and in the silence Hunter could hear the girl's irritation. "It's certain you are then?"

"Aye."

"Well, if you change your mind you've but to ask for Grace."

Hunter could almost hear his scowl. "Very well."

There was a moment of silence, followed by a few quick footfalls and the sound of the closing door.

"Odd lass," he muttered.

Hunter left her dirk on the chaff-filled mattress and pulled the blankets from her head. With an effort, she pushed herself to her elbow. Pain skittered through her and she failed to hide a wince.

"Here." His voice was still gruff though he hustled to her side. "Let me assist you."

She kept her tunic pressed against her breasts as she allowed him to help her sit up. Why was he all but rude to the maid and so strangely solicitous to her? What did he hope to gain?

"She is gone?" Hunter asked, and although the answer was obvious, it only prompted more questions.

"Aye."

She scowled at the door for a moment, then returned her attention to him. "Did you not find her . . . comely?"

He shrugged. "Nay. Not to me own way of thinking, but . . ." His scowl deepened. "Mayhap you would find her so."

She raised her brows. "I would find her comely?"

"Mayhap. I've no way of knowing."

How very strange. If he did not think the maid bonny, what *was* he attracted to? It didn't matter, of course, and yet she was curious. "How did she look?"

"Look?" He glanced up, not as if baffled, but more as if he were irritated.

"Aye. Was she slim, fair, tall, bonny?" Why the devil had he turned the girl aside? She'd all but crawled into his sporran and spent the night.

"She was bonny enough, I suspect. Though she didn't—" His hands lingered for a moment as he shifted the pillows behind her.

"Didn't what?" she asked, but in an instant he'd pulled his hands abruptly away.

" 'Tis naught. We'd best bind your wound."

She skimmed her gaze to the tray and saw the bandages there. "She brought them?"

"Aye. I told the gaffer you'd sustained a slight injury."

She nodded, too intrigued by the conversation just past to bother with her wound. "And it does not concern you that you . . . missed your opportunity with her?" she asked, still watching his face.

He'd retrieved the flagon of spirits. "This will sting," he warned, and sat on the bed behind her.

"So you don't care?"

"Are you ready?"

"Aye," she said, still distracted, but in a moment pain burned like lightning across her back. She hissed through her teeth and tightened her grip on her shirt, but it was over soon enough.

"Me apologies." His hand felt warm and unutterably strong against her arm.

She glanced at it, then his face. It was the face of a warrior tested in battle and found to be strong. His eyes were solemn, his expression troubled. "Why did you turn her away, MacGowan?" she asked.

"Who?"

"The maid," she said, exasperated. "If the bed hadn't been occupied, you'd have had to burn it down to be rid of her."

"The maid what brought the meal?"

"Aye. Grace, I believe her name was."

He shrugged as if that answered everything. His face was utterly sober, sculpted and square and a long way from pretty. But the power there and the ferocity! Emotion skittered up her spine, and her face felt flushed.

"Are you well?" he asked. "You look a bit feverish."

"Nay. I—am well."

He nodded and reached for the bindings. "I'll see you bandaged then."

She turned away with some relief, for the sight of him did naught to clear her mind.

He sat behind her, silent and motionless for a moment, then, "You'll have to shift the tunic a bit."

"Oh, aye," she said and drawing a breath, gathered the garment into a smaller bundle and clasped her right arm across her chest. Beneath her fingers, she felt the rough path of the scar she'd sustained from the Munro's blade. It was long and curved, slanting around the outside of her left breast, but it had been a small price to pay for the privilege of Knight's company.

Lachlan sat unmoving behind her. She tightened her grip on the tunic, covering the scar, and in a moment his hands brushed her back. His fingers stroked the side of her ribs, and she held her breath as the same hand skimmed, light as moonlight, against the underside of her breast. Reaching across, he retrieved the bandage with his left hand and began the process again. Still, he never crossed her bosom, but stayed well beneath it, only brushing it now and then with his knuckles or thumbs.

Heat spread upward like evening tide until she felt hot and restive. Against her neck, she could feel the warmth of his breath, and upon her skin, his hands were as steady and gentle as sunlight. She concentrated on breathing, on remaining still, on refraining from any type of stupidity. But it seemed almost as if he were not just bandaging her. It felt as though he were caressing her, stroking her, seducing her. When he leaned close, she could feel the heat of his body against her back, could feel his power as surely as if she had placed her hand to his chest, had felt the muscles bunch and shift against her flesh. Aye, he would be a powerful force to contend with if ever she decided to take a lover, but she would not. Nay. She was a warrior, tried in battle, accustomed to temptation, strong, and not about to weaken now when she was so near solving the riddle.

Evil comes to Evermyst.

Maybe it was true, and if it was she would stop it, for she was no different than MacGowan; she would not be content until she had repaid her dues, righted her wrongs.

Still . . . She shifted her gaze to his hands again. If ever she were to take a mate, he would not be a horrid choice. He would not be binding her wounds then, but skimming his hands reverently over her body. True, she was not the type of woman men swooned over, for she was strong and rough and scarred. Indeed, she was barely a woman atall, but perhaps he was different than most. After all, he had resisted the chambermaid's obvious advances. So it was possible he was looking for something deeper—perhaps a woman who did not quake when he scowled or swoon when he smiled, but one who met him as an equal. Aye, she was an exceptional fighter, but if she set her mind to it perhaps she could also be an adequate—

"Hunter."

She jumped at the sound of his voice. "Aye?"

"'Tis finished," he said, and she realized suddenly that his hands had stilled. He remained motionless behind her upon the bed. All but naked, she sat only inches from him. Her face felt flushed, her body the same as she sat frozen before him, but he made no attempt to touch her.

A thousand possibilities soared through her mind, but she had no experience in the ways of seduction. Indeed, she had spent much of her life avoiding any possibility of it. She glanced furtively over her shoulder at him. His eyes met hers, and she lowered hers hastily, praying he could not read her thoughts.

"You'd best clothe yourself," he said.

"Oh." The word escaped from her without thought, breathless, worthless, foolish. She cleared her throat and lowered her voice. "Aye," she said, and lifted the tunic. Her face felt damnably hot.

"You've . . ." He paused, then tightened his large hands to fists and scowled at her. "You've naught else to wear?"

She shook her head once.

"Here," he said and, turning abruptly, reached into the leather bag he'd kept behind his cantle. From it, he drew a fresh shirt. It was a simple garment, softened by time and use and faded to the color of aged bone. " 'Tis clean and dry and will be more comfortable for you."

"Nay," she said, and shook her head. She had no desire whatsoever to wear his clothing, to accept his favors, to make him believe she had some interest in him. 'Twould be far too personal to feel his shirt against her skin, to smell the essence of him surrounding her like . . .

"I will see yours mended, and if the village has a decent leather wright, I will tend to your jerkin as well."

"It is fine as it is," she said.

"Nay, 'tis not, for through the rend others will see either the bindings or your . . ." He paused. His gaze skimmed downward momentarily and when he lifted his eyes again they were darker than ever, with his brows pulled low and his expression hard. " 'Tis in need of repair," he insisted and shoved his tunic toward her.

"Very well then," she said and took the garment from him. Their fingers brushed.

Silence fell like spilled ink over the room.

"I will help you . . ." He drew a deep breath through his nostrils. "Don it."

She would have to release the garment she held to her breast like an iron shield. The thought went unspoken. But it was obvious. She stared at him, and he stared back, his eyes earnest, his mouth unsmiling, as if this was no more than an unpleasant chore, best done quickly.

Was it all a ploy to see her unclothed yet again? Did he only hope to compromise her? But nay, she most probably had no need to worry on that account, not once he saw her in the full light of day, scared as she was.

Tipping up her chin, she met his gaze and dropped the tunic.

His attention remained focused on her face.

His square hands were formed into fists and for several seconds he stood exactly as he was. She remained unmoving, unspeaking, waiting in silence. Ready.

But in the end he neither turned away nor came in a rush.

Instead, he approached slowly. Her heart beat at the same laborious rate as she watched him fill her sight, and then he reached out. His fingers brushed hers. Lightning sensations shivered up her arm. Her heart leapt and stopped. For a moment the world stood still, but finally he tugged the garment from her clenched fingers.

"Lift your arms," he ordered.

It was all she could manage to do. She felt absolutely

naked, as vulnerable as a babe—breathless and light-headed and foolish as she raised her arms toward the ceiling, revealing all.

For an instant, his nostrils flared, then, stepping closer still, he bunched the cloth in his fists and tugged the sleeves over her hands. The garment brushed along her arms, raising gooseflesh in its wake. His knuckles grazed her cheek as he drew the garment over her head and downward. For a moment her heart thrummed against the backs of his fingers. Then, soft as a butterfly's wings, she felt the brush of his hand against her nipple.

The entire world froze. They were inches apart, breathing in sync, and for just a second she thought she felt him tremble.

Desire roared through her.

"Lass." The word was no more than a whisper.

"Aye." Hers was the same.

"I need . . ." He paused. She tried to breathe, but there was no hope of that.

"What?"

For a moment he closed his eyes, then he clenched his jaw and straightened abruptly. The tunic fell to her waist in a hasty cascade.

"I need to be going," he said.

She exhaled sharply while she could. "Going?" she asked, and hoped he couldn't hear the insane intensity of her desire. "Where?"

But his gaze had fallen to her breasts, and for a moment she let her own attention be drawn there. Through the aged fabric she could see the dusky circles of her nipples as they strained against confinement.

Lachlan raised his eyes back to hers then turned woodenly and lifted her soiled tunic from the bed. "To get this . . ." He motioned vaguely, as if he were at a loss for words. "To . . ." he began again, then, "Anywhere!" he rasped, and turning mechanically, strode away.

The door rocked on its leather hinges as he disappeared into the hall.

Hunter sat unmoving, staring in bewilderment at the reverberating door and trying to catch her breath.

He had left. Abruptly. Almost as if he were escaping. Her face reddened. Was it her scars that revolted him or was it something else?

Not that she'd wanted him to stay. She'd never primped or perfumed for any man. It wasn't her place in life. Still . . . A gossamer shiver shook her as memories trickled back through her.

How long had it been she'd been touched as he had touched her? As if she were cherished. As if she were precious.

She stared at the door, thinking back, remembering, but not one instance could she recall. Perhaps it had never happened. Not in a score of years, not in all her life. Maybe there had never been a time when she had been touched with gentleness and caring.

The thought made her feel strangely hollow, as empty as the shell about her neck. But nay. It did not matter. She was a warrior, strong and independent.

Reaching across the bed, she retrieved her dirk. It felt good in her fist. She tightened her grip. Aye, she was a warrior, not some milkfed maid, and perhaps it was the lack of coddling that made her so.

She had no use for Lachlan MacGowan. The sound of his voice did not make her weak, and his touch did not make her want. She had no need for either his strength or his gentleness. But how was it that such a man as he could be so tender? How could such callused hands feel so soothing against her skin?

There had been a breathlessness, an excitement akin to the anticipation of battle. She had thought he felt it too, but he had turned away. Did she disgust him or . . .

Could it be that he was a man of integrity as well as strength? Long ago she had heard a rhythm. Or had it been a dream? *Peaceable yet powerful he must be* . . .

But no. She did not believe in foolish poems and the tales of old wives. Yet . . . perhaps there were yet men of substance. It seemed that Anora of Evermyst had found one—Ramsay MacGowan.

She had met him long ago, but they had been at odds. Indeed, they had battled, for she had planned evil against his love. Hunter closed her eyes. Guilt gnawed at her, but she thrust it aside, for guilt did no good. Actions were all that mattered—thus her need to keep Evermyst safe. It was a payment of sorts and had naught to do with emotions. After all, it wasn't as if Hunter hadn't caused others to suffer. She was a mercenary, but she chose her battles carefully, and long ago, she had realized her mistake. Anora Fraser did not deserve to die. Indeed, perhaps none who was loved by a man like Ramsay deserved to die. Aye, Hunter regretted her long-ago attack on Anora, for though she had longed to obtain revenge for her pathetic childhood, Anora was not the one to pay. And Ramsey had made certain of that, had, in fact, come to the maid's rescue, though Hunter had tried to take her from him, had dressed as a woman to distract him.

Ramsay with the soulful eyes. Ramsay whom she had kissed. Ramsay, with whom she shared a brief past, and yet he didn't know it, for disguise, in one form or another, had always been her protector. Never had he known her true identity, but it was not so with his brother. Nay, Lachlan knew far too much. Lachlan! Larger than life, solemn, breathtak—

Foolish! He was a foolish noble. Nothing more. After all, he had followed her with no other purpose than to prove his own ability.

Still . . .

She could not forget the look of his face in the moonlight when she'd first met him on the battlefield— wounded yet not defeated.

Hunter shook her head. Despite his prowess and his appeal, he was naught but a man, and men were weak.

And yet he had turned aside the bonny chambermaid in his rush to help her. Indeed, he had barely seemed to notice the girl's offer in his concern for herself.

But in the end he had turned away from her also. Even after she had dropped her tunic he had made no attempt to seduce her. Indeed, only after he'd pulled his shirt over her head with his own hands had he allowed himself to lower his gaze. So it could not have been her scars that offended him.

But he had fled.

Something curled tight and uncertain in Hunter's stomach. She lowered her own gaze. Through the sheer fabric of the borrowed garment, she could still see the dark, sensitized rings of her nipples. Below the pale tunic, the scarred leather of her breeches looked worn and rugged in comparison.

That was it then. She was too much the warrior even without the scars. 'Twas understandable. Preferable even, she told herself, and tightened her fist on her dirk again, but her thoughts roiled on.

He had turned aside the maid too and *she* had been naught but the picture of femininity.

He was gentle. Yet he had a ferocious need to prove his prowess in battle.

When he had thought her a man, he followed her relentlessly.

He spoke of his mother with rare reverence.

He remained unwed. Indeed, for one so appealing, he seemed strangely uncomfortable around females.

Hunter sat in stunned silence as her thoughts halted abruptly in her head.

Damn! The truth was suddenly clear. Lachlan Mac-Gowan favored men.

Chapter 7

It seemed to Hunter that she stared into space for an eternity, but finally hunger drew her from her trance. She lit a candle and ate.

The meal was simple fare, but it was hearty enough, and she felt a bit of normalcy return with each bite. When she'd eaten her fill, she washed in the water left in the basin and turned to stare numbly at the bed.

Aye, she was tired, but there was only the one mattress and she would not be sleeping alone. Then again, it was late already. Darkness had fallen long ago and MacGowan had yet to return. Perhaps he did not intend to. Perhaps he had turned back toward his father's keep, or even toward Evermyst. They would be awaiting his return—the brother rogues and their delicate wives. Ready to welcome him back into the fold—the men jovial with mock rivalry, the women fawning. Oh, aye, though the twin maids had come from far different backgrounds, they would both fawn. Indeed, 'twas most probably how they had won their husbands' attention. But perhaps not. Perhaps all that was necessary was for them to be *women*. She had seen how their husbands looked at them, had sensed the depth of feeling lying hidden beneath the surface. There was passion, yes, but there was more. There was caring, kindness, loyalty.

Why would MacGowan not return to Evermyst? After all, he had fulfilled his vow to save her life. He was probably on his way there even now.

Then again, maybe he was merely out enjoying a bit of revelry. Maybe he'd met a likely . . . lad.

She grimaced and paced fretfully as she tried to acknowledge the truth. The man was not attracted to *any* woman—much less *her*. Not that she cared. In fact, it was much preferable this way, for she no longer had to worry about keeping him from her. She glanced at the bed. Fatigue dragged at her limbs, but did she dare risk falling asleep when he might return at any moment?

Aye, she decided abruptly, for she would be perfectly safe there beside him. Her heart rate increased at the thought, but she ignored the rush of excitement, for she was only being practical.

If he did return to their shared chamber, he would not touch her. He could pretend he kept himself from her because he was a man of honor and she could pretend she did not know his secret. In fact, she would tell no one, for she bore him no ill will. He had done nothing to harm her. Quite the opposite, in fact. He had been rather considerate. But perhaps that made a bit of sense. After all, each sex had its weakness. Women were thought to be kindly, but tended to be weak when trouble brewed. Men were strong, but were wont to abandon all good sense when women were involved.

Perhaps it was those in between who had the best of both worlds. She, for instance, had obtained a man's skills, yet she could see their shortcomings, for she did not share their lust for women. Mayhap MacGowan was somewhat the same. Aye, he had been momentarily discombobulated when he'd first realized her sex, but his shock was understandable. If his interaction with the chambermaid was any indication of his steadiness, she could guarantee he would not play the fool for even the comeliest of lasses.

So surely he would keep his wits around *her*. She had no need to worry about his advances.

For a moment she glanced through the distorted glass of the window to the street below. The night looked dark and empty. She turned away, facing the bed alone.

The situation could not be more perfect, she told herself. She could get the first full night's sleep she had had in some time. In fact, there was no reason she could not remove her breeches and find some comfort. 'Twould be a relief.

Slipping back the borrowed tunic's lengthy sleeves, she pulled up the hem and pushed down her thick hose. It felt quite lovely to pull the leather from her legs and better still to slip into bed. The worn sheets felt soft against her calves.

Aye, this was good. She needn't worry, she told herself, and lay alone in the darkness.

Just down the rutted, winding street, Lachlan paid the leather wright and retrieved Hunter's jerkin.

The road back to the inn was muddy and dark.

She would probably be asleep by now. He nodded to himself. Aye, she would be sleeping. All would be safe. After all, he wouldn't be expected to touch her, or bandage her, or pretend that her presence didn't make him crazy.

He swallowed and tightened his fist on her vest. Though padded and tough, it was soft and supple. Like her. Strong and firm, but smooth as satin beneath his fingertips, and when he touched her—

Holy mother! What the hell was wrong with him? Had he no pride whatsoever? She wasn't interested in him. Damn! She wasn't interested in his entire gender!

How could he be so daft!

'Twas just like him to turn aside the chambermaid in his yearning for another who would never want him. Oh aye, in retrospect, he realized Grace had shown some interest in him when she'd brought their meals. But at that precise moment it had been impossible for him to concentrate on her, for he was a man to focus all of his attention on the task at hand, especially when that task involved a warrior woman with a siren's voice and an angel's body.

The maid had probably been bonny enough, but Hunter had been . . . well, she was Hunter! With her warrior's pride and maiden's softness. Hunter, with her endless legs and hidden bosom. Aye, he would be the first to admit he had always favored delicate women, but they made him . . . well, fidgety. Of course, Hunter made him fidgety too, but in a different way entirely.

If one looked at the situation in a certain light, she was right—they were alike. Indeed, it almost seemed that she understood him, and yet they were worlds apart. Her breasts—

Even now he ached at the memory of them. Even knowing she had no interest in him. Even knowing she had shown more interest in the maid than he had. In fact, maybe they were together at this very moment.

The thought literally stopped him in his tracks. A combination of raw emotions curled in his stomach. Part revulsion, part . . .

He didn't know what the other part was, but suddenly his feet were hurrying him back to the inn. He ascended the stairs two at a time. For a moment he paused at the door, then, taking a deep breath, he pushed inside.

Beside the bed, a candle still glowed, and upon the far pillow, the light shimmered like gold on Hunter's flaxen hair. It was spread about her in gilded waves. And now, in the auspices of sleep, there was no harshness in her face. Her lips were slightly parted, rosebud bright and bowed slightly as she slumbered. Her lashes were long and full, shadowing her ivory cheeks. One palm cradled her chin just so, showing the frail blue veins that criss-crossed through her wrist.

She was, in that moment, the very picture of woman-hood, and for a second, Lachlan failed to breathe. Without thinking, he took a step forward, but with that movement, he remembered his resolve. She was not for him. In fact, she was not for any man. Perhaps that real-ization should have made him feel better, but somehow it did not. Four and twenty years he had seen, and though he had been interested in a multitude of maids, never in all that time had he met one that seemed to match him so exactly. He had never met a woman he ached to call his own. What did it say for him that now that he had, he found that her interest lay in another direction entirely?

But perhaps that was best, he thought as he clenched

and unclenched his fists. Of course it was. She was not the type to get involved with anyway. She was more man than maid, he told himself, but at that moment, she sighed and shifted slightly in her sleep. The blankets were pushed aside and above them he could see that the tunic he had loaned her had not been closed. Instead, the metal-tipped laces lay lax, leaving the neck opening twisted askew so that the sweet slope of one breast was visible. His throat felt dry. His erection tightened with painful intensity.

More man than maid? Who the devil was he fooling? At that moment she looked more angel than human and suddenly he felt hot and cold all at once. He turned abruptly and paced silently across the length of the room.

What the devil was he supposed to do now? He could sleep on the floor, but glancing at the planks beneath his feet, he winced. It looked hard and cold and lone . . . Well, his back ached at the sight of it. The battle, after all, had taken its toll on him, too, though he had come out better than Hunter.

She had fought like a gladiator. In fact, regardless how she looked just now, he must not forget what she was: a warrior, trained and tested in the heat of battle. No more and no less. A few of his miscellaneous body parts were eager to dispute that idea, but he assured himself it was true. She was a warrior and he had shared sleeping quarters with other warriors innumerable times. 'Twas the way of the world. Accommodations were oft harsh. More than once he'd slept in stables or under the stars, but surely he would be a fool now to turn down the comforts of a bed. In fact, she might well be insulted if he did. She had gone out of her way to make him realize she thought of them as the same. He dare not induce her ire by implying that he disagreed.

Fatigued by his intense justification, Lachlan took a step toward the bed. She lay as before, but now, just past the edge of the tunic, he could see the darkened skin that encircled her nipple. Something hit him in the gut, or perhaps it was just lust, wound tight as a crossbow inside him. Heat flooded his face. He turned rapidly away, crossed to the wash basin, and splashed water on his cheeks. They felt coarse and unshaven. He exhaled through his mouth, straightened, and washed his hands with a bit more decorum.

All was well. All was fine. Retrieving the soap, he lathered his hands. She wasn't really a woman. Not really a woman. He ran the thought round and round in his mind like a mantra. His stomach settled. He kept scrubbing until his fingers felt raw, then, rinsing his hands, he dried them thoroughly and turned back toward the bed.

The candlelight still glowed on her face, shone on her hair, and turned her throat a golden hue. Below that—

Damnation, it was hot! He turned back toward the window, braced his hands on the edge of the sill and drew a deep breath.

Hot! Aye, that was the problem. He had but to cool off before he could find sleep. 'Twas simple enough.

Tugging his tunic from beneath his belted plaid, he whipped it over his head, then found the wash rag and applied it vigorously to his chest.

Upon the bed, Hunter lay very still, breathing softly through her lips, watching him. Oh, aye, she was awake.

She wasn't certain why she pretended to sleep. It was not because she was unsure of her feelings for him. Nay, of course not.

And obviously, she had no reason to worry about his arrival, for he could barely even look at her. Every time he turned toward the bed, she could feel his glower before he pivoted away again. She would not be atall surprised if he chose to sleep on the floor, but there was no need for such foolish chivalry, for it was plain she would be perfectly safe with him.

His back was toward her now as he washed his chest. His shoulders glimmered damp where he'd swathed the rag across them and when he moved they bunched with undeniable power.

He lifted one arm. Muscles swelled and danced beneath his dark flesh and for a moment she failed to breathe, but it was only because she was worried he would discover she was awake. It wasn't as if she were aroused. She squirmed a little, pulling her knees higher, and he turned, exposing his phenomenal torso.

Candlelight glimmered on his flesh like moonlight on waves. Shadows lay in the dells between his ribs and on the valleys of his abdominals. His belly was flat except for the hard hillocks that sloped down toward his lean hips.

Her throat felt dry, her stomach odd. She closed her eyes in earnest and refused to open them. He was just a man. A man with no interest in women. None atall. And . . .

The room was cast suddenly into darkness, and she knew he had extinguished the candle. In a moment he was moving, pacing toward the bed.

She dared open her eyes now, though only slightly,

and through her slitted lids she could see a vague outline of him. He stood beside the mattress with his back to the window, but what he did there was a mystery. And then, even in the blackness, she saw his arms move. The sound of his sporran hitting the floor all but shook the room, and then it was up to her imagination to guess the rest for she could see little and hear less. But finally the mattress creaked and bent as he sat upon its edge. She failed to breathe as he removed his shoes and when he lay down and rolled onto his side she remained frozen, not moving a muscle.

But the seconds ticked away and all was well. In fact, he had not come beneath the blankets, but remained on the surface, probably covered by his own plaid. Aye, all was well, she assured herself, but in that moment she deduced the truth.

Lachlan MacGowan, the Rogue Fox, was naked.

Chapter 8

Lachlan awoke groggily. He was tired. And sore. And as randy as . . .

But in that instant, memories stormed into his mind and he jerked to his elbow to stare across the bed.

Startled from sleep, Hunter awoke immediately, snatched her knife from beneath the blanket and sat bolt upright.

From their respective positions, they stared at each other for several hard heartbeats.

"Oh." Her voice was breathy, her eyes wide. She cleared her throat and lowered her voice an octave. "'Tis you."

He said nothing, but stared at her, hoping he looked casual, or maybe even bored. As if he awoke every morning to a wide-eyed warrior woman. As if his heart wasn't threatening to leap out of his chest.

"I—" she began and lowered the dirk, but all words were now lost to him for when she moved her hand, he saw that her tunic had slipped, revealing one creamy shoulder.

His gaze snagged on that ivory hillock, but beneath that, where the garment slanted sideways, much more was revealed, for one nipple was just visible in the tunic's opening.

Desire crashed through him like high tide, leaving him shaky.

He tightened his grip on his plaid and remained very still.

"MacGowan!" she said, but in that instant she realized his lack of attention and lowered her own gaze. "Oh." Her hand moved with poetic slowness, covering herself, but against the pale fabric he could now see that a flush of color brushed her throat and cheeks. "Me apologies," she said.

"Apologies?" He hadn't meant to say the ridiculous word aloud, but he was caught off guard and floundering rather hopelessly in the wild sea of desire.

"Aye." She tightened her fist in the shirt's front, pulling the fabric tight across her bosom.

God help him.

"I didn't mean to . . ." She paused. The color had faded from her cheeks a bit, but her eyes still looked large enough to drown in. Her hair framed her face in bright disarray and her lips seemed extraordinarily bright. She looked like nothing more than a startled archangel. Ethereal, but dangerous.

The dual image was disarming, but hardly unmanning. He shifted uncomfortably as he searched for something to say to fill the silence. Still, try as he might, he could think about nothing but that nipple.

She licked her lips. He watched her tongue dart out and in and wished he could swallow. "I did not mean to offend you. But . . ." She smiled a little sheepishly. "Highland warriors oft shed their garments before going into battle, do they not? Surely you are accustomed to it."

"Accustomed."

"Aye." She nodded curtly and cleared her throat. " 'Twas wise of you to share the bed."

He didn't respond. She would have to survive for a few moments without his clever repartee, for he felt entirely uncertain of his ability to talk. His body felt as tight as a crossbow, arched and ready for action.

"You must ache."

He stared at her.

"You fought bravely," she explained.

"Oh." It was difficult to breathe, but he managed it with a Herculean effort. "You speak of the battle."

"Aye." She scowled a little as if he were daft, and it was entirely possible that he was, for he felt as dizzy as a dervish and as dense as a rock. "I am not sure I thanked you properly."

He could feel his heart beating in his chest and wondered if she could see it pounding there, for now and then she glanced down from his face.

"Warriors are not always adept at . . ." She paused again. Her gaze darted lower, then she licked her bright lips and breathed through them for just a second. His erection thrummed to the rhythm. "I am not always good at expressing me gratitude."

She held her dirk against the mattress now, and her borrowed tunic drooped in that direction, covering her hand to the fingertips. It seemed a strangely erotic image. He stared, first at her fingers, then at her face, trying his damnedest to avoid everything in between, for if the truth be told, he could barely trust himself with those two innocuous body parts.

She cleared her throat. "And what of you, Mac-Gowan?"

It took him a moment to realize she'd asked a question. "What's that?" Perhaps quick-wittedness was not his forte, but he liked to think he was somewhat brighter than he sounded at that very moment.

"We are much alike, you and I. I but wondered if you have trouble . . ." She shrugged. Her shoulder nudged into view another half an inch. "Expressing your emotions. After all, I think we do not, either one of us, fit into the usual mold."

"And what mold is that?"

She shrugged again. The strain was beginning to tell on him as he waited with bated breath for the tunic to fall like the damned walls of Jericho.

"You were raised as a laird's son, used to fine trappings and willing maids, and yet you have turned them aside. Instead, you have chosen a warrior's path so that none will suspect . . ." She paused. A glimmer of worry troubled her brow.

He pulled his attention from her shoulder with an effort and concentrated on her expression. "Suspect what?"

She stared at him. "I do not mean to offend you, Mac-Gowan."

"And I am not offended," he said, though the first glimmer of foreboding was souring his stomach. "What will none suspect?"

"I know the truth," she said, holding his gaze. Her expression was resolute, her delectable lips slightly pursed. He waited for her to continue. She remained silent for some time and when she finally spoke her words were measured.

"Some think it a great advantage in a warrior," she said. "Indeed, in days of yore, your kind were much revered."

He canted his head at her, confused and still aching.

"The Roman army encouraged it in fact. I have done some study of history. I know it to be true. They considered their soldiers to be more content, indeed, more self-sufficient if they were . . . like you."

Something twisted in his stomach. He narrowed his eyes. "Like me?"

"You needn't worry," she said. "I'll tell no one."

"And what is it you'll not tell?"

She scowled at him, but delayed not a moment longer. "That you've a fondness for other men."

"Fond . . . !" He bounded from the bed in one leap and grabbed his plaid as he did so, but in his wild dismay, his fingers barely worked. The woolen slipped. He caught it before it hit the floor and dragged it back in front of his body. "You think I favor men?"

Her eyes had gone suddenly wide. She watched him unblinking, sitting rigid upon the bed. "As I said it matters not to me, MacGowan. I—"

"Holy mother!" he gritted and bunching the fabric sloppily about his waist, stormed from the room.

Hunter stole a glance sideways. He was still there and, truth to tell, she was surprised, for she'd thought he would leave her in Jedburgh after she'd discovered his secret. But she'd been wrong. Minutes later, she'd found him in the stable, silently throwing a saddle onto his stallion. In fact, he'd been silent most of the time since. And it had been many hours. But this was the end of their travels together. She would see to that.

"Well, MacGowan . . ." She halted Knight and faced him as the sun sank into the west. "This is where you turn back."

He glowered at her. There had been a lot of that recently, mostly in lieu of conversation. "I say when I turn back, *laddie*."

He said the word with some scorn, and she regretted again having spilled his secret. After all, it was obviously a sore spot, and he was trying harder than ever to prove his onerous masculinity.

"Nay," she said, and straightened slightly. Her back ached from hours in the saddle. She could only assume that his did too. " 'Tis me own decision, MacGowan, and I say you leave off here."

"Do you?" Perhaps he'd been difficult before, but now challenge seemed to flow from his every pore. "And why is that . . . *laddie?*"

"It matters not why . . . *champion*." Her own ire was rising steadily. After all, it wasn't her fault that he was attracted to men. In fact, if she could change that fact . . . Well, the point was . . . she didn't care who he was attracted to. She raised her chin and stared at him from beneath her helmet's visor. " 'Tis simply that I'll not have you trailing along any farther."

"Trailing along." He leaned toward her aggressively. His neck, she realized, was the approximate size of her waist. A vein throbbed in it just now. "So that's what I've been doing, is it?" he asked and pressed his steed toward her.

"Aye," she said, and stiffened her spine. Beneath her, Knight Star arched his neck and rumbled a warning as the other stallion sidled closer. " 'Tis. For I've not asked you to follow me."

"It's a nuisance I've been then, is it?"

" 'Tis not what I've said," she gritted and placed a hand on the hilt of her sword.

"But 'tis what you've been thinking."

"As I've said I did not ask for your company, Mac—"

"And as I've said, if I hadn't come along, chasing me horse the whole distance, like a bloody hound on your trail, you would be worse off than dead, laddie."

"Worse than dead! To a warrior there is no such thing."

"But to a woman there is," he gritted. "What do you imagine might have happened had I not shown up?"

She said nothing. He crowded his steed closer still.

"Might you think they would have wished you well and sent you merrily on your way?"

"I've seen trouble afore, Mac—"

"Nay!" he growled, and leaned from his stallion so that he all but rode hers. "They would have killed you. But not before they discovered the truth!"

Fury awoke in her like a sleeping lion. "And what truth is that, champion?" she snarled.

"What truth?" He looked as if she'd suddenly gone daft. "The truth that you are a maid and not a man atall. The truth that your skin is as soft as satin and your—" He curled one hand dramatically before him, but found no more words. "Sweet Mother Mary! What the devil were you thinking?"

She watched him from close proximity, her mind roiling, her body taut. "Perhaps I was thinking 'tis a man's world," she said. "Perhaps I was thinking that women have few options in that world, and perhaps . . ." She paused, feeling anger boil quietly inside. "Perhaps I thought it best to survive as best I could rather than perishing quietly like other well-born maids would have done."

He leaned back a mite. "What the devil are you blathering about?"

She stared at him. A thousand memories thundered like wild steeds through her head, trampling all in sight, but she'd tamed the beasties before and she did so again, easing them to a safe haven in her mind. "It matters not," she said and drew a deep, even breath. "It only matters that you leave now."

"Leave? Now?" He laughed. The sound was deep, incredulous, and entirely without mirth.

"Aye."

"Here? In the borderlands where the bloody reivers be more numerous than lambkins?" He laughed again. "I tell you what, laddie. How about if I just kill you meself and see the task done."

She drew out her sword in a flash and motioned toward him. "If you think yourself man enough, MacGowan, have at it."

His own weapon stayed at his side. He swore quietly and with deep feeling. "You are the most stubborn maid that has ever walked the Lord's green earth."

"Perhaps that is because I—"

He laughed, interrupting her words. "Because you are not a maid? Huh!" He leaned toward her again, nearly pressing his mammoth chest against the tip of her sword. "You are deluded is what you are. Aye, you are a warrior, you are brave, and you are competent, but you are also a woman."

"Shut your mouth, MacGowan," she said, and shifted her gaze side to side. Now was not the place to have her secrets aired.

"Or what? You'll shut it for me? You'll kill me? You'll cut me tongue from me head?"

"Aye," she said, and pressed her sword against his chest, but in an instant he had knocked the blade aside and snatched her from her horse. As quick as death he dragged her atop his pommel and crushed her against his chest.

For one fleeting moment his gaze seared hers and then he was kissing her. His lips slanted across hers, burning on contact. She tried to push away, but there was no hope of that. In fact there was nothing she could do except kiss him back, but as suddenly as he began, he quit and swung her like a sack of meal onto her waiting mount.

She found herself in her saddle, slightly askew and feeling as stupid as a hop toad with her sword drooping from a limp wrist.

They stared at each other, though his expression was more of a glare. There was no telling what her face showed. For all she knew, her eyeballs may well have popped clean out of her head.

"I'll be coming with you," he growled.

She continued to stare.

"Unless you kill me here and now."

She blinked once.

"And I'll not be apologizing," he warned, and turned his mount toward the south. "So don't be holding your breath."

Chapter 9

They rode in silence for some time. Off to the west a curl of smoke darkened the twilight sky. Lachlan loosened his sword in its scabbard and tensed, ready for trouble. Where the devil were they headed, anyway?

He would ask, but he knew better than to waste his breath. She wouldn't answer. In fact, he considered it damned fortunate that she hadn't tried to kill him for several hours. And after the kiss . . . Well, he was lucky to remain unscathed, but for one crazy moment he'd almost thought she'd kissed him back, almost thought she'd softened in his arms. Almost . . .

But no. He was being daft. He'd never been particularly astute at reading a woman's mind, and this woman was no different in that respect, apparently.

Favored men! Him! Didn't she realize that her presence all but made him explode with frustration? Didn't she know—

Something rustled in the bracken up ahead. He pushed his mind back to staying alive. There were few places, in Scotland or otherwise, that were more dangerous than the notorious border country, and if he hoped to remain alive, he'd best stay alert.

The sky was darkened and he had no idea where they were. That lack of knowledge made him nervous. After all, he wouldn't want to guarantee that Hunter had his best interests at heart. The fact that she hadn't spoken to him for the past three hours did little to make him feel more secure. Perhaps she knew there were reivers ahead. Perhaps she was leading him into an ambush of some sort. But would they not also ambush her? Unless she was one of them. After all, he knew next to naught about her. Perhaps she was not the only one of her kind. Perhaps there was an entire clan of women of her ilk— like the Amazon women of yore. Bold, hearty maids who welcomed men into their midst only to test their metal and see if they could withstand their challenges.

His heart did a trick beat in his chest. Aye, perhaps he would be tested. But what if he passed the tests? What reward would he receive? Might he then win what he most desired? Might not the object of his desire come willing into his—

"I am asking you to leave."

Her voice was low and quiet in the deepening darkness. His fantasies disappeared like smoke in the night.

"What's that?" he asked, and squinted through the gloaming, trying to see her face behind the metal ventrails she now wore.

She stopped her stallion and turned toward him. Even

in the daylight it was all but impossible to see her face past the metal links, but now he could only guess at her expression, hidden as it was by the lengthening shadows.

"I am asking you to turn back."

He watched her, wishing he could read her thoughts, could at least guess what the hell she was up to. He knew nothing about her, except that she desperately wanted to be rid of him.

"I would like you to leave me." Her voice was so soft it barely resembled her voice atall.

"Why?" he asked.

"I am asking . . ." She paused and drew a deep breath as if it were difficult to go on. "A favor."

"A favor," he repeated, and made no attempt to keep the surprise from his voice. After all, her asking a favor seemed tantamount to the sun falling from the sky and crushing them both like ants in an avalanche.

"Aye."

"Why?"

"It doesn't matter . . ." Her voice was slightly louder now. She lowered it and continued on. "I have saved your life and you have saved mine. The debt is paid. There is no reason for us to share our paths any longer."

No reason! Was she daft? Of course there was a reason. They traveled in the notorious borderlands, and she was a woman alone—with breasts and everything. He was merely doing his chivalrous duty accompanying her—and maybe hoping to get a glance at her . . . everything . . . again.

"Why part ways now?" he asked.

She said nothing for a moment. Her body looked stiff. Her tone was impassive. " 'Tis as good a time as any."

"Aye," he agreed, "if you are hoping to get killed. Or

hoping to get me killed," he added as an afterthought, remembering the Amazon scenario. It was an intriguing
one, but 'twas said such women cut off one breast to improve their ability as archers, and she most definitely had
two—

"So you're scared, MacGowan, is that it?"

"What say you?" The image of her naked plagued his
mind. She stood in the moonlight, her hair like spun
gold, her breasts pearly white, and her sword held aloof.

"You're afeared to ride alone," she said.

He smiled at her, for though he knew anger was the
safer course, his infamous temper was conspicuously
lacking. "And here I thought you had met me brother
Gilmour."

She said nothing as she waited for an explanation.

"If you're hoping to goad me into leaving, you'll have
to do better than such a paltry insult," he said. "For me
brother has used that ploy far too oft for it to remain ef-
fective."

There was no need to see her expression now because
he could feel her rising anger. "I'm asking you nicely,
champion. Leave me be."

"And I'm telling you nicely, I will not."

"I have been patient with you."

He canted his head in concession. "Aye. Not counting
the times you have tried to kill me."

"I have been patient," she repeated. "But I will not be
so charitable much longer. You will turn back now." He
expected her to draw her sword, or at least her dirk, but
she did not.

"And why would I be doing that, laddie? I already
know you are female," he mused. "What else have you to
hide?"

She was silent for some time. "What will it take to turn you aside?"

There was something in the way she asked the question that cranked up his interest. Almost a hint of suggestiveness. He swallowed, refrained from pouncing on her like a hound on a hare, and reminded himself where her interests lay. "What are you offering?"

"I did not say . . ." she began, then paused. The tension was as tight as a well-turned screw. "What would it take?"

He could not ignore the images that raced through his mind—the naked, provocative, breathtaking images. He'd spent the night with her, after all. None could blame him for being as randy as a lonely goat. On the other hand, most could expect him to at least be aroused by someone who would have some hope of returning his interest.

"I fear the price would be more than you are willing to pay," he said, and smiled grimly into the darkness.

"Mayhap I should be the one to decide that." Her voice was soft now, almost inaudible even to his foxlike senses.

Somewhere below his waist, his second brain screamed its agreement, but in the end good sense prevailed, surprising him immensely. It seemed he was not quite so foolish as to admit his longing for her. Not quite so desperate as to beg sex from a woman who wished nothing from his entire damned gender.

"I'll be accompanying you, laddie," he said, and his nether regions ached with disappointment. "I fear there's naught you can do to stop me."

"Naught I can do?" she rasped and yanked her knife from its sheath.

They faced each other in the darkness, barely two feet apart.

"Turn back, MacGowan!"

He sat unmoving, his gaze on the blade. "Nay," he said.

Something like a growl issued from her throat. There was the hiss of a blade as it passed not a full inch from his ear. For a moment his heart stopped in his chest, but even before it had picked up its beat, he turned Mathan and pulled the quivering hilt from the tree behind him.

Kneeing his mount to the south, then, he preceded her down the road.

It was shortly before midnight when Hunter first saw the lights of Penham through the misty rain that slanted from the north. Tension coiled in her stomach, but she stared straight ahead as she spoke casually to her unwanted companion.

"You will follow me own lead."

"What's that?" His voice was low and not particularly agreeable. Good, she was spoiling for a fight.

"We will be entering a village soon. You'll say nothing."

She sensed more than saw a shrug and scowled in disappointment. A rousing good battle might relieve her tension, but it looked as if she would have to wait, would have to bear his presence for a while longer, would have to endure her aching frustration for a bit more time. After all, he favored men. She knew it was true, regardless of the kiss. Regardless of the skill of the caress, it was obvious he'd only done it to disprove her theory. No man would ignore the chambermaid and show interest in her, for she was not truly a woman, not one to pique a man's interest, and certainly not one to excite a rogue like Lachlan.

The road beneath them became more tightly packed. Knight's iron shoes clipped against a rock, sparking on contact, regardless of the slanting rain.

From up ahead a voice called out. "Who goes there?"

She neither explained nor hesitated, but rode on toward the gate that barred the road to the village. "I am Giles come to see me uncle at Nettlepath."

There was a moment's pause. "My lord, it has been some time."

"Aye." She said no more, for she'd rarely had the luxury of making friends, and here less likely than any other.

"You'll be off to the old baron's manor then?"

"Aye."

"Who rides with you there?"

"This is me servant. He is deaf and mute." For a moment she thought MacGowan would argue, but he did not.

"As you well know I am to let no one enter so late at night, but since 'tis raining and all . . ." His words trailed off as the gate opened.

"Me thanks," she said, and loosened Knight's reins. He needed no more encouragement, but canting his head away from the wind, entered the village and turned of his own accord onto a barely visible path. Long ago Lord Barnett's estate had been swallowed up by Penham. It resided now within the village's wooden palisade. The trail that wound between the shops of a cobbler and a wainwright was course and uneven.

"A deaf mute?" MacGowan's voice rumbled from the darkness.

"What's that?" she said, and continued to stare between Knight's dark ears. "I fear I cannot hear you."

The other snorted and in a moment a hound barked and raced toward them down the winding road.

"Quiet, dog," she said. The cur wagged his tail at the sound of her voice, only emitting barks at intervals as he scampered and wiggled his way toward Nettlepath's ancient stable.

"Come no further!" warned a teetering voice, and a feeble light was unshielded.

Knight pitched his dark ears forward and stopped on command. Hunter dismounted without a pause.

"All is well, Shanks. It is I."

There was a moment of silence before the lamp was held aloft. An old man blinked in the glow of it.

"Lord Giles, is that you?"

"Aye. 'Tis."

Hanging the lantern on a nearby peg of the stable, Longshanks tottered out of the shadows, his pale night cap clearly visible in the enveloping darkness. "You have returned," he said, and dropping his walking stick, grasped Hunter's arms in a feeble grip.

"Aye," she said, and for a moment allowed a smile for the memories that soared through her. "That I have."

"And you are safe and well," he said, pushing her out to arms' length.

"I am hale."

"I prayed it would be so."

"It must have been your prayers that have kept me from harm then, Shanks."

"And your uncle's."

"Of course," she said, and pulled gently from the other's grip. "How is he?"

The old man's pause spoke volumes. "I fear he is not doing well. The ague took him this spring. He has not been the same since. But you have returned. Surely that will see him improved."

"Perhaps," she said. Leading Knight into the barn, she loosened his girth and slipped the saddle from his back.

"And who is this with you, Master Giles?" asked Longshanks. His voice warbled a bit more than she remembered, but otherwise, he seemed unchanged, built like a curved needle, with a nose like a fisherman's hook and eyes of palest green.

"He is me servant."

"Servant?" The old man squinted into the darkness, his head canted. "A brawny lad, he is."

"Brawny enough, I suppose."

"Do you have a name, lad?" he asked.

"He is deaf and mute," Hunter said quickly.

"Ahh. 'Tis unfortunate."

"Sometimes. So the old mare gave me uncle another strapping colt," she said, glancing into a large, well-bedded stall. Inside, the floor was piled deep with strew. Lying with her long legs tucked beneath her, the gray nuzzled her sleepy foal and nickered with maternal contentment. The world could be falling apart about their ears, but the horses of Nettlepath would want for nothing. Things had changed little since her departure.

"Aye, a bonny one he is too," Shanks said and followed her to stand in the doorway where she turned Knight loose. From the corner of her eye, she saw that MacGowan did the same with his steed. He was silent, but she would guess he was none too happy about it. The thought almost made her smile, but she turned away instead, searching for a grooming brush.

Longshanks turned stiffly toward her. "I will see to your steed, lad."

"I like to make certain—" she began, but the old man stopped her.

"Who taught you the ways of the horse at the outset?" he asked.

She paused a moment, allowing the memories in for another brief instant. "It was you, Master Shanks."

"Aye." He nodded. "Aye. And old age has not made me forget."

She watched him for a moment. Errant emotions filtered through her like chaff on the wind, but she put them carefully aside. "Me thanks," she said finally.

"Go to your uncle," he told her. "He does not sleep well these days."

She scowled, but the old man had already turned away.

"And take your servant with ye."

She considered arguing, but Longshanks spoke first.

"A fine mount you've given him. Near as good as your own."

Even without looking, she could feel MacGowan's glare. The silence was deafening, but the old man spoke into it.

"You were always more generous than others deserve."

She would have spoken, but he turned away with a gentle word for Knight, and finally she stepped out the door.

The path to the house seemed both endless and foreshortened. Striding up the stone stairs, she paused for a moment before letting herself in. The ancient hinges creaked as the weathered door swung open.

"Aileas?" The voice that called from the adjoining room was reedy and abrupt, as if just startled into lucidity. She stopped where she was, but in a moment she felt MacGowan's gaze on her and moved on, through the darkened house toward the light that glowed from within.

"Ai—" Lord Barnett began again, but his mouth froze in a soundless O when she entered the room. He lay on a narrow bed that seemed adrift amidst a sea of parchments and books that were scattered like seed upon every possible surface.

"Me laird," she said.

His pale lips moved, but no sound came forth. He looked old and frail, barely a shadow of the man she had once called father. "David," he rasped finally.

Memories stormed her mind. "Nay," she said, and braved a few more steps toward him. Liver-colored spots shone on the pale flesh of his sunken cheeks and his hand shook as he lifted it toward her. "David died of the fever many years since. Do you not remember?"

The house was as silent as a tomb, then, "Aye." He nodded and on his face was a lost sort of misery. "Me David. Gone. Like his mother," he mused to himself. "He was a bonny lad." A scowl tightened his brow, then he lifted his face again. "Who—"

"I am Giles."

He repeated the name without inflection, staring at her with his mouth slightly open. "Giles? Me nephew?"

"Aye." It was all she could do to force out that one lie, for her throat felt tight.

He did not seem at ease with the idea, but neither did he argue. "Long you have been gone." There was accusation in the words. She ignored it. Self-preservation had taught her well.

"I had much to do."

He nodded jerkily. "How did you find London?"

"I did not go to London."

"The king, he is well?"

She stiffened, but refrained from glancing at Mac-Gowan.

"I am weary," she said. "Is me old chamber unoccupied?"

"There will always be a place for you, David."

She paused. When last she saw him he had been lucid, but that had been long ago. "Very well then," she said, and turned away.

"But what of this fellow?" asked the baron, and turned ill-focused eyes toward Lachlan.

"You need not concern yourself with him," Hunter said.

"What be your name, lad?"

"They call him champion." She felt MacGowan's gaze on her, but ignored its heat with careful disdain. "He does not speak," she said, and finding a candle on the nearby table, set the wick to the living flame that lit the room from the arched stone hearth.

"Champion," mused the old man, and nodded rhythmically. "It suits you. You will see to me nephew's comfort."

MacGowan said nothing.

"There is pigeon pie and almond fritters in the pantry. Shanks has kept a cauldron hanging over the fire. You'll be wanting a bath, as was your way. The lad can fetch the water."

"Aye." She turned away, guarding her fragile flame with a curved palm.

"David," called the old man.

She glanced toward him, ready to correct his mistake. But age had made him thin and frail. His eyes looked bright and lost and, despite everything, something ached in her gut. She said nothing.

"What of Rhona?" His voice was weak, his bent fingers clutched and loosened in the blanket that was pulled high on his chest. "Any news of her?"

Seconds ticked away. Memories burned her mind. Some paces behind her, Lachlan remained perfectly silent.

"Nay," she said, and turned away with a hard effort. "I've not seen her for some years."

Chapter 10

Hunter stepped inside the room she had once called her own. It remained unchanged but for the dust that lay on the place. MacGowan followed her in, and though she focused on her surroundings, she could feel his presence like a looming sentry.

The arrow she'd won at the Braemar Gathering remained in its place on the wall. The plaid she'd received from the Munros lay slanted across her old bed. She lifted the candle and swept her gaze across the room to the narrow window. A bed, a desk, a copper tub. Aye, the place remained the same, as if she had just stepped out for a moment. But years had passed and she stood now in a warrior's garb with this vociferous mute looming in the darkness behind her.

The silence weighed like a firkin of barley against the back of her neck.

"What is it?" she asked and, setting her candle upon the narrow writing desk, faced him finally.

He stared at her, his brows slightly raised. "I've no idea what you speak of," he said.

"Have you a problem you'd like to vent?"

"Me?" He chuckled a little. "Nay."

She told herself to let it be, but she could not. "And what is it you mean by that, MacGowan?"

He said nothing for a long moment, then, "Your uncle . . ." He paused as if he could not quite believe his own words. "He acts as if you are a man."

"Aye." She clenched one fist. Her patience was short this night. "That he does."

"Why?"

"Because that is what I chose for him to believe."

He scowled at her, as if she must have mistook his meaning. "Your uncle," he repeated and stepped closer. "He acts as though you are a *man*."

She gritted her teeth. "Aye," she said. "And why not? He had no use for me as a lass. I have made a capable man."

"But surely he knows the truth."

She barked a laugh. "Laird Barnett?" she asked and laughed again, though it hurt her chest somehow. "Did he look the sort to know anything? Nay," she said before he answered. "He had no use for the truth."

He was scowling at her. She scowled back.

"Then who is privy to your secrets?"

She removed her helmet and ran her fingers through her hair.

"And what secrets might those be?" she asked and swung the cape from her shoulders.

"Who knows you are a maid?"

Hanging her cape on a peg beside the door, she turned to him with a shrug. "As I have told you afore, champion, I am a man in every way that matters."

Behind her, the candlelight flickered in an errant draft.

"I beg to differ," he said.

She faced him, arms akimbo. "Do you threaten to expose me?"

He shook his head. "I but ask who knows the truth."

"It seems that you are the only one who *doubts* the truth, MacGowan."

"What of your mother? She must have known."

Her heart twisted. "You talk a great deal for a daft mute."

"Who is she?"

She shrugged. "No one you would know."

"Then you've no reason not to tell me."

"And less reason to spill her name."

"Surely she knew she bore a girl child."

Her chest ached. "My mother is long dead and past the cares of this world."

"Then your uncle is your guardian?"

She said nothing, but watched him in silence.

"He is not your uncle," MacGowan said, his voice low.

She tried to look casual, removed, uncaring. "Is he not?"

"Nay."

"Then pray tell, who is he, champion?"

"That is what I would know. That and much more."

She turned toward the window. Against her breast, her tiny shell felt small and fragile. "Leave me be, MacGowan. I did not ask for your company."

"How is it that you took this guise as a man? Surely there are those who know the truth."

She said nothing.

"So you have none to return to but this old man and his servant. I am sorry."

"Sorry?" She turned to stare at him. "There is no need for that, champion."

"You do not mourn your family?"

"I did not even—" She paused.

"You did not even what?"

"I am hungry," she said and, pulling off her gauntlets, tossed them on the bed.

"You did not what?" he asked. "Know them?"

"No." She stared up at him. "In truth, I did not."

"Why? Did they die at your birth?"

"Fetch me some supper."

He remained perfectly still, watching her for a long moment before he spoke. "They sent you away," he said finally.

Her throat tightened up, but she did not break eye contact. Indeed, she dared not change her expression.

"'Tis the truth," he said. His voice was quiet now. "They sent you to another. Why?"

Her heart was pounding in her chest.

"Was it here that you were sent? Did they tell the baron that you were a lad and—"

She snatched her dirk from its sheath. "I did not invite you here, MacGowan, but since you have come, you will do as I command."

He said nothing. Neither did he back away. "And what do you command, laddie?" He was as big as a wall, powerful and hard and alluring. She swallowed.

"Fetch me a meal," she said.

"And what then, laddie? Shall I share your room?" He said the words as a challenge.

The tension cranked up a notch, but she shrugged, attempting to dispel her breathlessness. "And why not?"

"For all the most obvious reasons."

"I've no more interest in you than you have in me, MacGowan," she said.

He laughed out loud, throwing back his head slightly, so that the taut cords in his neck stood out hard and rigid against his tanned throat. " 'Tis a good thing to know," he said finally, and took another step toward her.

The room seemed strangely narrow. She swallowed and raised her chin. "You needn't pretend with me," she said. "I know where your desires lie."

He clenched one fist and remained where he stood. "With men," he said.

"Aye."

"Then by your admission alone I should be interested in *you*."

It was a convoluted truth. Still, she opened her mouth to deny it, but he stepped up close and spoke before she could. "But I tell you this, *laddie*, I am not what you think I am."

She shrugged as if unconcerned. "And neither am I what you think."

"Nay?"

"Nay. I am a warrior and naught else."

"A warrior," he said.

She canted her head. "Just so."

"And what if I forget meself?"

"What?"

"Whilst I sleep," he said. "What if I forget your sex and force meself on you?"

"Force yourself?" she said, and laughed as she lifted her dirk. "I think not."

"For you fight like a man."

"Aye," she said.

"And you live like a man."

"Aye."

"And you think like a man. Therefore . . ." He shrugged. "You are a man."

She nodded.

"So why should I not share your chamber?"

The room felt airless.

"And fetch your water?"

She managed a shrug.

"And tell me, Master Hunter, shall I bathe you too?"

"And why not?" She swung toward him. "No matter what you think of me, I've no interest whatsoever in you."

The room fell into silence.

"And I am your servant." His voice was quiet, and if she didn't know better she would almost think she heard humor in the tone.

"Aye," she said, and raised her chin slightly. "Aye, you are me servant."

He nodded perfunctorily. "Very well then, I shall fetch your meal and tote your water."

"Water?"

He grinned. "For your bath?"

She swallowed. "Oh. Aye. Of course."

"Very well," he said and, nodding once, left the room.

She closed her eyes and let her mind spin wildly

away. How had she gotten herself into such a tangle? Many years since she had taken this guise as a man, and in all that time she'd not yet been discovered. Never had another guessed her true identity. Even the fierce Munro had accepted her as a man. His sisters and all their warriors had done the same. But all had gone amiss now, spilling out a myriad of wild feelings she had not thought she possessed. Even now—

The door swung open, stopping her thoughts short.

MacGowan entered, pushed the door shut with his foot, and bore his burden toward the bed. "I fear the baron may have been imaging when he spoke of the pigeon pie and almond fitters, for I found none, but there is this," he said and, depositing a board set with dark bread and cheese, handed her a horn of ale.

"You are quick when the mood strikes you," she said, and he laughed as if she'd said something terribly witty.

"I did not wish to incur your lordship's wrath with my tardiness," he said.

She snorted.

He lifted one brow at her derisive sound. "You do not believe me?"

"Usually."

"Perhaps I was in a rush because I did not wish to miss anything then," he said.

She narrowed her eyes at him. "Anything?"

He caught her with his gaze. His eyes were dark, full of challenge and promise and a million other things she could not identify and dared not consider. "I am certain you are impatient. Indeed, patience is not me own greatest virtue, and it has been a long while for you."

She felt a bit breathless. Perhaps it was fatigue. "A long while since what?"

"Since you've bathed," he explained.

"Oh." She licked her lips and remembered to breathe. "Aye."

"Well then . . ." A muscle jumped in his lean jaw. "I'd best fetch the water."

She swallowed. "You must be hungry," she said, and indicated the board that held the impromptu meal, but he only stared at her, his eyes boring into hers.

"Aye," he said. "I am indeed."

Heat smote her like the blast of a smithy's furnace.

"Enjoy the ale," he said, and turned away.

It seemed but a moment before he returned with his arms full of wood. He said nothing as he set the faggots into the fireplace and nurtured a small flame. When it was doing well, he left again only to return but a few moments later. Each fist was wrapped about the rope of a wooden bucket. Both buckets steamed.

He emptied the first into the copper tub that occupied the corner of the room, then did the same with the second.

"I shall return shortly." She heard his words clearly, but whether they were a threat or a promise, she could not tell.

She wrung her hands until he stepped through the door once again. A few additional trips and the tub was all but full.

"There you be," he said, and indicated the bath with an open palm. His eyes seemed to smolder in the firelight. "Will me laird need help disrobing?" There was challenge in his voice. Challenge and anger and some other dark emotion that she dare not question too closely.

Her legs felt shaky and her mouth dry, but she raised her chin in response. "Why not?"

Chapter 11

Lachlan stood rooted to the floor. Nay, he was not one to turn away from a challenge, but neither was he one to rush in headlong where he could not win, and he was entirely uncertain he could be the victor in this, for he didn't even know the rules.

"You say you wish for me to disrobe you?" he asked.

There was a pause long enough to sing a half dozen Hail Marys before she finally spoke. "Aye," she said. "Unless it would be too difficult for you?"

"Difficult?" The muscles in his hands ached. He eased them open. "Nay. Why would it be? After all, you say I have no interest in women."

She shrugged, but her expression was taut. "Perhaps that is why then."

He shook his head in confusion.

"Mayhap you are repulsed."

"Repulsed!" he gritted, then calmed himself. The irony was not lost on him, but he did not feel like laughing. "You worry that I am repulsed."

"Nay." For the life of him, he could not read her thoughts. Her hand was gripped into a fist. He stared at it, and she opened it beneath his gaze. "I am not worried."

It seemed suddenly that he was painfully close to the truth, just a breath away. "Because you believe I am not attracted to women or because you believe I am not attracted to *you*?"

An unknown expression flitted across her face, but she shrugged finally. "It matters naught, for I've heard that great fighters are not oft great lovers."

"I am flattered," he said.

She raised her brows with a bored expression, and he leaned one shoulder against the wall and watched her at his leisure. It was a luxury he had rarely been afforded, for far too often she was armored and caped and defensive. But now, with her hair undone and her figure clad in leather, she was beautiful beyond words, even in warrior's garb. Or *especially* in warrior's garb. 'Twas a confusing thought. "I am flattered that you think me a great fighter," he explained.

Her lips curled upward slightly at the corners, and he could not help but wonder what would happen if kissed her just there at the edge of heaven.

"And not insulted that I think you a poor lover?" she asked.

"I've no need to worry on that account." He was too busy watching her lips to realize immediately that his response sounded roguishly self-assured.

She studied him with careful scrutiny. "So . . ." He stared back, arousal making him hard and impatient.

"You are confident of your skills in that arena, are you, champion?"

Lachlan crossed his arms against his chest and reminded himself that only a fool would show weakness to a woman of Hunter's ilk. "I've had no complaints," he said.

"If I cared I would be quite excited."

He shrugged. "I suspect your disinterest will only make me task the easier."

She drew a sharp breath and he smiled.

"I but meant the task of disrobing you," he said and, shifting his weight from the wall, approached her slowly. She watched him with ever widening eyes until he was mere inches from her. Had she ceased to breathe? Had he? "You are ready?" he asked.

For a moment, he thought she would back away but she did not, so he set his hand to the buckle of her scabbard with steely determination.

Their eyes met for an instant, but he pulled his away and cleared his throat. "You've a fine sword."

"As do you."

He skimmed his gaze to hers again, but if her words meant anything more than the obvious it did not show in her eyes. Slipping the blade from her hips, he set it aside and breathed carefully.

"Did your uncle give it to you?"

"Aye," she said.

He nodded and drew off her jerkin. It was padded heavily at the shoulders but had no closures and was simple enough to remove once the points were loosened. She stood finally in naught but a linen tunic and her calfskin hose. He reached slowly for the leather thong that closed the shirt at her throat, and to his surprise she did not stop him. Tugging gently, he pulled the lace loose. The garment opened a sparse few inches. He clenched his jaw and relaxed with a hard-won effort.

"Your back does not bother you unduly?"

"Me back?" She drew a careful breath. "It is well enough."

"Good." He nodded, unclenched his fists and reached resolutely for the hem of her shirt. " 'Tis good."

It came away without anyone passing out, though he felt a bit lightheaded as he tossed it to the bed. Her arms were bare now as were her shoulders. But her wound was bandaged and above that her bindings stood guard between her and the world in general—or him in particular. His teeth were beginning to sweat.

"If this is bothering you—" she began. Her tone was cool, but he interrupted.

"Nay! Nay," he said, and reached for the cloth that hid her breasts. At the last moment though, he changed his course, for if the truth were known, he was entirely uncertain he could touch her there again and maintain any semblance of control.

Thus, he dipped his fingers lower and untied the bandage that bound her most recent wound. He was close to her breasts, so very close that it was difficult to concentrate on the task at hand, but finally the knot worked loose and he was unwrapping her. He did so slowly, with a great deal of focus given to that specific part of her body, never letting his eyes stray from his mission, even when he set the bandages aside.

"If this makes you . . . uncomfortable I can finish the task meself," she said. Her expression was still set, but perhaps there was an edge of breathlessness to her tone.

"Nay." Focus. "Nay." He shifted in an attempt to ease the pressure down below. "Not uncomfortable atall."

For a moment he wondered if she failed to breathe, but finally she spoke again. "Your belt," she said, changing the subject without warning. "It bears the Mac-Gowan wildcat."

"Aye," he agreed and, reaching out, tugged at the cloth that bound her breasts. It sighed loose. He forced his hand to move, to circle, to unwind, to remain steady, and in a matter of moments her entire torso was bare. Nestled against her buttermilk skin was a delicate shell hung on a narrow chain. It was crafted of finest silver and shone in the firelight, but it could not retain his attention, for her breasts were as beautiful as he remembered. They were full and pale and capped with nipples the color of sweet wine, but along one delectable, outside curve, a jagged scar was revealed.

He tightened his jaw and carefully kept himself from reaching out to smooth his fingers along its course. "You were wounded," he said.

"Aye." Her tone was tense, and when he looked into her eyes he saw that her face had gone hard, as if she were steeling herself against some unseen force.

"It does not hurt you?"

"Nay."

"How did you sustain it?"

"A dispute with the Munro."

"A dispute?"

"He did not think I had a right to his favored stallion."

He eased his fists open again. "Damn him." He tried to keep his tone absolutely neutral, but perhaps he was less successful than he'd hoped, for her steely expression gave way to curiosity.

"You dislike him?"

"Dislike him!" The words rasped out, low and gritty, but he drew a deep breath and calmed himself. "He wounded you."

"I stole his steed."

"Good."

"Tell me, champion, do you resent the truce between the Munros and your people?"

"He wounded you," he reminded her.

"And I wounded him."

His jaw hurt. "Aye, but it matters not if you mar him, while you . . ." He paused, searching for words.

"I do not care that you think me ruined, MacGowan. Indeed—"

"Ruined!" He choked the word, but could find naught else to say that would not reveal the pain her presence caused him.

And thus they stared at each other in wordless immobility.

"The water cools," she said finally. "Let's see this done."

His erection waved its wild approval. Lachlan resolutely kept his gaze on her face, for although her breasts had been alluring before, the scar seemed to add a strange new depth to his feelings. It was all he could do to refrain from touching her.

"Get on the bed," he ordered.

"What?" Was there panic in her face?

He would have laughed if he'd still possessed the capabilities. "Sit," he said. "On the bed. I'll remove your boots."

She pursed her lips, then cleared her throat and did as commanded. "Of course."

His hands were remarkably steady as he set them to her first boot. It came away easily in his hands, as did the next. He swallowed and reached for the top of her hose. Beneath his fingers, her waist felt as tight and supple as an oak sapling. He concentrated on the task at hand, pushing the leather downward and remembering to breathe. Beneath the hose, she wore naught but a loin-cloth tied with a wide linen lace. He avoided it carefully and tugged her hose down and away, praying while he did so until her thighs and knees were utterly bare. Squatting soundlessly, he reached for the garter that held her stocking in place. It loosened easily and he rolled the woolen garment over the firm slope of her calf and lower. Her skin was smooth and pearly, her muscles long and taut.

His breathing was steady now and his sight clear. Undressing this woman was not unlike a battle. He only had to remain focused lest he make a terrible mistake and lose his head. Lifting her foot onto his knee, he trailed his fingers light as sunrise over the sharp bone of her ankle. The stocking fell before his fingers, smoothed away to reveal the fine curve of her foot by slow, careful increments. The instep was high, the tendons tight and as his hand skimmed lower, finally revealing her toes, he saw that they were small and perfect. He ran a finger down the lot of them. It was like striking the cords of a harp, for he felt her shiver as the instrument might.

The stocking fell away, but his hands remained, cradling her foot upon his knee. He glanced up. "Are you well?"

"Well?" she repeated, but around the word he could hear her quick, shallow breathing.

"Aye. All is well?"

"Of course. Why would it not be?"

Without glancing down, he skimmed his finger across the tidy row of toes. She shivered again and he scowled in fascination. "I do not know," he said. Their gazes melded. He seemed strangely calm now, as if he held his own life in the palm of his hand and did not worry for the outcome.

"Lass," he said, but in that instant she yanked her foot. In his surprise, he almost lost his grip, but he did not, for at Evermyst it was oft said that what he put his hand to did not easily go astray. "Whatever is amiss?"

"'Tis naught amiss," she said, "but that you refuse to release me foot."

"Ahh, well, I am your faithful servant after all." Reaching up slightly, he curled his palm around her calf. The skin felt warm and lovely beneath his hand. He kneaded it gently. "'Tis me duty to see to your care."

"You have done enough." She licked her lips and tugged at her foot again.

He tightened his grip even as he continued his kneading. "You seem a bit tense."

"And why would I not be? A great beast of a Mac-Gowan has got me foot."

"A great beast of a servant," he corrected patiently. "But you've no need to worry. After all, we are both men here, aye? There can be no indiscretions."

"No indiscretions. So I was correct; you have no bias about sins against nature."

"Sins against nature?" he repeated, and kneaded her

calf again. It was firm and long and smooth, nothing like his own bunched muscles.

She drew breath sharply through her nose. "You know just what I mean," she said.

"Aye," he agreed, and stroked her leg again with slow deliberation. "That I have more interest in men than women."

She nodded, but the movement was jerky. "And that is fine by me."

He trailed his finger along the crease behind her knee. Her entire leg jerked like the kick of a recalcitrant mule. Interesting.

"After all," she said. The words were raspy and quick. "You are a warrior of sorts."

He almost smiled. It was not unlike the calm he oft felt before battle. "Of sorts," he agreed.

"No offense meant, of course."

He ran the beds of his nails along the back of her thigh. The long muscle jumped.

"Of course," he agreed. His own tone was amicable.

"After all, you are certainly built—"

He skimmed his fingers down her leg from her knee. She rasped a sharp breath and he raised his gaze to hers. She was breathing through her mouth. The sight was not unbecoming, but seemed to escalate the beat of his heart.

"I am certainly built?" he began, reminding her where she'd left off.

She stared at him for several long seconds, then licked her lips. He watched the swipe of her tongue and felt the effects curl like smoky talons deep in his gut.

"Like a warrior," she finished. Her voice was as deep as night, shivering pleasantly through his system.

He circled her thigh with his palm and massaged firmly. "Is that a compliment, lass?"

"What?" She was watching his hand.

"Did you compliment me?" he asked, but it mattered little what she said, only that she remained as she was, supple and warm, and all but naked beneath his fingertips.

She swallowed. "I did not mean to. 'Tis just that you are . . ." His sleeves were rolled away from his wrists, exposing the working muscles of his sun-darkened forearms. "You are beautifully built—for a womanly man."

He paused in his massage, then raised his brows and laughed out loud.

"Something amuses you?"

He resumed his movements. "Apparently so. And 'tis strange," he admitted. "For if another said the same I may well feel the need to sharpen me blade on his skull."

"Are you challenging me, MacGowan?"

He smiled a little. "Not to a duel."

Their gazes met. Her eyes seemed unusually dark and her cheeks were flushed.

He slid his hand along her leg, squeezing gently over her knee and down the satiny length of her calf.

She watched his progress with enormous eyes.

"This isn't bothering you, is it?" he asked.

"Bothering—"

"Aye," he said and, easing her foot from his lap, reached for the other leg.

She jerked it from his grasp. "Nay!"

He glanced up, absorbed by his task. "What's that?"

She cleared her throat. "I am feeling quite guilty . . . for the things I said of you."

He stared up at her.

"After all, you are *not* me servant . . . exactly."

"Perhaps not exactly," he agreed and, capturing her second foot, set it upon his thigh.

She watched his movements and swallowed. "'Tis not your job to disrobe . . ." She failed to find any additional words for a moment. "'Tis not your job to see to me own comfort."

Her legs ran on forever, her waist scooped in with dramatic flare and her breasts . . . Half hidden by the wayward sweep of her flaxen locks, they appeared like fair glimpses of heaven. He felt his desire throb and he tamped down that familiar impatience.

"As it turns out, I do not mind so terribly," he said.

She licked her lips. He watched the movement with absolute absorption. "Just because . . ." She paused, breathed a few times, and continued. "Just because I conduct meself as a warrior does not mean I am . . . that sort."

He released her second garter at a leisurely pace, enjoying every brush of his fingertips against her flesh. "That sort?" he asked and, slipping his hands around her calf, eased the stocking downward.

She drew a careful breath between her teeth. "The sort we spoke of before. The sort that . . . dallies with their own type."

He studied her face in a long moment of silence. "And despite all hard evidence to the contrary you still believe *I* do." He eased her stocking over the arch of her foot, letting his fingertips skim along the scooped sole and over her toes as he slipped the garment from her.

"Why else are you here?" she asked.

He almost laughed, but the feel of her skin beneath

his fingers made it difficult to breathe, so he merely encircled her ankle and leaned toward her.

"Because despite your delusions to the contrary, lassie, you are a far cry from being a man."

Their gazes met with a jolt, and perhaps in his eyes she could see the hard edge of his desire, for in that instant, she jerked her foot away. Her toes brushed the burgeoning swell of his erection as she stumbled to her feet.

He rose more leisurely, still watching her.

"I am not the sort you spoke of, lass. In truth, I am the furthest thing from it, and I'll not pretend to be otherwise, no matter how safe that pretense makes you feel."

"You think I need pretense to make me feel secure?"

"Aye, lass, I do."

"Then you forget me abilities?"

She stood nearly naked before him. Through the brushed gold of her hair, her breasts rose and fell with the depth of her emotion.

"I forget nothing about you, lass."

For a moment he wasn't sure if she would flee or fight, but finally she spoke, her tone cool. "You needn't pretend to be what you are not, MacGowan. I care not either way."

He studied her carefully. For a moment while he touched her it had seemed that she too felt something. Had he imagined it or was that why she persisted with her foolish notions? To protect herself. To hold him at bay.

"Indeed," she said. "I do not think less of you because you prefer men."

He said nothing.

"You are a warrior," she continued. "Brave and

strong. You have no need to prove your sexual prowess, for as I've said, I have no interest in you." She lifted her chin and gave a single nod, like a punctuation of her decision.

An odd mix of emotions churned in Lachlan's stomach, but damned if he could keep them straight.

"So tell me, lass," he said. "After all this, you still believe I see you as a man."

"'Tis no great surprise," she said. "Others have been believing that very thing for years."

"Which merely proves me theory."

"Which is?"

"Most men are dolts."

She laughed. "Do not try to pretend you were unfooled by me disguise."

"Nay, I readily admit that at the beginning I thought you a man, for you make a bold warrior and a formidable enemy. Yet I cannot help but wonder what you would be like as a—"

A dirk appeared like magic in her hand. In truth, he had no idea where it came from, but she held it waist high, where it could do a good deal of damage.

He sighed. "Lass," he said. "I tire of this drama."

"As do I!"

He failed to do so much as glance down at the blade. Instead he met her eyes full on. "What are you so afeared of, lassie?"

"Afeared!" she snarled. "You dare insult me again?"

"Nay," he said, and took a step closer as he skimmed his gaze down the ethereal length of her body. His chest swelled at the sight of her, squeezing in on his heart. "I could not see you thus and insult you. I but wonder if you lie."

She shifted the knife slightly in her hand. "As if turns out, MacGowan, you are a bigger fool than I thought at the start."

"Truly?" he said and took a step closer still. The point of the knife pressed low on his abdomen, but he ignored it. "How so?"

"Few would be daft enough to cry liar in your current situation."

He shrugged. The movement felt slow and heavy, as if he were swimming upstream. "I readily admit that there are few like me, lass. And perhaps that is why . . ." He paused, and reaching up, brushed the back of his fingers against her cheek.

She didn't move, but remained absolutely still. "Why what?" she breathed.

"Why you must guard yourself against me," he said.

For a moment he thought she might actually stab him, might drive her blade into him without a second thought, but instead she threw back her head and laughed.

He watched her and waited for the anger. After all, he was not a man known for his patience. And yet the fury did not come, not through the long moments as her laughter rolled on.

"So you think yourself irresistible, do you, champion?" she asked at last.

Nay, he was not angry, but perhaps a bit of heat warmed his cheeks, a bit of embarrassment for her mirth at his expense. He would be the first to admit he was no lady's man—no coxcomb wont to draw the maids. And not one to put himself in a position to invite ridicule, but this once, perhaps for the first time in his life, it seemed worth the risk.

"You say you are not the least attracted to me?" he asked.

"I am not!" Her tone was scoffing. He remained absolutely still, and she backed away finally to indicate him with a wave of her dirk. "You are . . ." She skimmed him with her gaze, but for a moment he almost believed she hesitated, almost faltered. "You are hardly the sort to draw me own interest."

"Indeed?" He canted his head slightly. "Then 'tis *you* who is attracted to your own sex."

Her mouth opened and closed. He thought she would object, but she did not. " 'Tis none of your concern," she said instead. "But this much I will tell you . . ." She leaned forward to point at him with her dirk. "I've no interest in *you.*"

He forced himself to shrug. " 'Tis just as well," he said, "for then you will not be overcome with desire when I bathe you."

Chapter 12

Hunter held her ground. Her heart was beating like the hooves of a wild destrier, but she would not let him see her panic.

" 'Tis kind of you to offer," she said, making certain her tone was disdainful. "But I changed me mind. I need no help bathing."

He watched her. His eyes were dark and somber, his tremendous body still. " 'Tis no trouble. I have little else to do," he said and in one fell motion, yanked his tunic from beneath his belt and over his head.

Muscles bulged into view, capping his shoulders, rising from his chest, stretching from his throat to his waist in tight hard rows. She stumbled back a pace. "What the devil are you about?"

He shrugged. Muscles shifted like magic beneath his skin. Indeed, every inch of him bulged and danced as if set to music. His arms were broad and corded, his chest was hard and honed, and beneath the pronounced rows of his ribs, muscles rippled across his abdomen like marching soldiers.

Damn! she thought, and was completely uncertain whether she'd said the word aloud.

"You needn't be afraid."

His words spurred her gaze back to his. She was already shaking her head, though she couldn't remember why exactly. "I am not—"

"I'll not harm you."

She lifted her chin. "I believe we've proven that already."

"So we have, laddie. Remove your loincloth."

He said it not as an order exactly, but more as an offhand statement. As if he didn't particularly care if she obeyed, or rebelled, or ran screaming from the room like a deranged banshee.

"I'll not—" she began.

"You can hardly take a proper bath until you do."

"I've been bathing long afore—"

"Then you should know how it's done," he suggested, his tone mediational. "Remove your clothes."

She couldn't move.

"Tell me, lass, is it yourself or me that you fear the most?"

"I fear no one."

He stared at her for a moment longer, and in the depths of his eyes it seemed she could see her own emotions reflected as clear as sunrise. She shifted her gaze away and for an instant, from the corner of her eye, it almost seemed that she saw him smile.

"Disrobe now," he said, "unless you need me own help again."

She knew she should refuse, but his logic, her desire, and her own foolish words had conspired against her. She put her hand to the lace that held her undergarment in place, but her lungs felt compressed, her fingers unsteady. "Why do you just stand there, MacGowan? Have you nothing to do?"

"Ahh, but I *am* doing something," he countered. "I am watching you disrobe." He paused. His nostrils flared. "In order to be of more assistance to you in the future."

Future! In the future! As though she could bear to do this again without admitting her own shameful weaknesses. As though . . . She gritted her teeth and forced her mind onto safer ground. Her hands shook. She tightened them to fists and tried to ascertain how to keep them out of trouble. "Fetch me soap and towels," she ordered.

"Presently," he said. "As soon as you are safely in the tub."

"Now!" Her tone was brash and harsh, the command of a warrior.

He smiled. Her knees weakened.

"Nay," he said, and took a step forward. "Mayhap you are in need of assistance."

"Don't—" The harsh tone had weakened considerably, but she sharpened it quickly. "Don't come nearer."

"Tell me, me laird. Are you so aloof with all your servants?"

"I do not have servants, as you very well know."

He scowled as if puzzled. "And why is that? Surely you are not afeared they will mistake you for a maid."

"Nay. 'Tis because I oft find them troublesome."

He laughed and lifted a hand to indicate her loincloth. Muscles jumped like leaping steeds in his chest and arms. "Remove that ungodly thing. The water cools."

She swallowed hard. A million possibilities stormed through her head. Should she refuse, order him to turn around, challenge him to a duel? The options seemed limitless. Even swooning was a distinct possibility, though she'd rather die.

"Come now, laddie, surely you have naught I haven't seen a hundred times since. After all, we are both warriors, you and I. Unless . . ." He paused. "Unless you admit you are something more."

She lifted her chin and straightened her back. "Damn you, MacGowan," she said and, tossing her dirk onto the bed, set her fingers to the string that held the last vestige of her modesty. It came away easily in her hand, then slid down her legs to the floor.

They stared at each other from a few mere feet apart as Hunter chanted a soothing mantra. All was well. All was well. They were two warriors, just as he said. And even if he were not a womanish man, she was surely not the type to attract him. Men were wont to idolize another kind of maid. Not a scarred, steely warrior like herself, but the small and the dainty. Therefore, there was no reason for her to worry. She was not attracted to him. He was not attracted to her. She could step into the tub without fear of molestation. In fact, she ordered herself to do just that, but her legs refused to move.

She was frozen in place, her gaze locked on his. But finally his attention shifted. It traveled downward as slow as pain, touching her breasts first. She held her breath and refused to wince, for she did not care if he found her unbecoming. But if he were repulsed, his emotions failed to show in his face. Indeed, his eyes seemed to be lit by a fire from within as he skimmed his gaze lower, over her waist and beyond to the tingling cap of hair trapped between her shivering thighs.

She drew in her breath as if struck and he caught her gaze again.

His nostrils flared momentarily. "Get into the tub," he said.

She planned to refuse. Indeed, she opened her mouth to do just that, for no man gave her orders, but there was something in his eyes. Something dark and deep and just barely controlled. She hesitated just an instant, and then, like one in a trance, she stepped over the metal rim and into the water. It rose up her legs like a balm, and she sunk eagerly into its concealing warmth.

Their gazes never broke, but when she was beneath the surface, he exhaled softly and she wondered suddenly if he too had been holding his breath.

Might he be telling the truth? Might his desires be normal? But nay. He had turned aside the maid at the inn and concentrated on her. She shifted her eyes fretfully away and stared into the water. It was a smallish tub, just large enough for a good sized man to fit inside with his knees bent up. Still, the heat was soothing. She cleared her throat and tried to concentrate on that sensation, but she could feel his gaze like a brand on her face.

"What are you staring at?"

"Anything that is visible."

She spurred her gaze to his. His eyes were ablaze, his body taut, but finally he drew a deep breath and unclenched his fists. "Where do I find the soap?"

She found her equilibrium with some difficulty and fi-

nally managed to give him directions. Disappointment
and relief swelled in her when he finally left. She closed
her eyes and breathed heavily, then sank lower into the
tub and let the wilding panic take her.

Hell's saints, what had she gotten herself into? What
was she thinking? What—

But before she'd finished the garbled thoughts, he had
already returned.

She hunched her shoulders, but refused to cover herself. After all, she was a warrior, and wholly without
shame. Still, she had to force herself to meet his gaze as
she cleared her throat.

"You found it then?" she asked, though she knew he
had for he held the soap, along with an earthenware jar,
in his hand . . . just below the dark nub of his right nipple.

She swallowed hard and raised her gaze to his face
with a snap.

Not a word was spoken. Not a molecule of air seemed
left in the room. "Good," she said, and nodded. "'Tis
good. 'Tis . . . well . . ." She nodded. The movement felt
strangely disjointed. "I've no further need of your ser-
vices, MacGowan."

"Your uncle said to see to your needs."

"Aye, well . . ." She licked her lips, and he seemed to
follow the motion with his eyes. "Me uncle is clearly not
in his right mind, for 'tis certain I do not need you."

The silence lay as heavy as sin around them.

"Mayhap," he said finally, and took a step toward her,
his hard gaze raking her. "But I am here nevertheless."

Her ribs were constricting her lungs. She struggled to
breathe, to draw in air, to refrain from any kind of foolish

weakness. Instead, she gripped the smooth metal rim and raised her chin.

"Find your bed, MacGowan."

"Bed." His voice rumbled deep and quiet in the firelit room. "Nay. Not just yet. You are not ready."

"What?"

He raised his gaze slowly to hers. His eyes burned like living amber. "I will see you bathed first," he said.

Her fingers hurt from her grip against the tub's rim. "In truth, MacGowan . . ." she began, but the truth was not her ally. Nay, though she loved honesty, 'twas lies that had kept her alive these many years. "I prefer my privacy."

Nevertheless, he came nearer. Beneath the water, her body coiled in on itself, feeling tight as a drum beneath the gentle waves.

"How long has it been?" he asked.

She steadied her breathing and hardened her glare. "What's that?"

"How long has it been since someone saw you thus?"

"Why do you wish to know?"

He was near the tub now and in an instant he was seated on the rim, just beside her whitened knuckles.

Her throat closed up.

"How long has it been?" he asked and, dipping into the jar, scattered a handful of herbs over the water.

The sweet smell of lavender spilled into the air, and suddenly she could think of no lies. "Some years," she said, and even with those simple words, memories stormed her mind like evil birds of prey. She had been young when sent from Nettlepath. Young and scared and vulnerable, but there were those who did not care about a maid's innocence. Those who would take it by force, who would ruin a wee lass and cause her to defend herself anyway she could. She had been a lad ever since, and never regretted it. Not until now.

" 'Tis surely a sin," he mused.

"What?" Against her will, she covered her scar with her arm, squeezing her breast against her silver shell, but he leaned slowly forward. Grasping her wrist in gentle fingers, he tugged it away.

"Don't," he said simply. " 'Tis not right to hide such . . . 'tis not right."

Did he mock her? She speared her gaze to his, but his eyes were somber, his expression the same. She could only stare.

Reaching out, he brushed his knuckles along the path of the scar. Feelings darted through her like frightened harts, leaping for cover.

He raised his gaze to hers. "You made the bastard pay?"

It took a moment for her to find her voice. "The Munro?"

"Aye."

"He is not your enemy any longer," she murmured. "Not since Ramsay bested him in battle. Not since he gave up any hope of having Anora. And surely not since he met his own bride."

A muscle jumped in his jaw. "I'll be the one to decide if he is me enemy," Lachlan gritted. "Did he suffer?"

"He bears a scar on his cheek."

"His cheek." The words were softly scoffed. "It does not compare with the damage he has done."

She pulled her arm from his grasp, clamping it to her breast. "Do not look if you find it so hideous."

"Hideous," he breathed. "Is that what you think I believe?"

"I do not care what you believe." She forced the words out on a whisper.

He leaned toward her, his face sober. "But I will tell you nonetheless, for—"

"MacGowan!" she interrupted rashly, but he didn't listen.

"I will pretend to be mute." His voice was low. "I will feign servitude. But I will not pretend you are undesirable. And I will not pretend me own desire is unnatural. Not when you are what you—"

"Nay," she whispered, then, "nay," she said more forcefully. "We are the same, you and I. The—"

But in that moment, he grasped her hand and placed it against his chest. Beneath her palm, his flesh felt like living granite, as hard as stone yet soft as velvet.

Air escaped her lungs in one hard rush.

"The same?" he asked.

"Aye," she whispered and he pulled her hand lower. Her fingers bumped over his nipple. The faintest whimper escaped her throat, but he was already skimming her hand lower, over his ribs and down the rugged hills of his abdomen. He halted her fingers just above his belted plaid.

"The same?" he asked. The question was little less than a threat. Beneath his plaid, she could see the hard outline of his desire.

She snatched her hand away and grabbed the tub with frantic fingers.

"What do you want, MacGowan?" she rasped.

Absolute silence filled the room. For an eternity not a word was spoken. "You," he finally said.

She tried to formulate a thought, but nothing came.

" 'Tis you I want," he repeated.

She tried to force a laugh, but she could not. "You jest."

His eyes were as sober as death and failed to shift the slightest degree. "Do I look like I jest, lass?"

"I am not a lass. I am a warrior, scarred in battle and—" she began, but in that moment he touched his fingers to her lips, shushing her. Indeed, causing her to hold her breath.

He stared at her mouth for a moment, then lifted his attention back to her eyes as his fingers skimmed over the cleft of her lips and lower. Soft as a breeze, he trailed over her jaw and down the length of her neck.

Against her will, she shivered beneath his touch. Her eyes fell closed. Her hands ached against the metal as her head fell back. His fingers slipped into the hollow in her throat and against his flesh, she could feel the hard tattoo of her heart.

"Surely you know the truth." His words were no more than a whisper. "You are temptation itself."

"Nay," she moaned and tensed to rise, but already his hand held her shoulder.

"You cannot escape it, lass. You are beautiful and you are desirable no matter how long you hide from the fact."

She stared at him, her heart pumping wildly. "I am not beautiful."

"Aye, lass, you are, but why would you wish it otherwise?"

Moments stretched into silence, then, "Beauty is weak," she whispered.

He tilted his head and eased his hand slowly down the

length of her sword arm. His fingers remained on her biceps for a moment, then continued on until he reached her wrist. Once there, he lifted it upward so that her palm lay open before him.

"Weak?" he whispered and kissed the hollow of her palm.

She sucked air through her teeth.

"I think not."

Her hand tingled. Her breath came hard.

"What was your given name, lass?"

"I have many names." Her voice was raspy, unnatural.

"Aye." He trailed his fingertips along the tendons in her wrist, over the blue ridged veins and upward. "Hunter. Giles. Warrior. Good names. And well used, all. But what of the name your mother gave you?" His fingers bumped over the crease where her arm bent. She jumped like a startled hare beneath the rampant sensations.

"Mother gave me nothing."

His gaze felt sharp on her face, and though she knew she had said too much she could not seem to correct herself, to think, to focus on anything but the feeling of his fingers against her skin.

"Nothing?" he asked and, cradling her elbow in his palm, brushed his thumb across the bend.

She tried not to shiver. "She gave me life, but little else," she corrected and swallowed the spark of pleasure that radiated from his touch.

His gaze was as warm as sunshine upon her face. "I am sorry."

"Do not pity me!" she said, and yanked at her arm, but he held it firm.

"You? Nay, lass. 'Tis not you I pity, but your mother."

"What?"

"Do you think for a moment she could have wanted to give you up?"

She said nothing, but stared into his eyes. They were as deep as forever.

"I am not a sensitive man, lass. Nor do I have the gift of understanding. Me own greatest talent is in swordsmanship, but this much I know; there is not a mother of sound mind who could have given you up without relinquishing part of her very own soul."

"She kept me sister." The words were a whisper and for that weak tone as much as the words themselves, she hated herself.

"Poor thing," he said and kissed her wrist where the pulse thrummed like mad.

"I told you not to pity me." She jerked it out of his grip. Water splashed violently over the side of the tub, wetting his bared chest, but he did not retreat. Instead, he watched her from a proximity so close it seemed she could feel the heat radiating from his body.

"Look at yourself, lass," he said, and drew his gaze down her body and up. "None could pity you."

She scowled. Her eyes stung, and her throat felt tight. "And you will not pity her," she ordered.

"I will," he argued. "For not only did she give you up, she was forced to choose between you and another. How was she to know she would relinquish the best of the pair?"

She watched him in terror, barely able to breathe. "You do not know me sister!" she whispered.

"Nay," he said, "but I know you."

She forced herself to relax a mite. He did not know her secrets. All was safe, but the tightness in her throat did not lessen. "She's as bonny as the springtime," she informed him.

The smallest of smiles lifted his lips. "I meself like the winter," he said and stroked her wrist.

"Delicate as a flower."

"I've a weakness for strength."

Anger whipped through her. "Don't pretend you disdain her."

His brow lowered. "As you said, I do not know her." His eyes were suddenly hawkish. "Do I?"

"Nay." She dropped her gaze to the water and felt panic rise like an unfamiliar wave. "Of course not. I only meant that . . . you would worship her if you but met her."

The frown did not lessen. "What is her name?"

"It matters not."

"Then tell me."

"It would do no good."

"Neither would it do any harm."

"I have no need of her."

"You—" He paused. "She does not know of you?"

"Might you think we exchange Yuletide gifts, Mac-Gowan? Might you think we embroider bedsheets as we sit by the fire and speak of scented soaps and drink—"

"Mayhap she longs to."

The air left her lungs. "What?"

"Mayhap she is as lonely as you."

"I am not lonely," she whispered.

He didn't argue, but only watched her for an instant. "Maybe she is tired to death of embroidery and longs to ride free as you do."

"I doubt that," she said and her throat felt tight again. "Her embroidery is perfect."

He laughed and she started as he reached for her hand again. "As is your swordplay. Or nearly so." He smoothed her knuckles with his thumb. "So she is a noblewoman."

"Aye," she said, watching his hand upon hers. His skin was dark and when he moved, the muscles tightened like magic up the length of his mesmerizing arm.

"A family I know?"

She caught her breath suddenly. Only a fool spilled secrets at the simple touch of a man's hand. "She is not of noble birth."

"Oh?" His brows rose slightly.

"Nay. I but meant that she thinks herself quite noble."

"Ahh," he said. If he believed a word of it, that naïveté did not show in the strong lines of his face.

Indeed, he looked somber and sage and as powerful as a broadsword.

"You've met her then," he said and caressed her wrist with velvety softness.

Feelings skittered up her arm like summer lightning.

"Aye. Nay. I . . ."

"Which is it, lass?"

"I am not a lass!"

His gaze skimmed her body again, but in a moment it returned to her face.

"And you feel not the least bit of desire."

"Nay, I do not."

The corners of his mouth tilted a bit. Anger rose in her at the very sight.

"Is that so hard to believe, MacGowan?"

He said nothing.

"'Tis, isn't it! And why so? Just because you are strong and bonny and . . ." She stopped the words belatedly, feeling sick, expecting him to laugh, to howl at the evidence of her weakness.

But he did not. Indeed, even that devilish hint of a grin had been wiped clean from his face. He watched her with eyes slightly narrowed, his hands perfectly still on her arm.

She cleared her throat and kept herself from shifting her gaze away.

"You think me bonny?"

She could no longer hold his gaze, but let it drift to the side. The candle flickered atop her walnut writing desk, chasing shadows across the room. "I did not mean that."

It took a moment for him to speak, but finally he did. "What is it that you meant?"

"Some . . ." She scowled at the quill left atop her ancient desk. "Some maids might find you appealing."

"Me nose has been broken," he said. "Twice."

She nodded, but refused to look at him, for every inch of him spoke of strength and valor and all the things for which she cared.

"Me face is scarred."

There was a unnatural crease in the center of his chin and his left cheek was marred. She knew without looking at him. Still, something tightened far down below, making her want to squirm deeper into the water. Aye, he was a warrior clear to the bone, and yet, when he touched her . . .

"I am neither charming nor witty, despite me heritage. Not like me brothers."

"Your brothers!" she scoffed.

His scowl deepened and she wished to hell that she could sink beneath the water and not arise until he was long gone.

"What of me brothers?" he asked.

"Nothing." She refused to meet his gaze. "There is naught amiss with them, I am certain. Indeed . . . I do not know them well."

"You sounded . . ." His own tone was perplexed. "Disdainful."

"Nay."

The silence stretched around them. She fidgeted.

"Maids swoon at the merest glance from Gilmour. Indeed—"

"Gilmour," she scoffed again, then winced, mortified at her foolishness.

His scowl had deepened. " 'Tis said scores of maids fell to his charms before he met his Isobel."

She kept her mouth firmly closed and refused to lift her gaze from her own wrist. It seemed so ridiculously pale against his darkened skin. For a warrior she was uncommonly fair. And as weak as a Protestant. But who would not be weak where he was—

"You do not find him appealing?" he asked.

"He matches his steed's color to his own." She knew she made little sense.

"What?"

She cleared her throat. "He is too fair and too vain for me own taste, but as I have said afore, MacGowan, I've little interest in men, so I am not the one to ask."

"I beg to differ," he said, his voice low and his caress soft against her wrist again. "You are the only one."

There was something in his tone or his touch, or perhaps it was the very air around her that made her shiver. She closed her eyes and hid the weakness as best she could.

Silent seconds ticked away. "You seem to know a

good deal about me brother for one who has no interest in men."

She said nothing.

"And what of Ramsay? You must admire him; his steed is as ugly as sin," he said, and rubbed a slow circle into the palm of her hand.

She tried to think beyond the feelings his fingers caused. "He punishes himself," she said.

"What?"

The surprise in his tone brought her fully aware.

"As I have said afore, I've no interest in—"

Again he trilled his thumb across her wrist. She shivered from her shoulders to her knees. Coherent thought burned to ash.

"Methinks you protest too much," he whispered.

"I do not lie!" she said and yanked her arm from his grasp. "So do not think I long for you."

All the air had been sucked out of the room. One moment it was there and the next it was gone. Voilà. Like magic.

"Lass—"

"Nay!" Her voice sounded shrill, just short of panic. "Do not speak."

His gaze burned into hers. She held it as best she could, but for a warrior she felt pathetically naked—body and soul.

"Very well. I will let it be." His own voice was low, and he sat for a moment, entirely unmoving as he watched her. "Tilt your head back. I will wash your hair."

"I don't need your help."

He dipped his hand into the tub. She jumped and he raised his brows as he looked at her.

"The water is cooling," he said. "I will hurry you along."

"I am not a weakling maid what needs the help of some brawny—" She stopped before she spilled another compliment, stared at him for an elongated moment, then, in a wild attempt at self-preservation, slipped lower and dunked her head.

For a moment she felt more exposed than ever as her breasts rose into the cooler air. She straightened quickly. Water streamed from her hair.

MacGowan shifted his gaze to her eyes. A muscle danced in his jaw and suddenly her own face felt hot.

For a moment the entire world froze and for the same amount of time, she fought to remain where she was, safely out of his reach.

She thought for an instant that he would touch her, but he kept his hands away, rose to his feet, and walked behind her. In a moment she felt his hands in her hair, felt the soap rub against her scalp.

She closed her eyes to the world, to her own foolishness, to the feelings that raced through her like intoxicating wine.

He dipped his hand into the water, raised it and lathered her hair again. Then his fingers were against her scalp, easing away the tension. They skimmed her brow, caressed her ear, traced a path of suds down her throat and onto her shoulder. She held her breath. For a moment he paused. She could feel the shift in his attention, and then, like magic, his hand smoothed with velvet softness across her breast.

Hunter gritted her teeth. Sensations sparked like fireworks in her loins. She dared not look down, but she felt her nipple bend and rise in the soapy trail his hand made down her body.

He shifted around her. Their eyes met, then he pressed on her shoulder, and she slipped deeper into the water.

Soft as seal skin, her hair whipped against her back and neck, but in a moment she was up.

He reached for the soap again and dipped it slowly into the water.

There was naught but torture after that. Slow, nerve-shattering torture. He lathered her arms and shoulders. Then, with painstaking thoroughness, he washed her breasts and moved lower. Not a hollow nor a swell nor a dip was neglected until finally his hand skimmed lower still, slipping beneath the water along her belly.

She held her breath as magic raced over her hip and onto her thigh. Every fiber tingled as he caressed her calf, but finally he lifted her foot from the water.

Her foot! When her entire body ached to be—She stopped the thought, managing not to pant like a hound as she watched his progress. His hands were moving upward, lathering her leg as they went. Her calf muscles felt limp beneath his ministrations. His hands encircled her knee, sliding toward her bottom, smoothing, caressing, washing, until they reached the mound of hair nestled between her legs. He cupped her there. Fire burned, threatening to engulf her, but he was moving again, shifting so that his fingers slipped between her thighs. She closed her eyes and pushed against his hand, aching with need.

"Lass," he whispered, and it was that whisper that brought her awake.

She jerked to her feet. Water splashed over his chest. The candle's flame hissed and sputtered as she stumbled from the tub.

"I'm clean!" She all but shouted the words—like a newly washed Christian staggering from the Jordan.

He rose slowly to his feet, muscles flexing everywhere.

She swallowed hard. "Clean," she repeated.

"Lass—"

"Nay!" Her voice warbled as she hugged her arms against her chest. "I am not a lass."

His gaze lowered. Hers followed suit. Above her tightly pressed wrist, her nipples bulged toward the ceiling, bright red and ridiculously enlarged.

Retrieving a towel from the tub's edge, Lachlan advanced, and though she meant to retreat, she could not. Indeed, when he stepped up to her, it was all she could do to keep from climbing him like a well-broke steed. Instead, she merely tilted back her head and hoped her heart would not stop dead in her chest.

He wrapped the towel slowly about her body, letting his hand brush her breasts. Her knees went limp. She placed her palm against his chest. Perhaps she meant to push him away. But the feel of his flesh beneath her fingertips was horrendously magnetic, drawing her gaze, her attention, her entire focus. She slipped her hand lower, letting it ripple over the intense strength of his abdomen and rest just above his plaid.

Tension was cranked as tight as a windlass. Air was impossible to find. A muscle jumped in his cheek.

"Tell me what you want." The words were gritted, almost as if he were in pain.

She sucked breath in through her teeth and met his

eyes. They burned like hot coals in the firelight. "I want . . ." A thousand images soared through her mind. Every one of them showed him naked.

His belly felt as taut as a war drum beneath her hand. His hands were still where they held the towel together between her breasts and every corded muscle in his arm was stretched hard and strong.

But she was strong too. And she could not afford to be weak, not now. She closed her eyes to the heat of her desire.

"I want you to leave," she whispered.

The world stood still. She dare not breathe, but he spoke finally, his voice low in the shifting darkness.

"Swear to me that is what you want."

"I swear it."

For a moment she thought he would refuse and for a moment hope soared, but finally he pulled his hands away.

The high muscles in his chest jumped as though he was enduring some horrendous torture, but he stepped back, his eyes still blazing, and then, like a well-trained soldier, he snatched up his belongings and left the room.

Chapter 13

L eave.
   Lachlan marched through the house. The corri-
dors were dark but he knew his way to the door. Aye, he
would leave.

From the chaotic library he heard the old man start
and call out something incoherent, but Lachlan did not
stop. In a moment he was outside. The autumn air felt
crisp, and though it cooled his skin effectively, it did little for his ardor as he strode down the hill toward the stable.

From upwind the flop-eared hound approached on
cautious feet and growled as he circled Lachlan in the
darkness.

Lachlan growled back and continued on, into the barn
where the warm equine scents welcomed him. He
wouldn't wait until morning. Nay, 'twas far better to be

gone now. True, there were bound to be reivers and brigands on his journey north, but with the mood he was in just now, he would be far safer than they if any challenged him.

I want you to leave, she'd said. After glancing up through her lush lashes with those mercurial eyes. After allowing him to touch her siren body. After sighing like an angel beneath his—

"Lad?"

He started like an untried boy and spun toward the noise, sword drawn.

The old man didn't move so much as an eyelash. Instead, he glared at Lachlan with bloodshot eyes, his pale lips pursed.

"Jumpy you are," he said, "for a deaf mute."

Lachlan grunted, lowered his sword and exhaled softly. Apparently he *was* a bit tense, he realized and sheathing his weapon, turned to find Mathan's bridle. From the shadows, the hound growled again.

Longshanks shuffled along behind, his walking stick rapping on the hard-packed earth. "I've seen better performances from a peck of cabbages."

Lachlan glared at the old man. He had no idea what he spoke of, but neither did he care to.

"You'll never succeed on the stage."

MacGowan said nothing as he stepped into the nearest stall.

"If you're mute I'm a corpse," hissed Shanks.

Mathan accepted the bit with grudging reluctance, swishing his tail belligerently as he did so.

"So the brawn means naught."

Ignoring the old man, Lachlan let the reins dangle in the straw and went to fetch his saddle.

"'Twoud have been just as well if you'd been a scrawny lad with pimples and a lisp."

Lachlan didn't respond. Mathan grunted as the girth was pulled tight.

"Highlander! Pah!" spat the old man and stepped up close behind. "It's a coward you are."

Lachlan spun about, grasping the other's tunic in a fist that ached for activity.

"Tell me, gaffer, do you tire of living?"

Longshanks hung like an empty bag from Lachlan's fist, but his eyes never faltered as he glared with violent heat into his capture's face.

"So it's true—you are no more mute than I am daft."

"I disagree," Lachlan said and loosening his grip, pushed the old man away.

"I am not so daft as you are cowardly."

"You think me a coward?" Lachlan asked and bent to reach for his reins.

"Why else would you leave her?"

Lachlan straightened with a jolt. "Of whom do you speak?"

The old man snorted. "So 'tis just as I suspected— you are not only a coward, but a simpleton as well!"

"What are you playing at, old man?"

"No bigger than a lambkin, she was, when first she came to us."

"Who?" The word sounded unreasonably loud to Lachlan's own ears, but the other didn't seem to hear.

"Bundled like a precious gift when I brought her to me master. Even then he was not a young man, but mayhap events have aged him more than time."

Silence swallowed the darkened barn. Lachlan waited, but patience was not his virtue.

"A babe was left at Nettlepath?" he asked.

"Have you grapes in your ears!" rasped the old man. "She came as a babe, over a score of years ago."

Lachlan scowled. "Laird . . . Giles?" he guessed carefully.

"Rhona!" snapped the other. "Her name be Rhona, you half-witted toadstool."

"Tell me," said Lachlan, watching the other through narrowed eyes. "How is it that you have lived to such a ridiculous old age?"

Shanks snuffled a snort. "You think yourself a warrior! But a few years past Lord Barnett could have sliced you in twain with a feather. And his son . . . David." He drew a deep breath. "A right braw lad he was. Swift and sure as an adder. The best ever I'd trained, until . . ." He closed his ancient eyes for a moment. "We should not have sent her away."

Forbearance was certainly not Lachlan's foremost attribute. Gritting his teeth, he grasped the old man's tunic again.

"What the devil are you talking about?"

"The miller's goat," spat the gaffer and, raising his walking stick, rapped Lachlan's knuckles. Pain spurted through his arm, and he abandoned his hold. The old man stumbled away, holding his weapon high. "I speak of the girl, you feeble-minded imbecile."

"Rhona?" Lachlan guessed.

"Ahh, so you are not the complete lackwit."

"Don't test me, old man. You're one breath from death's door. I would feel little guilt for pushing you through."

"Huh! I would accept your challenge, young coxcomb, were it not for *her*," he said, and nodded jerkily toward the house as he began to pace. "Ach, your Lordship," he said softly, as if speaking to another. "He is a fool! Perhaps." He nodded, agreeing with himself. It seemed he had forgotten Lachlan's presence entirely. "But he has come. None other has done as much. So surely he possesses some cunning."

Lachlan watched in silent amazement as the old gaffer paced and argued.

"The wits of a turnip, he has. But what of strength? Strength is naught without intellect. You've said as much a score of times. Aye, but he has learned the truth, yet he feels no need to blather it about like a London fishmonger." He nodded to himself. "And she has accepted him. Perhaps he will bring her peace. Who else can say the same?"

The old man suddenly turned his glare on Lachlan.

Quiet fell like dust motes into the stable, broken only by the soft coo of a pigeon from the loft.

"Very well," said Shanks.

"So . . ." Lachlan began, "the lot of you—you're all mad as wild boars."

"I do not like it, but I suppose you must do."

"Must I?" Lachlan stared in mute amazement. " 'Tis wonderful to know. And what, pray—"

"You are acceptable, you fool. For our lassie."

"The one who calls herself the warrior?"

The old man slashed his staff upward. It hissed like a serpent inches from Lachlan's face. "Mock her and you will rue the day!" he warned.

Perturbed practically to the end of his limits, Lachlan half turned away, then pivoted back and snatched the staff from the ancient hands. "Do not threaten me," he said, pointing the staff back at its owner.

"So you are angry." The old man nodded. "Then you'd best strike me down if you can, for if you slander her name again I will surely feed you to the crows."

"Damnation!" stormed Lachlan and tossed the staff at the other's feet. "I do not slander her, old man, I—" he began, but he stopped himself.

"You what?"

Lachlan glared at him. " 'Tis none of your concern."

A gleam came into the gaffer's eye. "Perhaps he is peaceable, Shanks. Aye, me laird," he agreed with himself. "But perhaps he is naught but a coward as I first suspected."

"You do know I can hear you, don't you?" Lachlan asked.

The old man turned his rheumy gaze back to Mac-Gowan. "Have you not heard the prophecy?"

Lachlan glared. "What prophecy?"

"He does not know," said Shanks. "What do you say about his cunning now, me laird? I say there is none other and I have not much time left to see her content. Do not say—"

"What the devil is wrong with you?" cursed Lachlan.

The old man broke out of his conversation. "You are the chosen one then."

"Chosen for what?"

"To care for her, you dolt."

Lachlan threw back his head and howled at the ceiling. In the rafters, the doves took flight. "Believe me, old man," he said finally, "she does not want me to care for her."

"Then why did she bring you here?"

"In truth, I gave her little choice."

"Rhona?" Shanks said, then smiled crookedly. His

teeth were all but black. "You do not know her well if you think she be without options. Aye, she has chosen you whether you know it or nay, and you shall be the one."

Lachlan crossed his arms against his chest. "And if I refuse?"

Shanks clenched his bony fists. "The crows be hungry," he vowed.

"Holy mother," hissed Lachlan. "I see where she gets her charming temperament, but tell me this, why have you trained her to be a warrior if you now wish her to be a maid?"

The old man winced. "Me laird cherished her. Do not believe otherwise."

Lachlan remained silent.

"Aye, he cherished her, but he could not show it. His son was lost. His wife the same. We did not know how to nurture a lassie, and she had such spirit. Like a lion she was in a pinch. She took to swordplay like the king's firstborn and—" He paused. "It did not seem harmful to allow her to learn, but then she grew older. The face of a queen she had, but the fist of a knight." He clenched his own feeble hand. "The children of the village were afeared of her."

Quiet settled in.

"I did not know then what I know now of the Black Douglases."

Lachlan's mind spun, trying to keep up. "You sent her to the Douglas stronghold?"

"They were strong and well connected. We thought that even though she was . . . unique, they would find a place for her. A mate."

"Archibald Douglas? The earl of Angus?" Lachlan

glared at the old man. The name of Douglas was infamous amongst his kinsmen. For shortly after marrying Scotland's queen, Archibald had abducted the young king. Many months James had been kept captive in Edinburgh. Only good fortune and the king's own clever disguise had seen him freed. "In what year did you send her there?"

"She was tall even then, but her face . . ." His expression looked strange, a painful meld of happiness and horror. "She did not want to leave us. Said me master needed her, and I as well." His voice cracked. The bony hound nuzzled his leg. He cleared his throat and sharpened his glare. " 'Twas the last I saw of her."

"What do you mean the last? She is here now, old man."

"And what do you think she will do if I admit as much to her face?" he hissed. "Do you think she will return? She has chosen another path. Has turned us aside." He shook his head. Gray, scraggly hair protruded in every direction from beneath his form-fitting cap. "We should not have sent her away, me laird," he whispered. "I know that now," he answered himself. "Indeed, I have paid well for that mistake. But I will not suffer much longer. Do not speak like that," Shanks murmured sadly. "She is returned. All will be well. She is returned, but she has not forgiven."

"Has not forgiven what?" asked Lachlan. Frustration was now a constant in his life.

The old man jerked his attention toward the other. "You are a daft imbecile!"

"Aye," agreed Lachlan and, gathering Mathan's reins, turned toward the door. "But not so daft as some."

* * *

He planned to leave. Indeed, he *did* leave, but he had not yet reached the village gates when he turned back. The old man was no longer in the stable when he turned Mathan loose in his box.

The night was still dark, his mind still rolling like pieces of a chaotic puzzle. Her name was Rhona. She'd been sent to the traitorous Black Douglases, to the man who had abducted Scotland's king. She'd crossed swords with the Munro himself, and she had a penchant for appearing at a battle and leaving without warning. But who the devil was she really?

He glanced toward the house, but there was no solace there. Thus, he found a mound of likely-looking chaff, removed his plaid, and covered himself with the woolen.

Morning found him grouchy and chilled. Sitting up, he realized his legs were bare and his plaid gone. One glance about the stable showed him the reason. Not fifteen feet away, the hound lay curled upon the Mac-Gowan's clan tartan.

"What think you now, Longshanks?" the old man asked himself aloud. Lachlan glanced up at the sound of Longshanks' voice. "Might there be some kindness in him? Surely a man who shares his only blanket with a hound cannot be utterly lacking in compassion. Mayhap," the gaffer agreed with himself, "But if it's me own opinion you be wanting—"

"If you answer yourself, old man," Lachlan said, "I'm going to pick you up by your God ugly cap and toss you out on your bony arse."

Shanks looked momentarily startled, then laughed. Lachlan rose. The dog growled. And the day began.

Breakfast was simple fare—brown bread and warmed

ale delivered to Lachlan by Shanks himself in the dark and shadowed kitchen.

From the library, he heard Lord Barnett mumble something, but Rhona was nowhere to be seen.

Lachlan warmed himself by the fire for a moment, glanced toward the passageway that led to the bedchambers and scowled back into the fire. It didn't matter what she was doing. It wasn't as if he missed her. But the mystery intrigued him. Who was she? Had she truly lived with the Douglases? And what was the mission she had spoken of on their journey here?

He glanced down the passageway again, then grudgingly back to the fire. It was a small blaze with no logs available to make it larger. Perhaps he should gather wood. The old man was certainly too busy talking to himself to do the task, and since he seemed to be the only servant in the moldering manse, there was no other to pass the job on to. But Lachlan had no idea where to gather kindling in this area. He could ask Shanks, of course, but the old fellow was no longer anywhere to be seen, and besides, he was less than charming anyway. Whereas Rhona . . .

He ran the name around in his brain. Aye, it fit her, he decided, for it was neither weak nor masculine, but a unique blend of femininity and strength, of velvet and steel, of—

Damn it all, he thought and turning on his heel, marched determinedly down the hallway in search of her.

He didn't hesitate outside her bedchamber door, but lifted the latch and stepped inside. It was immediately evident that the chamber was empty.

He scowled, moved back into the dark corridor, and continued on. The next door opened into a storage room and the next was a small anteroom of sorts.

Deep in thought, Lachlan pushed open the next door, then stopped short and stared in silent amazement.

"What are you doing here?" Hunter asked.

He said nothing, but stepped quietly inside, shut the door behind him, and stared some more.

If he wasn't mistaken, she was, apparently, in the process of getting dressed. Leather breeches encased her endless legs, but above that she was bare except for a stiff, sleeveless bodice made of white linen and bone. It scooped upward from her hips, nipped in at her waist and lovingly cradled her spectacular bosom. Bare to the nipples, her breasts were pushed up high and pale, and her midriff was squeezed tight, making it difficult to breathe—at least for him.

Her neck, he noticed, was flushed the hue of a bonny sunrise and when he managed to bring his attention to her face, he realized that her cheeks too were bright.

She straightened under his speechless gaze with her hands still holding the laces tight behind her back, but this new position did nothing to diminish his interest. Indeed, he held his breath to see what might fall out.

"You said you were leaving." Her voice was a low accusation.

He shook his head, still not quite able to speak and not much more successful at keeping his gaze averted from her chest.

"Get out." Her hands remained behind her back. Her bosom still threatened to escape.

"What . . ." He drew a deep breath and noticed for the first time that a gown lay across the nearby bed. A trunk stood open and a tumble of strangely fashioned hoops lay upon the floor. "What is it you're doing exactly?"

Early morning light streamed through the nearby window and gleamed like gold on her freshly washed hair. She wore it loose this morn, neither confining it beneath a hat nor binding it in any way. Instead, it was spread across her ivory shoulders like a priceless net.

He cleared his throat and refrained from adjusting himself beneath his plaid.

"Leave me," she commanded, but he took a step nearer instead.

"Tell me, lass, who is this Rhona?"

For a moment he thought she paled, but just as quickly she rallied.

"'Tis none of your affair, MacGowan."

"I beg to differ," he said and, pacing soundlessly across the floor, placed himself upon the bed. Perhaps it was not entirely coincidence that he now sat between her and her abandoned tunic. "I hear she was sent to the Black Douglases at a tender age."

She was silent for a moment, then, "I do not know this Rhona you speak of."

"Truly? Then you know nothing of King James's abduction by the earl of Angus?"

She stared at him, then laughed. "I said I did not know the girl, I did not say I failed to have any knowledge whatever of politics."

"Politics." He studied her narrowly. "Is that what it is to you? Our young king was abducted by his mother's own husband and you think 'tis naught but a bit of interesting politics?"

She shrugged. The movement did nothing to steady his erratic heart rate. "I am, as you've said, only a lass."

He drew in breath carefully, lest he forget that important practice. "I never said 'only.' And had I seen you in that garment earlier . . ." He shrugged, feeling light-headed.

"Why are you here, MacGowan?"

He wondered the same himself. But if the way she looked in this foolish garment wasn't enough to keep him close at hand perhaps the mystery was.

"I wish for answers," he said simply.

She flexed her shoulders. Maybe her arms were getting tired, bent back as they were. But her discomfort was naught but a boon for him.

"Do you need help with that?" he asked.

"Answers to what?"

There were so many, and suddenly a half dozen squeezed in at once.

"Who you are, to start?"

"I have told you—"

"Aye. Hunter," he said. "Giles. The warrior. But 'tis strange, for a warrior should not look like you do in those stays."

She pursed her lips. "I am sorry if you disapprove."

"Disapprove?" He shifted slightly, trying to ease his discomfort. "You put words in me mouth yet again." He let his gaze drift downward and when he returned to her face it seemed to have colored once more. "You make a hell of a warrior, lass, but as a woman . . ." He let the words lie, for he had not intended to compliment her. Indeed, he had not even intended to return. Just now, however, with her breasts perched at the very brink of that ungodly bodice, it was difficult to regret his decision.

She stared at him for a motionless moment, then turned abruptly away as her fingers fidgeted with the laces. He watched for an instant, but her back was not nearly so entertaining as her bosom, so he approached and set his own fingers to the ties.

She froze at his first touch.

"Here then," he said, and pushing her hands aside, pulled the laces snug. He was close enough to smell the scent of the herbs he had strewn on her water the night before. Close enough to glance over her pearly shoulder and see the high mounds of her breasts capped in sunset hues.

He cleared his throat and tied the laces in a bow. "'Tis too small."

She stepped abruptly away and turned slightly toward him, her body stiff. "What?"

"The whalebone . . ." he began, but she was, it seemed, just as fascinating in profile as head on. "'Twas made for a smaller form."

Glancing down self-consciously, she crossed her arms against her waist. It looked amazingly narrow beneath the power of her well-honed arms.

"Was it your mother's?"

"As I've said, me mother left me naught."

"And what of the chain about your neck?"

She glanced down and curled her fingers over the silver shell. In an instant it was gone, hidden in her bosom. Lucky shell.

"From whence did that come?"

She stepped toward her tunic where it lay beside the gown. He did the same, then walked casually over and sat atop it.

"Tell me, MacGowan," she said, looking down her nose at him. "Are you always such a damnable nuisance?"

"Generally, aye. Are you Rhona?"

For a moment he thought she would deny it again, but instead she watched him before speaking. "If I tell you the truth will you leave me?"

"Nay."

"Then why should I tell you?"

"Because otherwise I will have to ask the others," he said, and nodded toward the all but empty house beyond.

A flash of anger crossed her face, but finally she spoke. "Longshanks has suffered enough for his loyalty."

"I did not intend to torture him, lass," he mused. "Though the idea bears merit and—"

"I am Rhona," she said. "Or at least that is the name I came with."

"Came with?" he said. "From whence?"

She shrugged. "I am told I was a wee thing. Not yet a year of age when I was left at Nettlepath."

"By whom?"

"You must think I have a marvelous memory, Mac-Gowan."

"Or that you were curious enough and bright enough to learn the answers."

She stared at him for one speechless moment, then, "'Twas an old woman that brought me. 'Tis all I know. She left me with some coin and took away a promise that I would be cared for."

"An old woman." Something niggled at his mind, but he wasn't sure what. "Where was she from? What was her name?"

"I know not. Give me my tunic."

"Nay. And the shell?"

She looked as though she considered a variety of stories. "It was around me neck at the time." She looked tense, nervous. Why?

"I've not seen the like."

She relaxed marginally. Again, why?

"May I take a closer look?" he asked and stood. They were face to face. Mere inches separated him from all that glorious flesh.

"You've looked close enough, MacGowan," she said.

He shifted his gaze to her bosom, luscious beyond compare, and stepped closer. "I may be missing something."

"Or you will be soon," she said, and in that instant, he realized her dirk was pressed against his hip.

"Tell me one thing, lass," he said, and though he knew himself a fool, he lifted his hand and brushed a golden lock away from her cheek. Her skin was as soft as moonlight. His fingers ached to touch her, to skim down her throat to the glories beyond.

"One thing," she agreed and pressed the dirk into his plaid so that he could feel it against his flesh.

He held his breath. "Did you do it for me?"

She narrowed her eyes.

"The gown," he said. "Do you—"

"You?" She laughed and choked at the same time. "Are you daft?" she asked and jerking the knife away, turned with a jolt.

Disappointment smote him. Aye, he should have guessed her answer, but when he was near her it almost seemed that she felt as he felt—except for the ever-present knife, which was disconcerting at best.

He remained very still. "Then why?"

A thousand thoughts seemed to flit through her mind. "'Tis none of your concern," she said finally.

"Then I am forced to believe you are lying, and that the feminine attire is indeed on me own account."

"Do you think yourself so important that I would don these foolish garments for you?"

He shrugged, hoping against hope that he looked unconcerned. "Then who?"

"A gentleman."

He said nothing. Indeed, he did his best not to think, for his was not a steady temper and the thought of her in another's arms . . . He pushed the image aside.

"So you've fallen for a nobleman, have you?"

"Fallen for!" she said and laughed again. " 'Tis just like a man to believe lust would be the reason behind me plans."

"Plans?" he asked, but in that moment she ran out of patience.

"Out of me way," she said and, pressing past him, snatched up her tunic and left the room.

Chapter 14

I t took Lachlan some time before he got his emotions under control. Longer still to cool his ardor.

A nobleman? What noble? And why? If not for lust's sake, what did she seek? Fortune? She didn't seem the type. So why had she donned that blood-stopping garment? Did it have some connection with the mission she had mentioned before?

He had no answers and a host of questions. Thus he finally sought her out again. But she was not in the house. Neither was she in the stable.

Letting Mathan rest, he strode down the muddy path toward the village. The day was warm, the clouds high and scattered. A chandler gave him a dark look from beneath a droopy cloth cap, and a wee lass skittered aside as he approached. 'Twas fairly clear they did not see a host of plaids down here in the lowlands. They were a different sort of Scotsman in the southern reaches, if they were Scots at all. Perhaps their loyalties lay with the English king instead of with James. Perhaps . . .

But in that moment a thought seized him. The Black Douglas was an earl. He was also condemned to death for his part in the young king's abduction, but perhaps that was not a deterrent for some. Perhaps it was seen as a badge of honor for those who sided with the English king. Perhaps this Rhona felt the same.

Up ahead, a cobbler hammered a nail into the sole of a shoe, and beyond that a shingle hung askew above an arched door. Etched into the wood was the picture of a woman's gown, pinched in at the waist and flared dramatically at the hips.

Lachlan glanced down the street. Rhona was nowhere to be seen. He looked behind him, then down at his plaid. He was not one to be ashamed of his Highland garb, but if Rhona was plotting some mischief he would be the one to learn of it, and fitting in with these lowlanders would only make it easier.

By the time Lachlan returned to Nettlepath, Rhona was standing outside the ancient manor house, but she was not alone. She was staring up at the roof, speaking to a man dressed in laborer's garb, but before Lachlan even reached the house, he had been sent on his way.

She had taken the guise of a man once again, wearing the broad-brimmed hat and leather gauntlets that belied her feminine form.

"Who was that?" he asked when he approached her.

She scowled at him, and he wondered suddenly if there had been an odd tone in his voice. Not jealousy, of course, but something else.

"If you insist on staying, champion, you might just as well do some good," she said.

And so his labor began. Nettlepath, it seemed, was in ill repair. Stones were loosening at the northwest corner, the thatch needed replacing, and the stable was crumbling.

They started with the loose stone. It was not a simple task, for mortar had to be mixed. The sand was heavy, the lime needed to be hauled a goodly distance, and even the water was not easy to come by. But finally the rocks were once more secured.

Darkness was falling fast by the time they ceased their labors and found their way up the winding path into the house. Rhona and Lachlan ate cockaleekie soup while the hound roamed cautiously about the table, and Shanks fed Barnett in the adjoining room.

They could hear his chatter as he served the old man.

"Your Giles is doing a fine job at the stonework. Labored all day with his hireling at his side."

The old man coughed and said naught.

"Aye. Aye, me laird," agreed Shanks as if the other had spoken. "He is hale and hearty. Strong as a pair of oxen, if a bit slow-witted."

Another cough.

"Ahh, you speak of your nephew," said Shanks. "He is well too. Healthy and bright of eye."

There was the sound of labored breathing and perhaps the hiss of a question almost formulated.

"He helped with the repairs, me laird. Worked well and long, he did." There were no more words for a long while, then, "Aye," Shanks said. "He may be the one."

Lachlan shifted his gaze to Rhona. "What one?" he asked, his voice low in the deepening darkness.

She drank the last of her ale and rose to her feet. "I've no more idea than you, champion."

Lachlan watched her walk to the hearth and stretch her hands toward the fire, but he noticed that her attention was tilted toward the two old men not far away.

"Me laird Giles . . ." Shanks's voice quaked when he spoke, but there was none of the scathing derision reserved for Lachlan. Nay, for Rhona, he had naught but respect . . . and barely hidden adoration. "I have changed the rushes on the floor of your chamber and opened the window to freshen the air."

"You are kind, Master Shanks."

It may have been a smile that stretched the old man's thin lips, Lachlan realized. But perhaps he was only experiencing a bit of gastric discomfort.

"And I have warmed water for your bath. Mayhap your lad could carry it hither for you."

"Certainly," she said and turned rapidly away from the two. "Champion."

He rose slowly to his feet. "I tell you," Lachlan said, passing her and speaking low. "This game gets old."

She shrugged. "There is none to make you play."

He grunted a response, wrapped his hand in a towel and, grabbing the metal arm that held the pot, swung the thing out of the fire. In a matter of moments, he had dumped the boiling water into the metal tub and not much later he had added additional water to cool it. It steamed with friendly repose into the air around him, filling the room with warmth.

"You'll sleep in the stable this night," she said, approaching from behind.

He glanced at her. She had removed her hat, but nothing else, and in the fading light, she looked as imperious as a queen, or perhaps a king.

"Mayhap," he said. "After I bathe."

She raised her brows at him. "Insolent for a servant."

"Or even for a nobleman," he said.

"Very well then. I shall wait elsewhere, but fetch a change of garments from the anteroom adjoining this. You smell like a draught horse," she said, and turned to leave the room.

He took a whiff of his shirt, refrained from passing out and went in search of the clothes she had mentioned. The anteroom was filled with trunks, leather, oaken, and iron. He opened them, rummaged through the contents, and came up with two tunics and a pair of hose that would suffice until his commissioned garments were complete.

Padding back to the bedchamber, he put his hand to the latch . . . and found it locked. He swore in silence, thought for a handful of seconds, then set the garments on the floor and exited the house.

Rhona's window was no more than twelve feet above the ground, and it was no great task to scale the wall. He did so without making a sound. In fact, she didn't even turn when he slipped into the room and crossed the floor. Instead, she sat in her tub, her back to him, her shoulders gleaming wet and luscious in the candlelight.

"The poor gentleman."

She jumped as if she'd been shot from a cannon. "Damn you, MacGowan!"

He could not quite help but grin, though he thought it might be poor judgment on his part. The girl had a fondness for her dirk.

"Rather jumpy this eve, aren't you, Rhona? Mayhap 'tis your guilt getting the better of you."

She raised her chin, but he noticed that her arms were crossed tightly against her chest. Lucky arms.

"And why should I feel guilty?" she asked.

Loosening his belt, he slipped his tunic over his head. "Probably for many reasons," he said. "But most recently for being too selfish to share your bath."

"If you dislike playing the servant you can run home to your mother, champion." Her tone was still disdainful, but her expression was not so certain. She gazed at him narrowly as he dumped his shirt onto the floor.

He approached the tub, not because he could trust himself there, but simply to see her eyes go round. "Does he know, sweet Rhona?" he asked and retrieved the soap from its place on the nearby stool.

She neither reached for it nor tried to catch it when he dropped it into the water. Instead, she let it sink along her leg and settle beside her bottom. Lucky soap. "Does who know what?" she asked.

"Your nobleman," he explained. "Does he know you are too selfish to share your bath?"

"He's not the sort to encourage sharing."

His mind buzzed. "I have heard the same of the Douglas from others."

She watched him for a long second. "The Douglas?"

Was she toying with him or did she truly not realize what he was referring to? "Is he not a bit long in the tooth for you, lass?"

"The Douglas," she said again.

"Aye. Archibald, the sixth earl of Angus. The queen's husband, divorced these many years." He watched her. She said nothing. "The king's abductor?" he explained.

"I know who he is," she said.

"And yet you go to him?" He could feel his anger rise, despite himself. Perhaps it was because the man was a traitor to the crown of Scotland. Or perhaps not.

"This I tell you, MacGowan," she said. "I would sooner kill the Douglas with me own hand than go to him now."

There was passion in her voice. Was it feigned? "Then the gown was not for him."

"Ahh, you are a hard one to fool," she said. "Even for a Highlander."

He let the insult wash over him. "Then who?" he asked.

" 'Tis not for you to know."

Emotion welled up in him. Merciful saints, she was a handsome maid. The candlelight glistened on her alabaster skin and her eyes were as bright as heaven's own stars. Aye, she'd labored like a slave this day, and yet, tonight, she looked like nothing more than a nobleman's pampered daughter. Why that stirred him he didn't know, but perhaps it was his own upbringing that made it so, for his parents had been careful not to allow him to get above his station.

He drew a deep breath and steadied his thoughts. "I will know," he said, and she smiled.

"That I doubt."

"Then move over, lass," he said and reached for his belt.

It came away in his hands.

"What are you doing?"

"I am coming in," he said.

"Nay."

"It will be a squeeze," he admitted, and eyed the narrow tub dubiously.

"You cannot."

"What will you do, lass? Fight me for the space? Or scream for Master Shanks? I don't doubt the old bastard would try to rescue you, be you maid or man this eve, but . . ." He shrugged. "The door is barred."

"Get out of me room."

"I would but it seems you've left your dirk out of reach. Very thoughtless for a warrior," he said, and stepped closer.

She tilted her head up at him. Her eyes snapped like firelight in the shadowed room. "Mayhap you would find I do not need it."

Intriguing, he thought, and stopped beside the tub. What was she going to do? Bite him? He wouldn't doubt it, but judging from his body's reaction, he didn't find the thought necessarily distasteful. Perhaps now would not be the best time to disrobe. She might well be flattered by the view.

"Who is the fortunate gentleman you've set your sights on?" he asked again. His voice was impressively low.

"Are you threatening me, MacGowan?"

"Aye."

"With what?"

"You'll soon find out if you fail to answer me question." He supposed he would too.

She gazed at him, then shrugged, and he stood like a statue, wondering what the hell to do next. Her brows were raised, her eyes steady. Honor dictated that he drop his plaid.

Her eyes popped open and she stiffened. For a moment he expected her to make a lunge for her knife but she did not. He took a tentative step toward her.

"The marquis of Claronfell," she said.

He stopped in his tracks. "Laird Turpin?"

Her gaze sprinted downward. His cock throbbed, and her eyes lifted, rather slowly, he thought, back to his face.

"You know him?" she asked. Her tone was husky now.

"We've not met," he said. "But I'm told he wooed Anora afore Ramsay came along, and I've met one of his knights. Sir Charles, I believe his name was."

"Where?"

"Why do you go to Claronfell?"

" 'Tis none of your affair," she said. He glared at her but she raised her brows. "What now, MacGowan? You've naught else to remove, unless you plan to peel off your skin."

"You know little of men, lass, if you think that disrobing is the worst I can do."

The room was silent. Her gaze skimmed him from bow to stern, then returned to his face. " 'Tis not true," she said. "I know a good deal of men, for I am one. Remember?"

" 'Tis difficult at times. Tell me why," he said and, reaching for a towel, wrapped it about his hips.

Her eyes darted down again. Was there disappointment in her face? "Why what?"

"Why do you don maid's clothes for the marquis and none other?"

" 'Tis like a man to assume it would be for a man."

"Ahh," he said, "Another of the sage Hunter's lessons about the evils of a man's vanity."

"Just so."

"If not for a man, then who?"

"Could it not be that even lassies deserve some attention?"

He scowled at her. "What?" he said but she seemed to be concentrating hard on the water that surrounded her. He stared too. There was little to see actually, for her knees were drawn tight against her chest and her arms were set atop them. Still, it did funny things to his heart.

"What lassies?" he asked, doing his best to concentrate on the conversation at hand.

He was surprised when she answered. "The marquis's daughters."

"Turpin has daughters?" He was trying to see some connection.

" 'Tis not so surprising, surely. Half the population of Scotland is female, after all."

There was anger in her tone and he scowled, uncertain of the reason. "And what has that to do with you?"

"Nothing surely. They are only girls. I am certain the marquis has seen well enough to their care since their mother's death. After all, he is not only a man, but a noble."

His mind ticked along, trying to piece together this erratic puzzle. But when those same pieces fell into place, it hardly seemed possible.

"Nay," he said.

She shifted her gaze rapidly to his, saying nothing.

"You do not plan to . . ." He paused, still thinking.

She didn't help the process, but shifted slightly, drawing his attention to any part of her being that might happen to escape her arms.

"Get out, MacGowan," she said. "I am ready to rise."

He didn't even respond, but sat upon the rim of the tub. "You plan to care for his children?"

There was something in her eyes. If he didn't know better, he would think it was fear.

"Girls?" he said. "A nursemaid? You?"

"Tell me, champion . . ." Her tone was deep and somewhat disconcerting. "What surprises you more, that I would be able to care for children, or that I would think girls worthy of the trouble?"

He watched her carefully. His erection, by the by, had not eased in the least. Also disconcerting. "Of the two of us, laddie," he said, "I would say you are the one who thinks girls unworthy. After all, 'tis not I who abhors them so that I abandoned me own sex."

"I did not say it was because they are unworthy."

"Why then?"

She did not answer. Indeed, she shifted her gaze away. "Mayhap I did so because I could. And yet, as simple as not, I can become a woman."

"And care for another woman's babes?"

"You think I cannot?" Her voice was challenging, her eyes the same.

"Would you even recognize a bairn if you saw one?"

"I've seen children afore."

"Truly? Shanks said you did not play with the other villagers for they were afeared of you even when you were a wee bit of a thing."

"I do not want you speaking to Master Longshanks."

There was true anger in her tone now. Why? Perhaps it would behoove him to speak to the daft old man more, no matter how onerous the task.

"Leave him be," she warned. "He has seen trouble enough."

"And the marquis's daughters have not?"

She glared at him. "You think I would be such a horrible nursemaid?"

204

"How daft do you think me, lass?"

She gritted a smile. "Those aren't taters between your thighs."

His jaw dropped and then he laughed, throwing back his head as he did so. "Shall I be flattered that you noticed?"

"Most probably. 'Tis the best you shall get from me and I see that you are needy."

He could only guess what she meant by that so it was surely best to ignore it altogether, for if he thought in sexual terms . . . well . . . it was hard to think atall. After all, she was right, they weren't taters.

"I but meant this," he said, "you are not going to Claronfell for benevolent reasons."

"Nay?"

He shook his head.

"Then perhaps I still hope to marry well. After all, I am not quite in me dotage."

His gaze skimmed her shoulders. Despite her best efforts he could still see the high portions of her breasts. Sigh. "Nay," he agreed, "not quite. So you plan to nurture his children and gain his title."

She batted her eyes at him. "I am, after all, a maid."

"Sometimes."

Her gaze held his. "You think I cannot do this?"

He didn't answer.

"You think I cannot gain his interest."

"I did not say that."

"But you think it, don't you, MacGowan," she said and rose slowly to her feet. Water sprayed over him, but his throat went dry and his cock went crazy. Every inch of her was revealed, absolutely naked, damp and glowing, with water running over her like loving hands.

"Don't you?" she repeated.

He rose stiffly to his feet. It was not a simple task. 'Twas easier to walk with a leg wound than an erection. "You do not plan to seduce the marquis, lass."

"Because I cannot?"

"Because . . ." It was difficult to think, harder still to put the thoughts into coherent words. "Because it is not in you. You might kill him or you might—"

"But I cannot seduce him," she repeated and stepped from the tub. They were inches apart.

Lachlan swallowed hard. From this distance his cock could almost reach her and it was giving it a hell of a try. Unfortunately, his towel was a deterrent.

"Because," she continued. "Although you've been telling me all along that I am a maid, you do not truly believe it. So what am I, MacGowan?" She took a brief step toward him, doing naught to cover herself. 'Twas impossible to know if he should grab her or run. "Not quite a man, but not a woman either. So I am nothing. Is that the case?"

"I did not say—"

"I tell you this, champion," she murmured. She was so near that her peaked breasts almost touched his chest. Her hair curled like magic against the cranberry hue of her nipples. His teeth hurt from clenching them. "I am what I choose to be, and I do what I choose to do. And if that includes seducing the marquis . . ." For one breathless moment she was silent and then she tilted her head to the side and pressed her lips to his. Her fingers slipped around his neck and her mouth moved, lightly, like a fairy's kiss. Like a maiden's kiss. Like utopia. But he fought the madness. She was playing him like a harp, using him, toying with him, and he knew better than to succumb. But just at that moment her nipple brushed against his chest.

Desire roared through him like a kitchen fire. He reached for her with a moan.

His hand curled about her waist, but in that instant the kiss was broken off, and something cold and sharp pressed against his ribs.

He gritted his teeth and closed his eyes. Damn, it was the dirk.

"Tell me again how I cannot seduce him, Mac-Gowan."

His erection throbbed between them. Perhaps she wouldn't notice.

"In truth, lass, I said no such thing."

She raised a brow. "Then you admit that I can?"

"I am certain you could seduce a hay fork if you set your mind to it."

Her lips parted slightly. It took every bit of his horribly lacking strength to keep from kissing her.

"But that is not why you plan to go there," he said.

"Then what is me plan?"

They were still close. So terribly close that he ached, truly ached to have her.

"I do not know," he said and releasing her, endeavored to take a step to the rear. Self-restraint was not his forte and for a moment he thought his legs might actually refuse to do his bidding. But in the end they did. Damn legs. "That is why I will be going with you to visit the marquis."

She raised the knife and her eyes narrowed. "This I tell you, MacGowan, you will not be traveling with me again."

He smiled and, touching his hand to his towel, let it fall to the floor. Between them, his erection sprang hopefully into the open air. There was not a tuber to be seen.

"Aye, lassie," he said and, turning painfully away, stepped into the tepid water. "I will."

Chapter 15

L aughter lilted through the solar. The room was wide and bright, filled with looms and music and unnamed treasures garnered from childhood.

A trio of fair-haired maids bent their heads together and laughed again.

"Look at the three of you." An old woman shuffled into the room. She was bent with age, bowed with wisdom. In the light from the high windows, her face looked as seamed as a patch of ancient parchment. "Did I not know better I would think you were plotting some mischief."

"Mischief?" The smallest of the trio laughed as she finished the braid in her sister's hair. "Nay, we are but preparing Rhona for her wedding."

"Ahh." The aged lady shuffled forward. "And so you are. The three of you together." She shook her head and *reaching out, smoothed her gnarled fingers down Rhona's cheek. "So bonny you are. Me three bairns— like princesses awaiting—"*

"Good eventide." Lachlan MacGowan filled the doorway. He was dressed in a ceremonial plaid, neither garish nor pompous, but so handsome it all but made her breath stop.

"Lachlan," said her sister and dancing forward, drew his hand into her own delicate fingers. He smiled down at her. "Come, see your bride. Is she not bonny?"

He went forward eagerly, but suddenly he stopped, and his expression of happiness became one of horror. It was then that she realized she was naked. Naked and vulnerable.

Rhona awoke with a start. She was breathing hard, and her heart galloped madly in her chest.

What had she done? Opened herself to the ridicule that would most certainly come. Begged for her sisters' acceptance when she knew they would never—

But nay! She glanced wildly about her old chamber. Little had changed. Her secret was safe. No one knew. No one but—

And at that moment her gaze fell on Lachlan. He slept on the floor, wrapped in his plaid. Below the fringed bottom of the tartan, one dark leg was exposed to midthigh. Even in repose, the muscles stood out hard and well defined, and though she knew she was foolish she was tempted to go to him, to touch him, to awaken him with a whisper. Power lay in his hand, yet peacefulness there was too.

Against her will, she moved across her bed toward him, but in that instant, just when she was staring down upon him, he awoke.

Their gazes met. Emotions steamed through her, and then, like a startled deer, she bound out of bed, snatched up her clothing and stumbled over him to the door.

She drove him hard that day; there was much to be done and little time to do it in, for she must leave soon, must learn the truth before it was too late. The masonry was finished before long, and soon the thatcher arrived. Although she'd not asked for MacGowan's company, they rode together into the woods and found timbers to replace the broken rails in the stable. Like a hero of old, Knight pulled the felled logs down from the hill to Nettlepath, and as Rhona stroked his bowed neck and murmured her thanks, Lachlan glanced up from his task of hewing the gargantuan logs.

He had removed his tunic. The dark hose he'd borrowed from Nettlepath's coffers hugged his hips and thighs like a second skin. His muscles gleamed in the misty sunlight, and for a moment, as her fingers snagged in the stallion's dark mane, she forgot to breathe.

Knight bumped her with his bowed nose, drawing her back to earth, and hurrying her to her next task.

Barely a word was spoken for the remainder of the day, but more often than not, she could feel MacGowan's gaze on her.

By nightfall, Rhona's every muscle ached. As for MacGowan, he did not look the least bit fatigued. He only looked irritable. In fact, he was not too tired to heat water or to carry it into her bedchamber and deposit it into the tub.

She glanced at him as she entered the room. He was just straightening from his task. Muscles flexed and tendons tightened in his broad forearms as he dangled the buckets from square fingertips.

Without the least bit of effort she could remember the feel of his hands on her skin. Could remember the skittering emotions that soared through her. Could remember how his chest felt beneath—

He cleared his throat and she jumped as if caught peeping through a knothole.

"Well . . ." She shuffled her feet and barely kept herself from leaping back into the hallway. "I will leave you to your bath."

"Nay." He set the buckets aside and nodded toward the steaming tub. " 'Tis for you."

She considered arguing. He had labored hard and surely deserved a bath. On the other hand, he had bathed yesterday and it had been all she could do not to stare, not to turn on her bed and watch his every movement, not to beg him for things she could not have.

She cleared her throat. " 'Tis . . . kind of you."

A muscle jumped in his jaw. His eyes were dark and ultimately solemn. "I fear kindness is not me most outstanding attribute."

She tilted her head in question.

"I did not offer to leave."

"I beg your pardon."

"I did not tote the water for selfless reasons," he said and continued to watch her.

Her heart picked up its pace. "You are planning . . . to stay?"

"I worked hard for you this day."

It was a statement simply made, as if he were certain he was deserving of some reward, as if she owed him something, when in truth she had done all she could to be rid of him. The injustice of the situation struck her, and yet, strangely, she could raise no anger. Indeed, she felt nothing but a breathless, shameful impatience. "So this is the payment you would ask?" She meant to say it with disdain, but something had curled tight in her stomach and her face felt flushed.

His eyes were the color of amber, lit with a fire from within. "I am but your servant. I come cheap, but I do not come free. Do you need help with your garments?"

"Nay," she said, but he stepped forward, and for reasons unknown, she lacked the strength to retreat.

"I worked *very* hard," he said and reached for the ties that closed her tunic.

She knew she should slap his hand away, or knee him in the groin, or challenge him to a duel, or chant Hail Marys or . . . something. But she did nothing. Instead, she stood like a frightened hare, or a cornered doe, or perhaps, God forbid, like an enamored maid.

His knuckles brushed her skin. The ties eased open and then he tugged the tunic from her. Inch by inch he undressed her until she stood naked and vulnerable before him.

"Lass." His voice was soft, and his palm, when he brushed it down her breast, was as gentle as a sigh. It was all she could do to keep from leaning into it. "You would give this to an aging marquis with waning strength and little honor?"

She shivered beneath his gaze, aching for the things she refused to receive. "What do you know of his honor?"

"He has none. Not where maids are concerned. He is a strange man with strange tastes."

"How do you know?"

"I knew his wife before she married him some years ago."

"Knew her?" She tried to keep her tone level, but it was not a simple task. "In what sense?"

He watched her narrowly. "Lorna was with child when he met her."

Drawing a careful breath, she forced herself to remain calm. After all, she had learned much of the MacGowan rogues in the past few months. The child had not been Lachlan's. She was certain of that, and yet she could not help but ask. "The babe . . . was it yours?"

His brows lowered still further. "Would you care?"

"Damn it, MacGowan!" she snarled, then loosened her fists and stepped into the tub. "I but wonder."

"Nay." He watched her closely, but it seemed now that his attention was on her thoughts and not on her body. "It was not mine," he said, "but me brother's."

"Ramsay does not seem the type—" she began, but he interrupted even before she'd finished the thought.

"How did you know?"

"What?" She glanced up, sensing her mistake.

"How did you know the child was Ramsay's? 'Twas Gilmour what had the roving eye."

"I . . ." She calmed herself. He knew nothing, not of her heritage, and not of her mission. "As I said earlier— Ramsay punishes himself. I but assumed that was why."

Perhaps he accepted that answer. In any event, he continued on. "Ramsay met her at court some years ago. He was young. She was beautiful. He thought himself in love, but he was called home to Dun Ard before he could declare his intentions."

"And there he met Anora."

"Nay, not for some time. Lorna sent a missive saying

she carried Ramsay's child, but he did not receive it until it was too late. When he next saw her she had already wed the marquis."

"And the babe?"

"He had no interest in the bairn," Lachlan said.

That was not exactly what her spying had revealed. Indeed, MacGowan was correct, the marquis had strange tastes, but though he may have wished to bed a pregnant woman, he did not wish to wed one.

"She had the babe taken before its time," Lachlan said. "It all but ruined Ramsay when he learned she had sacrificed the child. Indeed, had it not been for his Anora and the heir she bore him, he might never have recovered. Late in the year they will hold a gathering to celebrate their—"

"And what of his wee lass?"

"What's that?"

She had reason to hate herself again, for she had not meant to speak, had not intended to mention the tiny girl child Ramsay had claimed as his own and named Mary. Nay, she had no intention of remembering how the Mac-Gowan rogues fussed over the babe as if the wee lass were the most precious of children and not a bairn borne of shame and disgrace with no true parents to claim her. But recently her own childhood seemed so raw, so close to the surface. What would it have been like to be so adored by such a man? Adored instead of abandoned and forgotten. " 'Tis naught," she said. "I but find it interesting that you blame the marquis for your brother's loss."

"What lass?" he asked.

She kept her body carefully relaxed. "I heard he adopted a child when he first went to Evermyst, an unclaimed lass born out of wedlock to a Fraser woman."

Though she searched for more to say, she could find no words.

"How do you know of wee sweet Mary?"

"Rumors," she lied, but the memory of seeing the rogues with the child was strong. "Naught more. There is much talk of the MacGowan rogues among the very bored." He watched her strangely, but finally he spoke.

"Aye, when Ramsay first arrived at the high keep, a young woman died in childbirth. Though there had been enmity between he and the maid, he had no wish to see the babe suffer, so he claimed the infant as his own, perhaps as recompense for the life that was lost. Or perhaps he cherished the bairn from the first instant. 'Tis difficult to say with Ram."

Silence fell around them for a moment. Lachlan continued, "I believe wee Mary's father is a Munro, though none has stepped up to claim her. Still, her presence at Evermyst has done much to further the truce between the two clans."

She said nothing.

"Why the interest in her, Rhona?"

"Does she not warrant interest, MacGowan?"

"Do you think she should have been given to the Munros?"

"When even his sisters were nurtured elsewhere?" she asked.

"Were they?"

"Aye." She cleared her throat and calmed herself. "In France, I believe, with their aging aunt."

"It occurs to me that you know nearly as much about the Munros as you do of the MacGowans."

"Could it be that you are trying to divert me from the topic of your brother's daughter?"

He watched her closely. "She is, in fact, the very apple of me brother's eye," he said. "I but wonder what she has to do with you."

"And I wonder why you blame the marquis for the loss of Lorna's babe. Surely the choice was hers as much as his."

"For a woman so eager to protect her own sex, you are strangely anxious to condemn them."

It was true. Since meeting this man she felt all turned about, uncertain about a thousand things that had been so clear before. "Not atall," she said. "I but think it prudent to lay the blame where blame is due."

"Unless it be at the good marquis' knobby feet," he said.

His tone was strange, gritted. She raised her brows. "Do you know something of him that I do not?"

"Probably not," he admitted. "For you seem to know a good deal on many fronts, and as I say, I've not met the man. I only know he cannot be trusted."

"I will surely keep that in mind," she said.

"When you seduce him?" His tone was hard.

"I thought you did not believe I was capable."

"Do you go to prove your abilities?"

She shrugged. "Mayhap. If he has strange tastes as you say, perhaps I will prove to be to his liking."

A muscle jumped in his jaw.

"He has had many mistresses," MacGowan said.

"Many men do."

"And you would be content to be just one more?"

"I did not say as much."

"So you hope to wed him."

'Twas what she had told him, wasn't it? Her words were becoming tangled. Indeed, she had never liked to fabricate the truth. A warrior's path was a narrow one, and yet her life was built on lies. "A lass could do worse," she said.

"The man is aged." Lachlan's voice was dark. "But even in his prime he was not good enough to . . ." He stopped himself, tightened his fist and watched her closely. She forced her arms to unbend, to reach for the cloth, to wash water over her legs. His gaze followed her motion. "He has seen twice your years and does not possess a fraction of your strength. Yet, he would not be faithful to you."

"Most men are not faithful to the women they take to wife, MacGowan."

"But some are." His voice was tight, his expression the same, his eyes so intense it all but stole her breath away.

"Who?" she whispered.

"I . . ." He paused. His voice was as soft as a solemn vow. "Me father taught us . . . Me father has been faithful to the Flame."

"Your mother."

"You know of her?"

"Rumors again."

"They are most likely true."

"There are those who say she would kill him if he crossed her." She kept her tone carefully flippant, but her words were not quite true, for the tales she had heard spoke of love and loyalty and a dozen other things she could ill afford to believe in. "Perhaps that is why he stays close to hand."

He said nothing for a moment, but his gaze followed her fingers as they moved the rag across her shoulder.

"He has made a vow to protect her," he said, "has

promised to bind his life to hers forever and always. He would sooner take a blade to the heart than hurt her."

She searched for some dismissive word, some banal comment to prove she was unimpressed, but her throat felt strangely tight.

Silence echoed around them.

"Do not go to him, lass."

She swallowed hard and met his eyes with some difficulty. "I must."

"Why?" Mayhap he, too, tried for distance, but there was deep emotion in the question and dark lightning in his eyes.

She pulled her gaze from his and cleared her throat. "His daughters—"

"Do not tell me again of his daughters!"

"Why? Is it so difficult to believe that I care for them even though you do not?"

"Aye, it is, for you care for no one!" he said and jerked to his feet.

"And why should I?" she asked. "Was I not foisted on an old man with no wish for a daughter? An old man who had lost his only son. Who could barely see me for longing for his boy! What was I to do? Rumbling about in this withering manse with none but Shanks to care for me. 'Twas so much simpler for all if I acted the boy. Skilled as any young man, I became. Only then would Barnett acknowledge me. Indeed, he could almost pretend I was male, but in the end I was neither a lad nor a lass, and they could not accept me. Why then should I accept them?"

He turned toward her and exhaled tightly. "I am sorry," he said.

"Aye well . . ." She searched for the anger again, but it

was gone, lost in a wink in the depth of his amber eyes. She pulled her gaze from his. "The Douglases did not share your pity."

"How so?"

There was something in his tone that caught her attention, that pulled her gaze back to him. Something dark and ultimately male.

She forced herself to breathe, to turn back to her bathwater. "The Douglases did not think me so masculine. Indeed, Edmund . . ." She was not entirely certain what she had meant to say, but suddenly it was too difficult to go on.

"Edmund?" he asked and stepped aggressively toward her. She leaned away, pressing against the copper tub, forgetting her nudity.

"Let me just say that I've no wish for other girls to live me own mistakes, MacGowan."

"Edmund what?" he asked.

"Spoiled, and loathsome, he was," she hissed. "But his father loved him dearly. Indeed, he could do no wrong." She could remember his hands on her. Remember her drowning terror. But she put it firmly behind her, as she'd done a hundred times before. "So I became just like him when I left. Indeed, I took the name of me cousin, Giles of France, and suddenly all doors were open to me. Even Barnett's."

"What did he do to you, Rhona?"

She watched him for an instant, then looked away. "It was not so difficult really. I hated . . . I was not happy in the Douglas stronghold. I did not make a good lass." She shrugged. "But in the end it was easy to leave. Just a few stolen garments. Just a few spoken lies and I was gone. So unimportant was I, that they did not even care that I had left. But then I suspect they had their minds on other things." Finishing her washing, she rose to her feet. "Hand me a towel."

He did so. Their fingers brushed. She gritted her teeth and ignored any feelings that may have sparked from his touch, threatening to drown her.

"How old were you?" His voice was as deep as the night outside their window.

She shrugged. "Two and twelve perhaps."

"You returned here to Nettlepath."

"Eventually."

"As your French cousin."

"Aye."

"And they did not recognize you?"

She shrugged. "So much easier to have a nephew, a man, worth—" She stopped the thought, buried the self-pity. "Strong. Capable."

"You were worth a great deal." His tone sounded so ridiculously sincere, so painfully honest.

Her throat felt tight. "Was I?"

"Aye."

"What was I worth then, MacGowan?"

"Adoration."

For a moment she could not breathe, could not speak, could not turn away, but finally she forced a laugh. "Why would I be adored, champion? As a girl I could do nothing. Not weave, nor cook, nor even that damned embroidery."

"And as a man you could do anything."

"Aye."

"But in reality you are not a man, and still your abilities are unlimited. So as a maid you can do all. You slay the dragon, you *are* the princess." Silence settled in. "You need no one."

He was wrong. So painfully wrong. Her eyes stung. "I go to bed now, MacGowan."

He said nothing, only nodded. She held the towel before her like a limp shield, fighting herself.

"Perhaps . . ." She paused. He watched her. "'Tis cold on the floor."

He didn't respond. Made no attempt to make her words any easier.

"Perhaps you could share me bed if you . . ." She was losing her mind. "Bathe first." It was hard to force out the words. "After all, I'm in no danger from you, since you are . . ." She tried to finish the thought, but standing as he was, every muscle hard and every fiber taut, she could not pretend he was any less of the man he had proven himself to be. "You know that I . . . do not desire you."

He said nothing, made no movement to imply that he agreed or disagreed. She turned away and walked stiff-limbed to her bed. As she pulled a fresh tunic over her head, she didn't glance at him, didn't turn over when she heard him enter the tub. Instead, she stared at the wall and listened to the beat of her heart against the mattress.

Minutes or a lifetime passed. The mattress dipped behind her. She held her breath, but he kept his distance.

She cleared her throat. "'Tis rather chilly this night."

Not a sound could be heard in all the universe.

"Are you asking me to move closer?" he asked. The words rumbled from him like distant thunder, ominous, yet exhilarating.

"Nay," she said, but the naked lie lay between them like a hungry bear—large and dangerous and difficult to ignore. "Unless you are cold."

An eternity passed. He moved closer and finally she

felt his hand on her arm. She tensed, waiting, but he did not turn her toward him. Instead, he eased closer still. She could feel the heat of his body as he drew his palm down her arm and onto the slope of her waist.

"I am sorry."

His words were soft. She didn't respond, and he flexed his fingers so that his nails skimmed along the curve of her ribs and up her spine.

"For me mother again?" she asked.

"Nay. I am sorry that you cannot want."

"Is that what you think, MacGowan? That because I do not want you, I cannot—"

But in that moment he brushed her hair aside and kissed her neck.

Her moan escaped of its own accord. Aye, she was strong, but damn it all, she was a living, breathing woman, and no matter how hard she tried, she could not remember being gently touched by any but him. She felt him move closer, felt his erection brush her buttocks.

"What did he do to you, lass?"

"Who?"

"The bastard . . ." He drew a careful breath and skimmed his fingers down her spine again. "Edmund."

The memories stormed back, but she did not answer. He kissed her again where her neck curved into her shoulder. Feelings swamped her, threatening to drown the memories.

"Lass?" he said, and brushed his fingertips over her ear.

The shiver was impossible to hide this time, so she spoke, shielding her emotions with words. "Would the details be so pleasant for you, MacGowan?"

She felt him stiffen. His movements paused for a moment. She had wounded him. 'Twas good, she thought, and yet she almost turned to beg his forgiveness. Almost.

"If I could," he began, and touched her hair again. "I would undo the damage he has done. But I do not know the damage."

She did her best to ignore his gentleness, his words, the feel of his skin against hers. "What would you do?" she whispered, and suddenly she felt so small and fragile that the fear all but swallowed her.

"Whatever you like."

She closed her eyes and fought the weakness, but it was all around her, closing in. "Hold me, champion."

He drew her closer, so that her back was pressed tightly against his chest, his legs cradling hers, and his erection a hard force between them.

"You were to be adored," he said.

Her mouth twitched with unwelcome emotion, but she forced herself to relax, to remain unmoved. "They did not adore me."

"Did he force himself on you?"

She could barely manage a nod. Her gut was tied in knots and her throat ached.

His hand tightened for a moment in her hair, then loosened. "And you did not tell the Douglas of his sins?"

"Aye." She said no more.

He waited. His grip hardened on her shoulder.

"It seems there are punishments for young girls who would seduce their betters," she said finally.

She felt the muscles in his arm jerk and freeze, but finally he relaxed a bit and tightened his arm about her waist, as if he could hold the world at bay, could keep her safe within the circle of his strength.

"God forgive me," he murmured. "I cannot right the

wrongs you suffered at their hands, for they have long ago fled Scotland." He paused as if struggling with himself. "But I would keep you from being hurt again." He smoothed his palm down her arm, but she could yet feel the tension in his fingers. "I fear the marquis of Claronfell is no better than the men of your past. Do not go—"

"All the more reason for me to go then," she said.

"Why? To join his cause against Scotland?"

She turned in the darkness. "Do you call me a traitor, MacGowan?"

"I do not know what to call you!" His tone was rife with frustration. "I do not know why you go to Claronfell, but your reason seems urgent."

"So you assume I would turn me back on me homeland?"

"Your back is scared and there was none in all of Scotland to save you from the pain. Indeed, you trust no man as well as you trust your steed. Why should you be loyal?"

They lay face to face, inches apart, naught separating them but the sheer fabric of her tunic.

"Believe I am a traitor if you like, MacGowan. I have told you why I go to Claronfell."

"Aye. You have told me." There was anger in his face, passion in his tone. "You have told me of abuse and neglect and your intent to punish yourself again when you could be safe and lov—"

He stopped, his hand tight around her arm. She held her breath.

"What were you about to say?"

He gritted his teeth and loosened his grip. "Perhaps you want to be hurt."

"Is that what you believe, MacGowan? Is that what

you tell yourself? Go ahead then." She lifted her hand from between them. "Take me while you believe it is what I want."

He glared at her for a prolonged moment, then yanked her close. His lips crushed hers, his body was as hard as granite.

Desire and fear and a dozen unclaimed emotions burned through her, but in the same moment he drew away, breathing hard.

"You lie." His voice was soft suddenly, his eyes narrowed and his body tense. She wanted to pull him back, to push him down, to draw him inside and around and under.

But he remained as he was, watching her from a distant of several long inches. Damn him! She lay perfectly still, anger soaring through her. "Aye," she seethed. "I lie. I was not abandoned or forsaken or—"

"You do not prefer women."

Her mouth fell open. Her body ached with hollow longing. "What?"

"You long for a m—a *man*, just as I long for you, but you are not brave enough to admit it," he said and pushing back, sat up and gazed down at her. "So much easier to be the warrior than the maid. So much easier to threaten and—"

"Easier!" She sat up too, anger boiling like a toxic brew.

"Aye," he said, and his voice dropped again. "You do not detest men. You fear them."

She laughed out loud, throwing her head back and howling at the ceiling. "What an imagination you have, MacGowan. If only your memory where half so amazing. I fear no man. Have you forgot me own ability with a sword?"

"Nay, I have not, but neither have I forgot that you shiver at me touch."

"And because you are a MacGowan you are so certain that 'tis not with revulsion but with a desire so tremendous I can no longer conceal it."

He stared at her. "This I tell you, lass. I'll not take you if your desire does not match me own."

She felt the blood drain from her face, for the truth was painfully obvious. She wanted him with aching desperation, but pride, or something like it, would not allow her to say as much. She forced a laugh. "How chivalrous of you."

"Methinks you'll not get the same offer from the marquis."

"But I go anyway."

He tensed. Muscles rippled like living cords beneath his skin, and for a moment she was tempted almost beyond control to feel them beneath her fingertips.

He relaxed them one by one, but still they remained carved like stone just beneath his sun-darkened skin. "Then you'd best learn to be a maid," he said.

"Oh?" She curled her hands into fists and kept them to herself. "And who will teach me, MacGowan? You?"

He stared at her, then skimmed his hard gaze down her body. Heat followed his course. She felt the burn like a living flame. Her head dropped back and her breathing came hard.

"Aye," he said. "Get up."

"What?"

"Get out of bed."

"Nay."

"You do not say nay to your laird, lassie."

"But you are me servant."

"The fat marquis will be your laird, and he will expect to be obeyed."

"Then he can burn in hell." She smiled. "As can you."

He smiled back. "And what of the lassies for whom you care so much?"

She sobered, remembering her mission, remembering all.

"What do you think will happen to them if the good marquis learns that you have spent most of your life as a man?" he asked. "Get out of bed."

"Nay," she repeated, but in one smooth motion he stepped over her and onto the floor. Reaching down, he yanked her up beside him. They were face to face, and he was naked. She caught her breath and pressed her palm against his chest and for a moment their breath melded.

"Lass," he whispered.

"Aye?"

He cleared his throat and pushed her back a scant inch. "There is no time to lose if I'm to teach you to be a lady."

Chapter 16

"You? Teach me to be a lady?" She skimmed his body disdainfully. He was built like a Roman statue, big and solid and as hard as a breeding stallion. Her knees felt strangely weak. "You would hardly be the one to—"

"Who then?" he asked. "Shanks? Barnett? Or have you befriended some maid in the village that I know naught about?"

She was almost tempted to tell him she had indeed made a female friend, but merciful saints—he'd thought she favored women! She would have laughed if her mouth hadn't gone dry.

"Remove your tunic," he ordered.

She raised a brow. "Nay."

He snorted and turning on his heel, stomped to the door. His buttocks were as hard as autumn walnuts.

Bunched with rounded muscle, they sloped dramatically down to bulging thighs.

She held her breath as he reached for the door latch, but at the last moment he turned. A small hitch sounded in her throat. His erection rose nearly to his navel, engorged and long and throbbing. But he snatched up a towel, slapped it around his hips and marched out.

She barely had time to blink before he was back with a bundle in his hands.

"What's that?"

"Take off your clothes and I'll show you."

It was her turn to snort.

"'Tis a most unladylike sound."

She snorted again.

He shook his head. "Do you forget the lassies?"

She glared at him and reached for the bundle, but he drew it sharply back.

"What say you, lass?"

"Give me that damned thing!"

"Poor wee babes, left without a mother to—"

She gritted her teeth. "If you please."

"Better," he said and, nodding, handed her the package. It was tied with two strips of raw hemp.

She fiddled with it for a minute, then snatched up her dirk and sliced the cords with one aggressive stroke.

He laughed and she glared before unfolding the fabric. Something stiff and white fell to the floor, but beneath her fingers there was fabric of finest velvet.

"What the devil is this?" she asked.

"I am certain you know that much."

She scowled at him, then glanced at the garment again. It was a gown of burgundy and rose hue. The bodice was square and trimmed with ivory lace. It was as soft as a rabbit's hide and beautiful beyond words—if one was fond of such foolish things.

"From whence did you get it?" There was, mayhap, a catch in her voice.

"The tailor in the village."

She didn't glance up. "Why?"

For a moment she thought he wouldn't answer, then, "If you wish to catch yourself a wealthy husband, you'd best bait your hook carefully."

"You did not know of the marquis in time to have this commissioned."

"I thought you would look . . ." He paused. His eyes glowed in the candlelight. "The other stays were too small."

She stared and he motioned toward the floor. Lying at her feet was a corset, its tapes tied tight. She bent and lifted it.

"Put it on," he said.

"N—" she began, but he raised a brow and she stopped and forced a maidenly smile. "Only if you look away, me laird."

She thought he would laugh at her request, for he had surely seen in her in naught atall, but instead his nostrils flared slightly and he turned.

Her hands were a bit unsteady as she whipped the tunic over her head, and when she was clear of the garment she realized with some surprise that he was still turned away.

Scowling at the whalebone stays, she slipped into the thing, but once again it could only be laced from behind. She pressed it up beneath her bosom and pulled the laces tight. Her breasts squeezed upward and her ribs constricted, but tying the thing was damned near impossible. Still, she tried, bending forward slightly and struggling madly.

"Might you need some assistance?" he asked, still facing the wall.

"Nay," she said, and redoubled her efforts. But perhaps her scraping and grunting differed from her answer, for he finally turned.

She ceased her struggles and stared at him. He stared back, frozen in place for a moment, before clearing his throat.

"The fit appears to be . . ." He ceased talking to breathe for a moment. "Acceptable."

"'Tis tight enough to strangle a warthog."

The shadow of a grin lifted his mouth, but in a moment he was behind her. "I believe a well-bred maid might try to refrain from speaking of killing a warthog with her undergarments."

She felt his fingers brush the fabric of her stays and forced herself to keep her own breathing steady. "Neither do they allow themselves to be trussed up by an ungodly stubborn Scotsman who—" He yanked the laces, effectively cutting off her breath. She braced herself against the wall and glared over her shoulder at him. "Bloody hell, MacGowan, are you trying to kill me?"

He tied off the laces with a flourish. "I be but trying to prepare you for—" he began, and turned her. She watched him draw a breath, watched his eyes darken, and against her thigh, something brushed her skin.

"The altar?" she asked.

He cleared his throat and reached for the gown. "'Tis not nice to speak of the marquis such. He may be a balding, deviant pig, but surely he does not believe in human sacrifice."

She stared at him for a moment. "I meant the *marriage* altar."

"Ahh. 'Tis me own mistake then."

She eyed the gown as he spread the skirt and slipped it over her head. It dropped into place with a sigh and a rustle, falling around her like raindrops on a slate roof.

He secured the dress from behind, then laced the sleeves on separately. She stood like an impatient parade horse, but finally he stood before her, perusing his handiwork with a critical eye.

"Well?" she said.

He shrugged, but the towel about his hips seemed strangely mobile. "I am not a lady's maid, after all."

"Aren't you? 'Tis me own mistake then," she quoted, and took a step away, but in that first fledging movement she tripped.

She never saw him move, but suddenly his arms were there and she was being propped back onto her feet, their lips inches apart, their breath melding.

"Lass," he murmured.

She jerked out of his grasp. "What is it, MacGowan?"

"If you are to be successful you should learn to walk like a lady lest the good marquis mistake you for a drunken draught horse."

"And you should keep your hands to yourself lest I cut them off," she said, and spun away. Unfortunately, when she tried to stride off, her toe caught in her hem and she stumbled yet again.

His chuckle echoed in the room. " 'Twill indeed be

much more fun accompanying you to Claronfell than I anticipated."

She glanced back at him as she retrieved a pair of slippers from an iron bound trunk. "You will not be accompanying me."

"Oh? And what will our noble friend think when you arrive alone? He may be as old as black pepper and as daft as a turnip, but even he may suspect there be something amiss when you come riding astride and swearing like a foot soldier."

She sat on the edge of the bed and realized she truly hadn't given that much thought. Indeed, she had been riding alone and unfettered for so long that she had not considered the problem of arriving unescorted at Claronfell.

" 'Tis not for you to worry on, MacGowan." She glanced up, felt her mouth go dry at the sight of him, and shifted her gaze rapidly to her feet. "You've troubles enough of your own."

He was scowling at her. She could feel it.

"Oh? And what troubles are those?"

"Your towel is not big enough," she said.

He glanced down, then shifted the fabric so that the opening slanted across the side of his thigh instead of directly down the front. In a moment he lifted his gaze back to hers.

"It is entirely possible that a well-born maid would have turned away," he said.

"And a gently reared man would not be standing before me in naught but a frayed bathing cloth."

He shrugged. The movement sent a thousand muscles dancing in his torso. "At least I needn't worry that you'll be tempted to peek at Turpin."

She forced a prim smile. "Oh, me laird, surely you jest, for I find the good marquis to be ever so appealing."

He snorted. "And me, I thought 'twas the lassies you were concerned with."

"You can hardly blame me for being impressed by such a noble title."

"Aye I can," he said. "For in truth, I thought you were not the sort to be seduced by such things."

There was sincerity in his tone and she shuffled her skirts back into place, covering her legs quickly. "Not the sort," she said and rose to her feet. "How hypocritical you are, MacGowan."

"Hypocritical? Me?" He crossed his arms against his chest. His wrist brushed his left nipple, and although it was all she could do to force her gaze away, he seemed not to notice.

"Aye," she said, and retrieved a hairbrush from the trunk. "You complain that I would better me station by marrying well, but when I bear me own sword and fight me own battles, that too you find improper. What then am I to do, champion? Lie down and die for I cannot please the likes of you?"

"I never said you failed to please me." The words were little more than a growl. "And there is no one more surprised than I."

Her breath caught in her throat. "What's that?"

His mouth was tight, his eyes as dark as sin, and for a moment she thought he would approach, but he did not. "'Tis not the likes of me you wish to please," he said. "But a warty old bastard with little more to offer than a title and a—"

She felt her brows rise toward her hairline. He paused.

"Why such vehemence?" she asked. "You do not seem the type to fight your brother's battles. Especially when that brother is happily wed and lucky to be rid of the woman the marquis married."

He shifted under her gaze. The movement might have been boyish but for the muscles that bunched and knotted in his massive chest.

"I've naught against him."

"The devil you don't!" she said, and he laughed aloud.

"With language like that you'll be able to attract naught but a sailor."

"Oh?" she said and let her gaze drift down his hardened body. "Tell me, champion, have you ever sailed the seas?"

He titled his head at her. "Truth to tell, lass, 'tis not all that difficult to stir *me*."

"Perhaps it is me masculine demeanor."

"Perhaps it's your breasts!" he growled, and took a step toward her.

She retreated a cautious pace, and he did not pursue her.

Instead, he closed his eyes momentarily and said, "I've no wish to argue with you."

"What do you wish to do, MacGowan?" she whispered, and though she knew she shouldn't ask, she felt a thrill of excitement race up her neck at his darkening expression.

A muscle jumped in his jaw, but he remained where he was and gave her a cocky grin. "I wish for naught but to help you win a grand title, of course."

"How kind you are."

He nodded. "Come hither."

"Burn in hell."

He chuckled once as he approached, but his eyes were still dark, his expression still taut. "Laddie, it may behoove you to treat men with a bit more respect."

"And it may—"

"Shh," he said and placed his fingers gently across her lips. "'Tis best to speak only when spoken to."

She glared at him and he smiled. "Much better," he said and lifting a girdle from the trunk, placed it about her hips. Made of broad links of chain that ended in a circular pendant, it swung nearly to the floor. He stepped back a pace and perused her.

"When you are quiet one could almost believe you to be a lady."

She gritted a smile, bunched the skirt in her hand and paced toward the window. "How kind of you to notice."

"Good sir," he said.

She turned to glare at him.

"Good sir," he repeated. "'Tis something you might say to the marquis instead of cursing at him. And there seems little reason to throttle the gown."

Glancing down, she saw that she had indeed crushed the fine fabric. She loosened her grip and smoothed the velvet over her thigh.

"I suspect you are right," she said. "There are others much more worthy of throttling."

"I'm flattered. How will you carry your baggage? Your loyal Night might not care to have a trunk strapped to his noble haunches. And what of additional garments? I understand your father may not be thought to be particularly wealthy, but surely you will need a few gowns to supplement this one."

"And this from a man who spends half his days in a bathing towel."

"Your voice is low for a woman," he said. "You are no longer trying to frighten the wits out of your enemy, laddie. Soften your tone. And what the devil are you scowling at? It seems you are scowling all your life. There is naught a woman can wear that makes her more appealing than a smile. As for your—"

"I did not ask for your help."

He paused in his harangue and shrugged. "You have spent your life becoming a man."

"And hence I cannot be a woman?"

"Laird Turpin has had many maids. Pampered they are and soft."

She took a step toward him. "And I am not soft enough?"

His gaze lowered to her breasts for a moment, then rose again. They were close now. He narrowed his eyes. "It was not I who said you should seduce a paunchy old reprobate in an effort to gain his wealth."

"Women do so every day."

"And you said you were not a woman."

"Forgive me," she said, and skimmed her gaze down his body again. "I had almost come to believe that you believed otherwise."

He scowled at her. She softened her voice even more. "In truth, you had nearly convinced me that I held some attraction for you."

She could feel his hard gaze on her face, but he remained utterly silent.

"So I was right from the start; you are not interested in me," she said, and advanced slowly.

"I never said as much."

She took another step toward him. "So what is it you think of me, champion?"

"You know what I think."

"Do not be afraid to say it, MacGowan. I'll not hold the truth against you."

"You are beautiful," he gritted. "And any man who is a man would say the same."

She tried to laugh, to tell him he was a fool, to prove that she had been toying with him, but in that moment his fingers curled around the nape of her neck. Her head fell back and his lips descended on hers.

Feelings swarmed in like angry bees and against her belly, she felt his erection rise to the occasion. She raised her hand to his chest, but if she meant to ward him off she was far too optomistic, for his body was as unyielding as an oaken buckler.

Rhona moaned beneath the kiss and slipped her hand over his nipple.

Lachlan wrapped his arm tight and fast about her waist, pressing her up against the bare expanse of him. She clasped her arms around his back, pulling him closer, and he crushed her with his kiss. His tongue pressed inside. She met it as if in a duel and slipped her hand downward, only to find a towel in the way. She tore it off and in a moment he was naked. She sighed into his mouth as she curved her palm over his hard buttocks.

"Lass!" he growled. "Gentle maids might not do that."

"Shut up, MacGowan," she ordered, and he kissed her again. She moaned out loud, then broke away and trailed a hot path of kisses down his throat. He had been naked half the time she knew him, had been flaunting his chest and . . .

She found his nipple and laved it with her tongue. He jerked against her, then wrapped his fingers in her hair. Forcing her head backward, he growled a warning.

"You were made for me, lass. None other."

She met his kiss with desperation.

"Not some bloated marquis!" Lachlan growled and lifted her into his arms. She slipped her fingers behind his neck and kissed him with ravishing heat. "We shall travel to Dun Ard," he gritted. "Wed within the month. Live—"

But suddenly his words came through to her. She pressed against his chest with all her might and scrambled to the floor.

"What the devil are you about?" he rasped.

"Wed!" The word sprung from her lips. "Are you daft? I cannot marry!"

His brows lowered and he paced closer. She backed a step away.

"You did not seem to dislike the idea a moment ago," he said.

"I said nothing of marriage."

"So you would bed me but not wed me?"

She licked her lips. "This I tell you, champion. You'll not own me. Not now, not ever. I go where I will."

"And you go to Turpin?"

He looked enraged and indomitable. Ready for battle or sex or both. Just as she was.

"Aye," she growled. "I go to Turpin."

"Though you want me."

"I did not say as much."

"Nay," he said and let his gaze fall across her body, her heaving breasts, her clenched fists. "For there was no need."

"Get out of me room, MacGowan."

"Nay," he said and lunged for her.

She sprinted away. Her toes tangled in her skirts and

she almost fell, but once again he caught her. Bearing her to her feet, he turned her in his arms.

Their lips were inches apart. She felt her knees go weak, and anger rose like a flood with that weakness. Clenching her teeth, she snarled at him, "Leave me be or I swear you shall rue this day."

He grinned. "And what shall you do, lass? You've no weapon close to hand."

She turned her head, desperately searching for protection, and it was there—her dirk, almost within reach, but his grip was like iron about her waist.

She turned back to him. Their gazes met and fused, anger and passion and frustration all melding at once, and then, like one in a trance, he reached out and wrapped his fingers around the hilt of her knife. She leaned back, her heart thumping, her eyes never leaving his. Lachlan raised the dirk, and she tensed, but he only spun it into the air and caught it by the blade.

"Here then," he growled, and loosening his grip on her waist, offered her the weapon.

She took it in her trembling hand and backed away.

"Feel better now?" he asked, and advanced slowly.

She hefted the dirk's familiar weight and raised her chin. "Aye, champion. I do."

"'Tis good," he said and, reaching slowly forward, drew her back into his embrace. "For I suggest you use it if you wish to stop me."

He leaned toward her. His lips felt hot as fire upon hers. She trembled with desire, but she pressed the knife against his ribs.

"MacGowan!" she growled.

He drew back slightly, his teeth clenched. "Aye?"

Against her breasts, his chest felt as hard as sin and upon her thighs, he throbbed with unrelieved desire.

She breathed through her mouth, trying to find her wits, and in the silence, he leaned forward again.

She pressed the blade deeper into his side, piercing his skin. He drew back, slowly, his face a solemn mask.

"You've some request, lass?" His tone was deep, his eyes like amber fire.

"Aye," she growled. "Take me, MacGowan!"

Chapter 17

There was a moment's delay, and then he swept her onto the mattress. The dirk was in the way now, so she tossed it aside and reached for him, tangling her fingers in his hair, pulling him atop her.

He kissed her ferociously, and she did the same, lifting her knees as he pressed into her, arching up to meet him. Her skirts slipped up her thighs. His erection pressed against her bare skin. She moaned as she pulled him into her and he entered with a growl.

A wave of painful pleasure hit her like high tide. She rocked back, gritting her teeth and pulling him deeper. He rode hard, grinding into her, pressing in time and again. Planting his hands beside her shoulders, he reared up and drove deeper still. Muscles corded in his arms. She grabbed his wrists, pulling him in, aching for more. Between her legs, his thighs bunched and bucked, but sud-

denly he was pushing away. She grappled for him, wrapping her legs about his, pulling him back, but his teeth
were set. She felt him slip away, felt utopia slide past.

"Damn you, MacGowan!" she rasped. "Come back."

He shook his head. For a moment he couldn't seem to
speak, then, " 'Tis not right," he growled.

"Right?" She tightened her legs around him, desperate to quiet the ache. "Aye, 'tis. 'Tis quite right."

"And what of later?"

She was panting as she wrapped an arm about his
back. Power flexed beneath her fingers and she moaned
at the feel, then set her free hand to his chest.

Muscles jumped at her touch. Fascinated, she
skimmed her palm over his nipple and down.

"Rhona!" he gritted, but held very still as if he were
paralyzed by the touch of her fingers. "Stop. 'Tis time to
think."

"Think?" She may have laughed, though it was difficult to say for certain. " 'Tis time to do many things," she
said, and kissed his chest. Merciful saints, it was a
bonny chest, sculpted with power and rippling with life.
"But 'tis certainly far past the time for thought." She
arched her spine into the mattress, reaching for him
again, but he planted his hands on her arms, as if he were
holding the devil himself at bay.

"Nay, lass. I'll not have you hating me all the more for
what I've—"

"Hate you!" She skimmed her hand down his rippled abdomen and felt their shivers merge into a fine
dance of desire. She touched his erection, sweeping her
fingers up its length. "I do not hate you. In truth . . ."
She wrapped her hand around him, guiding him toward

her core. "Just now I believe I rather like you, Mac-Gowan."

He jerked away, all but jumping from the bed.

"MacGowan!" he growled.

She stared at him.

"MacGowan!" He was circling her like a ravenous beast, glaring at her, his erection pulled tight to his rippled belly. "You do not even call me by me Christian name. Do you not know me Christian name?"

"Lachlan." The name flew from her lips. "'Tis Lachlan. Now come hither, damn you."

She watched him tighten his fists, saw the muscles bunch in his thighs as though he were just about to step forward. But he did not. She gritted her teeth.

"And what if you become with child? What then? There are no bonds of marriage. No—"

She laughed, relief washing through her. "Is that your concern?" she asked, and sat up abruptly. "There will be no babe. You can rest assured."

He scowled. "How do you know?"

"Listen, Mac—Lachlan, there is none who knows her body better than I who has lived as a man for most of me days. I have to know lest I spill me secret with me blood. There will be no babe from this coupling, that I promise you."

Again she thought he would come to her, but again he refused.

"'Tis still not right."

"Not right!" She yanked her skirt past her knees and glared at him. "You have been teasing me since the first moment we met, flaunting your body, flexing your glorious . . ." She skimmed each dancing muscle with her gaze, but managed not to voice any more of her weak-kneed opinions. "You have been teasing me," she repeated, "making me all but daft with your bonny words, your tender touch, your damned mesmerizing eyes!"

His brows had risen toward his hairline, but she stormed on.

"You have been teasing me for days," she said and, swinging her legs off the mattress, reached for her dirk and rose to her feet. " 'Tis a bit late to stop me now."

She raised the blade, but his gaze never dropped to it.

"I have not been teasing you, lass. I have been doing me best to keep meself to meself."

"You lying bastard," she said, and took a step toward him. "Do not act the innocent lad with me now when I know you are a master seducer."

"Master—"

"Get your arse back on that bed."

His lips moved, but not as violently as other parts. She lowered her gaze to watch his erection buck against the hard expanse of his belly, then drew a deep breath. "I am not one of your tarts to tease until they swoon for wanting you."

"Tarts?"

"Me," she said, and raised the dirk, "you will satisfy."

His erection danced a little fling. "Very well then," he said, and loosened his fist. "But 'twill be by me own rules."

She pulled her gaze from his penis and gritted her teeth against her own impatience. "You have rules?"

He delayed a moment, then, "Of course."

"What are they?"

"You'll remove your clothing."

It took a moment for his words to sink in, but once

they did, she immediately began ripping at the gown, her fingers frenetically trying to work around her dirk, but he stopped her.

"Lass." He took her fingers in his own, brought them slowly to his lips and kissed them. "I may be a master swordsman, but I am not a master seducer."

She laughed. It sounded strange, perhaps because she was salivating.

"Here," he said, and releasing her hands, turned her about. " 'Tis no reason to hurry," he said and, sweeping her hair aside, kissed her neck.

She didn't tell him he was entirely wrong, that there was every reason to hurry. That she was burning up, that she ached, that the damn world might end at any moment and ruin everything. Instead, she gritted her teeth and let her eyes fall closed. Her gown crept slowly open and with every inch of skin that was bared, she received a kiss. Down her neck, across her shoulder, along the length of her arm. She trembled with impatient longing as the garment sighed away, stepped out of the ring of fabric and shivered as his hands slid over her buttocks.

"MacGowan!"

"Shh," he said, and set his hands to the ties of her stays.

They too eased open with horrid slowness until they slipped onto her hips. Her breasts spills out. He kissed her shoulders, then skimmed his fingers after the garment, slipping down her waist with mind-numbing gentleness, before turning her in his arms and pressing the thing to the floor.

"Rhona." He said her name like a prayer. "You are the most splendid thing I have ever set me eyes upon. Like sunlight against me skin."

"Nay, I—"

"Shh," he said again, and kissed her lips with tantalizing tenderness.

She pressed into the kiss but he was already drawing back.

"Aye, you are handsome," he said, and kissed the corner of her mouth. "And bright." His lips touched her throat. She moaned and let her head fall back, exposing herself to him. "And strong." Lightning scorched her breast. She gasped at the searing feelings and twisted the fingers of her free hand into his hair. The other still grasped the knife. He touched her with his tongue, lapping her nipple and she jerked against him.

"MacGowan!"

"Lachlan," he corrected and, setting his hands to her waist, dropped to his knees.

"MacGow—" she began, trying to pull him up, but he licked her navel and she hissed between her teeth. The sound ended on a moan.

"And desirable," he whispered and, cupping her buttocks, pulled her closer still.

He kissed her belly, spreading his caresses across her skin like magic, then working lower. She squirmed, but finally his mouth reached her hair.

She stilled in his hands, and he tilted his head to kiss her. She gritted her teeth and bucked against him, feeling his tongue against her ache for just a moment before he rose languidly to his feet.

"You are certain you wish to do this?" His voice was as quiet as the night.

"You jest." Her own rather resembled a croak. The dirk wobbled in her hand.

"Shall I take that as a yes?"

She nodded.

"Was *that* a yes?"

Perhaps she had forgotten to nod. She did so now and he reached down, cupping her bottom in both hands and lifting her up against him.

She wrapped her legs around his waist and kissed him. He moaned into her mouth, then strode forward and pressed her back against the wall. Their lips joined again, and in a moment he was inside her. He caught her groan in his mouth as she arched hard against him.

Muscles exploded beneath her hands, but she could think of naught except the ache now. He pumped into her. She pumped back. Her legs slipped. She dug her heels into his bunched buttocks and ground into him.

Tension mounted, winding like a clock inside her. She squeaked something unintelligible and dug her fingers into his back, desperate to stay astride, and he answered her frenetic energy with a power so deep it seemed to drive to her very core.

She gasped his name. He groaned, and then she exploded, pleasure and desire and fulfillment all bursting within her. She sagged against him, and would have fallen had he not held her aloft and carried her to the bed. Once there he lowered her to the mattress. She sank onto it, breathing hard, every limb loose, every fiber exhausted as she fought for air.

As for Lachlan, he dropped down beside her. His chest rose like a bellows, his sculpted arms lay unmoving at his sides.

"MacGowan." Her voice was as weak as her body. She breathed in, trying to settle her heart, but when she turned on her side, she saw that he was as glorious as ever and as naked as the truth. Never in all her life had she seen anything so spectacular. "You are a liar," she said and, managing to lift her dirk, ran the flat of the blade slowly up the dramatic slope of his chest.

"Liar?" If he was offended it did not show in his tone. Indeed, the word was breathy and faint.

"Aye," she said, and slipped her blade over his nipple. It peaked immediately. "You said swordplay was your forte."

He turned his head to stare at her. A slight scowl marred his brow. She slipped her hand lower.

" 'Tis," he said, and she smiled.

"Are you certain?"

"Aye."

She moved closer so that her thighs brushed his and her breasts caressed his arm. "I believe you are wrong, MacGowan. But we'd best be sure."

"You want a battle?" he said, but even as he said it, she felt his attention rise against her thigh.

"Aye," she agreed, and swinging her leg over his, kissed him full on the mouth. "Choose your weapon, champion."

Chapter 18

Lachlan awoke from a dream. Every muscle felt as limp as a steed's forelock, every thought was as rosy as dawn.

Master seducer? Him? Of course, there was some pain that accompanied the title. He moved his leg. The muscles in his thighs ached and when he rolled his shoulders, the scratches on his back burned.

He smiled. Aye, she was a lioness, but he should have expected no less. Could have wanted no more, and if he were lucky, mayhap she was also insatiable. Turning, he reached for her.

The other half of the mattress was empty. He sat up with a scowl. His balls bunched between his thighs. They were, he realized, the only part of his body that didn't hurt.

Swinging his legs over the edge of the bed, he rolled

his shoulders forward and back and rose to his feet. Finding the hose he'd purchased was no great difficulty. Pulling his tunic over his head gave him a bit of pause, but in a moment he was striding down the hall. The house felt empty and quiet. Lachlan snagged a chunk of dark bread from the table as he passed and hurried outside, but once there he stopped short as he gazed toward the cobbled lane.

There, seated behind a pair of matched bays, was Rhona, but she was not the woman he had loved the night before. Nay, this morn she was the warrior, solemn of face and dark of clothes as she glanced down at Shanks who stood beside the looming carriage.

Lachlan swore in murderous silence as he strode down the steps and approached the heavy vehicle.

"You should not go alone, me laird," said Shanks.

She replied, but Lachlan failed to hear her words.

The old man's fingers looked gnarled and white where they gripped the carriage seat. "But surely you will let me fetch your lad at least."

"Nay, Shanks. Fare thee well now. See to my Knight."

The ancient servant's grip tightened even more upon the edge of the seat. "But how long will you be gone? Me master will not last much longer, and then the manor will fall to you. Surely you will wish—"

"Where are you off to then?" Lachlan asked.

Rhona tensed, but he received little pleasure from her surprise. Indeed, no pleasure would ever seem so great after last night's.

" 'Tis about bloody time," Shanks muttered.

Lachlan ignored him, keeping his attention on the girl. "Where are you off to so early?"

She straightened slightly, though her hands remained

steady on the lines. "I have but a few errands to run. 'Tis naught to concern yourself with."

"Errands." He glanced behind the wooden seat. "With your trunks in tow."

Her expression hardened. "Aye," she said, and turned her attention back to the old man. "Take care of yourself, Master Longshanks."

"But won't you be taking your lad here with you?" asked the old man, and gave Lachlan a concealed jab in the ribs.

" 'Tis not for you to concern yourself with," she said, and her face softened a mite as she placed a gloved hand over the old man's. "You've worries enough."

"I will miss you," he murmured. "As will me laird."

"He is much blessed to have you."

"And you," he said. Were there tears in the old bastard's eyes? "He knows that now if he did not before."

For a moment Lachlan thought she might say more, but instead she lifted the reins and the steeds moved out.

Shanks hissed something, but Lachlan was beyond hearing for he was already swinging up beside her.

She kept her attention on the rutted lane in front of them. "You are not invited, MacGowan."

"Truly?" Anger crowded in on the pleasure that still haunted him. "And where am I not invited to?"

"As I have said, 'tis none of your concern."

He settled back. Rage made his body tight. Fatigue made it ache. "I thought I made it me own concern last night, lassie."

They passed a tanner with a fresh hide slung over his shoulder. The old man glanced up at the sound of the endearment, but Rhona kept her attention strictly on the road ahead.

"You got what you wanted," she said, " 'tis time to be on your way."

"What I wanted!" he rasped. Her expression changed not a mite, so he shifted his attention to the uneven road in an effort to refrain from throttling her. "What *I* wanted!" His words were louder now. She shifted uncomfortably on the wooden seat and carefully avoided the gaze of a passing blacksmith. "It seems to me 'tis what you wanted too, lass, unless I be mistaken about the knife wound in me side."

"Do you say you did not want it?" she asked, and glanced at him from below the broad brim of her hat.

Desire rekindled in him, for despite everything there was something about her manner that made him remember every moment of the night just past.

"I wanted it," he said.

She nodded once. "Then you should be well satisfied. 'Tis time we parted ways."

"I beg your pardon?"

"You heard me and you understand me, MacGowan. I will be gone for some time."

"So you are going to him," Lachlan intoned.

She said nothing. Neither did she glance his way as they rattled out of the village and onto the well worn path of the common thoroughfare.

Anger stirred with a dozen other emotions, twisting Lachlan's stomach. "So you are on your way to the fat marquis without so much as a thank you."

She did look at him now, but her gaze was disdainful, her eyes cool. "You are a vain cockerel, aren't you, MacGowan?"

"Vain! Me?"

"I may not be as desirable as some, but I am capable

of attracting others to me bed if I so wish. Do not think I cannot. Aye, you are gifted, champion. That much I admit, but do not think I will come begging for your attention."

He sat in absolute silence for several seconds, then, "You think I expect you to thank me for last night?"

She went stiff. Her eyes shifted rapidly toward him and away. Her gloved fingers tightened on the lines. "Nay."

He continued to stare. "Aye. You did. You entirely forgot to be grateful that I saved your life and—"

"Nay, 'twas what I was referring to." She glanced nervously toward him. "That and the fact that—"

He roared with laughter. Her brows lowered like a hand beaten portcullis.

"What the devil are you chortling about, Mac-Gowan?" Her voice was low and her expression angry, but the world looked utterly rosy again, as bright as a fresh tomorrow.

Lachlan chuckled to himself. Life was good. She continued to glower.

"Truly," he said finally. "I cannot think of a single other instance when I have been so flattered."

"I'm certain there's a reason for that."

"There must be," he agreed, grinning widely.

"I meant . . ." Her teeth were gritted. "There is probably naught else you do as well."

"Better still!" he said.

She stopped the team abruptly. "Get out."

"What's that?" he asked, and struggled to control his grin.

"Get out before I kick your arse off of here."

" 'Tis not that I think you frail, lass," he said, and refrained from doing cartwheels. "In fact, I have scratches from me shoulders to me arse to prove the opposite, but 'tis not likely that you can best me in hand to hand combat." Not that she wouldn't give it a go, and what a thrill that would be.

"So . . ." She leaned back slightly and studied him, her eyes narrowed. "You enjoyed last night, did you?"

He leaned closer. "Would you like me to show you how much?"

She glanced up at him and drew a breath through her lips. They were parted and waiting, and despite the attire, the attitude, the threats of physical violence, she looked like naught more than a bashful maid. "Mayhap later," she said, and though he knew it best to talk things through he could not help but move in for a kiss. "If you leave now."

He drew back with a start. "What's that?"

The shy maid was gone, replaced with a steely warrior who glared at him with battle-hardened eyes. "Leave me now, MacGowan, and you may feel again the burn of last night, but I tell you this . . . if you do not leave I will never bed you again."

Emotions stirred like a witch's brew inside him. "So that's the way of it, lass? You go to your marquis and perhaps, if I am tractable, you shall return to me bed some day."

She shrugged. "Perhaps."

He swore in silence and ground his hands to fists. "And meanwhile what will you be doing?"

For a moment she was silent, but finally she spoke. "I am not the spoiled son of a doting nobleman, Mac-Gowan. Therefore, I do what I must."

"And you must seduce Turpin?"

"Mayhap."

For a brief second he wanted to shake her until she promised otherwise, but he conquered the urge with a hard effort and nodded. "Then I must accompany you."

"Nay!"

"Aye."

"Damn you, MacGowan! This is not some game I play for boredom's sake. This is life and this is death!"

He studied her closely. "Whose life?" he asked. "Whose death?"

She paused for a moment, looking breathless. "Mine," she said finally.

He nodded once. "Then I shall go with you, and perhaps better your odds."

"You cannot—"

"I go!" He gritted the words into her face. "And there is naught you can do about it, unless you hope to end me life here and now."

For a moment she looked angry enough to do just that, but finally she fell silent. Slapping the lines against the team's broad haunches, she moved them down the road toward Claronfell.

Shortly before dusk, Rhona stopped the team and handed Lachlan the reins. Not a word was spoken as she slipped from the driver's seat and into the interior of the carriage.

It was not much later that they reached a village and when Lachlan opened the door of the vehicle he could not help but be shocked by the transformation.

Gone were her muddied boots and manly attire. She wore now a flowing lilac gown that laced up the front, displaying her breasts to her best advantage. He wondered momentarily if she had managed the stays he'd purchased for her, but with one additional glance he saw that her form was too soft, too feminine, too tempting to be wrapped in whalebone.

Nay, beneath the gown, she was unfettered. He pushed the image from his mind as he reached for her hand.

For a minute she missed his intent as she stared out over his head, but finally she glanced at him, scowled and accepted his assistance.

They walked to the inn together. Lachlan opened the door then gave her a mock bow, letting her precede him. She did so, her chin raised, and her fingers gloved in white kid leather.

Nearby, a stooped man with tremendous ears ceased his labor to stare at her.

"M'lady," he said, finally coming to his senses with a start. Lifting his rag from the table he'd been scrubbing, he bowed as though he'd just met the queen in disguise. "How may I serve you?"

"I'll have a room, and be quick about it," she ordered.

For a moment the innkeeper seemed taken aback. "Yer pardon?"

Lachlan chuckled, though he felt far from jovial. He could immediately feel her anger, but her voice softened nevertheless.

"My apologies," she said. Splaying a hand across her lovely bosom, she smiled shyly through her lashes. "I fear my throat is rough after such a long ride." The man's gaze followed her hand and held there for a moment after she'd removed it. Her voice was as sweet as elderberry wine. "I will require a private room for the night."

"For yourself and . . . your husband, me lady?"

"Husband?" She laughed. It was not the bewitching, silvery tone he'd heard only a few times before, but it was a fetching facsimile. "Nay, my good man. This fellow is naught but me servant."

The innkeeper wiped his hands on his apron and smiled happily. Lachlan momentarily considered beating him senseless. "A room for yourself then, me lady. Very well. And for your man we have a fine room with but a pair of others letting it."

Lachlan considered telling him what he could do with his room and his letters, but before he opened his mouth, Rhona spoke again.

"I am certain those arrangements will be perfectly acceptable. But for now I need a meal and someone to fetch my trunks. I fear I am not very strong."

"Certainly, my lady," he said again, and scurried into the kitchen to dispense orders.

They were seated in a moment, alone shortly after.

Rhona carefully removed her white kid gloves finger by delicate finger. Lachlan watched in silence as her digits were revealed, pale and talented and tapered. He was angry. Indeed, he was incensed, and yet he found that, against all good judgment, he longed to kiss those fingers, to take each one into his mouth and suckle it until she was wet and wanting.

"'Tis a fine inn," she said, using that girlish tone she had adopted only minutes before. "Don't you agree, champion?"

Resentment ground crankily in his gut. "You'll not manage it, laddie."

She turned her attention back to him, raising her brows as she did so. Surprise shone like sunrise on her bold features. "What's that, my good man?"

"Oh aye," he said. Doing his best to appear casual, he leaned a shoulder against the wall and watched her. "You can simper prettily and act the helpless maid now, but what happens when the fat marquis refuses to behave?"

"Refuses to behave?" Her tone was still perky. She giggled, and he found he missed her usual earthy tone with rare desperation. "Whatever do you mean?"

"I mean after you stab him with your dinner knife, he is unlikely to believe you are naught but a delicate maid bent on serving him."

"Stab him!" She looked aghast. Her eyes were ungodly wide, and she blinked several times before touching her fingers to her lips as if she'd heard something too hideous to believe. It made his hair stand on end. It was eerie how she could sound as if she had not a vile thought in her head. As if she were the most harmless of god's witless creatures. "Whyever would I do such a horrid thing?"

Lachlan carefully refrained from grinding his teeth. "Because it is your nature. Or do I have to show you me own wounds to prove it?"

She smiled. Her lips were perfectly bowed, and her thick lashes fluttered over the creamy skin of her cheeks.

"I know you are manly, champion," she said, and reaching out, placed her hand delicately atop his. Though it appeared refined and ultimately gentle, it was not a fragile hand. Nay, it was strong and talented, and when he thought about what she could do with those hands, a familiar ache settled into his groin. "But I do not think it would be quite proper to reveal your scars here at the inn."

"There is a hell of a list of things that are not quite proper," he growled and pulled his hand out from beneath hers.

She laughed again. At the table near theirs, two men stared at her with unconcealed admiration.

He glared at them until they turned away.

"Champion," she said and made a tsking noise as she glanced at him from beneath her lashes. "You are so peevish this day. Whatever has set you off?"

The men at the nearby table had doggedly resumed eating, so Lachlan pulled his attention from them and turned his scowl on her. "Turpin may be a fool, but even he will not believe you're nothing more than a comely maid," he warned.

"You think not?" she murmured and arching her back, let her eyes go dramatically wide as she spread her fingers in dismay across her startling bosom.

"Nay, I do not," he growled, but in his heart he knew the truth; it didn't matter if she fought like a foot soldier and swore like a whore, any man with a pecker and half a brain would want her.

And damn him—he had both.

Chapter 19

They arrived at Claronfell on the following afternoon. The manse loomed outside the carriage window like a gray storm cloud.

Rhona sat inside the coach, feeling sick to her stomach and pitifully weak. Oh aye, she had been on more dangerous missions, but never had the entire assignment depended on her ability to seduce. And never had she been accompanied by a growling Scotsman who refused to abandon her no matter how miserable she was to him.

Why would he not leave? The question haunted her, gnawing at her caution, tearing at her barriers, but she fortified her defenses, for she could not risk the answers. Indeed, she had fled Nettlepath for the very same reason. She could not risk. Could not delay, for if she did she may very well find she no longer possessed the ability to leave him. Indeed, one more touch of his skin, one more

kiss, and all might be lost. The memory of their time together rose up like a sweet-smelling mist in her mind,
lulling her, weakening her. But she knew the truth; she
should have left earlier, should have escaped before she
realized how he could make her feel, should have—

He opened the door now and stood there, staring at
her, as dark and taciturn as an ancient gargoyle, as powerful as a force of nature. His usual tunic was gone. In its
place he wore a sleeveless plaid jerkin. It had neither a
lace nor any fasteners, but was held in place by naught
more than a simple iron pin slipped through the fabric
near his navel. Upon his head he wore a dark tam
pierced with a single ostrich feather.

Perhaps he should have seemed ridiculous, too bar-
baric, too unrefined. But somehow the sight of him thus
only managed to take her breath away.

"We've arrived," he said finally.

She nodded and forced herself to lean forward, ready
to step down, but he refused to back away.

"I ask you again not to go through with this." His
voice was deep and earnest. His eyes were filled with
quiet solemnity, and for a moment she almost faltered,
but finally she steeled herself.

"I must," she said simply, and made to leave again. He
remained as he was, blocking her exit.

"And what if I do not let you?"

Perhaps she should declare her ability to do as she
wished, but standing thus, he looked as powerful as
Knight, though not so mild-mannered. "Why?" she
asked instead. She'd meant to say it simply, casually, but
emotion had somehow crept into her tone.

"I think you know."

She shook her head and he tightened his grip on the

door handle. Muscles rippled from his wrist to his shoulder. From somewhere, he had secured a pair of dark hose that fit to disconcerting perfection. But his shoes were scuffed and his simple jerkin showed an immense amount of broad, sun-darkened chest. She kept her gaze doggedly on his face, the better to concentrate.

"You are not meant for the likes of Turpin," he said.

She waited, saying nothing and feeling empty. But time was fleeting and she dare not delay. "Neither am I meant for you."

"Perhaps you do not know me so well as you think."

She smiled. "I know you, MacGowan," she said softly. "You are wealthy. You are gifted, and you will someday take a bride much like the ones your brothers have wed."

He paused. "And you?"

She stifled a shrug. From henceforth, she must be aware of every movement, and ladies of breeding did not oft display such common mannerisms. "Mayhap I will win me a marquis. Surely you would not deny me that?"

"As I said, you do not know me so very well."

His expression was as solemn as death, his eyes dark and earnest, and for a moment she wanted nothing more than to step into his arms, to believe that he would fight for her.

" 'Tis my choice," she said softly. "And I shall make it."

"Why?"

Anguish was in his tone. She hardened her heart. "Because I must." From the corner of her eye, she saw that two brightly liveried servants approached, pacing between the looming topiary that lined the walkway from the manse on the hill. "Because it is of utmost importance," she murmured.

"I disagree," he said.

She drew a deep breath. The servants were drawing nearer and behind them came another. "That is because you do not know the facts."

"I will not leave you," he said.

Anger spurred up and she was tempted to take him by the tunic and demand that he be on his way. But Turpin's servants were approaching, and she had no time. "You must."

"You have oft been wrong," he said. "But never more than now, for I will stay."

"Damn you!" she swore, and he smiled.

"A proper maid might not say such things, me lady. Not to her poor, humble servant."

"You make a horrible servant," she hissed. "No one will believe you are aught but what you are—a bull-headed Scotsman with more balls than brains."

His mouth twitched before he spoke. "Me leidy," he said, and suddenly his brogue was replaced by an outlandish accent. "Ye cut me ta the quick."

She longed to slap some sense into him, but the marquis' servants were nearly upon them, so she pursed her lips, accepted Lachlan's hand, and stepped into the afternoon's full sunlight.

"Good day," she said, and straightened outside of the coach. It took a moment for MacGowan to release her fingers, but she refused to turn toward him. "I am Lady Rhona, late of Nettlepath, come to care for my lord's poor wee daughters."

The two brightly dressed men stood at her horse's head, while the third fellow bowed regally.

"My lady," he said. He was dressed well but conservatively all in dark colors, and his face bore not a hint of a smile. "I fear we were not expecting you for some days."

"I myself did not plan to come so soon, but when I thought of the children . . ." She paused and spread her gloved fingers across her décolletage as if in wide dismay. His gaze didn't drift from her face for the barest moment. "How do they fare?"

"I am but the bailiff here, my lady. I know little of the children," he said. "But I can show you to your quarters if you desire."

"I would be eternally grateful," she said, and brushed an imaginary speck of mud from the wide skirt of her gown. "It has been a long and wearisome journey."

"Shall I send another to gather your trunks, or will your man be seeing to them?"

"I've no wish to trouble you further, Master . . ."

"You may call me Reeves, my lady."

"Reeves," she said, and gave him a small smile. "I've no wish to take you from your duties. I am certain your expertise is much needed elsewhere."

He made no indication that he had heard the compliment. She kept her smile firmly in place and felt as if MacGowan was about to burn a hole through the back of her head. Damn him and his Highland glower.

"My servant would be delighted to see to my trunks, Reeves."

Beside her, Lachlan remained absolutely silent. Tension cranked tighter in her gut, but she turned resolutely toward him.

"Wouldn't you, champion?"

For a moment challenge flashed in his eyes, but finally he lifted his face and gave Reeves a crooked smile.

"Delighted I'd be," he agreed, his voice unusually loud. "Just as me leidy says."

The bailiff seemed not the least bit disturbed by Mac-Gowan's boisterous demeanor. Neither did he deign to address him. "And will he be leaving us or shall I make a place for him in the servants' quarters?"

Rhona opened her mouth to speak, but Lachlan interrupted.

"It's staying I'll be," he said, and placing his fists on his hips, gave the somber bailiff a sharp nod. "Lord Barnett, 'e said, look after me daughter well or it's your 'ide I'll be tannin', so I'd best be stayin' 'ere with 'er for I've a fondness for me 'ide, but I've a strong back, I do, and I've a talent with the 'erbs if somemat should tek sick."

"Very well then," said Reeves and turning about, led Rhona toward the looming house.

She had no time to admonish Lachlan for his foolish display of rustic civility, but followed Reeves until she stood in the entryway. She'd been to Stirling Castle, King James's residence, more than once. Its size little exceeded Claronfell's, but she took no time to marvel at the grandeur of the place. Instead, she climbed the stairs behind the bailiff and was soon ensconced in her own chamber. It was almost bare, boasting little but a bed draped in deep blue velvet and a massive fireplace crafted of gray stone. Above the hearth hung a mace and a pair of battleaxes, both notched from use.

Pacing to the window, Rhona looked out at the property below. Vast gardens stretched out forever. Verdant hedges spiraled this way and that. Bushes trimmed in the shapes of every manner of wild beast capered across the lawn, and fragrant roses still bloomed along a rock wall that formed an archway near its center. But despite the manor's beauty there was a macabre aura about the place that disturbed her.

Suddenly, though, she heard laughter, and turned, thinking she would see the children.

" 'Tis the third door to the right. Some ways yet it be, but by the look of ye ye'll stand the distance," someone said, and in a moment Lachlan entered the room with a trunk upon his shoulder. A maid not yet twenty years of age followed. "Arms like that will come in handy round about now," she said as he straightened from setting the trunk on the floor.

"And a figure lek yours be 'andy year round," countered Lachlan with his odd accent.

"Hum, I'll have to keep an eye out when you're round about," said the maid. "And what shall I be calling ye?"

"Me mam named me Dafydd," he said.

"Dafydd." She rolled the name on her tongue. " 'Tis a strange name ye have."

"Not atall," he countered. " 'Tis a good Welsh name, it is."

"Aye well, I've not seen a Welshman the likes of you."

"Nor shall ye," he said, and winked. "For me veins also flow with the blood of the Scots and the Saxon and a wee dram of the red dragon's blood."

"Not to mention a bit of the blarney," said the maid, and laughed.

Emotions churned in Rhona's gut as she watched the two. The girl was as pretty as springtime, with dark wavy hair and a pert, turned-up nose. The pale color of her green gown showed her tidy figure to perfection.

"Not a bit of blarney is it, me leidy?" Lachlan asked as he turned toward Rhona.

"Oh!" The maid jumped, then bobbed a curtsy and

fidgeted as though she would be struck dead on the spot. "Me apologies, me lady. I thought you had gone to see the wee ones. I didn't see ye standing there."

Rhona said nothing.

"Well . . ." The maid cleared her throat and backed toward the door. "I'll be helping your Dafydd here with the rest of your luggage then if you've no need for me just yet."

"I do," countered Rhona.

The maid stopped as if she'd been stabbed.

Something akin to humor shone darkly in Lachlan's eyes.

Rhona dropped her gaze and cursed the deep timbre of her well-trained voice. "I do so hate to be a bother," she said, and tried an ingratiating smile. It may have resembled a snarl. "But as a matter of truth, I could use your assistance. And I'm certain Dafydd here can manage to fetch my trunks himself."

His attention didn't shift from her face. Neither did the gleam disappear from his eyes.

"Oh, of course," said the girl and bobbed again. "How can I assist you, me lady?"

She was so eager, so comely. It made Rhona's fists ache. "Aren't you the bonny one?" she said. "And what might your name be, lass?"

"I am called Colette."

Even the name was delicate. Not like Rhona. And already she was flitting her wide-eyed gaze back to Lachlan, as if he were her savior, just arrived on his champing white steed.

"If it is not too much trouble, I would like to meet the children, Colette."

"Oh. Certainly. The poor wee babes," said the other,

and turned with only one more glance at MacGowan. "If you'll follow me, I shall show you the way."

The halls were narrow and dimly lit, and it seemed a long distance from her chamber to the girls', but finally they arrived.

The nursery was a large room, mostly empty but for a narrow bed, two trunks, and a few well-crafted stools. A small girl sat upon one of them, her middle finger still wet from having just been jerked out of her mouth and half hidden in the folds of her white pristine gown. The hem was embroidered in soft shades of pink and green that twisted like living vines about the gown's outer edge. The lace at her wrists was snowy, as was the upright collar that reached her chin. She held a clay doll and in the corner not far away another lass sat cross-legged with her back toward them.

"Catherine!" scolded Colette and snapped her gaze to Rhona and back. "Get up off the floor, child, or there'll be the devil to pay."

The girl with the doll jumped to her feet, nearly falling over in her haste, then hurried over to stand nervously beside the other.

As for the elder of the two, she turned sullenly toward them, eyes narrowed. Her face was very pale but for a small blackish bruise on her temple. She was dressed identically to her sister.

"Come hither," ordered Colette.

Neither child moved a muscle.

"Come along now," said the maid, then started as another woman arrived. "Oh! Baroness!" she said and curtsied. "Lady Rhona has arrived."

The newcomer turned to Rhona with a shy smile. She was a small, pretty woman with large sad eyes and a slim body garbed in black. Her hair was gray, pulled back from her face and mostly hidden beneath a dark French hood that hung down her narrow back. In her hand she carried a string of wooden beads which she worried at with quick, delicate fingers. "Lady Rhona," she murmured, her voice dulcet. "I thank the Lord you have arrived safely. And what of you, my dears," she said, turning toward the children. "I hope you have welcomed her in due Christian fashion."

Rhona glanced back at the girls. Though they remained in the corner, the eldest had risen to her feet and turned now, her back to the wall. Defiance shone in every taut fiber.

"I am Lady Irvette Norval," said the baroness, and smiled bravely at Rhona. "So you are come to care for my brother's daughters."

"Aye."

"I pray it will work out for the best."

There was something about her tone that aroused Rhona's curiosity. "Has there been trouble, Lady Norval?"

"Trouble?" A mixture of sadness and worry lit across her aging features, but she smoothed her expression and smiled wanly. "Nay, no trouble. They are good children," she said. Her voice was soft. "They but take too much guilt upon themselves."

Rhona focused on the girls. They stood absolutely immobile, saying nothing, and she realized finally that the room had gone silent. "I beg your pardon?" she said, certain the baroness had spoken.

"I asked if you have cared for children before?"

"Not as much as I would have liked, your ladyship. But I did spend some time with my cousin's children."

"Your cousin?"

"Aye. I have been summering in Spain these past months with Lady Romona de Leon. Mayhap you know her."

"I've not had time for the luxury of travel," said Norval. "My brother's wife has been ill for some time as you may know. 'Twas my Christian duty to come and see my nieces gently reared."

" 'Tis good of you to leave your own affairs to care for them."

"We must do what we can. I've not been blessed with children of my own, but I cherish these two as if I had birthed them myself."

"I am certain I will feel the same."

The look of sadness creased the baroness's brow for a moment. "I pray 'tis true," she said softly. "Though Catherine . . ." She paused, then glanced at the girls and put on a brave smile. "Humility is a fine thing, surely, but . . . All will be well. I am sure of it."

Dread marched ominously down Rhona's back. "Is there something I should know, baroness?"

The older woman smiled wearily and shook her head. "Nay. I am being foolish. 'Twas only that Lorna needed much attention before her death. The children may have been neglected during that time, and I fear . . ." She paused, looking as though her heart would break. "I fear our young Catherine blames herself."

"Why?"

The baroness shook her head. "There is no reason," she said, staring directly at the elder girl as she did so, as though she could force her to believe the softly spoken words. "No reason atall. Not for the blame, and certainly not for the bruises."

The bruises? Rhona skimmed her attention to the blackish mark on the girl's brow. She abused herself?

"And . . . their father?" Rhona asked, her mind spinning.

"My brother is often busy with his affairs."

Lachlan's words swirled wildly with the information she herself had garnered about the marquis. "I am certain it has been difficult since their mother's passing," Rhona said. "But I will do my best to care for them."

"I am certain you will," said Lady Norval, "but you needn't tax yourself immediately. You must take some time to settle in. I will see to the little girls until you've become accustomed to the ways of Claronfell."

Rhona frowned. Time was fleeting, and if the marquis did indeed plan some evil, she didn't have much time left to learn what it was. "I've little to do but care for the lassies, Lady—"

But the other interrupted with a lift of her frail hand. "They are used to having me here," she said. "Indeed, we have become quite close and they do not need yet another blow so quickly upon the death of their mother." She glanced at the girls. They remained exactly as they were, not moving a hair, their expressions unreadable masks. "Nay," she said. "I will not be leaving just yet."

Chapter 20

The marquis was not what Rhona expected. He was neither balding nor paunchy as MacGowan had implied, but stood straight and elegant, before bowing over her hand.

"Lady Rhona," he said, and kissed her knuckles with fatherly gentleness. His hair was silver and when he smiled, fine lines radiated from the corners of his azure eyes. "How kind of you to come all this way on my account."

"'Twas the least I could do for an old friend of my father's," she said.

"Not so very old, I hope," he countered.

She scowled, remembered herself and endeavored to implement that wide-eyed gaze of adoration that other women seemed to accomplish so easily. "Of course not, my lord," she corrected quickly. "I should have said my father's *esteemed* friend. When I heard of your wife's passing I only wished to help your daughters through this difficult time, and relieve your pain some whit."

His eyes saddened. She pulled her hand carefully from his grasp.

"Aye, 'twas a terrible loss," he said. "She was with child, you know."

"Nay, my lord, I did not."

"Aye, she carried my son."

"You know the babe's sex?"

He smiled wanly and seated himself at the head of the table. "She already bore me two lovely daughters. Simple logic would suggest—ahh, but there are my princesses now," he said, and sure enough, they came, shepherded along by a darkly garbed Lady Norval toward the table. "Edwina," he said, his voice coddling as he addressed the younger of the two. "Come hither."

Rhona noticed now that the child's fingers were tangled in her sister's starched sleeve.

"Come," he said again, and without glancing down, the taller of the two tugged Edwina's fingers from her sleeve and urged her forward.

The tiny girl stumbled forth on wooden legs. Lord Robert lifted her onto his lap, where she sat stiff as a spear and stared up at him with eyes as round as guinea eggs.

He smiled down at her, then lifted his gaze as his sister urged Catherine toward a high stool.

The girl's pink mouth was pursed, but she did as told. Climbing reluctantly onto her perch, she pushed her hands rapidly beneath the table, then turned to glare at Rhona.

"I trust you have become acquainted with my dear sister," said the marquis.

Rhona pulled her attention from the girl. "Yes, my lord," she said, and turned her gaze toward the elder woman.

The other lowered her eyes demurely and lovingly stroked Catherine's hair. Fine and long, it gleamed red in the candlelight, but the girl's mouth remained pursed, and her eyes smoldered.

"Lady Irvette is baroness of Hanstone," said the marquis and set Edwina on her feet. The girl scurried like a field mouse over to her high chair, then scrambled onto the seat and rolled her eyes from one adult to the other while Colette hurried forward to fit a wooden tray into its place in front of her.

"Learn what you can from her," Robert suggested to Rhona, "for I fear she will soon be leaving us."

"You needn't worry immediately," murmured Irvette, glancing with concern at Colette's progress with the tray. "I am planning to stay a bit longer."

Edwina's round eyes got rounder, but Catherine's expression remained unchanged.

"Indeed?" said Lord Robert. "And to what do we owe this privilege, sister?"

"To Catherine," Irvette said, and smiled reassuringly at the girl. "It seems she is not yet prepared for me to leave."

"Ahh," said the marquis, and motioned to Reeves for the first course.

And so the meal began, but Catherine refused to eat, Lady Irvette barely spoke, and the marquis rambled on about wines and spices and the time he had spent at court.

The dining hall was large and well furnished. A host of ancient weapons adorned one wall. Rhona did her best not to admire them, but it would seem so much better to hold one in her hand and challenge all comers than to sit here in silence and try to untangle the nuances that flowed around her like spoiled wine. Was there a reason for her presence there, or was this naught but a waste of time?

After supper, the baroness insisted on taking the girls to bed herself, thus Rhona was left alone with the nobleman. He was richly dressed in a scarlet doublet with slashed sleeves. His tunic was the color of the evening sky. It too bore the stylish slashes, and about his neck he wore a heavy pendant of gold. He smiled over his goblet at her.

"How refreshing it is to have a maid like yourself at my table," he said.

Rhona lowered her gaze to the pewter plate she'd just used. Claronfell, it seemed, spared no expenses on its guests. "You are too kind, my lord."

He relinquished his wine and leaned closer as if to share a secret none other was privy to. "My sister is a boon with the children, but what with the sadness of the past several months . . ." He sighed. "She does not lighten the gloom as you do."

"She seems a godly person."

"She does, doesn't she?" he agreed and, smiling, reached for her hand. "Perhaps you would like a tour of the gardens."

" 'Tis kind of you to offer," she said and, tugging her fingers carefully from his, rose to her feet. "But it has been a long day, my lord. Perhaps I should bid your daughters good night and find my own bed."

He chuckled as he stood up.

Irritation rippled up her neck, but she had carefully

replaced her dirk in its place in her girdle. It was allowed, after all, since even Claronfell did not supply its diners with knives. "Why do you laugh, my lord?"

"Simple pleasure, I suppose," he said, and raised his hand palm up to indicate that she should proceed him from the room. "I hope you do not resent me for enjoying your presence."

"Of course not, my lord."

"After all, you are quite a surprise."

She passed him, finding there was little room between him and the table, so that her skirt brushed his legs. "A surprise? How so?"

"Well, unless I forgot, your father is not a handsome man."

She scowled and he laughed again.

"No need to look so uncertain, my dear. I am but saying that you are quite striking. Not beautiful exactly, but . . ." He paused. "Handsome. Like the warrior queens of yore."

She stared and he chuckled again.

"You needn't look so worried. I am not about to devour you, child."

"Nay. Of course not," she said.

He sighed. "Mayhap you have heard rumors of my . . . reputation."

She said nothing.

"I do not deny that I was not always . . ." He paused again, searching for words. "I was not the perfect husband," he said. "But I cherished my wife, and she me, I think."

"I am certain she did, my lord."

He smiled warmly, as if lulled by her assurances.

"You will find Edwina in the nursery," he said, and stopped as he swung open a heavy timbered door.

Inside, the room was as black as pitch, but for the light the marquis lifted high. The tiny girl snatched her finger from her mouth and lay huddled alone in bed. She looked no larger than a hare with her eyes gleaming in the candlelight and her knuckles white as she clutched her blanket to her chin. She said nothing. Indeed, if she could speak atall, Rhona had no proof of it. Then again, mayhap she was too young to have learned the Gaelic. The enormity of Rhona's ignorance suddenly came crashing in on her, but Lord Turpin w$\overline{as}$ staring, so she crossed the room and awkwardly patted the girl's shiny head.

"Good night, Edwina."

There was no response, but Lord Robert seemed unperturbed. His candlelight flickered on a pair of crossed broadswords that adorned the wall above her bed. It might be that the marquis favored weapons even more than she did.

"And what of Catherine?" asked Rhona. "Does she not share the nursery with her sister?"

The marquis lifted the candle as if to search the shadows, but Lady Irvette spoke up from the hallway.

"Catherine sleeps in the chamber down the hall."

"Oh?" said Rhona. It seemed strange, for the room was large enough for several children. "May I bid her good night?"

"I fear she is already asleep," said Lady Irvette and smiled wanly.

"I would not awaken her."

There was a moment's delay. Was there tension in the

air? "Then of course," said the baroness, and led the way down the hall. She said not a word as she raised the bar that held the door shut.

"It is locked from this side?" asked Rhona.

Lady Irvette glanced worriedly toward her brother. He shrugged, pleasantly. "Sometimes she wanders unknowing from her room at night."

"She walks whilst she sleeps?" Rhona asked.

"If it is sleep it is an unnatural one," murmured Lady Irvette, and made a furtive sign of the cross against her chest.

"Unnatural?" Rhona asked. "How so?"

"I . . ." She paused and lowered her eyes. "I cannot say exactly," she said, and without another word pushed the door open. Her candle flickered in the draft.

Inside, the chamber was dark, pierced only by the wavering shaft of light, but in that slim illumination, Rhona could make out Catherine's face.

She lay on her side with one hand cradling her cheek. Her rose-tinted lips were slightly parted, and she looked, Rhona thought, like a small sleeping angel. Whatever troubles caused her to wander the halls at night were not bothering her now.

They stood in silence for a moment, but finally Lady Irvette spoke. "I'd have a word with you, if you've a moment, brother dearest," she said.

"Certainly, sister," he said and, bowing masterfully, left the room. In a moment the doorway was empty.

"So you are another of my father's whores."

Rhona speared her gaze to Catherine. The girl lay as she was, but her eyes were open now and her small mouth was sneering.

"Why do you feign sleep?"

"You'll not last the week," said the girl.

"Why?" Rhona asked, but a shadow crossed the threshold and Catherine's eyes fell immediately closed.

"Come along, my lady," said the marquis.

Rhona went a bit shakily. She had hardly hoped to be met with huzzahs and kisses, but neither had she expected to be threatened by a child half her size.

The marquis closed the door behind them and escorted her down the hall to her own chamber. A candle flickered beside her bed.

"Here you are then, lass, safe and sound."

She tried not to scowl, but it had been an odd day and her mind was atremble. "My thanks, your lordship."

"There is no need for such formality."

"What would you have me call you?" she asked, and lowered her eyes, trying to emulate the delicate baroness.

"We shall see," he said.

She raised her gaze to his, and he only smiled.

"Such a sweet thing you are. I hope you will not be frightened alone in your room this night."

"I'll try to be brave, my lord."

"No need for that, lass." He moved the slightest bit closer. He smelled a bit like old whisky. Not an unpleasant scent, but not altogether soothing. "I am just down the hall."

"I will surely sleep better knowing 'tis so."

He eyed her carefully. "I look forward to getting to know you, Lady Rhona. I think you are a rare woman."

"You flatter me, my lord."

"I try."

She glanced up sharply, and he laughed as he bowed.

"Good night, lass," he said and turned away.

* * *

Although Rhona carefully studied the layout of Claronfell on the following morning, her day did not go much better than the last and the next still no better. She found no opportunity to safely investigate the manse. Reeves acted as if Rhona had come to burgle the spice chest. The marquis did his best to seduce her. Colette shamelessly teased Lachlan—not that Rhona cared. And the lassies watched her as if she were a slavering wolf, though she rarely saw them, for when they weren't in the small, high chapel with Lady Irvette "where nothing was between them and God," as the baroness informed her, they were closeted away in the nursery. Rhona had wandered into it once.

"Hurry up!" Colette had been saying. "Correct your stitches afore—"

She'd jumped nervously when Rhona entered, then executed a bow and turned to help the girl with her embroidery.

Perhaps Rhona would have stayed, but Edwina's wide eyes seemed to welcome her no more than her sister's narrow gaze, and if she were asked to join them, the truth would be out. She had fled the room in a matter of moments.

But on the third day Lady Norval left Claronfell for the village, and since the marquis was still about, this seemed the ideal time to draw the girls out of themselves. When Rhona ventured into the nursery, however, she found the room empty.

She considered asking about their whereabouts, but she did not altogether trust Colette. She was too bonny, too pert, too perfect. And if the girls were where they were not supposed to be, she dare not cause trouble for them.

Eventually she found them in the stable.

They sat in the dirt like two wayward urchins, their hands soiled and their shoes muddy. They were playing with twists of straw that vaguely resembled steeds.

"So there you are," Rhona said. She thought her tone was lilting and gay, but the girls reared back in unison as if flogged by the same whip. And in that instant Lachlan stepped out from behind a stall, a straw horse in his own capable hand.

"Ye've frightened 'em," he said, then leaned a brawny shoulder against the wall and glanced down at the girls as if they shared some secret to which she was not privy. "But ye needn't fear, lassies, she's not so fearsome as she appears." There was humor in his tone, but Catherine wrapped her arm about her sister's shoulder, pulling her to her feet.

"I'm not afraid of her," she said, backing away and tugging her sister with her. "Even though she be Satan." And with those words she broke and ran.

Rhona felt her face redden, but she could do little more than stare after them. Lachlan did the same, startled from his leisurely stance to watch them fly toward the house.

"I've no idea why I worried," he said, not losing his rough accent. "For it's a way with the children, you 'ave."

"She's not a child," Rhona said, feeling flushed. "She's the devil incarnate."

"Truly?" He gazed after the girls as if deep in thought, then turned that same expression on her. "And 'ere I be thinkin' that she reminded me of another I know."

Rhona drew herself up to lambaste him, but the truth of his words seared her. Maybe this Catherine was not so different from herself.

*   *   *

"You play the gitarn beautifully, dumpling."

The solar was filled with candlelight this evening. It glowed off the women's flaxen hair and gleamed like sunlight on the copper strings of Rhona's tall, slim-necked instrument. She set it aside and grinned at the foolish endearment. It seemed at times that there was happiness everywhere, and never more than when they'd christened each other with ridiculous pet names. "But not so well as Tart," she said.

The three of them laughed in unison, but a draft wafted mysteriously into the chamber. Chill it was, and somehow frightening.

"What was that?" Rhona whispered.

" 'Tis Grandmother. She warns us of something."

"Aye." A man stepped into the doorway. His face was shadowed, but his intent was not. Evil exuded from him.

Rhona reached for her weapon, but no sheath adorned her hip. Indeed, there was naught there but a silver girdle against the rich velvet of her gown. And in that moment her sisters screamed.

Rhona awoke with a start. Reality came more slowly, but she breathed deeply, settling her mind.

It was well past midnight. She'd been at Claronfell several days now, and though her disguise seemed well accepted, she had learned little, though she had spent some time in clandestine investigation. The strongroom stored Claronfell's treasures and seemed the place most likely to house any damning documents the marquis might possess. But it had shed no light on the situation. Indeed, it had given her nothing . . . except the key now hidden beneath her cape. The key that had opened none of the trunks in his strongroom and none of the containers in his bedchamber.

Although Rhona was doing her best to maintain her frail demeanor, she had not been idle since arriving there. Still, time was running out, but the house had long since gone silent, and now was the time for action.

Crafted of impenetrable rock and mortar, Claronfell's walls were several feet thick and would buffer all but the loudest sounds. Still, Rhona stood at her door for a long while, making certain not the slightest noise would be heard as she opened it and stepped into the hall. A corbel of candles flickered in the corridor around the corner, and she slipped toward it, making not a whisper of sound as she set her taper to a flame.

Circumstances would be much simpler if she knew what she searched for, but she did not. There had only been rumors that the marquis held a grudge against the rogue brothers. Whispers of planned evil. Still, she would learn the truth for she had impending evil against the lady of Evermyst. Indeed she had tried to implement that evil, and for that she would make recompense.

The house was dark. From somewhere down the hall, she thought she heard a woman giggle. She froze and waited, but nothing happened. No one accosted her. Not a soul spoke. She hurried on. The library housed innumerable books and parchments. Perhaps that was where Lord Robert kept his private papers, but she would check his solar first. Situated on the south side of the second floor, it offered much light during the day. Now it was dark and silent. The latch lifted with a groan. She held her breath, waited, then easing the door open, stepped inside and closed herself in.

Setting her candle aside, she slipped the key from beneath her cape and glanced hastily about. The desk was spindly-legged and simply made. Its surface held little more than an ink-blotched quill and a soft piece of rolled vellum. One glance at the flowing script told her it was of no importance.

A buckler hung on the wall, and on a small console near the door, an ancient helm was displayed. A tapestry, rich in reds and browns, hung near the window. Hurrying to it, she pushed it aside, but there was naught behind it except chilly wall. She spurred her gaze about the room, and then, nestled in the shadows of the writing desk, beside the cushioned stool, she spied a narrow trunk. It was made of rowan wood, bound in leather, and secured by a solid metal lock. Holding her breath, she drew out the small trunk and set it silently upon the desk. It opened with barely a sound.

Inside, she found a myriad of odd items—a silk sleeve, a worn rosary, a score of other feminine articles, and a dozen rolled parchments. Shifting through the bizarre personal effects, she hauled out the scrolls. The first was written in a woman's hand. Rhona's brows lifted in surprise as she read it, for though it was intimately personal, 'twas obviously not from his late wife. She shoved it quickly aside and unrolled the next. It was similar to the first and signed with naught but an *I*. So, MacGowan had been right about the marquis's wandering eye. Indeed, it was entirely possible that the trinkets that littered the trunk were tokens of his conquests while—

Hell's saints!

Her fingers trembled against the vellum just opened. She skimmed to the bottom, but the missive was unsigned. She read from the top, skipping over the mundane solicitudes and reading:

> *Per your request, I have begun some inquiries, and have learned a bit of information that you might find of interest. I have it on good authority that the MacGowan rogues will hold a gathering at the stronghold of Evermyst. 'Tis said it will celebrate St. Crispin's Day and the birth of Lord Ramsay's young heir. By all accounts, 'twill be a large assemblage. In fact, 'tis rumored that James himself may make an appearance.*
>
> *Mayhap this would be just the opportunity you had in mind.*

There were a few more sentences, but none that held her interest. She rolled it up, slipped its ribbon back into place and rummaged rapidly through the others. None were in the same hand until she had nearly completed her search. This note was no more than two simple sentences.

I have done as requested. All plans are set.

Although Rhona searched the trunk frantically, there was nothing else.

From somewhere far away, she thought she heard a scratch of noise. She jerked her head up, but no other sounds alerted her to danger. One more quick search assured her there was nothing else to be found. Rapidly replacing the scrolls, she locked the trunk and shoved it carefully back in place.

Once again she pinned the key out of sight, blew out her candle, and stepped silently into the hall.

There was a whisper of sound behind her. Fear stroked her neck. She turned, but a hand streaked out, covering her mouth and pulling her roughly backward. She tried to spin around. An arm encircled her waist. Raw instincts made her strike with her elbow, driving it hard into his ribs. There was a grunt of pain, then:

"Damnation, Rhona, it's me."

She stilled, rolled her eyes sideways and felt the hand slip off her mouth.

Lachlan stood before her, slightly bent over his injured ribs.

"What the devil are you doing here?" she hissed.

"Me?"

Candlelight flickered across his face. His eyes were dark and angry. He wore naught but black hose, and he rubbed his chest where she had struck him. His feet were bare, as were hers, and without the hindrance of her shoes she had been absolutely silent.

"How did you know I was here?"

"Perhaps I heard you," he said.

She shook her head, then stopped, remembering the sound of a woman's laughter. "Where were you?"

Even in the darkness she could see his eyes narrow. "'Tis a strange time to be inquiring about *my* whereabouts, laddie, when you are creeping around like a thief in the good marquis's private chambers."

They were standing but inches apart.

"So you were with Colette."

There was a moment's pause. "Are you thinking I've dallied with the maidservant?" he asked.

She pursed her mouth. "I would not care if you dallied with the marquis himself."

He stepped closer. The anger in his eyes had been replaced by another emotion. Something less sinister, but no less dangerous.

"You think I've slept with another," he said and, reaching out, brushed a wisp of hair from her face.

She pushed his arm away. "I care not what you do."

"You lie," he said, and reached out again. She swatted his hand aside and longed for her dirk.

"Are you jealous?" he asked.

"Nay," she said, and backed away. Absolute silence filled the hall. Time stretched into the blackness. Her nerves stretched with it. "Were you with her?"

"With who, lass?" he said and, with careful casualness, leaned his shoulder against the plastered wall.

If not for her need for secrecy she would have surely struck him. "Colette," she hissed.

He said nothing for a long while. She cursed him in silence.

"You'd best be careful, lass," he said finally. "For if one watches your window closely enough, one can tell when you leave your chamber."

She drew a careful draught of air. "You were watching me window?"

"I can see you quite clearly, except when the fat marquis blocks the light from the hall."

Jealousy? A despicable titter of glee soared through her. "In truth, champion, he is really quite charming."

"Charming!" A muscle worked in his jaw, but he relaxed it with a seeming effort. "Did you know he ordered a leech to open his wife's dead body?"

"What?" she hissed.

"They took out the babe."

"Mayhap he hoped to save it."

"'Twas three months early," he said. "But it was a lad."

"How do you know this?"

"I have a good deal of time whilst you flirt with your warty nobleman, lass."

She raised her chin. "I have no reason to suspect he is anything but what he says."

"Is that why you are sneaking about in his private chambers then, because you find him irresistible?"

" 'Tis none of your affair why I am here."

"I beg to differ, lass," he said. "For though the marquis acts too daft to be dangerous, 'tis said he is in league with the English king."

She stared at him in silence as a thousand thoughts whipped through her head: Evermyst, the rogues, the king! Was Lord Robert planning some evil against the crown?

"I but wonder where your loyalties lie."

"If you think you cannot trust me, you've no reason to stay," she said, and turned away.

He caught her arm and pulled her back toward him. "If only 'twere true," he gritted.

"Let me go, MacGowan," she said, and tried to push him away.

"God knows I have tried," he said and moved closer. His fingers touched her throat. Beneath her hand, his chest felt as hard and smooth as iron. Her breathing became labored. His lips brushed hers.

"Whore!"

Rhona ripped away from him. A blade flashed in MacGowan's hand, but their enemy stood some yards away and was not yet tall enough to reach his chest.

"Catherine." He said her name softly and with that strange Welsh lilt. She stood in the doorway. Clothed in naught but a white night rail, she looked like a small solemn archangel.

"Lass." Rhona breathed the word. "Why—" she began, but her thoughts shifted. "How did you escape your room?"

"Why were you in my father's chamber?" the girl countered.

"I—your father asked me to fetch something for him."

She shook her head. "He is busy with another just now. You have come to do mischief."

"'Tis not what you think, lass," Rhona began, and took a step toward her. "I've but come to care for you."

The girl backed away. "You lie, just as she said you would."

"Who said?"

The girl shook her head. "You'll not hurt us! Not when I tell Father I've found you with another." Though she tipped her head toward MacGowan, she did not look at him as though she could not and still betray him.

"Why are you awake?" Lachlan's voice was quiet in the dimness.

Catherine blinked. She chewed her lip, glanced indecisively down the darkened hallway, and turned her gaze on him finally.

"Come lass, you know you can trust me," he said.

"She does not cry out of fear," whispered the girl.

Lachlan was quiet for a moment, then, "Your sister," he said.

"We are not afeared of her."

Absolute silence filled the space.

"You go to soothe Edwina," Rhona murmured.

The lass scowled.

"You've—" Rhona began, but Lachlan interrupted.

"What happened to your feet, Catty?"

Catherine glanced down, then shoved one bare foot behind her ankle. "Naught," she said, but the other foot was still visible and across the instep, welts stretched like writhing serpents.

"And your hands," he added, but she had already tucked them behind her back. His face was as sober as death. "Who struck you?"

"No one. I scratched them whilst running through the brambles." The words were defiant, but her eyes glistened.

"I did not think you were allowed to run barefoot," Rhona said, but Lachlan already was shaking his head.

"Nay. She is not," he said. "And thus the stripes. Is it not so, lass?"

The silence that stretched through the room was as heavy as death, but finally the girl spoke. " 'Tis none of your concern."

"Nay," he agreed, " 'Tis your father's concern."

Her mouth twitched.

"But he was the one who did it, wasn't he?"

She shook her head violently.

"Aye." He tightened his fist, and it was not until then that Rhona remembered he held a knife. " 'Tis just like a coward bastard to treat a child so."

"He would not do such a thing," Catherine whispered, and though she did not cry, her mouth twitched as though she endured some silent torture.

Rhona exhaled carefully and extended her hand. "Give me the knife, MacGowan," she said.

Chapter 21

Lachlan shifted slightly. He didn't like the look in Rhona's eyes. Didn't trust her in the least. Aye, he was certain she had come here for reasons other than the girls' best interests, but perhaps just now, she didn't remember those reasons. "What is it you have in mind?" he asked, and kept his voice carefully steady.

"As the girl said," murmured Rhona, not shifting her gaze to his. " 'Tis none of your affair."

He tried a placating smile. But he'd been wounded by this woman more than once, perhaps making his grin suspect. "I believe if you kill the good marquis, I may well—"

"The marquis!" she said. "Nay, 'tis the serving maid that mistreats her."

"Colette? You jest."

"Just because she is bonny, does not make her good," Rhona said. "Give me the knife."

"Take the child to bed," he said and tucked the blade firmly in his belt. "Your head will be clearer in the morn."

Rhona stared at him. Her body was absolutely still, and in her eyes there was anger, dark and deep and just under control. " 'Tis because of me."

"What's that?"

She did not glance at the girl. Indeed, it seemed almost as if she could not bear to. "I knew something was amiss," she said. "But I did not question. Neither did I interfere."

"Demands would have been to no avail in this situation."

She smiled. It was not a soothing expression, probably no better than his own. "I can be quite convincing."

"Against the marquis and all he holds dear?"

She looked as tense as a bent bow, quivering with energy just waiting to be loosed. "Does Colette share his bed?" she asked, and it was strange, for her voice still contained that maidenly tone she had adopted since their arrival there.

"I know not," he admitted. "But she has been given a fine chamber. I heard her giggling there and methinks sleep is not so amusing."

"Then he has reason to stand behind her," she admitted, "but my duty is still clear."

"You cannot force this hand, Rhona. They be his own get."

"Then what good is the training of a warrior?" she hissed.

"To right what wrongs you can."

"I can right *this* wrong! Give me the bloody knife," she demanded, and stepping forward, reached for it.

He stepped back in tandem and nodded past her. "And what of the girl?"

"What of her?"

"Look at her eyes, lass."

Rhona glared at him, but turned finally.

Catherine stood like a pillar, not moving a hair, her eyes as wide as salt cellars.

"Who are you?" she whispered.

The world stood still, awaiting an explanation.

"This is the Lady Rhona," Lachlan said. "Tender nursemaid sent to care for you and your wee sister."

Catherine took a step to the rear and Lachlan turned his attention back to Rhona.

She took a deep breath, seemed to steady herself, and addressed the child. "Who struck you, lass?"

"No one," she whispered.

" 'Twas Colette, was it not?" Rhona asked.

"Nay."

A muscle jumped beside Rhona's full mouth. "Are your legs welted also?"

No response was forthcoming, but the girl's eyes were as bright as starlight, her mouth pulled tight in her pale face.

"So 'tis difficult to walk," Rhona said.

For an eternity, the girl stood absolutely still, but finally she nodded.

Rhona turned slowly toward Lachlan and upon her face was an expression that was beyond defining. An expression that said she had no alternatives.

He tightened his own hand on the knife's hilt. Anger broiled eerily in his gut, but he reminded himself with some sternness that, against all odds, he was to be the sensible one here. "You do not know who to blame."

Her mouth twitched with anger. She pursed her lip as though to still any outward signs of her struggle, and there in that second she looked so much like the child that he was left speechless. "Then what would you suggest . . . champion?" she asked, and let the title hang there as though it could not possibly be connected with him.

He ignored the insult. "Perhaps it as she says," he suggested. "Perhaps the welts be caused by naught but brambles."

"I heard the maid threaten the girls. And yet you would defend her," Rhona said. "Because she is female and because she is bonny."

He tightened his grip on the knife again, then loosened it with an effort. "Ye cannot kill her."

"Then what do you suggest?" she asked.

"We could bring it to the attention of the king."

"The king has troubles of his own!" she rasped.

"Troubles? What troubles?" he asked, but Rhona had already turned her attention away.

"Catherine." Her voice was low and commanding. "You must return to your room now, and say naught of this to your father."

The girl shook her head and backed slowly away.

Rhona frowned. "If you do as I say, I vow to protect you."

Catherine narrowed her eyes and took another cautious step to the rear. "Nay, you will not," she said. "You will but sleep with me father and hope for his fortune as all the others do."

"I assure you, I do not want his fortune."

"Aye you do. You are the devil," she said and, pivoting on her heel, leapt for the door. Her night rail billowed behind her like a windblown cape.

Lachlan bound after her, but in that instant, he felt the knife leave his belt.

"Nay!" he rasped, but Rhona had already thrown the thing. It flew toward the girl, spinning end over end.

Catherine stumbled to her knees and Lachlan almost cried out, but 'twas then that he realized the truth. She was uninjured. Only her gown was pierced, pinned to the wall behind her. She turned in bewilderment toward the reverberating knife.

"Catherine." Rhona's voice was no longer high pitched nor maidenly. Indeed, it was little more than a growl. "I can protect you."

The girl glanced back at Rhona and swallowed hard. Seconds ticked into forever. Her eyes were as wide as the heavens, and her nod was barely perceptible.

"But you must do as I say," Rhona ordered.

Another tiny nod.

"Do you trust me?"

She did not quite seem up to nodding this time, but remained frozen in place, still on her knees, with her scrawny calves bare and welted beneath her upswept gown.

Rhona's eyes snapped as she turned her attention back to the lassie's face. "You do not fear me, do you?"

Silence stretched out around them.

"Do you?" she asked again.

"Good Lord!" Lachlan said and pacing forward, ripped his blade from the wall. "The girl's not daft, Rhona. Of course she fears you." Shoving his dirk under his belt, he helped the child to her feet. Beneath the night rail, her bony wrist felt as frail as a swallow's wing. He clenched his jaw and dropped her arm, lest anger beset his good sense.

"Catherine," he said, keeping his voice steady. " 'Tis the truth I need from you now. Can you give me that?"

She straightened her back. Dark, haunted shadows were etched beneath her enormous eyes. "I am not a liar," she said.

He watched her face. There was pride there, so deep it seemed he could drown in it.

"Nay," he said. "You are not. Though the truth does not lessen your pain, I think. So I ask you, will you keep our secret hidden?"

Her face was as solemn as sin. For a moment she shifted her gaze to Rhona, then back. "Why are you here?" she whispered.

A lie would be handy now, but it seemed like sacrilege to sully her trust. "Is it the truth you want, lass?"

She nodded.

"I am here because Lady Rhona is here. I've is no other reason."

"And why is she here?"

The truth was becoming painful. "I do not know."

Her gaze flitted to Rhona and back again. "Can you not ask her?"

"I have asked," he admitted. "But she can be . . ." He searched for the proper word. ". . . stubborn sometimes."

The child absorbed that for a moment, then nodded solemnly, as if she understood all that was said and much that was not. "But still you love her."

"*Lass.*" He forced a chuckle and refused to glance at Rhona. "I did not say I love her," he said, but the girl was already turning toward the warrior maid.

"If I am silent . . ." she whispered. A dozen emotions flitted across her elfish face before she shoved her weathered mask back into place. "Will you teach me to use a knife?"

Her feet and hands were welted. Her forehead was bruised, and her expression tortured. "Why?" Rhona asked.

Catherine lifted her chin. It was small and pointed and pale. "Will you teach me?"

Rhona's answer was slow and cautious, but it came finally. "Aye."

The girl nodded and turned away.

The torn edge of her night rail dragged behind her.

"Lass," said Rhona, still seeming deep in thought. "I am sorry for your gown."

Catherine flitted her eyes backward. The trace of fear skittered across her face, but she lifted her chin and pursed her mouth, vanquishing any unwanted emotion with little seeming effort. "You will teach me?" she repeated.

Rhona frowned. "You have me vow."

Not another word was spoken. She slipped from sight as silent as a wraith.

"She does not trust me own word," said Rhona.

"She dare not," said Lachlan, and found some solace in the grip of his knife before turning to her again. "Why have you come here, Rhona?"

Quiet settled softly around them. "I cannot tell you," she murmured finally. It was the closest he had ever come to the truth, the first time she hadn't maintained that she had come for either the marquis or the children. Which was wise, for he had never seen a woman with less maternal ability. "But I will not let them suffer because of me," she vowed.

"I thought we had agreed not to kill anyone this night."

"Do you think that is all I am good at?" she asked.

He didn't answer directly. "You have another plan?"

Anger sparked like embers in her eyes. "The maid deserves to die."

"The lass denied Colette's part in this."

"She lied."

"You do not know that, and you cannot kill her even if 'twere true."

She raised one brow. "I do not like being told what to do."

"I shall keep that in mind. What are your plans?"

Her eyes narrowed. "Perhaps if I talk to her—"

"If you threaten her, the marquis will hear of it. 'Twould be better to kill her."

"Me own thought exact—"

"But you cannot."

"Then what do you suggest?" Her tone was rife with frustration, her expression tortured.

He shook his head. "I?" Perhaps the frustration came through in his own tone. He lowered his voice and began again. "I do not even know why we are here."

She drew a deep breath and stared into the distance, past him, toward something he could not determine. Duty, perhaps. But what duty he could not guess.

"Then 'tis up to me to find a way," she said.

"What have you in mind?"

She glanced at him from the corner of her eye. "There will be no blood."

"Not poison!"

"Hell's saints, MacGowan, I'm not about to poison her!" she hissed.

He shook his head. "I can think of nothing else."

"That is because you underestimate me."

"I doubt that," he said. "I still have me scars."

"And you are strangely obsessed with those little wounds."

He snorted, but she was already turning away. He caught her by her arm. "What will you do now, lass?"

Their gazes met and fused.

"I am about to return to me own bed," she said. "Alone."

He raised a brow. "I hadn't even considered an alternative," he said. "Not for several seconds."

She was holding her breath, and it seemed foolish to waste that effort, so he kissed her. Desire roared through him, but he stiffened his resolve and forced himself to be casual. "Well?" he asked again and slipped his fingers down her jaw to her throat. If felt as smooth as steel beneath his hand.

"I cannot," she whispered.

He kissed her neck where her pulse throbbed hard and fast. "Cannot what?"

"Sleep with you," she sighed, and despite himself he was hopefully flattered for the breathy sigh she made, for it sounded almost like disappointment.

He kissed her again, then forced himself to be content, to back away, to take no more risks. "I meant about the lassies," he said.

"Oh." She collected herself with some effort and now more than ever he longed to pull her into his arms and take the risks that needed taking. "I knew that," she said.

Seeing her uncertain and nervous was like magic. "Have you any idea how bonny you are, lass?"

She shook her head. Her eyes were as solemn and large as the child's had been.

"Irresistible," he said.

"Then why do you?"

"What?"

She cleared her throat. "Why do you resist?" she whispered.

She wanted him! The truth dawned like sunrise, and there was nothing he could do but pull her back into his arms. Once again, there was fire against fire. Her fingers were in his hair. Her other hand gripped his buttocks.

But a noise whispered in the hallway. They froze, neither breathing. Footsteps paused, then passed. An eternity followed before she spoke.

"I must return to me chambers."

"Aye," he agreed. "But promise me you will be cautious."

"They will not hear me."

"I meant with the marquis. You do not know what you are dealing with. A man who would mistreat his own child has no soul."

The manor went silent. "Do you bed her, Mac-Gowan?" she asked.

He shook his head. "How could you believe that when I have had you?"

She watched him closely in the darkness. "Because you refuse to believe she is to blame."

He tightened his grip on her arm. "Vow you'll not do anything foolish."

She nodded finally, her expression solemn. "Aye," she agreed. "Nothing foolish."

Chapter 22

Though the night was long and fitful, morning dawned as usual. With help from one of the maids, Rhona dressed in an ivory gown she had taken from Nettlepath's coffers. Perhaps it was well out of vogue, but Rhona was unconcerned, for the bodice was cut square and low and would surely catch the marquis' eye.

Dressed in a yellow and black doublet with puffed and slashed sleeves, Lord Robert was already seated on his ornate chair. His sister was some distance away, looking small and demure. A few inches from her, Edwina sat in her elevated chair, her eyes unnaturally bright. As for Catherine, she was there also, but her face was closed, her emotions unguessed.

"Ahh," said the marquis and rose to execute a graceful bow. His hose were a vivid green. "There is our bonny maid now. I trust you slept well, my lady."

"Aye, my lord," Rhona said. Keeping her gaze off the children, she lowered her lids and willed a blush. She was certain it didn't appear, but when she glanced up, he was smiling at her, so perhaps she didn't appear too ferocious. "I slept well indeed."

"I am glad to hear it," he said, and motioned for Colette to fill her goblet.

Lady Norval remained silent as she tasted her watered ale.

Edwina received the same, but Catherine's cup remained empty, as did her plate.

Rhona glanced at it, then at Colette. "You've forgotten the girl," she said.

The maid lowered her eyes. "Young Catherine asked to be allowed to fast this day."

Rhona's heart clenched. "Fast?" she said.

"Aye," Lady Norval said, and shifted her gaze quickly to her brother and back. "In atonement for her sins. 'Tis naught to concern yourself with. Do you fast, Lady Rhona?"

Rhona ignored the question and managed a smile. "What sins has she committed?" she asked.

The baroness glanced at the serving maid. "I am told she rent her gown during the night just past."

Anger and guilt burned in equal amounts in Rhona's gut.

"Have you any idea how that might have happened, Lady Rhona?" Lady Norval inquired, her voice barely a whisper.

Colette dimpled as she offered the baron a platter of cold venison.

"Me?" Rhona asked, and lowered her gaze from the servant. She lifted her knife. It felt lovely in her hand, but she forced her grip to remain light. "Nay," she said, and hated herself with a burning scorn. "I know naught of any mishap."

"You are certain, Lady Rhona?" Colette asked, her bonny brow furrowed with concern. "I thought I heard a noise in the hall."

"I am certain!" Rhona snapped then lowered her eyes and softened her voice. "I fear I sleep far too soundly to be roaming about at night."

"The sleep of the innocent," said the marquis, and patted her hand.

Rhona managed a smile.

"Indeed," murmured the baroness. "Blessed are the innocent."

Lord Robert smiled at his sister. "We were all innocent once," he mused, then seemed to pull himself from his reverie. "But what of you, Lady Rhona? I will be hawking this day. Would you care to accompany me?"

"I am honored, my lord," she said, "but surely I should see to the children."

"Nonsense," he said. "My sister thrives on the opportunity to see to my progeny. Hence we might as well take advantage of her presence here while it lasts."

Guilt pressed upon Rhona like a heavy weight. She could feel Catherine's accusatory glare on her face, but she did not glance toward the child, for duty was also a millstone against her back, and she dare not toss it aside. Instead, she flitted her eyes up to meet the marquis's.

"Certainly," she said. "If your lady sister will be here to see to the lasses."

"Of course," said Lady Norval. "I will enjoy their company, as always."

* * *

A myriad of worries nagged at Rhona. What was she to do about Catherine? Aye, it had seemed simple enough a few hours ago; she would demand the truth and right the wrongs, but after a sleepless night, she knew she could not risk such foolishness. Nay, she had come to garner information, and she could not risk being sent away. Thus, she must be cautious with her questions to the marquis, must learn if he knew the truth—or indeed, if he cared enough to be rid of his lover if it were she who caused the abuse. But he was easily distracted, and her questions regarding Colette went virtually unanswered. Still, perhaps her plan would work, for his gaze oft followed her, and he was wont to touch her whenever the opportunity presented himself. Maybe if she aired an ultimatum he would be rid of the girl.

Finally the day was past, and they returned to Claronfell. Behind them, the falconers brought the birds and the prey that had been killed.

Evening was beginning to fall around them when they halted their mounts near the house. Sidesaddle was a foolish and dangerous way to ride, but her borrowed palfrey was a sleepy beast, and not one to challenge her ability.

Lachlan exited the stable and strode up to hold her horse's head. Beneath the foolish droop of his tam, his expression was inscrutable. She avoided his eyes completely as the marquis strode forward to help her dismount.

"Here you are, my dear," Lord Robert said and, setting his hands to her waist, lifted her carefully down.

"Well . . ." She cleared her throat and glanced to the side, but she was trapped between her mount's barrel and the marquis. "It has been a lovely day." Behind her, the palfrey cocked a hip and sighed sleepily.

"It has indeed," agreed Lord Robert. His hands remained on her waist. From the corner of her eye she could see Lachlan's face darken.

"There is no need for it to end so soon," said the marquis and, relinquishing his hold on her waist, gently grasped her fingers. "I have not yet shown you my gardens."

There was slight movement behind Lord Robert's back. Startled, the horse grunted and sidestepped away.

Turpin scowled, and Lachlan smiled.

"Daft beastie," Lachlan said. "'E was crowding the lass."

The marquis turned back to Rhona, who smiled demurely as she tugged her hand from his grip and escaped into the open space.

"You have indeed been generous with me, my lord," she said, "but I have left the children all day and—"

"And a few minutes more will not harm them."

If only she were certain of that.

"Come with me," he said and, lifting her hand to his mouth, kissed her knuckles. "Humor an old man just this—"

"I 'ates to be worryin' ye, lassie," Lachlan interrupted. "But I fear one of yer steeds is not feeling 'is best."

"Truly?" She raised her gaze to his, but if there was concern in his face, she could not tell, for since their arrival at Claronfell, his expression looked as vacuous as the air.

"Aye," he said. "'E keeps cockin' 'is tail, but 'tain't naught ta show fer it if ye tek me meanin'. Perhaps ye'd best see to 'im."

"What's this?" asked the marquis, and laughed. "If

the steed is ill, my horse master will care for it. Go to the stable and tell Peter he is to give the lady's steeds the utmost attention."

MacGowan stood unmoving for a moment. He was still slumped in the manner he had adopted for Claronfell, but there was something in his eyes that boded ill. Rhona held her breath.

The marquis was not so astute. "Go," he commanded, and with a brief bow, Lachlan turned away, taking her mount down the hill toward the stable with him.

"Meanwhile," said the marquis, and reached for her hand again, "I will be giving you *my* utmost attention."

"You are too kind," she said.

He laughed as he tucked her hand beneath his arm. "The face of a queen and the voice of a dove. 'Tis easy to be kind to one so bonny."

"Surely you flatter me, my lord."

He stared down at her as they walked along. "If I didn't know better, lass, I would almost think you believe your own words."

Her heart fluttered. "What?"

He laughed, apparently at her abrupt tone. "It almost seems that you do not realize how striking you are. Tell me, sweet Rhona, how have you escaped the marriage block so long? Indeed, I would think you would wish for children of your own by now."

"Surely there is time yet for that," she said. "But when I heard about your girls, left motherless at such a tender age . . ." She forced a shudder. It felt like the shiver of an aging cow to her, but perhaps he did not think it seemed odd, for he wrapped his arm about her back and pulled her closer.

"You're not to worry yourself about them, my dear. They have been well attended since their mother's passing."

This was her opportunity then. A gift sent from heaven. "I've been meaning to speak with you about just that," she said.

His hand slid down her arm. "Have you now?"

She stopped and turned toward him, hoping the movement would cause him to release her arm, but she was disappointed. "Perhaps . . ." She smiled tremulously. "I do not mean to offend you, my lord."

"Nay," he said and, touching his fingers to her lips, traced the crease between them. "Lips so lovely could never offend me. What have you to say, my dear?"

"Perhaps things are not just as they seem."

A light shone in his eyes and fear sparked in her heart. She hurried on, praying he did not suspect her of being aught but what she appeared—a mousy maid with naught to do but ply her pitiful hand at seducing a marquis.

"That is to say, Catherine's welts—"

He shook his head, his brow creased. "It began the very day her mother died. She wanted a brother so badly." He paused and closed his eyes for a moment. "Indeed, I myself yearned for an heir. I do not deny it, and mayhap 'tis my fault. Mayhap she knew of my yearnings, and wanted it all the more to make me happy. I'm not sure. But this I know; she blames herself for her mother's death."

"You truly believe she abuses herself?"

His expression was anguished. "If I could change her thoughts, I would," he vowed. "I am a marquis. Wealthy, powerful." He tightened his fist. "Skilled with every kind of weapon. And yet . . ." His palm fell open. "I cannot seem to help her."

If he was acting he was very accomplished. "I am sorry, my lord," she said, and was surprised at her own earnestness. She'd never had a father that truly cared, and seeing it in another made her heart twist.

"Perhaps your gentle presence here will help her."

Guilt seemed to come from all directions these days. Perhaps she was a fool to be here. Then again, just because he cared for his daughters did not mean that he was not planning some evil against the crown.

"In truth, my lord," she said, careful now, and admittedly uncertain. "I am not altogether sure that Catherine abuses herself."

He stiffened. "What?"

"Think of it," she said. "It makes little sense for the girl to cause harm to herself. And she is so thin already. To miss another meal because of a torn gown . . ." She let her words fall away with a shrug.

He smiled. "So sweet you are, and young enough to believe you can set things right," he murmured, and touched her face. "Soft as a dream. Yet, not quite so, aye?" Brushing his knuckles across her cheek, he propped his fingers under her chin and lifted her face so that her eyes met his. " 'Tis very touching that you would wish to defend the girl," he said. "But to accuse my sister—"

"Nay. Not your sister!" she said. " 'Tis Colette I suspect."

"Colette!" he gasped.

She watched him closely and kept her tone carefully soft. "I understand she may be dear to you, but—"

"Dear to me?" he asked, then sighed. "Ahh, so you are not so naïve as you seem, my lady."

She forced herself to be calm, to *appear* just as naïve as she seemed. "She is a comely maid, my lord," she said. "And you are a . . . charming master."

"I admit that I have been lonely since my wife's passing," he said, and shook his head. "But if she is mistreating my children—"

"I am sure a gentleman like yourself will have no trouble finding a . . ." She searched wildly for the proper words. "Replacement."

She slanted her gaze up through her lashes toward him. Up ahead a stone archway frowned down at her.

" 'Tis certainly good to hear," he said and smiled wearily as he followed her. "But I can hardly dismiss the maid without proof."

"My lord—" she began, but he interrupted her.

"I will confront her this very evening. You have my vow, though I think you are far wrong."

"Thank you, my lord."

"You are most welcome. I but wonder if you might do me a favor in return."

"A favor!" she said, then lowered her eyes and reestablished her breathy tone. "You wish a favor, my lord?"

"Aye," he said, and gently pulled her to a halt in the archway. "If the truth be told, I wish many favors from you, Lady Rhona. But for now I only ask—"

"Your greatness!"

Lachlan's jarring voice seemed to yank the marquis away by his collar. He turned to glance over his shoulder. "What is it?" His tone sounded less than congenial now.

"Master Unter bade me tell ye that yer dinner be 'ot."

"What?"

"Yer dinner," he repeated. He shuffled his feet. They

looked strangely large and ungainly against the tight fabric of his hose. " 'Tis 'ot."

"Hot? Oh. Very well," he said, and returned his attention to Rhona.

MacGowan cleared his throat.

The marquis scowled as he turned again. "There is something else?"

"Aye." MacGowan had removed his tam and squeezed it between his huge hands like an uncertain lad before his master. "Beggin' yer pardon, yer grace, but do ye 'ave an answer?"

"What?"

Lachlan jumped. "I be but wonderin' when 'tis that you'll et?"

The marquis stiffened and Rhona stepped away from the arch.

"In truth, your lordship," she said, and found it difficult to stifle a grin, for seeing the MacGowan rogue acting like a cowed lowlander seemed far beyond belief. But then, the marquis had not seen him with a short sword in his hand. "I am quite famished and would eat soon rather than late."

Lord Robert's mouth softened slightly. "Very well then," he said, and nodded curtly toward Lachlan. "Tell Unter we shall dine shortly."

"Aye, yer grandness. Aye, I'll tell 'im just that, I will," MacGowan said, and without so much as glancing toward Rhona, bowed gracelessly and departed without another word.

Lord Robert glanced at her sheepishly. "Is your Welshman always your staunch defender?"

"Always, my lord," she admitted.

He laughed, brushed his lips across her knuckles and escorted her to the dining hall. It took only a moment for Rhona to realize both girls were absent.

"Shall I fetch the wee ones for dinner?" she asked, addressing Lady Irvette.

" 'Tis kind of you," said the older woman. "But that won't be necessary. They were fatigued. Colette already put them abed."

Without another meal? Rhona could feel her spine stiffening. "Perhaps they are still hungry."

"You are sweet to worry on their behalf," murmured Lady Norval, and smiled shyly. "But you needn't. Truly."

"In truth, sister," said the marquis. "Lady Rhona thinks Catherine is not abusing herself."

The baroness's eyes went wide, and when she drew her hand to her throat, it trembled slightly. "Whatever do you mean?"

The corner of his handsome mouth shifted slightly. "She thinks another is causing her injuries."

She turned her large, faded eyes on Rhona. "Who then?"

"Lady Rhona thinks Colette may be the source of our troubles."

"Colette?" Lady Irvette gasped. "Nay. Surely, it cannot be."

"I spoke to Catherine," Rhona said softly. "I am certain someone has struck her."

"You spoke to her?" asked Lady Irvette. "And she accused Colette?"

Rhona drew a deep breath. "I am not certain—"

"If I have been mistaken I shall never forgive myself," Lady Irvette whispered and rose awkwardly to her feet.

"Excuse me," she said. "I go to confront her this very moment."

Rhona awoke early, for worry had prevented her from sleeping well. She had checked on Edwina the previous night, and although the girl had moaned in her sleep, she had seemed well enough. Catherine's door, on the other hand, had remained locked.

She descended the stairs now, eager to talk to the girl.

"My bonny maid." The marquis stood at the bottom of the stairs. "You must have read my mind. I was just now thinking about you."

"Me, my lord?" She glanced past him toward the dining hall, hoping to catch a glimpse of her wards.

"Aye," he said. "I was wondering if you would favor a bit of a ride. There is a fair outside the village and I would appreciate your company."

"I thought I would spend some time with your daughters this morn."

He took her arm. "I've given a good deal of thought to our discussion last night, and I've spoken to Colette."

"What did she say?"

He shrugged. "She denied it."

"She lies!"

He raised his brows at her sharp tone. "I am pleased that you have taken so much interest in them in such a short time, but Colette is a trusted—"

"She is bonny and she is willing and—" She stopped herself abruptly. "I am sorry, my lord," she said and calmed herself. "But I think you may not be seeing things clearly."

He looked at her closely. "Perhaps you are right," he

said. "Perhaps I have been blind to what is right before my very eyes. Ride with me, Lady Rhona."

"I had planned to talk to your daughters."

"Perhaps now would not be the best time. Besides, my sister has things well in hand. Indeed, I have rarely seen her so angry as she was last night."

"So she spoke to Colette too."

"Aye, we both did."

"What did she say?" Rhona asked.

"The same that she told me."

She said nothing, but perhaps he saw her anger.

"Sometimes I think you are not so mild as you seem, sweet Rhona," he said.

"She struck your daughter," she said.

"Are you so certain the girl does not harm herself?"

"Aye, I am."

"Very well then," he said, and nodded. "Then you have my word, if the girl shows new bruises, I will relieve Colette of her duties."

"Thank you, my lord."

He smiled. "Come then," he said. "I will teach you much about my children's former years. Colette's departure will only increase your responsibility. I will arm you for the challenge."

She was tempted to refuse, but her mission loomed large in her mind, and in the end, she knew what she must do.

Although she had not expected it, the day was not completely unpleasant. They rode together down the winding avenue of the open countryside. The weather was fine with a scattering of clouds overhead and the lightest of breezes from the southwest. The field maple and beech trees were showing the first signs of yellow in their uppermost leaves and a hint of autumn brightened the air.

The fair was good-sized, brightly colored and noisy. Seated on his cloak in verdant grasses, a troubadour played a vielle. The copper wires shone in the sunlight and on his golden hair. Across the way a fishmonger hawked his wares while his wife shooed off a beggar.

For the most part, Lord Robert ignored it all, but when Rhona stopped to admire a small leather purse, he purchased it without hesitation and handed it to her with a bow.

"Nay, I cannot accept it," she said with sincerity, but he laughed away her objection and they continued on.

By nightfall, her emotions were in a strange tangle. She had not come here to enjoy herself. Hardly that, but during the day she *had* learned a good deal about the girls' formative years. It seemed Lorna was not a doting mother, and Catherine had sorely missed the lack of maternal attention. Lord Robert was oft busy elsewhere and had had little time to see to their needs himself.

'Twas a sad tale, and one close to Rhona's heart, but when she inquired about the girls' well-being that day, she learned they had eaten well. Still, she felt it necessary to check on them herself. Edwina was fast asleep, breathing softly through parted lips. Crossing the hall, Rhona found that Catherine's room remained unlocked. A spark of hope lit her heart. Hanging her lantern in the hall, she opened the door and pattered quietly to the girl's bedside. Catherine lay on her side, her lean face shadowed, her eyes closed, looking small and pale and lonely.

Strange emotions twined through Rhona, feelings she was not accustomed to, feelings she had no place for. Nay, not she, for she had deeds to do and little enough time to do them.

Who had written the letters to the marquis? What did they mean? Was evil truly bent on Evermyst, and if so, from what quarter? Were the fierce Munros involved? And how did the king figure into things? She was certain Lord Robert harbored some sympathy for King Henry of England, but was he bold enough to plan King James ill?

Her mind in a jumble, Rhona crossed the chamber and shut the door quietly behind her. At least she had done some little good here, she thought, for the girls looked undisturbed.

Her own room was empty and quiet. Stripping off her gown and undergarments, she slipped into her night rail and crawled into bed. Despite everything, she soon found sleep.

Laughter filled the lofty hall. Even Grandmother seemed content this night, for there were no whisperings, no drafts, only a feeling of contentment. Before the huge, open hearth, a wispy lass played chess with her uncle. Her hair gleamed red gold in the firelight.

"Check and mate," said the Highlander.

Her tiny mouth fell open. Her solemn eyes were wide. "You cheat!" she said, and he laughed as he left his stool and scooped her high into the air.

"Not I," he argued. "I would never. Ask your father."

"Da, your brother cheats," she accused.

Lachlan's eyes gleamed and his lips lingered on Rhona's for just a second longer before he rose to his feet. His hair shone like sable in the candlelight as he crossed the hall and took the child from her uncle's arms.

"Aye," he said, "that he does, wee Catherine."

"So you have returned."

Rhona awoke with a start, grappling for her dirk as she searched the room for the source of the voice, but she already knew who had breached her chamber.

"MacGowan," she said, and hoped her tone sounded casual. "Have you nothing better to do than climb me damned wall?"

Her fire had dwindled to little more than embers, but its erratic light gilded his hair to an amber hue. He shrugged as he stepped toward her. The tam was gone, as was his foolish expression and his inarticulate accent. He looked large and solemn and more than a bit dangerous in the moonlit darkness. "I thought perhaps you had forgotten the lassies and would spend the night elsewhere with your fat marquis."

She shrugged. "Indeed," she said, and faced him as he paced closer. "It was an enjoyable day. Lord Robert is quite good company."

"If you do not care that he abuses his children."

"In truth," she said, and scowled at her own thoughts, "he talked of little but them this day. I think he cares for them a good deal."

"Did he tell you that?"

She was tired and cranky and fidgety, with a thousand worries running like wild bullocks through her head. "Aye he did," she said, then hurried to add, "I'll admit that he has been neglectful, but when I suggested that Catherine is being abused, he assured me he would see to it."

"So he didn't know."

"Nay, he believed she was torturing herself. It seems she bears the blame for her mother's death. Lorna was not strong, and Catherine badly wished for a brother. The pregnancy was more than she could bear and—"

He chuckled. The sound was low and humorless in the deep night.

"You find something amusing, MacGowan?"

"Amusing?" he growled. "Nay. Pathetic! The marquis spews his lies and you would walk through fire to believe him. You have been here but three days. Yet *you* know the truth."

"You think he will refuse to relieve Colette?"

"Nay," he said, "I think he will gladly let her go."

"Then—"

"For the maid does not share his bed. She sleeps with another."

She felt herself go pale. "So you would vouch for her because she spreads her legs for you?"

His brows lowered. Anger rippled through the room. "'Tis Reeves she spends her nights with."

"You—" She halted. "Reeves? The humorless bailiff?"

"Aye. Apparently not every lass is enamored with your ugly marquis's grand title."

"Still . . ." Her mind was racing. "That hardly makes her innocent, Mac—"

"She was with him all last night and she did not touch the girl this day. Of that I am certain."

"That is because Lord Robert warned her—" She stiffened. "What do you imply?"

"Were you not so busy winning a fortune, you would know."

"Something happened to Catherine."

"Aye."

"But I checked on her." Her voice was pale. "All is well."

"You are right, I suspect. After all, you are the warrior, callused and hard. A lassie's blackened eye means little to you."

"Nay," she whispered.

He stared at her, his expression unreadable. "Call me a liar if you like, warrior, but the truth is in her face."

"Nay," she whispered again and, swinging her feet to the floor, lit an iron lantern and rushed from the room.

She swung the girl's door wide and in that instant Catherine sat up and blinked against the light.

But only one eye opened, for the other was swollen shut. Inflamed and blackened, it puffed away from her face in dark, ominous colors.

The girl said nothing. Instead, she sat absolutely silent, her expression inscrutable.

"Who did this to you?" Rhona growled.

The child said nothing.

"Did your father strike you? Tell me, Catherine, and I swear I'll make it right."

Another second passed in silence, then she turned her back and lay down.

Rhona stood frozen for some moments as her stomach roiled. Then, steadying her emotions, she pushed herself from the room and back down the hallway.

Aye, she had a mission. Aye, it was of the utmost importance, and aye, she had tried to protect the children while maintaining her disguise.

But she had failed. The child had suffered.

Rage boiled like black tar inside her.

Damn diplomacy!

Chapter 23

The lantern flame wavered as Rhona dropped it onto the floor. It hissed and went out, but she failed to notice, for she was already flinging open her trunk.

"So you saw," said MacGowan.

She didn't answer, but dug furiously to the bottom of the chest, tossing garments aside as she did so. She found them in a moment—her leather hose and dark tunic.

"Lass." His voice was less certain now. "What is your plan?"

She was already tearing off her night rail.

"Rhona!" he said and grabbed her arm. "What are you doing?"

"I'll tell you this much!" she hissed. "I am not being diplomatic."

"Don't be foolish."

"Foolish!" she snarled and snatched her arm from his grasp. " 'Twas foolishness to wait so long."

"What are your plans?"

She didn't answer. Her hose were already in place. In a second she had slipped her tunic over her head and belted on her sword. She was once again Hunter the warrior. Hunter the man.

"Rhona," he said, and caught her arm again. "I'll not let you do this."

"Won't let me?" Her dirk was in her hand. It felt lovely and right and proper. "I go to find answers, Mac-Gowan. Stop me now if you can, but know this, if they see you here you will ruin everything and the girl will suffer all the more."

He stared at her for the briefest moment, then backed away. She thrust her knife into her belt, crammed her helmet onto her head, and flew down the hall. In a moment she was at the marquis's door.

It sprang open beneath her hand. She charged inside, sword drawn, but the room was empty.

She turned a circle, searching. He wasn't there. Rage boiled anew as she leapt into the hall. Throwing open Lady Irvette's door, she rushed inside.

"Who struck the child?" she hissed.

A low fire crackled in the hearth. A candelabra gleamed on the crossed swords above the bed. The baroness sat up. "Who's there?" she asked, but her voice was neither mousy nor restrained, and her breasts gleamed bare in the firelight.

"I'll have answers," Rhona growled.

"Get out of this house!" ordered Irvette.

"Who is it?" rasped the marquis.

And in that instant, Rhona realized they were both

there, together in bed. She stepped back a startled pace, but found her balance in an instant.

"I am vengeance," she growled, and sweeping her sword sideways, sliced the candles in two. They fell hissing to the floor, burning for an instant against the carpet. "Come for retribution for your sins."

"She seduced me," whispered the marquis. "When we were yet children. I—"

"Shut up, Robert!" ordered Irvette. She was crouched on the mattress now, wholly naked and making no attempt to cover her nudity. "You're naught but a sniveling cur. Surrounded by tools of war, yet too weak to produce a single heir."

" 'Tis because we sin against nature," he hissed. "The devil has come."

Irvette laughed aloud. "There is no devil, you whimpering—"

"Who struck the child?" Rhona snarled.

"No one. She abuses herself," whined the marquis, but Rhona swept her sword forward, slicing through the coverlet between them. Feathers littered the air like wind-tossed snowflakes. " 'Twas my sister! She did it!"

"Damn your cowardice!" Irvette swore and leaping to her feet, tore a sword from the wall above the bed. Silver flashed in the moonlight. Pain ripped across Rhona's arm. She jumped back, blade in hand.

"Who are you?" snarled the baroness, and lunged again. Rhona leapt away, but Irvette came on, blade held high. She slashed out, but at the same moment, Rhona slammed her arm across the other's hand. The sword clattered to the floor, and Rhona pressed her blade to the woman's ribs.

"Did you strike the girl?"

"She is nothing! The bitch's foul seed and better off dead. 'Twill be myself that gives him an heir."

"Hear me!" Rhona warned. "And hear me good, for I'll not say it twice. If ever again you lay a hand to the wee ones, it was cost you dear."

Irvette strangled a laugh and drew herself straighter. "I am Lady Norval, Baroness of Hanstone, and there is no devil, just as there is no God."

"Aye, there is a devil and you are his handmaiden, but you've tortured the girl for the last time."

"Now!" Irvette shrieked, and in that instant Rhona sensed a movement behind her. She spun about, but Lord Robert was already striking. His sword gleamed in the firelight, and then, like a falling demon, he crumbled to the floor. MacGowan loomed dark and hooded behind him. Rhona spun back toward Irvette, grabbing her by the throat and shoving her up against the wall.

"Leave on the morrow and I will spare you."

The baroness clawed desperately at the warrior's hands, but through the gauntlets, Rhona felt not the slightest twinge. Indeed, she smiled as she squeezed harder.

"But if you stay, I swear by all that is holy, you will die bloody, and naught but hell awaits you."

Irvette's eyes widened as she gasped for breath. Against the wall her face shown a pale blue. Perhaps it was naught but a trick of the moon.

"What say you? Do you go or do you die?"

"I go!" The words were rasped and painful.

"And you'll not touch the lassies again. Not so long as your soul walks this earth."

"Damn you—" she swore, but it was so simple now to

tighten the pressure. She rasped for breath and struggled weakly. "Nay! Never."

It almost hurt to loosen her grip. In fact, Rhona held it a while longer. The baroness's legs jerked, then went still.

Rhona backed away, letting the body fall limply to the floor.

"Irvette," the marquis groaned from the floor.

Rhona spun about. " 'Tis your fault as well!" she hissed.

"Nay!"

"Aye," she said and, drawing her dirk, sent it quivering across his ear and into the floor beneath. "Next time 'twill be through your worthless skull!" she warned.

A flash of white shifted her attention. Catherine stood in the doorway, her face was pale and her one good eye was wide with terror.

The marquis twitched but did not rise. From a distant hallway, shouts were heard.

"Go," Lachlan ordered, but Rhona was caught in the girl's stare. Footfalls rushed nearer.

"Go!" Lachlan gritted again and grabbing her by the arm, pushed her toward the door. With one more glance at the girl, Rhona dashed down the hallway away from the footsteps. MacGowan followed, her cape billowing like a dark cloud around his giant shoulders.

A shout sounded from ahead. She turned wildly, searching for an escape route, but Lachlan grabbed her by the arm and dragged her into her own chamber.

"Take off your clothes," he ordered.

Blood pumped like alcohol through Rhona's veins. Wrapping her hand about the back of his neck, she kissed him with hot passion.

He dragged her closer still, crushing her lips with his before drawing abruptly back. "I'd gladly be your bloody spoils of war," he growled, "but either you hide your warrior garb or your damned mission will fail."

She came back to reality with a jolt and realized the marquis was yelling. Footsteps were running in all directions. Doors slammed open and closed.

She froze, listening intently, but his hands were already busy, snatching off her helmet, tearing off her tunic. She unlaced her hose and shoved them downwards.

Lachlan grabbed her discarded night rail and whipped it over her head, pinning her arms to her sides before pivoting away. Her cape billowed about him.

"What—"

"Shut up!" he ordered and bundling up her garments, tossed them out the window.

Voices clambered in the hall. Lachlan leapt for the window, jumped to the sill and nodded.

The plan burst in Rhona's head and she screamed as she pushed her arms into her sleeves. Her door slammed open, and in that moment MacGowan soared from sight.

Servants armed with candles and cutlery were pushed, quaking, into the room.

"Where is he?" someone sputtered.

"There! There!" she said and pointed shakily toward the window.

One intrepid servant hurried forward. The rest hung back, barely guarding the marquis.

"There he goes!" rasped the brave one, and then others streamed forward with the marquis behind.

"Seize him!" he shrieked.

The servants milled and gasped and finally bustled from the room. The place fell silent.

"What happened here?" rasped Lord Robert.

"I was asleep, then I was awakened," Rhona babbled and glanced shakily toward the window and away. "Big as a mountain he was, with black teeth and—"

Irvette stumbled into the doorway. Her face was gray and a lovely red bruise stretched like a rope burn across her neck.

"My dear Lord!" Rhona rasped and made the sign of the cross against her breast. "What happened?"

"'Twas Satan!" The words were little more than a croak from the lady's alabaster throat.

"The devil!" Rhona stumbled back, clutching her neck. "Whatever did he want with you?" she shrieked, but the baroness was already stumbling away and the marquis went with her, shouting for every door to be barred and every window secured.

Rhona stood in silence, breathing hard and willing away the tension. All in all it had gone quite well.

She flexed her wounded arm, turned toward her bed and stopped in her tracks.

Catherine stood in the doorway.

The silence was broken only by the marquis's distant shouts.

The child's gaze never faltered, then, "Do you want it back?" she murmured.

Rhona scrunched her gown to her bosom as if terrified beyond all reason. "What are you talking about, child?"

"The knife," she said and bringing her hand from behind her, hefted the blade she'd found stabbed into the floor. The blade that had skimmed past her father's ear just moments before. " 'Tis yours."

Silence descended, accented by distant shouts and the sounds of a hurried exodus.

"No," Rhona said, and held the child's gaze as she did so. " 'Tis my gift to you."

Dawn had not yet arrived when Lady Irvette's carriage rattled away from Claronfell. There were few explanations, perhaps because it was impossible for her to speak.

As for the marquis, he did not appear for the morning meal, but remained closeted away.

In fact, the stools around the table remained absolutely empty. Thus Rhona wandered from the dining hall to the nursery. Catherine's bed was empty too, so she hurried down the passageway to Edwina's room. The door was ajar, and from the hallway, she could hear two tiny voices whispering from within.

"There were noises in the night . . . Frightful noises." Edwina's voice was the tiniest scratch of sound.

"Aye." Catherine's was barely louder. "But you needn't fear. 'Tis past now. Go back to sleep."

" 'Twas the devil, wasn't it?"

"Nay."

"He will come again," Edwina's voice was rising to a low panic. "He will come and eat my liver just as Lady Irvette—"

"Nay," argued Catherine. "I will keep you safe."

"But Catty, your face!" she said, and began to cry softly. "He has already beaten you."

'Twas then that Rhona stepped into the room. The girls jumped like frightened hares, huddling together beneath the blankets, their fingers gripping each other like tiny birds' claws. She stopped where she was, her throat constricted.

"The devil is gone," she said simply.

They stared at her in silence. She shrugged. "He left." Still no response. "Forever," she added.

Silence again, then Edwina spoke very softly, as though her voice might stir the dead from their restless hiding place. "But Lady Irvette said he would come if I was disobedient like Catty. He would beat me, just as he did her."

"She is gone too," said Rhona, and carefully quieted her anger.

The girls glanced at each other then back at her. Their grip in each other's sleeves tightened slightly.

"She'll return . . ." began Catherine, her tone not daring to hope. "After the nooning?"

"She'll not be back," Rhona corrected.

"Perhaps the devil ate her," Edwina whispered. There was the whisper of hope in her tone.

Rhona stepped closer, her mind spinning. She knew nothing about easing a young girl's fears.

"You needn't worry, lass," she said. "God is watching—"

But in that moment a noise sounded from the doorway. She turned, expecting trouble, but it was only Mac-Gowan who shadowed the door.

"The devil did na want 'er," he said.

The wide eyes had turned to him. He smiled, and with that simple expression the room seemed to lighten somehow.

"He did not want her?" Edwina whispered.

"Nay. She was that bitter, she was."

"How do you know?"

"I spoke to 'im." He entered the room with easy casualness, his stride long and relaxed. "Afore 'e left."

"You spoke . . . to the devil?"

"Aye. I told him that an angel of the Lord guards these lassies and that there is no room for his evil here."

"But Catty's face," murmured Edwina. Her eyes were bright with unshed tears, her knuckles white against the coverlet.

A muscle twitched in Lachlan's cheek and Rhona threw herself into the breech.

" 'Twas not the devil who struck your sister, wee Edwina," she said, "but one of his minions, a person of flesh and bone. A person just like one of us, but evil."

Catherine seemed to have drawn into herself, but she spoke finally, her voice little louder than the silence. "She warned me not to tell. Said Edwina would suffer for it."

For a moment no one spoke. Rhona noticed that Lachlan's fingers tightened upon the hilt of his dirk, but finally he cleared his throat and loosened his grip. "Aye well, she be gone now," he said. There was a forced cheeriness to his tone, but his face was hard. "And the archangel 'as vowed to keep it so."

"Will he eat her gizzard?"

He laughed a little now. "Sooner than let 'er return, lass. But enough of this talk. I have been sent to fetch you down to break the fast."

And so the day began. The girls ate their fill while Lachlan looked on, and then, because the marquis was reported to have injured his leg in his "valiant defense of his home," Rhona suggested that they venture outside.

Edwina shook her small head vehemently. Catherine pursed her lips.

"You've no fondness for the out of doors?" Rhona asked.

Catherine's scowl deepened. Edwina spoke in a whisper.

"It rained," she said.

Rhona stared in bemusement and Catherine explained. "We might sully our gowns."

"Sully your gowns! Well, I should hope so," she said, and laughed.

"Filth is the devil's garden," Edwina quoted.

"But the earth is the divine Lord's playground," Rhona said.

Finally, dressed in their ugliest rags, they tripped through the endless gardens to the burn that babbled over its rocky bed toward the sea. Once there, they followed its wending course, their toes slithering in the mud as they went, and when they found a particularly lovely spot of muck, Rhona turned them loose to play.

Instead, they looked at her with eyes wide and faces wary.

"Play," she repeated, but Lachlan shook his head.

"Nay," he said. "These two wee ones are not the sort to waste their hours such. They 'ave been taught to work, have you not, lassies?" They were still clinging together like tiny spider monkeys. "So 'tis best to simply let 'em 'ave at it." Rhona stared at him, and he shrugged. "I am 'ungry, me wee lassies. Perhaps you could bake me a pie."

Edwina's little mouth circled. Catherine frowned before she spoke. "But we have no meat."

"Ahh, well, mayhap you'd best use mud, then."

"Mud?" Edwina whispered.

"Or twigs or grasses or whatever lies close t' 'and."

"You cannot eat twigs."

"You think not?"

Edwina shook her head. Catherine only stared.

"Then you have not yet been to Dun Ard."

No one spoke.

" 'Tis me father's . . ." He paused, seemingly remembering he was to be naught but a servant here. " 'Tis the castle where I used to labor before I came to serve Lady Rhona."

"They eat twigs there?"

" 'Tis like this, you see," he said. Narrowing his eyes, he leaned closer as if he were sharing some wondrous truth. "The lady of the keep is a great 'orse mistress, greater than all the lords of Christendom. 'er steeds eat like kings, but 'er subjects . . ." He shrugged. "Sometimes we 'ad to make do."

Catherine studied him as if he were some strange new creature, but Edwina spoke again, repeating the question that haunted her. "You ate twigs?"

He laughed as he straightened to his full height. "This I tell you, wee one," he said. "You make it . . . I will eat it."

They set to work finally, and although their movements were uncertain at first, they soon caught the spirit of the morning.

As for Rhona, she had never been adverse to filth, so she settled herself on a nearby hillock and scooped up the soil with them. In a matter of minutes they had three pies set atop a rock.

" 'Tis ready," whispered Edwina and turned her attention to Lachlan. Her dimpled hands dripped with slime.

He eyed their masterpieces with judicious sobriety, then, "Nay, they be not yet baked," he said, but just then the sun, seeming willing to play, skirted a bubbled cloud and shone down hot on the trio of pies.

"Well then," said Rhona, "they'll be done soon enough. What shall we do until 'tis time for Champion to sample the fare?"

Neither spoke, but from beneath her tattered gown, Catherine drew out the dirk she'd rescued the night before. Rhona met her gaze.

"Very well," she said finally, and thus the lessons began.

Although Edwina soon tired of tossing a sharpened stick into a circle of branches, Catherine practiced until her narrow arm shook and Rhona deemed she had had enough. Retracing their steps toward the house, they came upon the mud pies.

The girls stopped, eyeing the feast in tandem. Neither spoke for a long second, but finally Edwina lifted her gaze to Lachlan. The tiniest hint of a smile curved her soft lips.

"Look," she murmured. "Dinner is served."

Chapter 24

The days took on a singular cadence, for the marquis was busy nursing his injuries or an ale or both, and Lady Norval did not return, leaving Rhona to care for the girls. As for Lachlan, he rarely left their sides, but stayed close, acting as guard or jester as the moment demanded.

For Rhona this time was a revelation, like moments stolen from her secret dreams, like sunlight on her skin. The days were warm and lovely, the evenings irrevocably sweet, for it seemed almost as if they were a family—as if the girls were her daughters and the looming Highlander, her love.

As Lachlan finished his duties in the stables, Rhona laughed and tucked the girls into Catty's narrow bed.

"Aye," she said. "Now that you mention it, lass, Champion does indeed sound like a fine name for a steed."

"Then why does it belong to a man?" Catherine asked. "Is it because he came from a place with fine horses?"

"Nay," said Rhona.

"Is it because you ride him?" asked Edwina, who had mounted his shoulders just that day.

Rhona kept her fingers busy on the blankets and her eyes averted. "Of course not."

"Then it must be because he is your champion," said Catherine.

"There you are," said the marquis, and stepped into the room.

Rhona straightened with a start, then remembered to curtsy. "Aye, my lord, just seeing your daughters abed."

"Bed," he said. His words were slightly slurred. Since the night of the warrior's visit, he seemed inebriated more often than not. "What a fine idea."

"Aye," Rhona agreed. "I too am tired."

"You must have been busy indeed. I've barely seen a hint of you these past days. Where have you been hiding?"

"We were not hiding, my lord. 'Twas a bonny day. We ventured past the gardens to the river."

"So you are not afraid?"

"Afraid, my lord?"

"Of the bastard who broke into my house some nights hence."

Hell's saints, she had not even considered the fact that she should be afraid. "Oh," she said, and carefully lowered her eyes. " 'Twas a frightful thing. But nay, I do not fear, for I am certain you will protect me."

"Aye, and so I shall," he said and straightened slightly. He had changed since his sister's exodus, or perhaps it was only her perception that changed.

"I am but sorry your sister felt the need to flee," she
lied.

"She was always the frightened little mouse," he said.

Rhona's stomach turned at the thought of their
twisted lives. Still, there was no proof that he was guilty
of aught but deviant sex.

"But what of you, mistress?" he asked and watched
her with eyes half mast. "You act the gentle maid, but
things are not oft what they seem."

She swallowed her worry and smiled shyly. "I am but
trying to continue your sister's education. Your eldest is
becoming quite proficient at her needlework."

"My eldest," he said, then shifted his gaze to the girls
and away. "Ahh yes, my daughter." He said the word
strangely. "And what are you proficient at, bonny
Rhona?"

"I fear my needlework needs some improving."

"Well . . ." he said, and laughed. "I believe I can toler-
ate that." Taking her arm, he steered her round the corner. He limped slightly, but in a moment they had
reached her door. It stood ajar. He escorted her inside.

Nerves cramped in Rhona's stomach. "Excuse me,
my lord," she said and drew her hand carefully from his
arm. "But as I have said, I am quite fatigued."

"Of course you are," he said, and leaned a shoulder
against the wall as he watched her walk away. "For you
have the entire responsibility of my progeny since my
sister left."

"They are not a burden, my lord."

"Still, you should not have to care for them alone. Although I've warned Colette not to be too harsh with them
in the future, they are not as sweet as they seem at times

and will need disciplining. Perhaps I had best call someone in."

"That won't be necessary."

"You prefer to be absolutely responsible for their care?"

"Aye."

He smiled. The expression was a bit sloppy. "And you would be grateful for that opportunity?"

She fluttered her lashes and tried to remain calm, for although she did not doubt her ability to defend herself, she was concerned about the probability of being sent away if his balls became mysteriously lodged between his noble ears.

"I would indeed be grateful," she said. "But—"

"Me marquiship."

They turned in tandem toward the hall. MacGowan stood in the doorway, his gaze on Lord Robert, his expression solemn. "I dunna mean t' disrupt ye."

The marquis scowled. "Then why do you constantly insist on doing so?"

MacGowan bowed again. "Me apologies," he said, "but there be a wee bit of a problem in the kitchen."

"Then have Unter see to it."

Lachlan shuffled his feet. But there was a gleam in his dark eyes, as if his charade was growing thin. "As yer wishin', sir," he said, and turned indecisively away. But finally he shifted nervously back around. The marquis had already returned his attention to Rhona. "But ye may be wantin' to leave the 'ouse soon."

"And why the devil would that be?"

"Because 'tis 'bout t' burn down."

"What?" The marquis drew himself up with a start.

MacGowan drew back a pace as if frightened to utter the next words. "There be a fire, yer goodness."

"A fire!" rasped Robert, and left the room at a gallop, yelling as he went.

Lachlan watched him go for a moment, then straightened his back. Placing a hand on Rhona's door latch, he studied her with steady eyes. "Do you bar your door?" he asked, his voice ultimately low and deceptively casual. "Or do I kill him?"

Something tripped in her stomach, but she kept the joy from her face. "I can fight me own battles, Champion."

"Then you'd bloody well better do so, lass," he said. "For if I take on the task your slimy marquis will be keeping his head with his pipe tobacco."

For the next few days, the marquis was less of a worry. He confined himself mostly to his bedchamber, for either the pain in his head or the pain in his leg kept him busy. It was a relief to have him preoccupied, for lately he had had entirely too much time on his hands, and too many hands on her.

With this boon, Rhona found it much easier to poke about the house, but she found nothing. Even so, she had a good deal of time to spend with the lassies. Edwina became less timid, even laughing once, and causing Rhona's heart to swell in her chest. And Catherine, though still quiet and lean, seemed less tense as she became more proficient with a knife.

And it was all Rhona's doing. She knew that, felt that. It was not a reason for any great amount of pride, of course. After all, she was a warrior, trained for battle and not for nurturing young lasses. Yet sometimes, in the

evening, when the day stretched out full and lively behind them, and the girls were sleepy and soft-eyed, there
was a strange kind of feeling that curled in her stomach.
It didn't hurt exactly, but it was not a comfortable sensation either.

Still, Rhona tucked them in brusquely, knowing it
was best to be gone.

"Tell us a tale, Lady Rhona," said Edwina. But she
still did not speak well. *Lady* was said with a strange *w*
sound and Rhona sounded much more like Ro. Something tripped in Rhona's heart. She tromped it down.

"I have told you a half dozen tales already today," she
said, and though she meant to be firm, she found she had
already settled onto the edge of their straw-filled mattress. "'Tis time to sleep now."

"But you tell the best of tales," said Edwina. Catherine merely looked on. The swelling was lessening in her
face, and she could see out of both eyes again, but from
her brow to her cheekbone, the skin was brushed with
bright hues of magenta and lime. Her hair, red as firelight and fine as gossamer, lay across her brow. Without
thinking, Rhona reached out to push it back.

Catherine scrunched away, and Rhona slowed her
movements, but when her fingers brushed the girl, she
did not refuse the contact.

Rhona's throat felt tight as she pulled her hand away.

"One more tale?" Edwina whispered.

Rhona cleared her throat. "I . . . cannot think of any
just now."

"Refusin' to sleep are they?" asked Lachlan, and entered the room with two steaming mugs. He raised them
perfunctorily. "Colette said to bring by a bit of tea to 'elp
the wee lassies sleep."

Rhona eyed him dubiously. Aye, she knew now that the maid was not to blame for the girls' troubles, but it did not completely quell her distaste for Colette. The knowledge that she shared Reeves's bed, however, had gone a goodly way to easing Rhona's dislike.

Bowing slightly, Lachlan offered a horn mug to each of the girls. They scooted up in bed and took the proffered tea, but after one whiff they made identical faces of disgust and eyed Lachlan askance.

"Go on then," he said. "'Tis na so bad as all that. I drank it meself when I was a lad. Me auntie would brew it over the open fire. It makes you sleep like a babe, and the dreams you'll be 'avin' . . ." He shook his head as if remembering. "Never 'ave I seen such images. 'Twere like walkin' in the wakin' world, it were. Yet more real like. And the things I would see . . . Unicorns there were. But not your everyday sort. Nay." He shook his head. Catherine scowled into her mug, then chanced a sip. "The unicorns of me dreams wore wings of gold, and when I mounted one . . ." The girls drank in unison. He watched them with an expression of such tenderness that for a moment Rhona failed to breathe.

"What would happen?" Edwina asked, sipping again.

Reaching for the coverlet, he pulled it up slightly. His arm brushed Rhona's and lightning shimmied up her spine. He turned toward her for a moment, his eyes dark.

"Champion," said Edwina, calling him back to the present. "What would happen when you mounted one?"

"Oh." He cleared his throat. "'E would tek me to a place where there was no sorrows."

"Heaven?"

He shrugged. "Mayhap 'twere like heaven, but since I have na seen the Lord's land, I canna say for certain."

"Tell us about it," lisped Edwina.

" 'Tis late," he said, "and you've 'ad a long day what with all your . . . needlework practice." He lifted his gaze to Rhona. She said nothing. Knifeplay might well prove more worthwhile than embroidery in the long run.

"Please," said Edwina, but Lachlan shook his head.

"What would your dad be a sayin' if 'e saw Lady Roe 'ad kept you up too late?"

"He won't know," said Catherine. "He'll be drinking with Sir Charles into the wee hours, most like."

Rhona froze. "What!" How could she have missed the arrival of the marquis's mercenary knight? This was the entire reason for her coming to Claronfell, but somehow she had become foolishly distracted.

Catherine eyed her solemnly. Already, there was worry on her face, a frown between her brows.

Rhona smoothed her tone. "What say you?" she asked.

"Sir Charles," Catherine said after a moment's hesitation. "He arrived this eve."

"Oh?" She kept her tone carefully steady now, but Catherine's gaze was still on her, and though she daren't look at MacGowan, she feared he too was watching her suspiciously. "And why did he come to Claronfell?"

The girl blinked. "I know not. But they soon will be closeted away in the library if they are not already."

"Well . . ." Rhona said and stood. She tried to keep her movements casual, but her body felt stiff and her mind was racing. "Good night to you," she said and, being unable to think of a single other thing to say, hustled from the room.

Once in the corridor, she paused to listen, but the passageway was silent. One glance behind assured her that MacGowan had remained with the girls. She fled on silent feet toward the library and in a moment she realized Catherine had been right. Even now, she could hear the marquis's questions mixed with the knight's quieter answers as they came toward her.

She had no time to waste in thought, but stepped rapidly into the library. One glance around told her there was only one place to hide. Near the back of the room a wall jutted out, separating the books from the rest of the chamber. Skimming across the floor, she sprinted behind the wall, breathing hard.

A whisper of sound echoed from the far side almost immediately, and she froze with a hand on her dirk, but in that instant, MacGowan slipped in beside her.

They stared at each other from inches apart. "Cozy," he said.

"What the devil are you doing here?" she hissed.

"The same could be asked—" he began, but in that instant, she slapped her hand over his mouth.

"So all is well with you and yours?" said the marquis. The sound of the door was distinct, rather like the final closing of a stone casket.

"Aye, well enough," said Sir Charles and continued to tell about his father's father who lived in Newbury.

Pressed up against MacGowan like an ardent hound, Rhona held her breath and watched his eyes. The dialogue droned on.

"More wine?" asked the marquis.

Rhona could only assume the answer was affirmative,

for in a moment they heard the clink of glass against metal.

"And what of you, my lord?" asked Charles. "I trust you and yours are doing well."

The conversation continued with talk of taxes and rents and news of ever increasing wealth.

Rhona shifted her weight carefully to her opposite foot and forced herself to ignore the feel of MacGowan's biceps against her breast, though they felt as hard as living granite. Neither did she fail to notice when his fingers skimmed her hair.

"The harvest is bountiful."

His lips brushed her ear. Against her will her eyes fell closed.

"Aye. The weather has been favorable."

Lachlan slipped his hand behind her neck. Beneath his fingers, magic sparked. His lips found hers. Her knees felt weak.

A scrape of noise alerted her. MacGowan jerked away. Footfalls drew closer. She held her breath. They shuffled off. Against her breast, she felt Lachlan's hard body relax marginally.

"And your daughters, they are doing well?" asked Charles.

The marquis didn't respond immediately, and when he did his voice was slurred. "Young Lady Rhona of Nettlepath arrived to care for them."

"Lady Rhona?" The knight sounded interested in a bored sort of fashion. "I don't believe I've met her. Is she fair?"

"She is a strange lass," mused the marquis.

"To your liking then."

"She wears a silver shell I plan to add to my collection."

"Just one of many then? Or shall I be expecting Claronfell to have an heir soon?"

"Don't speak to me of heirs!" rasped Lord Robert. The rustling sound was more labored now, and Rhona knew it was the marquis who had found his feet. He roamed about the room as she held her breath.

"My apologies," said Charles. "But you do have two bonny daughters."

"To hell with my daughters and Lorna as well!" hissed the marquis, and they could hear him pivot about. His footsteps faltered.

"I did not mean to offend, my lord," said Charles.

"Leave me be," said the marquis. He was not a charming drunk. "I ask only one thing of you."

Sir Charles drank and sighed. " 'Tis a fine wine," he said. "Is it from your own vineyards?"

"Damn you and this senseless prattle," said the marquis. "Are the plans set or nay?"

"Aye, they are set, but I have been reconsidering the price."

"I have already paid you well."

"But you have asked a large . . ." Charles drank again. There was a shrug in his tone. "Shall I call it a favor?"

"Call it whatever you like. Just see that the job is done."

"It shall be. For a bit more coin."

"More!" the marquis growled. Someone paced the room. Rhona's arm felt cramped against MacGowan's side, but she dare not ease it. "We had an agreement."

"That was before I learned more of the situation."

"Frightened, Charles?"

The other laughed. It sounded no more sober than his companion. "Let me just say that I am not a fool."

"How much more do you want?"

"Double the amount."

The marquis swore.

"I will need it to pay the others," Charles explained.

"They can be trusted?"

"They too were wronged, it seems, and though they have the perfect opportunity, none will expect trouble from that front. You know how he cherishes his bonny Highland rabble."

Glass clinked against metal again. There was the sound of drinking, then pacing. Rhona held her breath as the footfalls came closer.

"Very well," said the marquis. He was very close, just on the far side of the wall. "But I want to see it with my own eyes."

"There will be a puppet show and a man dressed in naught but rags. I suggest you stay close to the puppeteer."

"A puppeteer," said the marquis, and laughed. His footfalls sounded closer, and suddenly he was there, gazing at the books. In a moment, a fragment of a second, he would turn and see them. But in that instant, MacGowan reached out. Quick as a serpent, he was. Grabbing the marquis by the back of his skull, he slammed the man's head against the bookshelf. Before Rhona could stop him, he'd stepped into the open, but one glance told him Charles was still turned away. Lachlan was back in hiding before the marquis's back struck the floor.

There was a moment of absolute silence, during which Rhona dared not breathe.

"Damn," drawled Charles. "A coward *and* a drunkard." There was the sound of a satisfied sigh as he finished up his drink and left the room.

Chapter 25

The footsteps had no more than disappeared when MacGowan stepped out of hiding. Taking one glance into the chamber, he snatched up Rhona's hand and dragged her out with him.

She scrambled over the marquis and rushed to the door. In an instant they were in the hallway and only a few moments later Lachlan had closeted them away in her room.

The door shut with a click behind them, and then he turned to her.

"Explain," he said.

She lifted her chin and held his gaze as her mind raced round and round like a carousel gone mad. *A puppeteer. A man in rags.* "Explain what?" she asked.

He smiled, but the expression was hard.

"What were you doing in the library?"

"I went to borrow a book." *None will expect it from that front.* What front? Who?

"Truly?"

"Aye."

"You lie," he said.

She shrugged. "You may believe whatever you wish to believe."

"Whatever I wish!" He slammed his palm against the wall beside her head. "I'll tell you what I want to believe," he growled. "I want to believe that you have come to Claronfell to care for those wee lassies. I want to believe that you have not lied to them, that you are not lying to me, but I tell you true, warrior, I am having a bit of trouble with that."

"Then try harder, champion," she gritted, and moved to slip away from the wall.

He caught her arm and pulled her back. "What are your plans, woman?"

"Plans?"

"Why are you truly here?"

Her mind spun like a wooden top. Surely she could trust him with the truth. Indeed, she longed to, for she needed help to untangle the clues. But she must do what she must and that meant danger, and though he seemed willing, nay, almost eager to risk himself, he was adverse to the idea of any danger for *her*. The thought sent a strange, melancholy feeling sweeping through her, and for a moment she was almost tempted to reach out and touch his face, to feel the hard planes of his strength against her palm. But she had not survived so long by being either foolish or soft, and she would not be so now.

"Tell me, champion," she said and carefully steadied her emotions. "What are your feelings for me?"

"Feelings?" His grip loosened on her arm, and he leaned back the slightest degree as if wary of standing too close.

"Aye," she said, and pressed on, though her heart was pounding like a charger's hooves. "Do you cherish me?"

He glared at her. A muscle jumped in his lean jaw, but finally he spoke. "You are like ale," he said. "The more I have of you the more I want, and yet, I think, you are not good for me."

It was difficult to breathe, but she forced herself to go on. "If I were in danger . . ." She paused, searching for words.

He narrowed his eyes and upon her arm his grip tightened a bit. "What kind of danger?" he asked.

"It matters not. If my life were at risk what would you—"

" 'Tis the marquis, isn't it?" His free hand was clenched, his face intense. "What has he done?"

She drew a careful breath as she watched him. Aye, there may be bonnier men, but never would there be one who embodied ferocity and tenderness to such a breathtaking degree.

"What has he done?" His voice was a low growl.

"MacGowan," she said, steeling her voice. "He has done nothing, I only—"

"You may as well tell me, lass, for I'll kill him either way, whether you admit the truth or nay."

Perhaps she should have been scandalized, or angry, or at least frightened, but somehow she was only flattered. Who else had there been in the entirety of her life who would risk himself for her? "Lord Robert is the Saxon king's second cousin," she said evenly. "The punishment would be death."

His expression changed not the least. "Tell me what he has done so that I may do what I must."

She watched him as a wild, indefinable range of emotions rushed through her, but when the chaos cleared all that remained was a tightening tinge of something that felt frightfully like happiness.

She bundled all the emotions up and set them aside. A warrior had no place for emotion.

"I am not for the likes of you," she whispered.

"And why is that?"

She shook her head, her mind racing. "You know nothing of me, MacGowan."

"Then enlighten me."

"Suffice it to say that your kind do not marry mine."

"Mayhap you know little of me own kind."

"There you are wrong."

"We MacGowans do not wed your average maid."

"Mayhap not average," she said. "But at least your brothers' wives are maids, while I—"

"Their mother was accused of witchcraft."

"Witchcraft?" She felt herself go pale, felt her stomach churn as the memory of the tale came burning back to her mind.

"Aye," he said. "Some think the birth of twins ungodly. Others said the lady of Evermyst had an unnatural attraction for the sea. As for the elder Munro, he accused her of killing his father. Thus she was condemned to death even though the king himself owed her," he said.

"Owed her?"

"Aye," he said. "Long ago one of His Majesty's ships was endangered. She made certain it returned safely to shore."

They too were wronged!

348   Lois Greiman

"Nay," she breathed. "It cannot be."

He scowled at her. "Did you know her?"

"None came forth to save her?"

"What?"

"No one stood by her?" she said. "Not even King James?"

"Our king was occupied with troubles of his own."

Puzzle pieces fell together like the clang of an iron cell. *'Tis said the king himself will be there.* There was a plot against the king. *There will be a man dressed in naught but rags.* He would be in disguise, dressed like a commoner as he oft was when visiting his subjects. *I suggest you stay close to the puppeteer.* He would be near the puppet master. *And though they have the perfect opportunity, none will expect it from that front. You know how he cherishes his bonny Highland rabble.* It was Anora and Isobel Fraser who planned the king's murder, for James had forgotten his debt and abandoned their mother to death.

She felt sick to her stomach, dizzy and weak.

"Rhona. What is amiss?"

She raised her chin, fighting the panic. His brothers' beloved wives planned treason, and she must expose them or let the king perish.

"Peaceable yet powerful he must be. Cunning but kind to thee and me," she muttered.

"What are you talking about?"

"Return to your father's keep, MacGowan," she said. "Find a maid who appreciates such qualities."

"I dunna know what you speak of."

"Aye you do," she said. "You may be powerful, but you are also peaceable. Cunning you have, but not in such a great degree as kindness."

He was scowling again.

" 'Tis not the same with me," she said. "Kindness is not my path. I will make the choices that need making, and damn those who suffer for it."

"Aye," he scoffed. "It's a demon, you are."

"Perhaps," she said and steeling herself, spoke again. "For I do not cherish you."

He said nothing. Indeed, she thought he had ceased to breathe.

She tried to speak again and finally succeeded. "Lord Robert is neither peaceable nor kind nor loving. But he is a marquis."

"You cannot stay with him." He gritted the words.

"Aye, I can and I shall."

"He is deviant and he is cruel."

"Aye," she said. " 'Tis a match made in heaven."

"Damn you, Rhona," he growled. "I'll not leave you. Not to him."

Her stomach clenched. Love, it appeared, was not a gentle suitor as she'd suspected, but a damned knave that twisted your gut and strangled your breath.

"Listen now," she said, "for I tell you the truth." It was difficult to force out the words, to breathe past the lie, to keep living. "I do not cherish you, MacGowan, and I never shall. Do not shame yourself further by pursuing me."

An eternity passed between them. Not another word was spoken. His fists clenched, his body tightened, and then he turned and silently left the room.

She did not sleep that night, and by morning, he was gone. Sir Charles left shortly after.

Rhona sat in silence at the breakfast table, her mind numb, her stomach sick. The marquis appeared, looking no better. His face was a peculiar shade of green. Upon his brow was a swelling the size of a swan's royal egg.

"Troubles, my lord?" she asked, and tried to put some feeling into it. But worry was a raw ache inside her. He planned murder and there was no way to stop it but to punish the Evermyst maids.

"Aye," he said, and put his hand to his brow. "I am in dire need of a tonic. Where is that blasted Welshman when I need him?"

"In truth, my lord, I have sent him away."

He seemed to brighten immediately. "Away?"

"Aye," she said, and lowered her lids with an effort. "I felt he was becoming . . . too attached to me."

A grin shifted his greenish lips. "He was rather in the way."

"Aye, my lord," she said, and returned his smile with careful shyness. "And it was impeding on my chances of getting to know you better."

"Better . . ." He brightened still more. "Indeed, 'tis a fine idea. But . . ." His face clouded. " 'Tis a poor time for this, for I will be leaving in but a few days."

Her heart thundered in her chest. "Leaving, my lord?"

"Heading north. To the stronghold of Evermyst." His tone was reflective. "The brothers MacGowans are hosting a gathering."

Dear God, she was right. Meara had not lied. Evil stalked Evermyst, but it came from within as well as without. "You are invited to this gathering, my lord?"

"I am the king's cousin." He laughed as if there were some irony she missed. "I am wealthy and powerful and welcome everywhere, and yet 'tis the Highland rogues who are favored." His tone had become strange, as if he spoke to himself, but he glanced up and gave her a tight smile. "There will be games and drink and merriment."

She forced herself to continue to breathe. "I do not believe I have met the brothers."

He turned his attention back to her. "Nay, I suspect you have not, my little steel mouse, but . . . perhaps it is time."

She said nothing.

"Aye," he said. "You shall travel with me, as will my progeny." He nodded as if to himself. "Aye. A man with his bonny daughters in tow. 'Twill be so much the better."

And so it was set. Rhona ate little and slept less for the next several days. When she was not fending off the marquis, she was caring for the children, and when she was not with the girls, she was planning, scheming, trying to see some way she had misread the clues. But she could not.

They left in two days' time. And the pace was laborious. Not for many years had Rhona journeyed such a distance as a woman. And never in her life had she traveled with children. Her nerves felt as raw as open wounds.

She wished now that the girls had stayed at Claronfell. Indeed, she had wished so all along, but they offered a shield of sorts, a garnish to her costume, aiding her mission.

Catherine was utterly silent in her father's presence. Edwina returned to sucking her finger, but for the most part, the marquis ignored them. He too, seemed preoccupied. Too preoccupied to make his usual advances, and finally they arrived.

Evening was fast falling when she first saw the heights of Evermyst soaring fifty rods above the sea. For a moment she could not take her eyes from it, could not look away. Against her breast, her small silver shell felt warm and heavy.

Although the road wound round an outcropping of

rock and up to dizzying heights, they did not climb up that rugged course, on the verdant nearby hills, pavilions of every bright hue had been erected. Lord Robert stopped their carriages there.

Soon servants were scurrying about like bees, setting up their camp, preparing meals. Reeves and Colette had accompanied them, for the marquis liked his comfort.

Edwina stayed close to Rhona's side. Even Catherine seemed loath to stray too far, though her eyes were round with wonder as she took in the sights that surrounded them.

From her vantage point, Rhona could see the banners of a score of clans—the Forbeses, the MacGregors, and near the mountain's very roots, the Munro's white destrier on a field of green.

Warhorses with heavy feathering and high steps jolted past. Women laughed. Men cursed, and from far off, Rhona heard the high eerie sound of the pipes playing to the sky.

Her heart felt bound up in her chest. Emotions cluttered in, squeezing her breath away. Evermyst, warriors, competition, death. She could all but taste the impending drama. While beside her, two small girls looked to her for comfort. But who would comfort her?

"Me lady," said a voice.

Horror and fear and soaring hope sparked in her chest at the sound of Lachlan's voice. She spun around, her heart thrumming hard. But he was not there. Only someone who looked vaguely like him, someone who would soon hate her.

"Me lady," he said again and bowed. "I am Laird Ramsay of Evermyst and this is my wife, Lady Anora."

Lady Anora—mistress of lofty Evermyst. Lady Anora—bonny and bright. Lady Anora—with the silver shell about her neck. Lady Anora—Rhona's sister.

Chapter 26

Rhona stared, struck to silence, and in that silence the marquis stepped forward.

"You must be Lord Ramsay, one of the brother rogues," he said. "I have heard much of you and your bonny bride."

"Then I fear your knowledge exceeds me own," said Ramsay. "What was your name, sir?"

"I am Lord Robert Turpin, sixth marquis of Claronfell."

"Lord Turpin," said Ramsay. "'Tis good to meet you."

"So you know of me."

"I knew your wife. I was sorry to hear of her death."

"'Twas a terrible loss, of course," he said. "But let us speak of happier things. Your lady has given you an heir, I hear."

"Aye, I am much blessed, for I have both a son and

a daughter. Wee Mary is but two years of age," Ramsay said and, reaching out, stroked his hand down Anora's back. There was a stiffness to the pair, as if there were some contention between them, and yet the caress seemed almost unconscious, as simple as breathing. And when he glanced into her eyes, the adoration was as clear as a hearth fire. "Tearle is not yet a year old, but already he possesses a temper to rival his mother's."

"And good sense to rival his father's," Anora countered, and though she raised a regal brow toward her husband, the adoration was returned in full. A rare hint of a smile lifted Ramsay's lips as he touched her again, and for a moment it seemed that they had forgotten the world entirely, but the lady drew herself into the present quickly. She was small and bonny, nothing like the sister they had sent away long years ago. But there was steel in her, that much even Rhona would admit. "You are most welcome here at lofty Evermyst, my lord. And you, my lady," she said, and paused as she shifted her bright gaze. Rhona's breath caught in her throat. "To what do we owe the pleasure of your visit?"

"Forgive my rudeness," said the marquis. "Let me introduce Lady Rhona, late of Nettlepath. She has been so kind as to care for my daughters these past days."

"Lady Rhona." Anora said and took her sister's hands between her own. " 'Tis good indeed to welcome you to Evermyst."

Emotion burned like acid through Rhona. A thousand dreams rushed by, torn by hate and fear and hope. "My thanks," she said, and could manage nothing more. No recriminations, no questions, no apologies. Long she had known of the bond between them, and long she had resented it. Indeed, resented it enough to wish the lady ill. But now . . .

"We've not met before," Anora said. "But I am eager to remedy that."

"Lord Turpin," Ramsay said, "We are proud of our achievements here at Evermyst for we've done much to improve our stronghold in the past years. Would you care to see the results?"

"'Twould be my pleasure," said the marquis.

"And you, my lady, you must come as well," said Anora.

Rhona nodded and said nothing as her sister tucked her hand beneath her arm and led her toward a nearby wagon.

It was broad and boxy and pulled by two powerful sorrels. Matching they were, with flaxen manes that reached their forearms and heavy locks that all but covered their nostrils. Bells jingled on their harness as they leaned into their collars, but Rhona could hear naught but the crash of the nearby sea and her own haunted accusations. Still, the sorrels bore them up through the narrow passage to the castle far above.

Rhona's heart jolted in her chest, feeling tighter with every step they took toward the summit. *Evil comes to Evermyst.* Nay, evil had already arrived. 'Twas no surprise it came with the warrior maid. Perhaps that was the very reason they had sent her away. Perhaps they had known even then.

Between the sheer walls of natural stone, the portcullis remained raised, for this was a day of celebrations. Ramsay pointed out the defenses and fortifications, but Rhona heard barely a word, for the beat of her heart challenged the crash of the sea far below.

She must think, must plan, must concentrate, for so much was at stake here. But as they reached their destination, the chaos only grew. Within the inner sanctuary of Evermyst, jugglers and musicians and tumblers mingled with dukes and monks and gentlewomen. Where was the king? Had he already arrived? How would she prevent his death? Who would strike the blow and how?

"My lady," said Anora. Rhona barely refrained from jumping, so tight were her nerves. "Tell me, was your journey here difficult?"

"Nay." She brought her attention back to the immediacy, but could think of no other words as her mind tumbled madly over itself. What of King James? Did he know there was a plot against him? Perhaps he had gotten word and would not come to Evermyst, or perhaps that same plot would never be tied to this woman. But nay, why would she care? These people had exiled her long ago, had sent her away and kept Anora to live in luxury as lady of the keep. Sent her away to fight her own battles, to hew her life out of nothing but an old man's bitter sorrow.

"And you ventured here directly from Claronfell. Is that correct?"

"Aye."

Anora smiled as if Rhona had said something clever, as if she weren't bumbling along like a draught mule in a grand parade.

"What of the marquis's children? Did they travel with you? Two girls he has, aye?"

"Aye." Panic was rising in her chest, as if she were being slowly smothered, as if she were drowning.

"How long have you been at Claronfell?"

"Naught but a few weeks."

"And before that did you live with your foster father?"

"Nay, I—" Rhona began, but Anora's words stood out suddenly in her mind like emboldened letters of fire. "How did you know the baron fostered me?"

"We have mutual friends, you and I."

"I have no friends." The words came out unplanned, unchecked.

"Never believe that," Anora murmured. A tiny frown furrowed her brow. "For 'tisn't true. There are those who would give their lives for you."

Rhona lifted her chin. "I fear you have mistaken me for another, Lady—" she began, but Anora interrupted her.

"Isobel speaks highly of you."

"You are mistaken," insisted Rhona. Fear constricted her heart. Fear and horror and sadness. They had sent her away, and they'd not tried to find her, had not tried to right the wrongs. "I know no one named Isobel."

Their gazes held for an eternal moment.

"You soon shall," said Anora and, dismounting the wagon, led Rhona through the crush toward the keep.

The crowd pressed in around them. The colors were overwhelming, the music suffocating. Inside the great hall, it was close and noisy and disorienting as they fought their way through.

And still a wisp of a draft caught Rhona's hair, lifting it from her neck like invisible fingers.

"Senga," said Anora.

"What?" asked Rhona as the mob pressed in on her.

"'Tis Senga you feel. Grandmother. She has been gone these many years and yet she remains."

Dreams haunted her, crushing in, stifling her. "A shade?"

"Aye. Some think she cannot bear to leave the high keep, and some . . ." Anora smiled as she led the way up the stairs at the far side of the hall. "Some think she remains to look after her kindred."

Rhona held her breath. Duty clashed with a strange, misbegotten loyalty, though long ago, she had wished naught but death for this delicate maid. Long ago she had followed her and hoped to accomplish just that. How ironic that ever since she had spent her life guarding her, only to come full circle. "This Senga, she protects you?" she murmured.

"Aye," said Anora, holding her gaze. "Me and my sis—*Bel*," she said as her sister appeared suddenly from around the corner of the stairs. She was as fair and fragile as her twin. "Isobel, I would introduce you to Lady Rhona."

For a moment not a word was spoken. Indeed, the entire world seemed to go silent, and then Isobel stepped forward and clasped Rhona's arms.

"Lady Rhona," she murmured. Her grip was strong, and tucked into her silver girdle was a wooden sling. It seemed strangely incongruous against the rich cloth of her gown. "I have waited long for this day. Welcome to our home."

Rhona drew herself from the other's grasp. "I fear you may be under some delusion," she said. "For I've not met you afore today."

"Aye," Isobel breathed, "Aye, of course not, and yet I feel I have known you forever, but I must away now. God be with you, Rhona. I will speak with you again soon."

They continued up the stairs. There were questions,

questions which Rhona answered, but never truly heard.

Finally, however, she stood at the very top of Evermyst, at the very peak of the world it seemed. The wind blew crisp and clean from the west, ruffling her hair against her shoulders, and she turned to feel it against her face. From here she could see eternity. From here she could shoot an arrow into the stars or into the heart of the earth. From here she could feel her very soul crumbling in her chest.

"'Tis beautiful, is it not?" asked Anora.

Rhona said nothing, but stared unspeaking into the far silvery distance where the sea blended magically with the sky.

"To my own mind, 'tis the most beautiful place in the world. What of you, my lady?"

Rhona jerked from her reverie. "Aye, 'tis a bonny sight," she said, her tone brusque, her throat strangely tight as she shifted her attention to the melee below.

In the courtyard, a host of entertainers laughed and parlayed, and a lifetime below that the sea crashed in frothing glee against the ancient feet of the mountain.

"You like the sea?" Anora asked.

"What?" she breathed.

"Those of us born to Evermyst have a fondness for the sea," she said. "Isobel was drawn to the lofty keep even before she knew she was born to it."

"You were separated at birth," Rhona said.

"Aye."

"And yet you did not try to find her." The words spewed forth.

Anora's eyes were solemn. "I did not know of her existence. Only Meara knew, and she kept the truth to herself in the hopes of protecting us all."

All? She almost laughed, but she could not. "So you did not want the high fortress for yourself?"

"Perhaps I did," she murmured. "But I would give it up for my sister. Blood is strong. Kinship is a bond that cannot be broke, not by the passing of time nor the struggle of hardships." Was there a tinge of sadness in her tone? A touch of desperation? "Do you not agree, Lady Rhona?"

She couldn't speak. Couldn't move. Noise boomed around them, and yet the world seemed utterly silent.

"I could not help but notice your pendant," Anora whispered.

Rhona slipped her hand over the silver shell.

" 'Tis an unusual piece," she said. "Do you—"

"I must go!" Rhona blurted.

"Nay. Already?"

"Aye," she said, and fled toward the stairs. She was not running away. 'Twas simply that she must remember her mission, must not get caught up in foolish sentiment and girlish ramblings. But when she reached the bailey she did not delay, but balled her ungainly skirts in her fists and rushed through the crowds toward the outer wall.

The mob pressed in about her. From the corner of her eye she caught a glimpse of an earth-toned plaid and sable hair. Lachlan! She spun around, but he was only a mirage swallowed by the crowd.

A handsome gentleman dressed in bright plaids stood near a woman with flame-colored hair. A slim lass skipped by, elegantly attired except for the black-nosed martin peeking from her sleeve. Two blushing maids teased a dark-haired lad with a cat-faced brooch. These were Lachlan's people. These bonny folk who laughed and cared. But she would still the laughter, and he would never forgive her.

She was running, stumbling through the crowd, her skirts wrapped like serpents about her ankles. Breathless and shaking, she reached Turpin's pavilion.

"Lady Rhona." Colette touched her shoulder. "Are you well?"

"Aye." She calmed herself, tried to breathe, to think.

"Someone came searching for you."

Lachlan! He was here. He had come—to keep her safe, to help her through. "Someone?" she breathed, barely about to force out the word.

"Aye," said the maid and, ducking into the pavilion, brought forth a bulky package. It was wrapped in linen and tied with hemp. "A woman brought this by."

"A woman." Her heart plummeted.

"Aye, she said that Lachlan of the MacGowans bade you take this and use it as you must."

Rhona felt herself pale, for she already knew the contents. Beneath the linen she could feel the hard metal of her warrior's helm.

He was here. And he knew. Knew she had come on some mission, but he could not know what. And yet he believed in her. She closed her eyes to reality. She could not betray his truth, but she had little choice. Turning like one in a dream, she bore her garments to a private place, shed her womanly garments, and donned her warrior's garb.

The bailey bustled with revelers. The crowds milled and lurched. Hours passed. Torches were lit, illuminating the courtyard, but Rhona remained in the shadows, her heart constricted, her muscles tense, waiting.

A dark-haired scoundrel stood upon a rope and juggled wine-filled mugs. From across the courtyard, an acrobat blew flame from his mouth, and not far away Ramsay MacGowan strode through the crowd, his swaddled son held close to his chest.

But there was no puppeteer. There was no king. Perhaps she was wrong. Perhaps—

But then she saw the puppet master. He was dressed in common gray. In rags! The marquis was nearby, halfway up a flight of stonework stairs, and from the light of the fire eater's hissing flame, she could see the hatred in his eyes.

Truth smote Rhona like the strike of a double-edged sword.

'Twas not the king Robert hated. 'Twas Ramsay Mac-Gowan!

From a window far above, a movement caught her eye. *Evil comes to Evermyst!*

She shrieked a warning even as she leapt from the shadows and struck Ramsay at the waist, bearing him to the ground. A man bellowed. Women screamed. The baby flew from his arms. An arrow hissed past, piercing the swaddling.

Rhona gasped and sprang toward the child, but when she pulled the cloth aside, 'twas naught but a bundle of rags.

"Nay," rasped the marquis.

Rhona straightened and drew her sword, but in that instant, the world disintegrated to cold ash, for there, beside Turpin, stood Catherine.

He turned toward the girl as if in slow motion and smiled as he pulled her close. Time slowed to a crawl.

Rhona could do nothing but watch as he wrapped his

arm about the girl's waist and lifted her against his chest. Could do nothing as his left hand disappeared murderously behind her back.

The warrior had failed! Had lost, and suddenly there was nothing she could do—nothing but hope for a miracle.

"Champion," she whispered. And somehow, he came, stepping out of nowhere, looming behind the marquis at the top of the stairs.

The world was as silent as death, and yet she could not hear the words spoken from the stone steps.

"Let the lass go," ordered Lachlan. Rhona was safe. Ramsay was safe! And by God, Catherine would be the same, for Rhona loved the girl, whether she knew it or not and he would not see her heartbroken. "Let her go, or I swear by that's holy, you will not last the day."

The marquis darted his gaze from one to the other. "Who are you?" he rasped.

"I am Lachlan of the MacGowans."

"The Welshman!" he hissed and jerked his head toward Rhona. "And him?"

"She is vengeance."

Even in the firelight, his face went pale.

"Let Catty go," Lachlan ordered. "She has naught to do with this."

"And neither do I," hissed Robert, his chest heaving, his hands atremble. "Do I, MacGowan?"

"Do not harm her."

"Harm her? Nay. I would not, for she is my progeny. My heir," he whispered and laughed demonically. "Damn you MacGowans for taking all I had."

"We took nothing from you, Turpin."

"The Fraser bitch should have been mine, but your brother seduced her. Her son should have been my son, but he was sired by another. I am the marquis of Claron-fell, the king's own cousin. You are naught but Highland rabble, and yet I get your brother's cast-asides. The haughty Lorna carried his brat. A boy it was. A boy! Yet she gave me naught but a pair of worthless maids."

Catherine's face was as pale as death, but in her hand, hidden in folds of her narrow skirt, was Rhona's dirk.

Lachlan eased his fist open and breathed a silent prayer.

"Let her go and we will do the same for you, Turpin."

"Ahh, the renowned mercy of the MacGowan clan," he said, and laughed. His voice shook. "I think not, Dafydd," he whispered and backed up the steps. Lachlan eased away, giving him room. "I will take her with me. But she will be safe—so long as you keep your secrets to yourself."

Lachlan dropped his gaze to Catherine's. A single tear slipped down her cheek, but her gaze never faltered—and he nodded.

She delayed a moment, a heartbeat of time, and then she tightened her grip on the hilt and stabbed.

The marquis screamed. His hands loosened, and in that instant, Lachlan snatched his own blade from its sheath.

It snarled into the air and plowed into the marquis's chest. He staggered backward. And suddenly arrows hissed from every direction, striking him like body blows. He drew his last breath before he struck the ground.

"Catty," Lachlan rasped and snatched her from her feet. She hid her face against his chest and clung to him with all her strength. "Sweet Catty."

"Champion!" Rhona stumbled up the stairs. Her face

was wet with tears, her voice raspy. "My champion, you came," she whispered.

"Aye. Aye, lass. I will always come," he said and, drawing her into his embrace, kissed her with wild desperation.

She touched his cheek, her fingers trembling against his skin. "How did you know? How—"

"And what is this then?" asked an imperial voice.

Rhona tried to step away, but Lachlan pulled her against his side, not able to let her go for the briefest moment.

"Your Majesty," he said and bowed.

"The Rogue Fox, kissing a warrior," said the king. " 'Tis a sight worth seeing."

Lachlan cleared his throat. Catherine still clung to his chest like a tattered doll. He tightened his grip across her back and closed his eyes to the fierceness of his emotions. "I can explain this, Your Majesty."

"Can you?"

"Aye. The warrior is not what he seems. What *she* seems. In truth, Your Highness—"

"Could you explain this better, Lady Rhona?" asked James.

She removed her helm. Firelight danced across her noble features. "The marquis of Claronfell plotted a murder, Your Majesty. I thought it was you he meant to harm."

James smiled and, reaching out, took her hand between his own. "And thus you hurried to my rescue once again, Rhone?"

"It seems his venom was not bent on you, my liege, but on the MacGowans instead. He positioned an archer in the window. He had best be caught," she said and scowled upward. "Although I know not who loosed the arrows that killed the marquis."

"The shaft through his heart is me sister Shona's," said Gilmour, and stepped suddenly from the crowd. "The others are from assorted clansmen."

"You knew," Rhona gasped, and stared at Lachlan. "You knew there was a plot aimed at Evermyst."

"I thought you were in danger," Lachlan said. "I too searched the marquis's belongings. Read his missives."

"He believed Ramsay was targeted," said Mour. "Though he wasn't sure. Thus me brother's clever baby of rags. Anora was mad enough to kill him herself for the risk he took, but we thought it best to let the drama play out, for we could not accuse Turpin without proof."

"You knew," she said again.

"The archer has died," announced a soldier, stepping from the crowd. "We tried to take him, but he chose death on the rocks below instead."

"Who was he?" asked James.

"'Twas Caird of Windemoor, my king."

"The Munro's captain."

"He has never been pleased with Windemoor's truce with Evermyst," Gilmour said. "Lord Turpin's coin only made the proposition more tempting."

"Sir Charles is also involved," Rhona began, but Lachlan interrupted her.

"You hurried to our king's rescue *again*?"

James turned toward him. "Did you not know it was the lady warrior who helped me escape from the Black Douglases many years ago?"

Lachlan shook his head.

"MacGowan," he chided. "You should learn a bit about a woman before you kiss her so fiercely."

"Me apologies, Your Majesty," he said. "But she can be a bit closed mouthed."

"It did not look that way to me."

Chuckles issued from those around them.

"Indeed," said the king, and sobered. "Our lady warrior was as much a prisoner of the Douglas as I. She dressed as a groom and brought me the same type of garment to aid my escape from Edinburgh."

"She must have forgotten to mention that," Lachlan said.

The king laughed. "I owe you much, Lady Rhone," he said. "In fact, I recently received a request regarding you."

"A request, my liege?"

"Aye," he said. "It seems that your foster father would like to bequeath Nettlepath to you instead of giving it to his closest male heir. I suspect I will have to grant his wish."

She said nothing, but shifted her gaze first to Catherine and then to Lachlan. Her eyes shone in the firelight, filled with an emotion so strong it was all he could do to keep from taking her into his arms and forgetting their royal audience.

"In truth, Your Majesty," she said softly. "There is another favor I would ask."

"Speak," he said.

"The marquis of Claronfell sired two daughters. We would take them as our own if you will allow it."

"*We?*" he asked.

"Lachlan and myself," she said.

Joy and passion smote Lachlan like a fist to the chest and perhaps it shone in his eyes, because the king laughed.

"And have you told the rogue fox of your plans yet, Lady Rhone?"

She blushed. Actually blushed, though she raised her gaze to his. "Champion," she whispered. "I know I am not what you hoped for in a bride. But the lassies need—"

"You are mine!" he growled, and pulled her back into a tight embrace. "Forever and always."

"Aye," agreed an ancient voice, and as they watched, Meara of the Fold pushed her bent body through the crowd. "Peaceable and powerful. Cunning and kind. Loving and beloved. Welcome back, wee Rhona." Her faded eyes were filled with tears. "I knew you would return for duty's sake if none other."

Rhona shook her head. "You knew I was the warrior."

"I am old, but I am not daft." She twisted her ancient face into a scowl. "And . . . your sisters recognized you some time ago."

She lifted her gaze to the firelit maids who stood together at the crowd's edge. Anora and Isobel Fraser. Her sisters. Her blood. "How?" she breathed.

Meara shrugged. "I do not know. They possess some strange power. 'Tis unnerving is what it is. But 'twas *I* who told you of the evil, was it not?"

"How did you know evil stalked Evermyst?"

"I didn't," she admitted. "But I could think of no other way to keep you close." She nodded. Her ancient eyes were misty, but she held her chin stubbornly high. " 'Tis about time you come home, lass. We have waited long."

Chapter 27

It was a Yuletide wedding, and Evermyst's great hall reeled with happiness. Although Rhona might never become accustomed to the feeling of family around her, she found also that she cherished it like none other. Anora and Isobel stitched her wedding gown themselves, laughing at every foolish stage and drawing her into the joy of their reunion. Meara and the kitchen staff argued relentlessly over who would care for Catty and Edwina, and Lachlan's kindred arrived by the score to tease and bully and congratulate.

Master Longshanks rode Knight Star alone from Nettlepath to give his blessings, for the baron had passed on, leaving the manor to her by the king's decree. His gigantic, flop-eared hound circled the tables, growling at Lachlan when they happened upon each other.

Beside the waning light of the crackling Yuletide log,

Catherine and Edwina played hoodman's bluff with their new found cousins. They remained quiet and shy, but their faces were no longer gaunt and the haunting fear was gone from their eyes.

Along the far wall, beside the wassail tree, a group of overly enthused youngsters performed the mumming, acting out skits to the crowd's delight, and near an iron bowl of heather ale, the brother rogues gathered.

Even from a goodly distance, Rhona could see mischief in their eyes.

"So," said Gilmour. "Shall I assume that I was correct? She *is* a woman?"

Lachlan took a sip from his horn cup and let his gaze skim from his brother to his bride. Happiness was his in such a vast degree that sometimes it felt all but impossible to believe. "Assume what you like, Mour," he said.

"Ho!" crowed Gilmour to Ramsay. "Mayhap our wee brother has tastes we know nothing about."

"Watch your mouth, Mour," Ramsay said. "The lass is armed."

Gilmour nodded, took a drink, and narrowed his eyes as he glanced at the newest Fraser bride. "Aye. She is that, but I believe me own Bel be the most dangerous of the three once her temper's up."

Ramsay thoughtfully rubbed an aging wound. "You *have* met Nora, haven't you?"

"Is it a wager you'd have than?" Gilmour asked.

"Methinks we may have enough wagers already."

"Ahh Ram, ever the cautious one. And what of you, Lachlan? Are you game for some sport?"

She was watching him, staring across the crowd with those mercurial eyes. The eyes of a warrior, the eyes of an angel, the eyes of his wife. His chest swelled.

"Lachlan," Gilmour said, and elbowed him. "What of a wager?"

She was coming toward them now, making her way through the mob. Gowned in blue velvet, she looked like a Highland queen. Regal and strong and so bonny it all but stole the breath from his chest.

"Lachlan!"

"I think he may have other things on his mind just now," mused Ramsay.

"Aye, it might well be," agreed Mour, "and I can well understand his enthusiasm, but I hate to see the lass disappointed."

And then she was there, beside him, filling his senses like a fragrant draught of wine. "Champion," she murmured. "I have missed you."

Their hands met. Their fingers twined. Lightning sizzled up Lachlan's arm, searing his thought. "Mayhap we have spent enough time among the rabble," he suggested.

Her lips lifted in impish agreement, but Gilmour spoke up.

"Nay, you must stay. The king and queen of bean have not yet been chosen."

"I have me king," Rhona murmured, and Lachlan leaned close. Her lips felt soft as a prayer against his.

"The wassailing has yet to begin," said Mour, and raised his cup. "You'll miss a good deal of drinking."

"You can have me share," Lachlan murmured.

Gilmour scowled. "Listen, lass," he said. "I do not mean to be the harbinger of ill news, but . . . 'tis your wedding night after all, and I feel I should prepare you for the ordeal ahead."

They turned to him in unison, their arms brushed. Lightning struck again, burning pleasantly.

Gilmour shook his head sadly. "Our Lachlan," he began. "Aye, it's built like a minotaur, he is, and he's a fair hand in a battle. In truth, I admit I'd rather have him on me side than against me, but . . ." He sighed with long suffering drama. "As you may have heard, great fighters are not oft great lovers and since you have agreed to wed him I assume you have not tested that theory, but I fear you will not be pleased with his ability in—"

But in that moment she kissed Lachlan again and every dram of his attention was drawn away, pulled to her, captured by all that she was—strength and softness, wit and kindness.

"Come," she whispered. "Your brother is rambling, and I feel a need to do that which you do best."

"I am yours. Forever and always for as long as I draw breath," Lachlan vowed and, lifting her against his chest, headed for the stairs.

"Damn," mused Ramsay solemnly, "unless she speaks of arm wrestling, I think you lose the wager, Gilmour."